THE ACCIDENT

C.L. Taylor lives in Bristol with her boyfriend and toddler son. She started writing fiction in 2005 and her short stories have won several awards and been published by a variety of literary and women's magazines.

C.L. TAYLOR

The Accident

AVON

AVON
A division of HarperCollins*Publishers*
77–85 Fulham Palace Road,
London W6 8JB

www.harpercollins.co.uk

A Paperback Original 2014
1

A catalogue record for this book is
available from the British Library

ISBN-13: 978-0-00-754003-7

Typeset in Sabon LT Std by Palimpsest Book Production Limited,
Falkirk, Stirlingshire
Printed and bound in Great Britain by
Clays Ltd, St Ives plc

MIX
Paper from
responsible sources
FSC **FSC˚ C007454**
www.fsc.org

Acknowledgements

Huge thanks to my editor Lydia Vassar-Smith and the team at Avon/HarperCollins for their support, encouragement and enthusiasm. You transformed this book from a figment of my imagination to something tangible and I couldn't be more delighted.

Massive thanks to Madeleine Milburn for supporting me every step of the way. You kept believing, even when my own belief faltered, and that marks you out as a very special agent indeed.

A big thank you to my friends and family – particularly my parents Reg and Jenny Taylor and my brother and sister David and Rebecca – for continuing to ask 'how's the novel?' even when the answer was little more than a sigh. And lots of love to Suz, Leah, Sophie, LouBag, Steve, Guinevere, Angela, Ana, Nan and Granddad.

Grateful thanks to everyone on Twitter and Facebook who helped me out with research – particularly Andrew

Parsons for his hospital procedure/drug expertise and Kimberley Mills for sharing her experience of caring for a coma patient. Thank you – and sorry – to Emily Harborow. The video research footage you surreptitiously filmed for me ended up on the editing room floor but I'm sure I'll be able to use it in another book.

Big thanks to Jim Ross for taking my lovely new author photos and to Rebecca Butterworth for doing my makeup.

A huge thank you to my writer friends. Writing can be such a lonely business and you keep me sane (and watered with booze). Special mention must go to Carolyn Jess-Cooke, Sally Quilford, Leigh Forbes, Helen Hunt, Helen Kara, Karen Clarke, Rowan Coleman, Miranda Dickinson, Kate Harrison, Julie Cohen and Tamsyn Murray for being particularly lovely.

Lastly, and by no means least, all my love and thanks to Chris and Seth. I wrote this book while I was on maternity leave – not because I had a very sleepy baby and lots of time on my hands – but because I thought I was going to go mental from sleep deprivation and writing was the only thing that kept me sane. I couldn't have done it without you Chris. Thank you for pushing the baby around town at 5a.m. so I could sleep, thank you for taking him to visit your relatives so I could write and thank you for telling me, over and over, that I *could* do it. It looks like I did.

http://cltaylorauthor.wordpress.com
www.twitter.com/callytaylor

For Chris Hall

Chapter 1

22nd April 2012

Coma. There's something innocuous about the word, soothing almost in the way it conjures up the image of a dreamless sleep. Only Charlotte doesn't look as though she's sleeping to me. There's no soft heaviness to her closed eyelids. No curled fist pressed up against her temple. No warm breath escaping from her slightly parted lips. There is nothing peaceful at all about the way her body lies, prostrate, on the duvet-less bed, a clear tracheostomy tube snaking its way out of her neck, her chest polka-dotted with multicoloured electrodes.

The heart monitor in the corner of the room bleep-bleep-bleeps, marking the passage of time like a medical metronome and I close my eyes. If I concentrate hard enough I can transform the unnatural chirping into the reassuring tick-tick-tick of the grandfather clock in our living room. Fifteen years fall away in an instant and I am twenty-eight again, cradling baby Charlotte to my shoulder, her slumbering face pressed into the nook of my neck, her tiny heart out-beating mine, even in sleep. Back then it was so much easier to keep her safe.

'Sue?' There is a hand on my shoulder, heavy, dragging me back into the stark hospital room and my arms are empty again, save the handbag I clutch to my chest. 'Would you like a cup of tea?'

I shake my head then instantly change my mind. 'Actually, yes.' I open my eyes. 'Do you know what else would be nice?'

Brian shakes his head.

'One of those lovely teacakes from M&S.'

My husband looks confused. 'I don't think they sell them in the canteen.'

'Oh.' I look away, feigning disappointment and instantly hate myself. It isn't in my nature to be manipulative. At least I don't think it is. There's a lot I don't know any more.

'It's okay.' There's that hand again. This time it adds a reassuring squeeze to its repertoire. 'I can pop into town.' He smiles at Charlotte. 'You don't mind if I leave you alone with your mum for a bit?'

If our daughter heard the question she doesn't let on. I reply for her by forcing a smile.

'She'll be fine,' I say.

Brian looks from me to Charlotte and back again. There's no mistaking the look on his face – it's the same wretched expression I've worn for the last six

2

weeks whenever I've left Charlotte's side – terror she might die the second we leave the room.

'She'll be fine,' I repeat, more gently this time. 'I'll be here.'

Brian's rigid posture relaxes, ever so slightly, and he nods. 'Back soon.'

I watch as he crosses the room, gently shutting the door with a click as he leaves, then release the handbag from my chest and rest it on my lap. I keep my eyes fixed on the door for what seems like an eternity. Brian has never been able to leave the house without rushing back in seconds later to retrieve his keys, his phone or his sunglasses or to ask a 'quick question'. When I am sure he has gone I turn back to Charlotte. I half expect to see her eyelids flutter or her fingers twitch, some sign that she realises what I am about to say but nothing has changed. She is still 'asleep'. The doctors have no idea when, or even if, Charlotte will ever wake up. She's been subjected to a whole battery of tests – CAT scans, MRIs, the works – with more to come, and her brain function appears normal. There's no medical reason why she shouldn't come round.

'Darling,' I take Charlotte's diary out of my handbag, fumble it open and turn to the page I've already memorised. 'Please don't be angry with me but . . .' I glance at my daughter to monitor her expression. '. . . I found your diary when I was tidying your room yesterday.'

Nothing. Not a sound, not a flicker, not a tic or a twinge. And the heart monitor continues its relentless

3

bleep-bleep-bleeping. It is a lie of course, the confession about finding her diary. I found it years ago when I was changing her sheets. She'd hidden it under her mattress, exactly where I'd hidden my own teenaged journal so many years before. I didn't read it though, back then, I had no reason to. Yesterday I did.

'In the last entry,' I say, pausing to lick my lips, my mouth suddenly dry, 'you mention a secret.'

Charlotte says nothing.

'You said keeping it was killing you.'

Bleep-bleep-bleep.

'Is that why . . .'

Bleep-bleep-bleep.

'. . . you stepped in front of the bus?'

Still nothing.

Brian calls what happened an accident and has invented several theories to support this belief: she saw a friend on the other side of the street and didn't look both ways as she ran across the road; she tried to help an injured animal; she stumbled and tripped when she was texting or maybe she was just in her own little world and didn't look where she was walking.

Plausible, all of them. Apart from the fact the bus driver told the police she caught his eye then deliberately stepped into the road, straight into his path. Brian thinks he's lying, covering his own back because he'll lose his job if he gets convicted of dangerous driving. I don't.

Yesterday, when Brian was at work and I was on bed watch, I asked the doctor if she had carried out a pregnancy test on Charlotte. She looked at me suspiciously and asked why, did I have any reason to think she might be? I replied that I didn't know but I thought it might explain a thing or two. I waited as she checked the notes. No, she said, she wasn't.

'Charlotte,' I shuffle my chair forward so it's pressed up against the bed and wrap my fingers around my daughter's. 'Nothing you say or do could ever stop me from loving you. You can tell me anything. Anything at all.'

Charlotte says nothing.

'It doesn't matter if it's about you, one of your friends, me or your dad.' I pause. 'Is the secret something to do with your dad? Squeeze my fingers if it is.'

I hold my breath, praying she doesn't.

Friday 2nd September 1990

It's 5.41 a.m. and I'm sitting in the living room, glass of red in one hand, a cigarette in the other, wondering if the last eight hours of my life really happened.

I finally rang James on Wednesday evening, after an hour's worth of abortive attempts and several glasses of wine. The phone rang and rang and I started to think that maybe he was out when it suddenly stopped.

'Hello?'

I could barely say hello back I was so nervous but then:

'Susan, is that you? Gosh. You actually called.'

His voice sounded different – thinner, breathy – like he was nervous too, and I joked that he sounded relieved to hear from me.

'Of course,' he replied. 'I thought there was no way you'd call after what I did. Sorry, I'm not normally such a twat but I was so pleased to run into you

alone backstage that I . . . Anyway, sorry. It was a stupid thing to do. I should have just asked you out like a normal person . . .'

He tailed off, embarrassed.

'Actually,' I said, feeling a sudden rush of affection towards him. 'I thought it was funny. No one's ever thrown a business card at me and shouted "Call me" before. I was almost flattered.'

'Flattered? I'm the one that should be flattered. You called! Oh God,' he paused, 'you are calling to arrange a drink, aren't you? You're not ringing to tell me I'm an absolute prat?'

'I did consider that option,' I laughed, 'but no, I happen to be unusually thirsty today so if you'd like to take *me* out for a drink that could be arranged.'

'God, of course. Whenever and wherever you want to go. All drinks on me, even the expensive ones.' He laughed too. 'I want to prove to you that I'm not . . . well, I'll let you make your own mind up. When are you free?'

I was tempted to say NOW but played it cool instead, as Hels had ordered me to do, and suggested Friday (tonight) night. James immediately agreed and we arranged to meet in the Dublin Castle.

I tried on dozens of different outfits before I went out, immediately discarding anything that made me look, or feel, fat and frumpy, but I needn't have worried. The second I was within grabbing distance, James pulled me against him and whispered 'You look beautiful' in my ear. I was just about to reply when he abruptly released me, grabbed my hand

7

and said, 'I've got something amazing to show you,' and led me out of the pub, through the throng of Camden revellers, down a side street and into a kebab shop. I gave him a questioning look but he said, 'trust me' and shepherded me through the shop and out a door at the back. I expected to end up in the kitchen or the toilets. Instead I stumbled into a cacophony of sound and blinked as my eyes adjusted to the smoky darkness. James pointed out a four-piece jazz band in the corner of the room and shouted, 'They're the Grey Notes – London's best-kept secret' then led me to a table in the corner and held out a battered wooden chair for me to sit down.

'Whisky,' he said. 'I can't listen to jazz without it. You want one?'

I nodded, even though I'm not a fan then lit up a cigarette as James made his way to the bar. There was something so self-assured about the way he moved, it was almost hypnotic. I'd noticed it the first time I'd seen him on stage.

James couldn't be more different from my ex Nathan. Whilst Nathan was slight, baby-faced and only a couple of inches taller than I am, James is six foot four with a solidity to him that makes me feel small and delicate. He's got a cleft in his chin like Kirk Douglas but his nose is too large to make him classically good looking and his dirty blond hair continually flops into his eyes but there's something mercurial about his eyes that reminds me of Ralph Fiennes; one minute they're cool and detached, the next they're crinkled at the corners, dancing with excitement.

I knew something was wrong the second James returned from the bar. He didn't say anything but, as he set the whisky tumblers down on the table, his eyes flicked towards the cigarette in my hand and I instantly understood.

'You don't smoke.'

He shook his head. 'My father died of lung cancer.'

He tried to object, to tell me that whether I smoked or not was none of his business, but his frown evaporated the second I put my cigarette out and the atmosphere immediately lightened. The band was so loud it was hard to hear each other over the squeal of the trumpet and the scatting of the lead singer so James moved his chair closer to mine so we could whisper into each other's ears. Whenever he leaned in, his leg rested against mine and I'd feel his breath against my ear and neck. It was torturous, feeling his body against mine and smelling the warm spiciness of his aftershave and not touching him. When I didn't think I could bear it a second longer James cupped his hand over mine.

'Let's go somewhere else. I know the most magical place.'

I barely had the chance to say 'okay' when he bounced out of his seat and crossed the room to the bar. A second later he was back, a bottle of champagne in one hand and two glasses and a threadbare rug in the other. I raised an eyebrow but he just laughed and said, 'You'll see.'

We walked for what felt like forever, weaving our way through the Camden crowds until we passed Chalk

Farm. I kept asking where we were going but James, striding alongside me, only laughed in reply. Finally we stopped walking at an entrance to a park and he laid a hand on my shoulder. I thought he was going to kiss me. Instead he told me to shut my eyes because he had a surprise for me.

I wasn't sure what could be quite so astonishing in a dark park at silly o'clock in the morning but I closed my eyes anyway. Then I felt something heavy and woollen being draped over my shoulders and warm spiciness enveloped me. James had noticed I was shivering and lent me his coat. I let him lead me through the entrance and up the hill. It was scary, putting my trust in someone I barely knew, but it was exhilarating too and strangely sensual. When we finally stopped walking he told me to stand still and wait. A couple of seconds later I felt the softness of the worn cotton rug under my fingers as he helped me to sit down.

'Ready?' I felt him move so he was crouched behind me, then his fingers touched my face, lightly brushing my cheekbones as they moved to cover my eyes. A tingle ran down my spine and I shivered, despite the coat.

'I'm ready,' I said.

James removed his fingers and I opened my eyes. 'Isn't it beautiful?'

I could only nod. At the base of the hill, the park was a chequerboard of black squares of unlit grass and illuminated pools of yellow-green light cast by glowing streetlamps. It was like a magical patchwork of light and dark. Beyond the park stretched the city, windows twinkling and buildings sparkling. The sky above was the darkest navy, shot with dirty orange clouds. It was the most breathtaking vista I'd ever seen.

'Your reaction when you opened your eyes . . .' James was staring at me. 'I've never seen anything so beautiful.'

'Stop it!' I tried to laugh but it caught in my throat.

'You looked so young Suzy, so enchanted – like a child on Christmas Day.' He shook his head. 'How is someone like you single? How is that even possible?'

I opened my mouth to reply but he wasn't finished.

'You're the most amazing woman I've ever met,' he reached for my hand. 'You're funny, kind, intelligent and beautiful. What on earth are you doing here with me?'

I wanted to make a joke, to ask if he was so drunk he could remember leading me up the hill, but I found I couldn't.

'I wanted to be here,' I said. 'And I wouldn't want to be anywhere else.'

James's face lit up as though I'd just given him the most wonderful compliment and he cupped my face with his hands. He looked at me for the longest time and then he kissed me.

I'm not sure how long we kissed for, lying there on a rug on the top of Primrose Hill, our bodies entwined, our hands everywhere, grasping, pulling, clutching. We didn't remove our clothes and we didn't have sex, yet it was still the single most erotic moment

11

of my life. I couldn't let go of James for more than a second without pulling him towards me again.

It grew darker and colder and I suggested we leave the park and go back to his.

James shook his head. 'Let me put you in a taxi home instead.'

'But—'

He pulled his coat tighter around my shoulders. 'There's time for that, Suzy. Plenty of time.'

Chapter 2

I wait until Brian leaves for work before I go through his things. It's nippy in the cloakroom, the tiled floor cold under my bare feet, the windowed walls damp with condensation but I don't pause to grab a pair of socks from the radiator in the hall. Instead I thrust my hands into the pockets of Brian's favourite jacket. The coat stand rocks violently as I move from pocket to pocket, pulling out the contents and dropping them to the floor in my haste to find evidence.

I've finished with the jacket and have just plunged both hands into the pockets of a hooded sweatshirt when there's a loud CRASH from the kitchen.

I freeze.

My mind goes blank – turns off – as though a switch has been thrown in my brain and I'm as rigid as the coat stand I'm standing beside, breathing shallowly, listening, waiting. I know I should move. I should take my hands out of Brian's fleece. I should kick the contents of his wax jacket into the corner of the room and hide the evidence that I am a terrible, mistrusting wife but I can't.

My heart is beating so violently the sound seems to fill the room and, in an instant, I'm catapulted twenty years into the past. I'm twenty-three, living in North London and I'm crouching in the wardrobe, a backpack stuffed with clothes in my left hand, a set of keys I stole from someone else's jacket, in my right. If I don't breathe he won't hear me. If I don't breathe he won't know that I'm about to . . .

'Brian?' The sense of déjà-vu falls away as the faintest scraping sound reaches my ears. 'Brian, is that you?'

I frown, straining to make out anything other than the rhythmic thump-thump-thump of my heart, but the house has fallen silent again.

'Brian?'

I jolt back to life, as though the switch in my brain has been flicked the other way, and I pull my hands out of his sweatshirt.

The hallway carpet is warm and plush under my feet as I inch forward, pausing every couple of seconds to listen, as I head towards the kitchen. The smell of bleach fills my nose and I realize one hand is covering my mouth, the scent of disinfectant still fresh on my fingers from cleaning the bathroom earlier. I pause again and try to slow my breathing. It is coming in small, sharp gasps, signalling a panic attack, but I am no longer afraid that my husband has come back to retrieve a forgotten briefcase or a lost house key. Instead I'm scared of—

'Milly!'

I'm almost knocked off my feet as an enormous Golden Retriever bowls down the hallway and launches herself at me, front paws on my chest, wet tongue on my chin. Normally I'd chastise her for jumping up but I'm so relieved to see her I wrap my arms around her and rub the top of her big soft head. When her joyful licking gets too much I push her down.

'How did you get out, naughty girl?'

Milly 'smiles' up at me, tendrils of drool dripping off her tongue. I've got a pretty good idea how she managed to escape.

Sure enough, when I reach the kitchen, the dog padding silently beside me, the door to the porch is open.

'You're supposed to stay in your bed until Mummy lets you out!' I say, pointing at the pile of rugs and blankets where she sleeps at night. Milly's ears prick up at the mention of the word 'bed' and her tail falls between her legs. 'Did silly Daddy leave the door open on his way to work?'

I never thought I'd be the kind of woman who'd refer to herself and her husband as 'Mummy and Daddy' when speaking to a pet but Milly is as much a part of our family as Charlotte. She's the sister we could never give her.

I shut Milly back in the porch, my heart twisting as she looks beseechingly at me with her big, brown eyes. It's eight o'clock. We should be strolling through the park at the back of the house but I need to continue what I started. I need to get back to the cloakroom.

The contents of Brian's pockets are where I left them – strewn around the base of the coat stand. I kneel down, wishing I'd grabbed a cushion from the living room as my knees click in protestation, and examine my spoils. There's a handkerchief, white with an embroidered golfer in the corner, unused, folded neatly into a square (given to him by one of the children for Christmas), three paper tissues, used, a length of twine, the same type Brian uses to tie up the tomatoes in his allotment, a receipt from the local supermarket for £40 worth of petrol, a mint imperial, coated with fluff, a handful of loose change and a crumpled cinema ticket. My heart races as I touch it – then I read the title of the film and the date – and my pulse returns to normal. It's for a comedy we went to see together. I hated it – found it rude, crude and slapstick – but Brian laughed like a drain.

And that's it. Nothing strange. Nothing out of the ordinary. Nothing incriminating.

Just . . . Brian stuff.

I sweep his belongings into a pile with the side of my hand, then scoop them up and carefully distribute them amongst his pockets, making sure everything is returned to where I found it. Brian isn't a fastidious man; he won't know, or care, which pocket held the change and which the cinema ticket but I'm not taking any chances.

Maybe there is no evidence at all.

Charlotte didn't squeeze my hand when I asked if her secret had anything to do with her father. She didn't so much as twitch. I don't know what I was thinking, imagining she might respond – or even asking the question in the first place. Actually I do. I was following up a hunch; a hunch that my husband was betraying me, again.

Six years ago Brian made a mistake – one that nearly destroyed not only our marriage, but his career too – he had an affair with a twenty-three-year-old Parliamentary intern. I raged, I shouted and I screamed. I stayed with my friend Jane for two nights. I would have stayed longer but I didn't want Charlotte to suffer. It took a long time but eventually I forgave Brian. Why? Because the affair happened shortly after one of my 'episodes', because my family is more important to me than anything in the world and because, although Brian has many faults, he is a good man at heart.

A 'good man at heart' – it sounds like such a terribly twee reason to forgive someone their infidelity, doesn't it? Perhaps it is. But it's infinitely preferable to life with a bad man and, when Brian and I met, I knew all about that.

It was the summer of 1993 and we were both living in Athens. I was a TEFL teacher and he was a widower businessman chasing a big deal. The first time Brian said hello to me, in a tatty tavern on the banks of the river Kifissos, I ignored him. The second time I moved seats. The third time he refused to let me continue pretending he didn't exist. He bought me a drink and delivered it to my table with a note that said 'Hello from one Brit to another' and then walked straight out of the pub without a backward glance. I couldn't help but smile. After that he was quietly persistent, a 'hello' here, a 'what are you reading?' there and we gradually became friends. It took me a long time to lower my barriers but finally, almost one year to the day after we first met, I let myself love him.

It was a warm, balmy evening and we were strolling beside the river, watching the lights of the city flicker and glow on the water when Brian started telling me about Tessa, his late wife, and how devastated he was when she lost her battle with cancer. He told me how shocked he'd been – the disease had progressed so rapidly – and then how angry, how he'd waited until his son was staying with his granny and then he'd smashed up his own car with a cricket bat because he didn't know how to deal with his rage. His eyes filled with tears when he told me how desperately he missed his son Oliver (he'd left him with his grandparents in the UK so he could fulfil a contract in Greece) but he made no attempt to blot them away. I touched his face, tracing my fingers over his skin, smudging his tears away and then I reached for his hand. I didn't let go for three hours.

I push open the door to Brian's study and approach his desk, instantly feeling that I have intruded too far. I wash my husband's clothes, I iron them, some of them I buy, but his study represents his career – a part of his world that he keeps distinct from family life. Brian is a Member of Parliament. Saying it aloud makes me so proud but I wasn't always that way. Seventeen years ago I was bemused when he'd rail against 'Tory scum', 'class divides' and 'a failing NHS' but Brian wasn't content to sit on society's sidelines and moan. When we returned to the UK from Greece, still flushed with happiness from our impromptu bare-footed wedding on a beach in Rhodes, he was resolute. We'd settle in Brighton and he'd start a new business – he had a hunch recycling would be big – and then, when it was established and making a profit, he'd run for Parliament. He didn't have so much as an economics O-Level but I knew he'd do it. And he did.

I never stopped believing in him, I still do in many ways, but I am no longer in awe of him. I love Brian but I can also see only too well how vain and insecure his career choice has made him. Flattery goes a long way when you're approaching your mid-forties, sixteen stone and balding – particularly when the person doing the flattering is young, ambitious and works for you. Brian has changed since Charlotte's accident. We both have, but in different ways. Instead of our daughter's condition bringing us together we've been forced apart and the distance between us is growing. If Brian's having another affair I won't forgive him again.

I take another step towards my husband's desk and my fingers trail over the brushed silver frame of a black and white photograph. It's of Charlotte and I on a beach in Mallorca, taken on the first day of our holiday. We've still got our travelling clothes on, our trouser legs rolled up so we can paddle in the sea. I've got one hand raised to my forehead, protecting my eyes from the sun whilst the other clutches our daughter's tiny hand. She's staring up at me, her chin tilted, eyes wide. The photo must be at least ten years old but I still feel a warm swell of love when I look at the expression on her face. It's pure, unadulterated happiness.

A floorboard in the corridor squeaks and I snatch my fingers back from the photograph then sigh. When did I become so neurotic that every creak and groan of a two-hundred-year-old house sent me catatonic with fear?

I look back at the desk. It's a heavy mahogany affair with three drawers on the left, three on the right and a long, thin drawer that sits in between. I reach for the brass handle of the centre drawer and slowly ease it open. Another floorboard squeaks but I ignore it, even though it sounds closer than the last. There's something in the drawer, something handwritten, a card or letter maybe and I reach for it, being careful not to disturb the mounds of paperclips and rubber bands on either side as I attempt to slide—

'Sue?' says a man's voice, directly behind me. 'What are you doing?'

Sunday 4th September 1990

James and I had sex.

It happened on Saturday night.

He called me in the afternoon and the first thing he said was 'I've barely slept for thinking about you.'

I knew exactly how he felt. I hadn't stopped thinking about him either. I'd woken up on Saturday morning with the most terrible feeling of dread that I'd never see him again. I was convinced I'd said something unforgiveable on Friday night and that, in the cold light of day, he'd realized that I wasn't the woman for him after all.

So sure was I that, when James rang and said he couldn't stop thinking about me, I was totally floored.

'Absolutely,' I said when he said he needed to see me ASAP. 'If I jump in the shower now then hop on the tube I could be in Camden in—'

'Actually I was thinking that we could meet for dinner this evening.'

What must he think of me – taking him literally like I had no life and no self-control? He didn't laugh, thankfully, instead asked if I'd ever been to some fancy restaurant in St Pancras. I'd never heard of it and said as much, so James explained that it had come highly recommended by a friend.

*Of course then I had **another** clothing dilemma (finally settling on my tried and tested little black dress) and was twenty minutes late as I walked in the restaurant at 8.20 p.m., trying not to ogle the stunning décor, the linen and crystal dressed tables and the immaculately turned out maître-d' who was showing me to my table. James stood up as we drew near. He was dressed in a three-piece grey suit with a lilac cravat at his throat and elegant silver cufflinks at his wrists. I felt dowdy in my three-year-old dress and scuffed heels but, when James looked me up and down and his eyes widened in appreciation, I felt like the most attractive woman in the whole restaurant.*

'I can't stop staring at you,' he said after the maître-d' seated me, handed us our menus and then left. 'You always look beautiful but tonight you look,' he shook his head as though dazed, 'ridiculously sexy.'

I felt myself blush as his eyes flicked to my cleavage. 'Thank you.'

'Honestly Susan, I don't think you have any idea of the effect you're having on me, and every other man in the room.'

I thought that was a bit over the top but when my eyes flicked to the two men having a business meeting at the next table they nodded at me appreciatively.

22

'So,' James reached across the table for my hand as I drained my first glass of wine. 'What do you like?'

I glanced at the menu. 'The scallops sound nice.'

He shook his head and slipped his fingers between mine, sliding them back and forwards. 'That wasn't what I meant.'

I tried to swerve away from the question, to a more neutral conversation, but James topped up my wine glass and fixed me with that intense look of his.

'I haven't been able to get you out of my head all day,' he said.

'Me neither.'

'I don't think you understand.' He tightened his grip on my hand and lowered his voice. 'I only spent one evening with you but I haven't been able to do anything because my mind and body have been craving you.'

I nodded, too shy to admit how many times I'd luxuriated in the fantasy of him lying naked beneath me.

'It's killing me,' he continued, 'sitting opposite you at the table, not able to touch you, not able to kiss you, not able to,' his voice became gravelly, 'fuck you.'

I didn't look away. Instead I ran my hand over his, lightly tracing my fingers over the contours of his knuckles and whispered, 'There are rooms upstairs.'

'So there are.' He smiled widely. 'But now I know how much you want me, I'm going to make you wait.'

I squealed in protest but he shook his head, still grinning, and poured me another glass of wine.

'Shall we order?' he said. 'The scallops look nice.'

The non-sexual mood didn't last long and by the time our starters arrived, the air was blue. It wasn't the sort of thing I'd normally talk about in a fancy restaurant but James kept slipping his fingers in and out of mine, I was circling his ankle with my stockinged foot and we were on our second bottle of wine and when he asked me if I'd ever had sex alfresco I was feeling bold so I admitted to sex in a tent, sex in a back garden after a party and a sandy attempt at oral sex on a beach. James listened to my stories, his eyes shining with excitement then urged me on, asking me if I'd ever indulged in S&M or role play, demanding I tell him what my favourite position was. I giggled as I told him that Nathan and I had messed around with silk scarves and handcuffs.

'How about you?' I asked after the waiter had placed our main courses in front of us. 'What have you tried?'

'Very little,' James raised an eyebrow, 'compared to you.'

He was smiling when he said it but there was a judgemental tone in his inflection that rankled me.

James noticed my change in mood immediately.

'Oh Suzy.' He grabbed my hand. 'Suzy-Sue. Are you sulking? Darling, I was only playing. Look at me, please.'

I raised my eyelashes then laughed at the pouty expression on James's face – an obvious imitation of my own.

'I've been very naughty,' he said, running his thumb

over the back of my hand, 'and I've done some terrible things but,' his eyes glittered with promise, 'not as terrible as the things I'm going to do to you.'

'Is that a threat or a promise?'

He released my hand, cut into his steak and smiled. 'Both.'

How we managed to check in, make it upstairs in the lift and operate the door mechanism to the room with our clothes still on, I have no idea because the second the door slammed behind us we tore at each other's clothes, ripping off shirts, dresses, stockings and underwear. The sex was fast, furious, animalistic and over quickly, so desperate was our desire to fuck. We lay in each other's arms, sweaty and panting for all of ten minutes before James rolled me onto my side, his erection pressed against my lower back, and fucked me again. At some point in the night we had sex in the bathroom. We were supposed to shower together to get clean but the lure of the water, the soap and two slippery bodies was too much. By the time we collapsed onto the bed again, the sun was peeping through the curtains.

'I feel like I'm in a dream,' James said, tracing his finger down my forehead, along my nose and resting in the dip of my cupid's bow. 'I don't think I've ever been this happy.'

'I know.' I stroked his arms, wrapping my hand around the contour of his bicep, cradling the muscle in my palm. 'I can't believe this is really happening.'

'It is.' He leaned towards me and kissed me tenderly,

then parted my lips with his tongue and kissed me again, harder this time, his hand on my breast. Seconds later he was on top of me again. It must have been after six before we finally fell asleep.

Chapter 3

'What?' I snatch my hands from the drawer and spin around to face my accuser. 'I wasn't doing anything. I was just looking for—'

'Got you!' The tall, auburn-haired man standing in the doorway points and laughs uproariously. 'Brilliant! You should compete in the Olympics, Sue. I've never seen anyone jump so high!'

'Oli! You frightened me half to death.'

My stepson laughs again, his freckled face lighting up with amusement. 'Sorry, I couldn't resist.'

I force a smile but behind my back my hands are shaking. 'Aren't you supposed to be at university?'

'I was. Am. Sort of.' He adjusts the weight of the rucksack he's wearing on one shoulder and smiles. 'Field trip in Southampton. I thought I'd drop in and see Dad en route.' He peers around the study. 'I've missed him, haven't I?'

'By about twenty minutes. He's in London today.'

'Damn.' He casts another look around, hoping perhaps that Brian will magically materialize, then looks back at me and frowns. 'You okay, Sue? You look like you've seen a ghost.'

'I'm fine.' I push the drawer closed and cross the study. 'Honestly.'

Oli's eyes dart over my face, trying to read my expression as I approach him. 'How's Charlotte?'

I sigh, deflating as the air leaves my body. I've been so pumped on adrenalin searching through Brian's things that now I've stopped I feel drained.

'She's . . .' I want to tell him the truth – that Charlotte is no different than she was yesterday, or the day before, or the day before that but he looks so worried I lie instead. His exams are coming up soon and he's worked so hard. '. . . She's looking a little better. There was more colour in her cheeks yesterday.'

'Really?' His expression brightens again. 'That's good, isn't it?'

'It's . . . progress.'

'And has she, you know, shown any signs that she might wake up?'

'No, not yet.' The secret's the reason she's still asleep, I know it is. Maybe once I know what it is I'll understand why, and then I'll be able to help her.

'Something . . . something . . . music,' I hear my stepson say.

'Sorry? What was that, darling?'

Oli smiles the same indulgent smile I've seen a hundred times since Charlotte's accident – it's the one that says it's okay for me to be away with the fairies, considering what's happened. 'Music. Have you tried playing Charlotte her favourite songs? It works in Hollywood films.'

'Music.' She adored Steps and S Club Seven and their ridiculously catchy tunes and simple dance routines when she was a toddler but that was years ago. 'I haven't bought her a CD for years. It's all MP3s and downloads these days, isn't it? I don't suppose you know what she likes?'

'No idea.' He shrugs. 'Lady Gaga maybe? Jessie J? Doesn't everyone under the age of sixteen worship her?'

'I don't know.'

'Or you could check her iPod to see what her highest rated or most frequently played songs are.'

'You can do that?' I make a mental note to find Charlotte's iPod.

'Or maybe ask one of her friends?'

'Yes, yes I could,' I say but the suggestion makes me frown. There's been an outpouring of teenaged concern on Charlotte's Facebook page – lots of 'luv u m8' and 'gt wl sn ☺ ♥' – but I haven't heard so much as a peep from the two most important people in her life – her boyfriend Liam Hutchinson and her best friend Ella Porter. How could I have failed to notice?

Oli glances at his watch. 'Shit. I didn't realize the time. I've got to run. Next time I'm down I'll pop in to see Charlotte.' A shadow crosses his face. 'Sorry I haven't been there for her more. Life's just been really—'

'I know.' I put a hand on his forearm. 'You've got a lot on your plate. The best thing you can do right now is study hard and make us all proud.'

We walk in companionable silence down the stairs, across the hallway and into the kitchen where Milly, our hairy Houdini, is waiting for us, her tail thumping the tiles. I reach up to Oli for a goodbye hug and it strikes me for the umpteenth time how quickly time passes. It seems only yesterday that we shared our first hug and his arms embraced my knees instead of my shoulders.

'I'll tell your dad you called in,' I say into his shoulder.

'Cool.' He kisses me on the top of my head then reaches down and scratches Milly behind her ears. 'Be a good girl, Mrs Moo.'

'Drive carefully!' I shout after him as he lollops out of the kitchen and crosses the porch in two long strides. He raises a hand in acknowledgement and is gone.

I'm still standing at the kitchen window staring out into the front garden long after Oli's little red Mini has pulled out of the driveway and disappeared down the road. Our brief conversation in the study has cleared my mind and I suddenly feel ridiculous for searching Brian's pockets. Other than some emotional detachment on his part, and a hunch on mine, I've got no reason to suspect that he might be cheating on me. Of course Charlotte's accident was going to change the dynamics of our relationship – how could something so terrible not? They say leopards never change their spots but Brian was a broken man when I found out about the affair. He cried and said he was 'no better than that monster you were with before you met me' and swore he'd never hurt me again. And I believed him.

The shrill sound of a phone ringing slices through my thoughts and, before I know what I'm doing, I've shut Milly in the porch and I'm taking the steps to the landing as fast as I can. Brian's private line rarely rings and only then when it's something very important.

'Hello?' I'm gasping for breath by the time I burst into the study and snatch up the receiver.

'Mrs Jackson?' I recognize the voice immediately. It's Mark Harris, Brian's personal assistant.

'Speaking.'

'I'm sorry to interrupt you Mrs Jackson but I was wondering if I could speak to your husband. I wouldn't have disturbed you but his mobile's off.'

'Brian?' I frown. 'He's on his way to work.'

'Are you sure?' There's a clunk and the sound of papers being shuffled, then another clunk. 'It says in the diary that he won't be in until this afternoon.'

'The diary must be wrong . . .' I swallow hard, my throat suddenly dry. There has to be a rational explanation for the fact that my husband told me one thing and his PA another. 'Brian definitely said he was going to work when he left this morning.'

'Oh.' Mark pauses. 'Did they open early for him or something?'

'Sorry?'

'The hospital. He mentioned yesterday that he was going to see Charlotte this morning. I presumed that was why he couldn't make it in until the afternoon.'

I sink into Brian's black leather chair, the phone limp in my hand.

When we visited Charlotte yesterday evening, the consultant told us they'd be running more tests on her and we wouldn't be able to visit until the afternoon at the earliest. He was very sorry but there would be no morning visits today.

'Mrs Jackson?' Mark's voice is so faint it's as though he's a million miles away. 'Mrs Jackson, is everything okay?'

Wednesday 6th September 1990

I haven't heard from James for three days and I'm starting to worry. He left the hotel room before me on Sunday morning because he had to go home and get changed before rehearsal and I haven't heard a word from him since.

I keep running the time we spent together over and over in my head but I can't find anything wrong. I did ramble on a bit over dinner about how excited I was that Maggie had given me the opportunity to design costumes for the Abberley Players and how the bar job meant I'd finally be able to ditch TEFL and sew in the daytime but I asked James plenty of questions too. And I didn't smoke once. Not even with my coffee.

Sunday morning, before he left, he leaned over the bed and kissed me on the lips. He said he'd had the most amazing night of his life, that he couldn't bear to leave me and he'd ring that evening.

Only he didn't.

And he didn't ring on Monday evening either.

By Tuesday night I was so stressed I called Hels. She talked me down off the ceiling and said there were all kinds of reasonable explanations why James hadn't called and he'd ring when he got the chance. She told me to relax and get on with my life. That's easy for her to say. She hasn't been single for years. She can't remember how torturous it is, sitting in, trying to watch a film but all the time staring at the phone, wondering if it's working – then getting up to test it to find that it is.

*Oh God. The phone is ringing **right now**. Please, please let it be him.*

Chapter 4

I'm curled up on the sofa when Brian gets home, a book in my hand, a glass of wine on the coffee table and my feet tucked up under my bum. It's a familiar scenario, and one that would normally signal a happy, relaxed Sue, but I'm on my third glass of wine and I've read the same paragraph at least seven times.

'Hello, darling.' My husband pops his head around the living room door and raises a hand in the same easy manner as his son, twelve hours earlier.

I smile in acknowledgement but my body is tense. It's not the thought that he's having another affair that's tearing at me, it's the fact he's been using our daughter's accident to cover his tracks. I've been torturing myself all day – poring through my diary and the one in Brian's study (there was nothing in the drawer, just some headed notepaper), looking for anything to back up, or even discount, my suspicions – but I found nothing. If it wasn't for the phone call with Mark this morning I wouldn't have a shred of evidence.

'You okay?' He raises a hand as he strolls into the room with Milly at his side. When he reaches the sofa he kisses me gently on the lips and sits down. 'How's your day been?'

'Okay.'

He reaches for the cushion behind his back, throws it onto the armchair, leans back with a sigh and then looks at me. 'Just okay? I thought you were going to go into town and treat yourself to a new dress?'

'I . . .' For a second everything feels normal – my husband and I, having a chat about our day – but then I remember. Everything is far from normal. 'I didn't go. I was too busy.'

'Oh?' He raises an eyebrow and waits for details but I change the subject.

'Oli popped by, this morning.'

'I missed him again?' He looks genuinely gutted. 'What did he want?'

'Nothing in particular. He was on his way to Southampton for a field trip. I think he's going to call in again on his way back.'

'Oh, good.' Brian brightens again. His relationship with his son is different from his relationship with Charlotte, it's more complex. They were joined at the hip when Oli was a child, clashed furiously when he was a teen and have developed a mutual respect since. Theirs is a comfortable friendship, tempered by a similar sense of humour and challenged by different political views. They laugh easily but when they clash it's Titan-like. Charlotte and I always run for cover.

I twist to place my book and my wine glass on the coffee table, temporarily hiding my face from my husband. I feel sure he must have noticed the strained expression on my face. Trying to appear 'normal' when all I want to do is rage at him is exhausting, but I can't scream at him. The last thing Charlotte needs is for me to suffer another of my episodes. I have to be calm. Logical. One lie does not an infidelity make. I need more evidence.

'You okay?' There's concern in Brian's voice.

'Great,' I twist back. 'How was work?'

'Urgh.' He groans and runs a hand through his hair. It was once as bright a shade of auburn as Oli but it's now ninety per cent grey, what's left of it. 'Hideous.'

'How was the train journey?'

He casts me an enquiring look. I'm not normally so interested in the details of his daily commute. 'Same as normal,' he says then reaches across the sofa and pats one of my knees. 'You okay, darling? You seem a bit . . . tense.'

My fingers are knotted together. Was I twisting them while Brian was talking? It's amazing, the little messages a body can leak. I look from my fingers to my husband. His body isn't saying anything unusual. He looks as relaxed and calm as normal.

'Why did you lie to me, Brian?' So much for staying calm and logical.

His mouth drops open and he blinks. 'Sorry?'

'You made out you were going to work.'

'When?'

'This morning. You didn't go, did you?'

'Yes, I did.'

'That's odd, Mark said you weren't there.'

'Mark?' Brian snatches his hand from my knee. 'Why would you ring my PA?'

'I didn't,' I say. 'He rang me.'

'Why?'

'He said he had something important to discuss with you. Didn't he mention it when you went into the office in the afternoon? *If* you went in.'

'Of course I did. And yes,' he shifts position so he's turned square towards me, 'now I come to think of it, he *did* have something fairly urgent to discuss with me.'

'Great. So,' I maintain eye contact, 'where were you this morning, Brian?'

My husband says nothing for a couple of seconds. Instead he runs a hand over his face and takes a few deep breaths. I wonder if he's steadying himself, hiding his eyes from me so I can't see the lies he's fabricating now I've confronted him.

'I . . .' he looks at me, a frown creasing his forehead. 'I was going to see Charlotte.'

'You didn't! We were both there when the consultant said—'

'Sue.' He holds up a hand and I bite my tongue. 'I was *planning* on seeing Charlotte this morning. I planned it days ago. I know you can't bear it when she's left alone so I was going to surprise you, suggest

38

that you take yourself into town to get a manicure or a haircut or a new dress or something while I sat with her. Then, last night, the consultant told us about the tests and that pretty much scuppered my plans so . . .'

'So?' I say the word so loudly Milly lifts her head from carpet and looks at me.

'So I went into town instead. I visited the library, went for a swim, did a bit of shopping and just had a bit of . . .' he cringes, 'I guess you'd call it "me time".'

'Me time?'

'Yes.' He looks me straight in the eye.

'So you took the morning off to give me some . . . *me time* . . . and when the consultant told us that we couldn't visit Charlotte you decided to have some . . . *me time* . . . for yourself instead?'

He shrugs uncomfortably. 'Yes.'

'Why didn't you mention it?'

'When?'

'When you came in just now? Why didn't you mention it?'

'Oh for God's sake, Sue.' Brian slumps forward, his head in his hands. 'I really don't need this. I really don't.'

'But . . .' I can't finish my sentence. The whole situation suddenly seems faintly ridiculous and I'm not sure why I'm continuing to argue. Brian planned a treat for me and it fell through so he took a few hours to himself. That's perfectly reasonable. So he didn't walk through the door and tell me all about it – so what? I'm not his keeper, he doesn't have to report his every move to me – I'd never do that to him, not after what James put me through.

I look at the hunched, tired shape on the other end of the sofa. He looked so fresh, so optimistic when he walked in ten minutes ago. He looks ten years older now.

'I'm sorry.' I reach out a hand and lay it on his shoulder.

Brian says nothing.

'I'm sorry,' I say again.

The grandfather clock in the corner of the room tick-tocks the minutes away.

'Brian,' I say softly. 'Please look at me.'

After an age he peels his fingers away from his face and looks up at me. 'I don't want to argue, Sue, not after everything that's happened.'

'Me neither.'

I squeeze his shoulder and he reaches a hand around and lays it on mine. The warmth of his palm on my skin has an immediate calming effect and I exhale heavily.

'Okay?' Brian says, his eyes searching mine.

I'm about to nod, to pull him close for a hug, to lose myself in the warm, musky scent of him when a thought hits me.

'Was the pool busy?' I ask. 'When you went for your swim?'

Brian looks confused then smiles a split second later. 'Rammed. Bloody kids everywhere. Half term isn't it, so what did I expect?'

I don't know what you expected, I think as he wraps his arms around me and pulls me closer, but I'd have expected it to be pretty damned empty considering it closed for renovations two weeks ago.

We sit by Charlotte's bedside in silence; Brian holding one of her hands, me holding the other. The heart monitor bleeps steadily in the corner of her room. We didn't speak on the way in but we often keep a companionable silence in the car, particularly when the radio's on, and Brian had no reason to think there was anything unusual about the fact I spent the whole journey staring out of the window. I was trying to decide what to do – to confront him about his swimming pool lie or bite my tongue and pretend everything is fine. I chose the latter – for now.

'They still haven't fixed the emergency button,' I say. My voice sounds horribly loud in the small room.

Brian looks at the grubby yellow tape covering the red button above Charlotte's bed. 'Typical. I don't suppose they've sorted the TV either.'

I reach for the remote control and press a button. The TV flickers to life and we watch *Bargain Hunt* for all of thirty seconds before the screen fills with white noise. I turn it off again.

'It's a bloody joke.' Brian shakes his head. 'I've campaigned for – and achieved – a three-fold budget increase for this hospital and it's still falling down around our ears. And don't even get me started on MRSA. Have you seen the grime on the windowsill?

What do the cleaners actually do here? Mist each room with eau de bleach then go for a fag?'

'That's a bit harsh.' I pull an antiseptic wipe out of the packet on Charlotte's bedside table and wipe down the windowsill, then the frame of Charlotte's bed and the door handle. 'I think they're just overstretched.'

'They should still fix that bloody button. What are we supposed to do in an emergency? Wave a white flag out the window?'

Brian sighs and shakes out his newspaper. Sometimes he reads the more interesting or controversial articles aloud. They have no effect on Charlotte but it helps fill the visit.

With the cleaning done I turn my attention to our daughter. I straighten her sheet, untucking then re-tucking it, then I brush her hair, wipe her face with damp cotton wool and rub moisturizer into her hands then hover at the side of the bed, my hands twisting uselessly in front of me. Charlotte's hair wasn't tangled, her face wasn't dirty and her hands weren't dry but what else can I do? I could hold her hand. I could tell her how much I love her. I could beg her to please, please open her eyes and come back to us. I could cry. I could wait until I was all alone in the room, lean over the bed, gather her in my arms and ask her why. Why didn't I notice she was in so much pain she'd rather die than live one more day? My own child. My baby. How could I not know? How could I not sense that?

I could plea bargain with God. I could beg him to

let me switch places with her so she could smile again, laugh again, go shopping, chat with her friends, watch films and spend too much time on the internet. So she could live instead of me.

But I've done all of those things. I've done them so many times over the last six weeks that I've lost count and nothing, nothing has brought her back to me.

'I'm sorry, we can only allow a maximum of three visitors at a time. I'm afraid one of you will have to—'

I twist round to see who's speaking. A nurse is standing with a young couple, just outside the door. I recognize the tall, blond man she's talking to. It's Danny Argent, one of Oliver's friends. I don't recognize the girl with him.

'But—' His eyes meet mine. 'Hi Sue.'

'Danny.' I glance at Brian. He's frowning. 'What are you doing here?'

He takes a step into the room. The nurse tuts loudly but he ignores her.

'We,' he glances back at the attractive mixed-race girl in the corridor, 'Keisha and me, we wanted to see Charlotte. Is that okay?'

Brian clears his throat. He's had a problem with Danny ever since we were called to A&E to witness Oli having his stomach pumped after a teenaged drinking binge. Brian went white when he saw his son lying semi-conscious on a hospital trolley, then purple when he spotted Danny leaning against the wall nearby, one grubby trainer on the paintwork, the other kicking

43

the wheel of the trolley. He's never forgiven him for getting his son so drunk he was hospitalized but Oli won't hear a bad word said against his best friend. As far as he's concerned, nightclub promoter Danny can do no wrong.

'Sue?' Danny says again. He jerks his head towards Keisha who smiles hopefully at me.

I look at Brian. To an outsider he looks perfectly normal but I know what's going on behind his eyes. He's wondering if Danny's got anything to do with Charlotte's accident. His protective hackles are rising just seeing him in the same room as his daughter. I've got nothing against Danny. He's vain, self-obsessed and materialistic – and he's not someone I'd *choose* to be Oli's best friend – but he's not a bad person, he's not dangerous. He's always treated Charlotte like a kid sister, much to her disdain, but I can't go against Brian on this, even suspecting what I do. This is about what's best for Charlotte, not the two of us.

'I'm not sure . . .' I start, my eyes flicking from Danny to Brian and back. 'I don't know if—'

Brian's chair squeaks on the bleached lino as he stands up. 'I need a coffee.' He shoots me a meaningful look. 'I'll get you one, Sue. You stay here.'

Danny looks as surprised as I feel as Brian gives him a cursory nod and then leaves the room. Several silent seconds pass as we all wait for someone to decide what happens next.

'Come in, come in,' I say at last, waving my hand to beckon Keisha in. She falters then drifts towards Danny and stands as close to him as she can without knocking

44

him over. I've seen Milly do the same with Brian. She'll press herself so tightly against his knees he struggles to stay upright. With Milly it's a sign of her utter devotion and, from the look on Keisha's face, I'm fairly certain the motivation is the same.

Danny barely acknowledges his girlfriend's presence. If it wasn't for the fact he just swung an arm around her shoulders and rested a hand on the back of her neck I'd say he wasn't even aware she was in the same room. He hasn't taken his eyes off Charlotte for the last five minutes.

'How is she?' he asks.

I shrug. It's a well-practiced response – half hopeful, half realistic. 'The doctors say the worst of her injuries are healing well.'

'So why . . .' he frowns. '. . . hasn't she woken up?'

'They don't know.' I squeeze Charlotte's hand. She's so still and silent you'd imagine it to be cold but it's not, it's as warm as mine.

'Really? You would have thought that they'd be ab—'

There's a loud sniff and we both turn to look at Keisha.

'Oh my God,' Danny looks appalled at the tears spilling down her cheeks. 'Stop it, would you. You're embarrassing me.'

I tense at his tone. James was the same, cold in the face of tears.

Keisha covers her face with her hands but she can't hide her tears. They drip off her jaw and speckle her pink top with red splashes.

I reach out a hand but I'm sitting too far away to touch her. 'Are you okay?'

She shakes her head and swipes at her cheeks with her right hand; her left clutches the hem of Danny's leather jacket. She must be eighteen, twenty tops, but the gesture is that of a five-year-old child.

'It's just,' she swallows back a sob, 'it's just so very sad.'

I'm surprised by her accent. I didn't expect her to be Irish.

'Yes it is. It's very sad. But we're still optimistic. There's no reason why she shouldn't pull through.'

Keisha wails as though her heart is breaking and wrenches herself away from Danny.

'Keish,' he snaps, a muscle pulsing in his cheek. 'Keisha, stop it.'

'No.' She wraps her arms around her slender waist and steps backwards towards the door. 'No.'

'Keisha?' I stand up and take a slow step towards her. I hold out a hand, palm upwards as though I'm approaching a startled foal. 'Keisha, what is it?'

She looks at my hand and shakes her head.

'I'm sorry.' She takes another step towards the door, then another. She's trembling from head to foot. 'I'm really sorry.'

'We all are.' I'm trying to stay calm but my heart is beating violently in my chest. 'But there's no need to be so upset. She really will get—'

'That's not what I mean. I'm sorry that—'

'Keish!' Danny's voice is so loud we both jump. 'Calm the fuck down.'

'No.' She tears her gaze from Charlotte's face to look at her boyfriend. 'She needs to know.'

'Know what?' What's she talking about? 'What do I need to know, Keisha? Tell me.'

She and Danny stare at each other, their eyes locked. His eyes narrow. He's warning her, silently ordering her to shut up.

'Keisha!' I need her to look at me. I need to break whatever spell Danny has cast on her. 'Keisha!'

'Sue? Why are you shouting?' Brian appears in the doorway behind Keisha, a cup of steaming coffee in each hand.

I stare at him in astonishment. How long has he been there?

'I knew it.' He glares at Danny. 'I bloody knew there'd be trouble if I let you—'

He's interrupted by Keisha who moans softly, then shoulders Brian out of the way and sprints out of the room. Hot coffee slops onto the cold, vinyl floor.

'Keish!' Danny's after her in a flash.

There's a horrible moment when he and Brian face off in the doorway and I think someone's going to throw a punch but then Brian steps to the side to let Danny pass. I hear Keisha shriek something as her boyfriend's trainers pound the corridor then the room falls silent again.

The heart monitor beep-beep-beeps in the corner of the room.

Brian looks at me, confusion and shock etched onto his face. 'What the hell happened?' There's an unspoken accusation behind the question and he looks at

Charlotte, concerned. 'I could hear that girl screaming from the vending machine in the corridor. I'm surprised the nurse didn't come back. Or security.'

'What did she mean?' He places the coffee cups on the bedside table and takes Charlotte's other hand.

'Who?'

'The girl with Danny. She shouted something as she was running down the corridor.'

'I didn't hear anything.'

Brian fixes me with a look. 'She shouted, "Stupid fucking girl. She trusted me, she thought I was her best friend, and look what happened to her".'

Saturday 9th September 1990

*It **was** James on the phone on Wednesday. He was terribly apologetic, said some awful things had happened in his personal life and asked if I'd ever be able to forgive him for leaving me hanging. I wanted to be angry, to tell him that I deserved to be treated better and that he couldn't just expect me to forgive him because he'd deigned to pick up the phone. Instead I said, 'Buy me a beer and I'll think about it.' He called me an 'angel' then and said it was typical of the amazing person I was that I'd be so understanding.*

When we met for a beer I tried to find out more about these 'personal things' that had stopped him from calling but he skirted the issue, telling me he'd reveal all once we'd been together a bit longer. (So we're 'together' are we? Interesting!)

Almost inevitably we ended up in bed together. Again.

We'd been to the Heart and Hand in Clapham Common and, as last orders were called, I suggested we get the tube back to my flat because I had a couple of bottles of wine that needed drinking. James jumped at the idea. He said he couldn't wait to see my flat and what my things said about me. As it turned out all he saw as we spilled through the front door, into the bedsitting room and onto my futon was a couple of magnolia-painted walls and the white ceiling.

Afterwards, as we lay in each other's arms, listening to 'Monkey Gone to Heaven' by the Pixies on repeat (we were both too lazy to get out of bed and change the CD), I asked James when I'd get to see his place. A cloud passed over his face and he said, 'Never hopefully.' When I asked what that meant he shrugged and said he needed the loo. When he came back he said something that made me laugh and that was it, subject changed without me even noticing.

I won't give up so easily next time the subject comes up . . .

Chapter 5

'Keisha Malley?' Oli reaches across the table for a biscuit and bites into it. He's only been back in the house for ten minutes and he's nearly demolished an entire pack of chocolate Hobnobs. 'Fit black girl? Yeah I know her, goes out with Danny.'

It's the day after the incident with Keisha and Danny in the hospital but I'm still reeling. What did she mean – *She trusted me, she thought I was her best friend, and look what happened to her.*

Brian and I talked about what had happened all the way home and for hours into the night but we still couldn't unravel it. It took all my self-restraint, and Brian's firm hand on the phone, not to call Oli at midnight to ask him for Danny's number so I could get some answers there and then.

'Did Charlotte ever mention anything about Keisha being her best friend?'

'Keisha? Her best friend? You're kidding me, right?

What about Ella? Those two are as thick as thieves.'
He raises an eyebrow. 'Or did they fall out?'

I shake my head. 'I don't know. Charlotte never mentioned falling out with Ella but then . . .' I tail off. I'm starting to get the impression there's a lot I don't know about my daughter's life.

Oli pulls a face. 'It's a bit unlikely, isn't it? A fifteen-year-old and a nineteen-year-old being best friends? Or is it different with girls?'

'I don't know.' I shrug. 'But why would Keisha say that if it wasn't true?'

'She's a woman. She's mental!' He laughs then looks contrite. 'Sorry Sue, present company excepted.'

'Oliver James Jackson,' Brian bellows from the porch. 'Are you insulting your mother again?'

He fixes Oli with a steely stare but he can't stop his lips from twitching into a smile and giving him away.

His son doesn't miss a beat. 'Thought I'd give you the day off, old man.'

'Oi!' Brian crosses the kitchen and lightly cuffs him round the back of his head. 'Less of the old thank you very much.'

I smile as they slip effortlessly into their roles for the father-son banter-athon. Information is swapped, insults are traded and jokes are told and never once do the grins slip from their faces. I adore watching the two of them together but a tiny, hateful part of me is jealous. Theirs is a closeness I could only dream of sharing with Charlotte. When she was born, when I held her in my arms for the first time, my head was full of happy imaginings for the future – the two of us shopping together for shoes, gossiping over manicures, cooing over Hollywood hunks in the cinema, or just sitting around the kitchen table chatting about our days. But it never quite turned out that way.

I was Charlotte's favourite person in the whole world until she turned eleven but then something changed. Instead of skipping home excitedly from school to tell me all about her day she became sullen and withdrawn. Instead of giggling on the sofa together at an episode of *Scooby Doo*, she'd hole herself away in her room with her laptop and mobile phone for company. She'd scowl if I so much as peeped my head around the door to offer her a cup of tea. Brian tried to reassure me that it was normal, all part of her becoming a teenager. He reminded me of the way his relationship with Oli had suffered at a similar age and, although I could vaguely recall them clashing it was always over things like bedtimes and pocket money. It didn't seem as personal as it was between Charlotte and I.

Her refusal to talk to me was the reason I bought her her first diary. I figured it would give her an outlet for all the new, confusing feelings she was having – including ones of resentment towards me.

'Isn't that right, Sue?' Oli waves a hand in front of my face and laughs. 'Anyone home?'

'Sorry?' I look from him to Brian and back. 'What was that?'

'Dad just made a joke. Well . . .' he raises an

eyebrow, '. . . he thinks it's a joke and I was trying to get you on side because . . .' he tails off and laughs, presumably at the blank look on my face.

'Did Sue ask you about Keisha?' Brian asks, changing the subject.

Oli nods but he's just shoveled in the last Hobnob and his mouth is too full to answer.

'Yes,' I say. 'He knows her – she's Danny's girlfriend – but Charlotte never mentioned her.'

'Hmmm.' Brian reaches for the empty plate, deposits it in the sink then returns to the table. 'And she didn't mention anything about falling out with Ella? Was there an argument or a disagreement of some sort?'

Oli shakes his head. 'Charlotte never really texted me with news and updates about her life. She only ever got in touch if she needed advice or . . .' he tails off.

'Or what?' Brian and I ask simultaneously.

Oli shifts in his seat. 'Or if she wanted stuff buying off the internet.'

Brian and I share a look.

'What kind of stuff?' he asks.

'Nothing dodgy! Gig tickets, magazine subscriptions, eBay purchases, just stuff you need a credit card or PayPal account for.'

'Was there anything strange or unusual she asked you to get her? Before her accident?'

'Nope.' He shakes his head. 'Like I said, just gig tickets and celebrity signed photos and tat like that.' He reaches across the table then pauses, realizing the plate has disappeared. A frown appears between his eyebrows.

'What is it?' Brian asks.

Oli looks from one of us to the other. His lips part as though he's about to say something, then close again.

'What is it?' Now I'm worried too. 'You can tell us anything, Oliver. You know that, don't you? We won't judge and we won't be angry. I promise.'

Well, *I* won't be angry. Brian is sitting on the very edge of his chair, his elbows on the table, his eyes fixed on his son's face.

'I . . .' He can't meet his dad's gaze.

'Please,' I say softly. 'It might help.'

'Okay.' He sits back in his chair and drums his thumbs on the table, his head down. 'Okay.' He pauses again to clear his throat and I think I might explode if I have to wait one second longer. 'She asked me if I'd pay for a hotel room for her and Liam.'

'She WHAT?!'

'She said she didn't want to lose her virginity in a car or the playing fields behind the school like everyone else and—'

'A hotel room?!' The back of Brian's neck is puce. 'She's fifteen, for fuck's sake. What the hell was she thinking? If you bloody—'

'I didn't do anything, Dad!' Oli holds up his hands. 'I swear. I wouldn't.'

I can tell by the horrified look on his face that he's telling the truth.

'Why didn't you tell us this before?' I ask.

'Why would I?'

'Because your FIFTEEN-YEAR-OLD SISTER was planning on having sex with her seventeen-year-old boyfriend in a hotel room!' Brian is halfway out of his seat, his hands splayed on the table, the tips of his fingers white.

'Brian.' He doesn't so much as look at me so I say his name again as he continues to rant. Then again. 'Brian, stop it! Stop shouting. It's not Oli's fault.'

Both men look at me in surprise. I don't think either of them have heard me raise my voice before.

'Sorry.' My husband's voice is gravelly as he sinks into his chair and rubs the back of his neck, his eyes closed. He opens them again and reaches for my hand. 'Sorry, Sue.' He looks at Oli. His chin dimples and he presses his lips together in contrition. 'Sorry, son.' Oli shrugs but says nothing. He's smarting, I can tell. 'I just find it all so—'

I put my hand over his. 'I know.'

Brian's eyes search mine. 'You don't seem surprised by all this.'

'I'm not.' I squeeze his hand. 'I've read Charlotte's diary. I know how she felt about Liam.'

He frowns. 'She's got a diary? When did you find it?'

'This morning,' I lie.

Brian sits up straighter in his chair. If he *is* somehow responsible for Charlotte's accident he doesn't look worried by the fact I may have had an insight in our daughter's most private thoughts.

'Does it . . .' He leans forward, 'Does it reveal why she might have wanted to . . .'

He can't bring himself to say the words 'tried to kill herself'. He refuses to entertain the thought that our daughter may have been so unhappy she chose to end her life rather than share her unhappiness with us. I can understand why he'd feel that way, completely understand.

'No,' I say and he visibly deflates with relief.

It's another lie of course but I can't share the truth about the diary until I know for sure if he played any part in 'the secret' that weighed so heavily on her. Right now I don't know what – or who – to believe.

'Can I see it?' he asks.

When I raise my eyebrows, he shakes his head.

'No, you're right, of course you are. She still deserves her privacy. But . . .' his eyes flick back to Oliver who's observing the two of us with a curious expression on his face. This is the first time we've been open about Charlotte's accident in front of him. The 'everything is fine' façade has finally dropped.

Brian shakes his head and slumps back in his seat. We lapse into silence and I find myself staring at the pile of crumbs in front of Oli. I wasn't surprised to read the entry in Charlotte's diary about how much she wanted to lose her virginity to Liam and how excited and scared she was. I didn't think much to it. I certainly didn't wonder whether it might be connected to 'the secret' Charlotte mentions on her final entry – I assumed that was to do with Brian – but now that Oliver has brought up this hotel business . . .

I tear my eyes away from the biscuit crumbs and glance at Milly who's half asleep at my feet. We need to take a walk – to Liam's house.

Saturday 30th September 1990

James told me he loved me last night – four weeks to the day after our first date.

He took me to a fabulous Mexican restaurant in Camden – all low lighting, intimate tables, flickering candles and not a cactus in sight. I was trying to eat my fajita without it flopping all over the place but the harder I tried to angle it into my mouth the more food fell out the end and the more I laughed. When I looked across the table at James he had a terribly serious look on his face. I glanced behind me to see if he was reacting to some terrible accident out in the street but cars and people were streaming past as normal.

I put down my fajita. I suddenly didn't feel very hungry any more. 'What is it, James?'

He shifted in his chair. 'You.'

'What about me?'

'You're the most incredible woman I've ever met in my life.'

His eyes were fixed and unblinking, his mouth set in a straight line, his hands folded neatly in his lap. It was like he was looking beyond my flowery red dress, black beads and curled hair and peering straight into my head.

'I love you, Suzy,' he said. 'I've never loved anyone the way I love you and it terrifies me, loving someone this much. I can't sleep, eat or think because of you. I can barely act. I've lost control of who I am and that scares the shit out of me but I can't run away because I love you so much. I can't ever be without you.'

He searched my eyes, looking for a reaction. I'd never seen him look so worried. I smiled, desperate to relieve his discomfort, and reached across the table for his hands. He unfolded them from his lap and held my fingers.

'I love you too, James but I've never felt more scared or vulnerable in my life. I've got no defences left, nothing to stop you from hurting me if you wanted to.'

'I'd never hurt you Suzy-Sue.' He let go of one of my hands and reached across the table so he could cup the side of my face. 'Never. I'd rather hurt myself than see you in pain.'

There were tears in his tears but he brushed them away brusquely.

'Let's just go.' He took a handful of notes out of

his wallet and threw them down on the table. 'Let's go back to yours, put on a record, crawl into bed and block out the world.'

I couldn't think of anything I'd rather do.

Chapter 6

I didn't go to Liam's house last night. Just as I was about to announce my intention to take the dog for a walk Brian shot out of his seat and disappeared into the hallway. When he returned a couple of minutes later he was wearing his jacket with Milly's lead dangling from his hand. He said the briefest of goodbyes to Oliver and then he was gone, out of the porch door like a shot.

Oli raised an eyebrow. 'Not like Dad to take Milly for a walk.'

I said nothing. Instead I offered him another cup of tea and more biscuits but Oli shook his head, said it was getting late and he needed to get back to Leicester.

I glance at the kitchen clock. Brian left for work ages ago and it's still only 8.50 a.m. If Liam is anything like Oliver was as a teenager there's no way he'll be awake at this time during half term. I should visit Charlotte first and then go and see him. I put down my cup of coffee and stand up. But what if he goes out for some reason and I miss him? Better to try and get hold of him first and *then* go and see Charlotte. Maybe if I take the long route to his house he'll be awake by the time I get there. It'll be at least 9.30 a.m. if I go through the park.

No, I change my mind again as I step into the cloakroom and reach for my coat. I should ring first. Or maybe I should text. That way I won't disturb his family. But I don't have a mobile number for him, just a landline.

Charlotte would though.

I fly up the stairs and head for her room, then pause in the doorway. Where's her mobile? I haven't seen it since before her accident.

I didn't touch Charlotte's room for two weeks after she was hospitalised, not one thing – not the mascara-stained makeup removal pads strewn across the dressing table, the dirty bras and knickers kicked under the bed or the magazines scattered across the floor – nothing. I thought that if I tidied up I'd regret wiping all traces of her personality from her room if she never woke up. It sounds ridiculous but I was in shock. How else could I have failed to notice that her phone wasn't in the clear plastic bag of her things that the nurse handed me? It contained all the normal things she'd take out with her – purse, keys, makeup and hairbrush – but no phone. Why? Like most teenagers she was umbilically attached to her mobile.

Three weeks after her accident, my shock finally dissipated and with it my insistence that Charlotte's room remain untouched. Instead of seeing the mess as a sign of normality it became a morbid shrine. My daughter wasn't dead – she was just ill – so I tidied up, ready for her return. And that's when I found the diary.

I throw open the wardrobe doors and root around in the pockets of some of her clothes. There are several items I've never seen before – a jacket that looks like it's Vivienne Westwood and an expensively cut dress with a VB label. I stare at it for several seconds. What's Charlotte doing with a Victoria Beckham dress? I push it along the rack and turn my attention to the pockets of a pair of Diesel jeans instead. I'll have to have a word with Oli the next time I see him.

I close the wardrobe door. The bus driver didn't mention anything about a mobile phone and neither did any of the other eye witnesses and the police immediately cordoned off the area so if it was lying crushed or broken nearby they'd have found it. So it must be in the house somewhere.

Charlotte must have deliberately hidden it. And if she did that then maybe she had something to hide.

I yank open Charlotte's sock drawer and root around at the back. Nothing. I tip up the box of folders and school work under her desk and sift through the papers. No phone. It's not hidden in any of her shoes or boots or secreted behind the novels on her bookshelf. I return to the sock drawer, squeezing each bundle but still find nothing. I search the room for fifteen, twenty minutes, going through every drawer, bag and shoebox but there's no sign of her mobile.

Where is it?

I reach under the pillow for her diary and flick through the pages. I must have read it ten, twenty times but whatever secret she was keeping, she didn't share it with her diary. She shared other worries – anxieties about her weight, nervousness about sleeping with Liam for the first time, concern about exam results and indecisiveness about the career she wanted but nothing huge, nothing so terrible she'd consider taking her own life.

I close the book and tuck it back under her pillow. There are no answers here, maybe Liam will have some.

White Street is completely deserted apart from a bad-tempered ginger tom who hisses at us as we walk past. I've been to Liam's house dozens of times but I rarely go in. I normally sit in the car, engine running, as Charlotte rushes in to grab him so I can take them bowling or to the cinema. She never stayed overnight with him and he never stayed at ours but I told her that, if she was still with Liam when she turned sixteen, I'd accompany her to the doctor so she could go on the pill. Then, once it was safe, her father and I would go out for the evening and she and Liam could have the house to themselves. I thought I was being very reasonable (or 'ridiculously liberal' according to Brian) but Charlotte told me it was the 'grossest thing she'd ever heard' and that, if she wanted her parents to know when she was having sex she'd put an advert in the local paper.

I open the gate of the blue house at number fifty-five. The front garden looks lovely – the beds are awash with colour, not a single weed to be seen. Claire, Liam's mum, must have been very busy. What I'd give for her green fingers.

I knock lightly when I reach the front door. The curtains are closed in the living room but I can make out the shadowy shape of a person moving about. I knock again, louder this time, and keep an eye on the curtains. A moment later they twitch and a pair of bright blue eyes peers out at me then they're swiftly pulled shut again. I hear the sound of a wooden floor creaking and then the front door swings open. Liam Hutchinson, Charlotte's seventeen-year-old boyfriend, stands in front of me in nothing but his navy and white striped boxer shorts. He looks confused, so I smile warmly.

'Hello, Liam.'

He nods. 'Mrs Jackson.'

'Could I come in? I was wondering if we could have a little chat?'

It feels strange to be sitting in the Hutchinson's living room. I've never been in here before and I can't stop myself from staring around, drinking in the unusual lithograph prints on the walls, the colour-coordinated scatter cushions and the large, expensive-looking rug in front of the original Victorian fireplace. Liam is slumped on the sofa on the other side of the room, his knees spread wide. If he finds this situation odd he isn't letting on. We've been sitting here, sneaking looks at each other, for the last couple of minutes, neither of us saying a word. I rehearsed my opening line dozens of times on my way over but now the time has come to say it, my mouth has gone dry.

'So . . .' I manage at last. 'You're probably wondering why I'm here.'

He shrugs. 'Something to do with Charlotte?'

'Yes. Have you been to see her? I'm surprised we haven't crossed paths.'

'No.' He picks at the ivory and gold throw covering his chair, plucking out the metallic threads and then dropping them on the floor. His mother will have a fit when she gets home. 'I haven't seen her. I didn't think I'd be allowed.'

'Really?' I sit forward. 'Because you're not a relative? That's fine. Friends *and* family are allowed in and,' I smile warmly, 'you're more than a friend.'

He shifts in his seat. 'No, I'm not.'

'Sorry. I meant – you're her boyfriend.'

'No. I'm not.'

I frown, certain I must have misheard him. 'I'm sorry. I thought you just said—'

'We're not going out any more.' He glances away, as though embarrassed. 'Charlotte dumped me.'

'No!'

I can't believe it. Charlotte ended it? *Charlotte* did? I felt sure that if anyone had called time on the relationship it would have been Liam. She idolized him. Tall, dark, two years older than her, handsome in a scruffy hair-in-his-eyes sort of way and in a band, she'd almost collapsed with excitement a year ago when one of his friends approached one of her friends in the school canteen to tell her that Liam thought she was 'fit'.

She didn't give the slightest hint anything was wrong in their relationship although . . . I look from Liam to the clock on the mantelpiece, distracted by the tick-tick-tick filling the room . . . and time slips away.

It's three weeks before Charlotte's accident – a Saturday afternoon – and she's just returned from a shopping trip in town. I'm in the living room, reading, when I hear the door to the porch open. I call out, asking her if she's bought anything nice but I'm ignored. I don't ask again but I do keep an eye on the open living room door. Seconds later Charlotte slams up the stairs looking white as a ghost. I call after her, asking if she's okay but the only reply I receive is the sound of a bedroom door slamming. I half-rise from the sofa, unsure what to do. Charlotte's not one for mollycoddling, especially when she's upset. She won't let me hug her and flinches if I so much as stroke her arm. She's stressed, all the kids are. You just have to stand at the school gates for a couple of minutes to work that out. Their GCSEs are fast approaching and coursework is mounting up. Charlotte even had to go into school in the holidays so her teacher could help her complete it on time. I sink back into the sofa. I haven't been sleeping well recently. My nightmares have returned and the last thing I need is a screaming match with a fifteen-year-old. *She knows where I am*, I think as I pick my book back up again.

'Did you split up on a Saturday?' I ask Liam. 'About nine weeks ago?'

He runs a hand over his face. 'No, it was . . .' he pauses and I sense that he's struggling to suppress his emotions, '. . . she ended it the day before her accident.'

'Why?' I lean forward in my seat, my hands gripping my knees. Why didn't I contact him sooner? It's as though I've been sleepwalking since Charlotte's accident – longer than that – and I'm only just waking up. Splitting up with her boyfriend *has* to be the reason she stepped in front of the bus. You never feel heartache as keenly as you do when you're young. You think it'll destroy you and that you will never love, or be loved, again. She didn't write about it in her diary though.

Liam stands up, crosses the room and picks up his guitar from the stand next to the bookcase. He sits back down and strums a few chords.

'Liam?' It's as though he's forgotten I'm in the room. 'Why did Charlotte end your relationship? How was she?'

He looks at me blankly.

'When she ended your relationship, how was she?'

He shakes his head. 'I don't know, I wasn't there.'

'Sorry?'

He looks back at his guitar, strums a few more chords then slaps the strings with the palm of his

69

hand, silencing the sound, then looks across at me. 'She dumped me by *text*.'

I can sense that he doesn't want to talk about it. That he wants me to leave. But I can't. 'What did she say? In her text? If you don't mind me asking.'

'Not much.' He reaches into the side of the sofa and Milly starts to her feet as a small, black, plastic object whizzes through the air and lands on the sofa beside me. Liam's phone. I look at him, to check it's okay for me to go through it. He nods then looks back at his guitar.

Charlotte the open message is titled. I read it then look at Liam in surprise.

'That's it?'

He nods.

I look back at the text message:

It's over between us Liam. If you love me you'll never contact me again.

'Did you ask why?'

Liam doesn't answer. He's staring at the carpet, tapping his foot repeatedly.

'Liam?'

'What?' He doesn't look up.

'Did you contact her?'

'Of course I did.' He moves as though he's about to put his guitar on the ground then changes his mind. He hugs it to his chest instead, the side of his cheek pressed against the fret board. 'You don't get a text message dumping you out of the blue like that and not ring up to ask what the fuck's going on, do you? Not if you still love the person.'

Milly snuffles at my feet.

'What did Charlotte say?'

'She didn't.' Liam looks at me blankly, like the fight has gone out of him. 'She wouldn't answer her phone. I texted her loads, but she didn't text back. Not once.' He shakes his head. 'I know she's your daughter but I didn't deserve that, Mrs Jackson. I didn't deserve to get dumped by *text* with no explanation and then get ignored like I didn't even fucking exist.'

I'm torn. Part of me wants to cross the divide between us and wrap Liam in my arms and take away the hurt. The other part wants to ask if they argued, if he did anything to warrant Charlotte ending the relationship in such a brutal way. I decide to do neither. He looks close to tears and I don't want to upset him more than I already have. Not if I want him to talk to me again. I stand up and pull on Milly's lead so she rises too.

'I'm sorry, Liam,' I say. 'I had no idea about any of that. Charlotte didn't breathe a word.'

He sighs heavily, then crosses his arms and looks away. Conversation over.

It's only when I'm halfway home that I realize I didn't bring up the one subject I'd traipsed all the way over to White Street to discuss. Sex. There's no way I can turn back and knock on the door again, not with Liam the way he was when I left. I don't know what drove Charlotte to do what she did but I can't help but feel that it was cruel, even for a teenager. But maybe Liam had done something to deserve it?

Sometimes you have to escape from a relationship as stealthily and quietly as you can.

'Here we are, Milly,' I say as I fit the key in the lock, turn it and twist the handle of the porch door. 'Home again. Home ag—'

My voice catches in my throat. There's a postcard, picture side up, on the mat. I start to shake as I reach down to pick it up.

'Stop it, Sue,' I tell myself. 'Stop overreacting, it's just a postcard,' but as I turn it over in my hands and look at the other side my ears start to ring. My vision clouds and I grab the doorframe, blinking hard to try and dispel the white spots that have appeared before my eyes but I know it's too late. I'm going to faint.

Friday 13th October 1990

Nearly two weeks since James told me he loved me and I still haven't been to his place. All I know is that he lives in a three-bedroom terraced house near Wood Green. Hels is worried. According to her, you don't date a man for six weeks without seeing his place unless he's got something to hide. I told her that I wasn't bothered – that going to hotels was exciting and staying at mine was convenient, but she knew I was bullshitting. You can't be friends with someone since you were ten and lie to their face and get away with it.

'Has it occurred to you that he might be married?' she asked me over lunch the other day.

I told her it had, but there was no mark on the third finger of James's left hand and he hadn't slipped, not even once, and mentioned a wife or children. He hadn't even mentioned an ex-girlfriend. I'd told him all about Nathan. I'd even told him about Rupert and the fact we'd had a drunken shag at uni, long before I introduced him to Hels and they got it together but he'd never so much as mentioned another woman's name. Helen thought that was odd – that his silence meant he was obviously hiding something. I argued that some people are private and prefer to keep the past buried.

'What then?' she said. 'Ex-con? Prisoner on the run?' We both laughed. 'Maybe he still lives with his mum and dad?'

I stopped laughing. That wasn't such a ridiculous suggestion. James did keep running off from my place at the most bizarre hours, claiming he had 'things to do' and 'stuff to sort' and, no matter how much I interrogated him, he refused to expand on his vagaries, saying instead that what he had to do was 'dull' and I 'really wouldn't be interested'.

'Definitely married,' Hels said when I told her that. 'Why else would he suddenly rush off and not tell you where he's going?'

Before she went back to work she made me swear that I'd stop 'fannying around' and demand that James take me to his place or I'd end the relationship. I wasn't sure about throwing ultimatums around but I promised her I'd bring up the subject when I meet him for dinner tomorrow.

I'm sure there's a perfectly innocuous reason why he hasn't invited me back to his place. So why do I feel so sick?

Chapter 7

I come to on the floor of the porch. One of my cheeks is pressed against cold tile, the other is strangely damp. I glance up to see Milly standing above me, her big, brown eyes fixed on the empty dog bowl in the corner of the porch, her tongue dripping with drool. She senses me looking at her and smiles down at me before enthusiastically licking my cheek.

'Hello Milly Moo.' I sit up slowly, gingerly checking my body for injuries. Nothing appears to be broken, though by the way my left temple aches, I think I'm in for a pretty impressive bruise. For a split second I assume I tripped and fell but then I spot the postcard on the floor beside me and it all comes flooding back again. The image on the front shows James Stewart sitting on a step smiling a goofy smile whilst, behind him, a shadow of an enormous rabbit is projected on the wall. It's an image from the film *Harvey*. The postcard could so easily be innocuous – a simple hello from one friend to another – only there's no chatty text on the other side of this postcard, there isn't even an addressee. There's just a stamp, postmarked Brighton and an address, *my* address.

This isn't someone forgetting to write a postcard and slipping it into the postbox with a handful of letters by mistake. That's the explanation Brian would come up with if I told him about it. He'd give me a look, *the* look, the one that says 'you're going to have another episode, aren't you?' and then he'd throw it in the bin and tell me that everything's fine and I'm safe. Only I'm not safe, am I? *Harvey* was James' favourite film. I lost count of the number of times we watched that film together.

Milly startles as I kick out at the postcard, sending it spinning and scuttling under the shoe rack. If I can't see it then maybe I won't think about it. Maybe I'll be able to ignore the fact that, twenty years after I left him, James has finally tracked me down.

I try as best I can to forget about the postcard but it's like trying to forget how to breathe. Whenever my mind pauses, whenever it's free of thoughts about Charlotte, Brian and what to cook for dinner, it returns to the porch, peers under the shoe rack and pulls out the postcard. No matter where I am in the house it haunts me from its dark, dusty corner. I want to visit Charlotte but I'm too scared to leave the house. What if James is waiting for me? If he's been watching the house he'll know I'm home alone but all the doors and windows are locked – I've checked three times – and there's no way for him to get in. I've got my mobile phone in my hands, primed and ready to key in 999 if I hear the slightest noise.

There won't be time to call for help if I leave the house and James attacks me. If he's hiding in the bushes opposite the front door he could get me as I get into the car or, if he's in a car down the lane, he could follow me to the hospital and attack Charlotte. It's been less than twenty-four hours since I last saw her and I'm already consumed by fear and guilt because I haven't seen her today. What if, deep in her subconscious, she knows I haven't been to visit, and it makes her retreat deeper into her coma? What if she wakes up and I'm not there? What if she dies?

For the next couple of hours I don't know what to do with myself. I jump when the phone rings and start when the wind rattles the letter box. When there's a knock on the front door I run up to Brian's study and peer down from behind the curtain, only to discover the electricity man pushing a card through our letter box. What am I doing? I'm allowing the memory of James to terrify me, to stop me from visiting my own daughter. I am not 'Suzy-Sue' – I haven't been her for a very long time.

I return downstairs and fish the postcard out from its dusty hiding place with the fire tongs and burn it in the fireplace in the living room. I sit on the sofa, watching as the flames lick at the corners, dance across James Stewart's lolloping smile and then envelop him. When he and his strange rabbit sidekick have turned to dust I sweep them up.

As I pour the ashes of the postcard into the kitchen bin a new thought occurs to me. What if the postcard was meant for Oli from one of his uni friends? What if they were too stoned to notice they hadn't put his name or a message on it and I just burnt it! What if he asks where it is? How do I explain what I just did without sounding certifiable? My hands shake as I reach for my car keys and I steady myself on the kitchen table. I drop my head to my chest and inhale slowly – one, two, three – then out again. I do it again – one, two, three – then out again. I need to be calm. I need to think clearly, otherwise I'll have another episode. This is how they start, this is how I go from normal, sane, rational Sue to neurotic, paranoid 'I'd better lock Charlotte in her room for the weekend because Brian is away at a party conference and BBC news has reported a child abduction in the next town' Sue. One, two, three. One, two, three. Slowly my breathing returns to normal.

I feel calmer and happy when I return from the hospital. The knots in my shoulders disappeared the second I stepped into Charlotte's room and saw that she was still safe, warm and being cared for. There was no change in her condition and the nurses reassured me that she hadn't had any visitors since Brian and I were with her yesterday. There is no reason to think James has found me. The blank post-card is just that. An innocuous blank postcard, sent to us in error or mistakenly delivered by the postman. I've barely slept since Charlotte's accident. I can't sleep at night for trying to work out why she did what she did. It's no wonder my mind goes into overdrive sometimes.

For the second time today I attach a lead to Milly's collar and lead her out of the house. She smiles up at me, delighted to be out in the fresh air again. We only tend to walk her early in the morning and late at night so an afternoon sojourn in the spring sunshine is an unexpected treat.

Judy, Ella's mum, opens the door with a scowl.

'Sue?'

I force a smile. 'Hello Judy. How are you?'

'Fine.'

I wait for her to ask what I want. Instead I am subjected to a long slow eye sweep that starts at the top of my head with my grey roots, pauses at the wrinkles and dark circles that line my unmade-up eyes, flits over my best M&S coat and settles, unimpressed, on my comfy brown Clarks slip-ons. Judy and I were good friends until we fell out when she took both girls to get their ears pierced for Ella's thirteenth birthday without checking with me first. In retrospect I may have overreacted but we both said some pretty ugly things and the time for mending fences is long past.

'Great,' I say as brightly as I can manage when really I want to bop her on her sneering Chanel-smeared nose. 'I don't suppose Ella's in, is she?'

'Ella?' She looks surprised.

'Yes. I'd like to talk to her about Charlotte. If that's okay with you.'

Judy's eyes narrow and then, just for a split second, a look akin to compassion crosses her face. I imagine she's heard about the accident.

'Okay,' she says after a pause. 'But keep it brief because she's supposed to be studying for her GCSEs.'

When I nod my assent she turns back towards the hallway, pulling the front door towards her so it's only open a couple of inches and then shouts for her daughter. There's a muffled cry in reply and then the door slams shut in my face. A minute or so later it opens again. Ella peers out at me.

'Hi.' She looks at me suspiciously, just like her mother did.

'Hi Ella.' My face is aching from smiling so widely. 'I was wondering if we could have a chat. About Charlotte.'

Her expression changes lightning fast – from suspicion to anger – and she crosses one skinny-jeaned leg over the other. 'Why would I want to do that?'

First Liam, now Ella. I only have to mention my daughter's name for a black cloud to descend. It doesn't make sense. When her class made their yearbook at the start of their GCSE year and predicted where everyone would be in five years' time Charlotte was voted 'girl everyone would stay in touch with' and 'girl most likely to be successful'.

'Because you're friends,' I say. 'Unless . . .' I study her face, '. . . unless you're not friends anymore.'

Ella raises a thin, penciled eyebrow. 'Correct.'

'I see.' I pause, trying to decide how best to continue. From the set of her jaw I can tell Ella's as keen on communicating with me as Liam was and yet . . .

'Charlotte's still in a coma,' I say.

'I know.' She raises the eyebrow again but the flash of light in her eyes betrays her. She's interested. She wants to know more about her ex-best friend.

'Her lungs are getting stronger which is a very good sign.'

Ella says nothing.

'We've tried everything to try and help her wake up,' I continue. 'I've talked to her about the family and what we're all doing. Brian reads her articles from the newspaper—'

'Grim. She'd hate that.'

'I agree,' I suppress a smile at the look of disgust on her face. 'I suggested he read out *Heat* magazine instead but he wasn't keen. I don't think he's as big a fan of celebrity gossip as Charlotte is.'

Ella pulls a face – like the mental image of my husband reading *Heat* magazine repulses her.

'So anyway,' I soldier on. 'Oli came up with the idea that we should play Charlotte her favourite song. He said he'd seen people do that in films and that it helps wake someone from a coma.'

Ella's face lights up at the mention of my stepson's name. Until recently she and Charlotte were like shadows to Oli and Danny. I have an inkling the boys may have been the subject of the girls' first ever crushes.

'Yeah?'

'Yes,' I say. 'So I was wondering if you could help. With the song. I haven't got the first clue what Charlotte was into.'

'"Someone Like You" by Adele.'

'Great.' I've actually heard of that song. They play it on Radio 2 all the time. 'Anyone else?'

She shrugs. 'That's her favourite but she likes "I Love the Way You Lie" by Rhianna and Eminem, "Money" by Jessie J. Oh, and "Born This Way" by Lady Gaga. We used to dance to that in my room before we'd go out to Breeze, to the under-eighteen night,' she adds quickly.

Her whole demeanour has changed. She's not a young woman propping up the doorway with her legs and arms crossed and a defiant look on her face anymore. Instead she looks like the little blonde five-year-old I found Charlotte hand in hand with in the playground at the end of their first day at school.

'You could see her,' I say softly, 'if you'd like. I could give you a lift to the hospital. I'm sure Charlotte would appreciate it.'

'No, she wouldn't.'

A scowl has fallen over Ella's face, all traces of vulnerability and tenderness gone.

'What makes you say that?'

'She just wouldn't.'

'Is this about Keisha?' I venture. A look of surprise

82

crosses her face at the mention of the other girl's name. 'Is that why you're angry?'

'It's none of my business who Charlotte hangs out with. She can do what she wants.'

'But you're her best friend. Surely you—'

'No, I'm not.'

'You're not?' I feign surprise. 'What happened?'

'Nothing.'

'Well, something must have—'

'Nothing happened, alright! Just leave me alone and stop asking me—'

'Everything okay here?' Judy appears in the doorway, alerted by her daughter's raised voice. 'Ella? Are you okay?'

'No.' Her daughter feigns a pained expression. 'Sue's hassling me and I haven't done anything wrong, Mum. I was just—'

'Have you been hassling my daughter?' Judy attempts a frown but too many Botox injections prevent her.

'No!' I can't help but laugh. 'Of course not. I was just asking her why she and Charlotte aren't best friends anymore.'

'And?'

'According to Ella, nothing happened.'

Judy glances at her daughter who shrugs as if to say 'that's what I said'.

'If Ella said nothing happened,' she says, looking back at me, 'then nothing happened.'

'But it must have. Those two have been friends since they were—'

'Nothing happened, Sue!' Ella screams. 'Okay? We just stopped being friends.' She looks at her mum. 'I don't want to talk about this anymore.'

'Okay, darling.' Judy puts a heavily manicured hand on her daughter's shoulder. 'Go back to your room and—'

'Please.' I beg. 'Judy, please. I need to know what happened. It might help Charlotte. Did you know that she'd split up with Liam or that—'

'Mummmm,' Ella looks at her mother with beseeching eyes. 'Mum, I really need to get back on with my revision.'

'Okay darling, off you—'

'Please.' I grab hold of Ella's wrist. 'Please. You need to help me.'

'Get your hands off my daughter!' I feel a sharp sting on my forearm and four white stripes appear on my skin from where Judy swiped at me with her false nails. 'Now.'

I'm so shocked I instantly let go.

'Thanks, Mum.' The smallest of smirks crosses Ella's face as she ducks out from the doorway and takes the stairs two at a time. Judy looks back at me.

'I'd like you to leave now please, Sue,' she says in a measured voice.

'Judy, look. I'm sorry if I overstepped the mark but—'

'Leave.' She takes a step back into the hallway and begins to close the front door.

I press my hand against it to stop it being slammed in my face. 'No, Judy, wait. Listen!'

'No! You listen!' The door swings open again. 'I'm sorry about what happened to Charlotte, really I am but it's not my fault and it's certainly not Ella's. Perhaps you should look a bit closer to home instead.'

I stand on the doorstep open-mouthed. And not just because Judy slammed the door in my face.

Sunday 15th October 1990

James and I had our first argument this evening. He and the rest of the theatre group popped by the bar, as they do every Sunday after rehearsals, and James took up his customary stool at the end. I said hello, got him a pint, gave him a kiss and got on with my job, just as I always do – having a bit of banter with Maggie and Jake, catching up on gossip with Kate and taking the piss out of Steve – but I could sense that something wasn't right. Whenever I looked across at James, instead of reading his script or his book, he was staring at me with a sour expression on his face. I shot him a smile then pulled a face. When that did nothing to crack his frown I went over during a quiet spot to ask what was wrong.

'You know,' he said.

'Know what?'

'I shouldn't have to tell you because you already know.'

'If I knew I wouldn't be here asking!'

He shrugged like I was an idiot and, thoroughly pissed off, I went off to serve someone else.

The next time I turned round to look at James he'd gone. I asked the others if he'd been in a bad mood during rehearsals. Far from it, they said. He'd been in fine form, practically bouncing across the stage.

'I think someone's in love,' Maggie had winked.

I thought he was too; he'd been hugely affectionate this morning and had insisted on shagging me not once but twice before he'd let me get out of bed to have a shower. He'd even replied 'soon' when I'd asked him when we were going to spend an evening in his place instead of mine.

So what had changed?

I couldn't wait for kicking-out time so I could put all the glasses in the dishwasher, wipe down the tables and get home to ring James. He didn't pick up for eight rings and then:

'Hello.' His voice was devoid of emotion.

'James, it's Suzy.'

'Hello Susan.'

That stung. He **never** called me by my full name.

'Why were you so off with me in the bar tonight?'

'You know.'

'Actually no,' I fought to keep the hurt out of my voice. 'I don't. That's why I'm ringing because I'd like you to tell me.'

'If you don't know there's no point discussing this.'

'Oh, for God's sake. Could you **be** more

exasperating? James, please tell me why you were in such a bad mood or I'm going to put the phone down.'

'Go on then.'

'Fine.'

I slammed down the phone then stared at it, waiting for him to ring back. Five minutes passed, then ten, then fifteen. By twenty I was fuming and snatched the receiver back up.

'Hello.' Same flat voice from the other end.

'What was it? Something I said? Something I did? Someone I talked to?' James sighed and I knew I'd hit the nail on the head. 'Who? And if you say "you know" one more time I'll never talk to you again.'

'Steve.'

'Steve Steve? Steve MacKensie?'

'Yes.'

'You were in a mood with me because I spoke to Steve MacKensie? That's ridiculous. Why would you be jealous of him?'

'No one said I was jealous, Susan.'

'Then why—'

'You were flirting with him. I saw you, leaning across the bar so he could look down your top.'

'What?'

'Don't try and deny it. Everyone saw and I won't allow the woman I love to make a laughing stock of me in front of my peers.'

'Allow? What is this, the 1930s? And I wasn't flirting with him, we were just bantering, like we always do.'

'Then why was his nose in your cleavage?'

'It—' I let out a deep sigh. 'This is ridiculous, James. Absolutely ridiculous. We were in bed this morning, lying in each other's arms after the most amazing sex *ever* and I was telling you how much I love you and now you're accusing me of . . .' I shook my head. 'Forget it. If you think I'd jeopardize what we've got, what we **had** to flirt with a second-rate actor then you're more than a fool, you're a . . .' my eyes filled with tears. 'Forget it, James.'

I slammed down the phone.

Less than a second later it rang. I let it ring nine times then picked it up. When I didn't say anything James sighed.

'I'm sorry, Suzy-Sue. I'm so sorry. I don't know what got into me. I've just had a lot on my plate recently. I've got a few . . . personal things . . . I'm working through at the moment, things I haven't talked to you about.'

'Well, that's no reason to take it out on me.'

'I know and I'm sorry. You don't deserve that. You looked beautiful in the pub tonight. I couldn't keep my eyes off you in that red top, your cleavage looks amazing, but it made me angry – when I saw other people admiring you too – because they have no right to ogle you like you're a cheap piece of meat and—'

'So you don't want me to wear low-cut tops anymore? Is that what you're saying?'

'Yes. No. No, that's not what I'm saying. What I'm trying, clumsily, to say is that it was obvious to me *that Steve was flirting with you because you looked gorgeous, and that made me angry – that your physicality was all that he could see. I'm not just in love with the way you look, I'm in love with the woman inside.'*

I said nothing. I was still trying to make sense of what he was trying to say. I think he was finding fault with Steve rather than me so why did I feel bad, like I'd done something to encourage him by wearing the wrong thing or being overly friendly.

'Suzy?'

I didn't say anything.

'Suzy?' James said again. 'Please don't be angry. Please don't hate me.'

'I don't hate you. I just don't understand you sometimes.'

'Let me rectify that.'

'How?'

'Let me take you home. Let me show you where I live.'

Chapter 8

'They're teenagers, Sue. What did you expect?'

'I know.' I dip a piece of cotton wool into the bowl of warm water next to the bed then wring it out and dab it gently across Charlotte's forehead. Three days have passed since I went to speak to Liam and Ella and I'm still smarting from Judy's parting remark.

'Show me a teenager that opens up to adults and I'll introduce you to Santa,' Brian adds. 'Honestly Sue, would *you* have spilled your secrets to some middle-aged woman when you were in your teens? I know I wouldn't.'

'No.' I meet my husband's concerned gaze and shake my head. 'I wouldn't. I just thought they might open up to me because Charlotte . . .' I tail off. Neither of them showed the least interest in helping our daughter.

Brian shrugs. 'I don't know why you're surprised, Sue. Kids fall in and out of love all the time and they switch their friends like they're going out of fashion. Teenagers are fickle, darling. Surely you know that?'

'I do but . . .' I place the cotton back in the bowl of water and pick up Charlotte's hairbrush. '. . . she'd been friends with Ella since primary school and they've had their spats but they always made up before. And as for Liam,' I tease the brush through Charlotte's long dark hair, 'she'd have done anything for him. She adored him. And I'm supposed to believe she dumped him because she's a fickle teen? It doesn't make sense.'

Brian turns another page of his newspaper then shuts it, folds it in two and rests it on his lap.

'Sue . . .'

I continue brushing Charlotte's hair, smoothing it down with my hands so the ends lie flat over her shoulders.

'Sue, look at me.'

'What?' I don't look up.

'You don't think you're getting a bit . . .' he pauses. '. . . obsessed, do you?'

'Obsessed?'

'With Charlotte's accident, acting like there's some big conspiracy when the truth is . . .' he pauses again. '. . . it was just an accident. A terrible, unpreventable accident. I understand how helpless and powerless you feel – I feel exactly the same way – but giving her friends the third degree isn't going to make her magically wake up.'

'You don't understand,' I start, then fall silent. I still haven't told him what she wrote in her diary.

I nearly told him about it a couple of days ago but then he snuck out of bed at six o'clock in the morning. At first I thought he was in the toilet but when he hadn't reappeared after half an hour I got up to look for him. He wasn't anywhere in the house, neither was Milly. It was the second time in as many years that he'd taken her out for a walk.

Something's going on and there's only one person I can talk to about it.

Mum's sitting in her favourite place, by the window in the hard-backed armchair I covered with a lovely Laura Ashley print a few years ago. She doesn't look up when I walk into the room.

'Hello Mum.' I move a pile of towels and laundry onto the floor and perch on the edge of her single bed. There's nowhere else to sit.

My mother doesn't acknowledge me so I try a different tack. 'Hello Elsie. How are you today?'

This time she turns around. Her forehead creases with confusion. 'Who are you?'

My heart sinks. She doesn't recognize me. Mum has good days and bad days. Today, it seems, is not a good day.

'I'm Sue,' I say. 'Your daughter. I bought you a present.'

I hand her a box of Turkish Delight, her favourite. She takes the tin wordlessly but her eyes light up when she spots the familiar Eastern Princess illustration on the front.

'How are you?' I ask. I want to put a hand on her

93

knee or make some kind of physical contact but I don't want to risk scaring her.

'A little bored,' she says, tracing a finger over the Princess's face. She looks up at me, a playful light shining in her pale blue eyes, 'but at least I'm not dead.'

I love that the disease hasn't totally stolen her sense of humour. Not yet anyway. There was a time when I thought it was gone for good – back when she was in a home in York and I lived so very far away in London and she went through the transition phase. Her grip on the present was slowly slipping away but she was still aware enough to realize what was happening to her. I can still remember hearing the terror in her voice when we talked on the phone. The present was scary and unpredictable, the past a safe refuge, but she didn't want to fully let go, to lose herself into the abyss of the disease. There would be no turning back then.

It's easier for Mum now, in some ways. Both of her feet are firmly rooted in the past and her trips to the present are so fleeting she barely registers them. She rarely recognizes me but when she does, it makes my day.

'Who did you say you were again?' Mum peers at me over her spectacles, the box of sweets clutched to her chest.

'I'm Sue.' I smile, desperate to reassure her, to assuage the fear in her eyes. 'I'm your daughter.'

'No, you're not.' A flash of anger crosses her face. 'Why would you say that? Why would you be so cruel?'

'I'm sorry.' I need to talk quickly, to calm her down before she works herself up into a state. 'I confused you with someone else. My mother looks very much like you.'

'Clever, is she?' Mum says, 'This mum of yours? Pretty too, I don't doubt.'

There is it is again – the playful twinkle in her eye.

'The cleverest,' I say. 'Not much gets past my mum. And as for pretty – well, she won Miss Bognor Butlins in 1952 so yes, she was stunning. A real beauty.'

Instead of being flattered, Mum looks cross. 'I won Miss Bognor Butlins in 1952.'

'Of course you did.' I correct myself quickly. I forget that, while Mum often doesn't know what day it is, she can recall events in the past with impressive accuracy. 'My mother must have won in 1951.'

Mum says nothing. Instead she fumbles with the cellophane wrapping around the Turkish Delight.

'Can I help?' I wait for a nod then pick away at the cellophane and open the box. Mum pops a dusty sweet into her mouth and closes her eyes in delight.

'I bought you a present,' I say, rummaging in my handbag and pulling out a CD. 'It's some music. I thought it might remind you of the tea dances you went to when you were younger.'

Mum shows no signs of either pleasure or displeasure; her eyes are still tightly closed. I cross the room and load the CD onto the small portable player I bought her last Christmas. I press play, wait for the sound of a double bass, overlaid with banjo and the crackling crooning of the male singer to fill the air, then sit down again. A small smile plays on Mum's lips and her slippered foot tap-tap-taps on the beige care home carpet.

'I found a million dollar baby,' she sings softly in her thin, warbling voice, 'in a five-and-ten-cent store.'

I sit silently beside her, holding my breath as her eyes flick open and she stares up into the corner of the room, her head nodding gently from side to side. It's a magical moment – seeing her so quietly happy, wrapped in a precious memory. I wonder if she's in Dad's arms, her hand on his shoulder as he twirls her around the dance floor. He's been dead for over thirty years now and I know she still misses him. For Mum, marriage and family were everything. She dedicated her life to Dad and me. She told me once that she'd been dreaming of having a family since she was a little girl.

I was the same and I was overjoyed when I fell pregnant with Charlotte. Brian and I had barely even started trying when I felt a strange pricking sensation just above my pubic bone and a pregnancy test confirmed what I already suspected. Brian was over the moon. He'd always wanted Oli to have a little brother or sister. My pregnancy only increased Brian's protective side and he wouldn't let me lift a finger for nine months. I'd never felt so precious or so loved in my life. I was twenty-eight when Charlotte was born and Brian and I loved being parents together so much we tried to conceive again, six months after she was born. But the luck we'd had first time around deserted us and, as the months rolled into years the doctors told us that there was no reason, other than our advancing age, why we shouldn't conceive again. After countless late-night chats and a lot of soul searching, we decided that what would be would be. If we were only meant to be a family of four then so be it. I ached to be pregnant again, to feel another child tumble turning in my womb but it wasn't to be. Three miscarriages in two years saw to that.

Neither of us could bear the heartbreak of another failed pregnancy so, the day Charlotte turned five, we took her to the home of a local Golden Retriever breeder and, out of a squirmy mass of soft, yellow fur, we chose Milly. Now our family really was complete.

'Hello Susan.'

Mum says my name so softly I think I must have dreamed it but no, there she is, sitting beside me, her pale blue eyes fixed on mine, the tin of Turkish Delight on the table beside her, her hands loosely gathered in her lap.

I want to jump off the bed and wrap my arms around her. I want to talk nineteen-to-the-dozen, to fill her in on everything that's going on in my life, to beg her for her advice, to listen intently, to feel small and safe and protected again. Instead I remain where I am and I take her hand. It's not fair of me to inflict my fears and worries on her. Mum's the one that needs to feel safe and protected now, not me.

'Hello Mum.' I gently squeeze her hand. Her skin is paper thin and speckled with age spots. 'How are you feeling today?'

'Old,' she says, shifting in her chair and changing position as though checking for aches, pains, clicks and twinges. 'How's Charlotte and that handsome husband of yours?'

Mum's always had a soft spot for Brian. Her fondness for him was part of the reason I took him back after the affair.

'Brian's fine,' I say brightly, reaching for a Turkish Delight even though I've never really been a fan. 'As busy as always. And Charlotte . . .'

I can't tell her the truth. I don't want to upset her and have her disappear on me again. What if she never comes back from the past? What if her last moment with me is a horrible one? I'd never be able to forgive myself.

'. . . Charlotte is studying hard for her GCSE exams.'

'Good girl.' Mum looks so proud. 'She's going to go far. What is it she wants to be now? Psychologist, was it?'

'Physiotherapist. She wants to work with premiership footballers. She says she admires their athleticism and dedication to the sport but I think she just wants to touch their thighs.' I laugh. 'I wouldn't be surprised if she wanted to be an air hostess tomorrow and a marine biologist the day after that. Charlotte changes her mind about what she wants to be so often I can't keep up.'

Mum chuckles. 'You were exactly the same, Susan. I always thought you'd be a teacher but Dad was convinced you were more cut out to be a seamstress.'

'You were both right,' I say. 'In a way.'

I trained to be a TEFL teacher after university – it was the easiest way to fund my travels – but my heart was never really in it. I'd graduated with a 2:1 in textiles and I really wanted to work in the theatre as a costume designer but jobs were worse than scarce. It was all about who you knew and I knew no one. That's how I ended up with the Abberley Theatre Players.

'You were very good at both,' Mum says, startling me back into her small, magnolia-walled bedroom at Hays-Price Retirement Community Home. She pats her chair. 'You should do this professionally, upholstering. People will pay good money for beautiful things.'

I smile. I abandoned my dreams of designing for the stage twenty years ago. I didn't pick up a needle again until a tearful five-and-a-half-year-old Charlotte came home from school one day and asked why she was the only one in the nativity play who didn't have a costume.

'Maybe I should.' There are a million things I want to tell her while she's still here, in the present, but I don't know where to start. I don't want to tell her that I suspect that Brian is cheating on me or that I think Charlotte's ex-best friend and boyfriend may have something to do with her accident. What I want to do is tell Mum how much she means to me and how I wish I could take away the terrible disease that, day by day, is stealing another part of her away from me.

'I love you, Mum,' The words tripping off my tongue so quickly they run together. 'I don't say it enough but I do. We all do. And I appreciate all the lovely things you've done for me in my life and I'm sorry I've been a terrible daughter—'

'Susan!' The smile slips from Mum's face and she purses her lips. 'Don't you dare say such a terrible, untrue thing. I couldn't have asked for a better daughter than you.'

'But I ran away.' Tears well in my eyes and I frantically swallow to try and dispel them. 'I ran away to Greece when you needed me and—'

'Susan!' She crushes my hand between her two smaller hands. I'm surprised at her strength. 'Don't you dare. Don't you dare apologise for that when that . . . that *monster* . . . did the things he did to you. I just wish your dad had been around to stop him from—'

I stare at her in horror. She wasn't supposed to know about James. She wasn't supposed to remember. I phoned her from Gatwick airport while I was waiting for my flight to Greece and told her everything. I needed to talk to someone, to purge myself of three years of hell but I didn't think for one second that she'd take any of it in. I didn't even think she'd know who I was. How could I have been so selfish?

'Charlotte sends her love,' I say, desperate to change the subject. 'She'll be along to visit as soon as she can.'

'Oh, that would be lovely.' Mum's face lights up and I say a prayer, begging whoever is in charge of the universe to make my daughter well so they can spend some time together, so it's not a lie.

'I'd like that,' Mum says. She rummages in a little drawer in the table beside her and presses a brooch into my hand. It's glass and paste, a bouquet of flowers with a ribbon tied around the stem. It's terribly old-fashioned but very pretty and sparkly. 'Give this to Charlotte with my love. Tell her it's to bring her luck in her exams.' She fixes me with a meaningful look. 'I was wearing it the day I met your dad you know.'

I open my mouth to thank her, to tell her how touched Charlotte will be but find I can't speak.

'I have something for you too,' Mum says, twisting back to her drawer. I try to object, to tell her she mustn't when Mozart's Symphony Number 40 in G Minor fills the air and I rummage in my handbag for my phone.

'Brian?' I say, standing up and walking across the room, my back to Mum, my voice hushed. 'Now's not a good time. I'm with Mum.'

There's a pause then,

'It's Charlotte,' he says. 'You need to come to the hospital. Now.'

Tuesday 18th October 1990

*Tonight I finally got to see James's house. And now
I know why he kept me waiting for so long . . .*

*We were supposed to get to his house for one
o'clock, the times Mrs Evans had said we should come
for lunch (yes, he lives with his mum!) but we'd hit
the pub early and James, who was ridiculously nervous
but wouldn't admit it, insisted we have one more for
luck. His mum wouldn't mind if we were late, he said.
She was probably too busy watching 'Murder She
Wrote' to notice the time.*

*Two hours later we finally rolled up at his house
in Wood Green. James could barely get the key in
the lock and I couldn't stop giggling.*

*'Shoes,' James said, nudging me in the ribs as we
fell into the hallway.*

*'Socks!' I nudged him back and burst out
laughing.*

'No,' he glanced down at my beautiful red, patent

heels. 'Take off your shoes. Mother doesn't allow shoes on the carpets.'

I reached a hand down and yanked one shoe off. I had to brace myself against the wall to stop myself from tumbling over. 'I thought you were playing a word association game. You know – shoes, socks, toes, feet . . .'

'Why would I do that?' He gave me a look. 'I'm not a child, Susan.'

I shrugged and reached for my other shoe, unsure of what to say.

'Kidding!' He poked me in the side and I instantly lost balance and tumbled to the floor. 'Feet! Cheese! Beans!'

I laughed as he helped me back onto my feet but it felt forced. The joke wasn't as funny anymore.

'Slippers,' James said.

I assumed he was still playing the word association game so ignored him and glanced around the hallway instead. It was a wide space but the deep red textured wallpaper and mahogany furniture that lined one wall made it seem small and dark. A single light bulb, smothered by a dark brown velveteen lampshade, hung from the ceiling and framed photographs decorated one wall, some in black and white, some technicolour but faded with age. There were a lot of a small blond boy with a wide smile and sparkling blue eyes so I stepped towards them to see if they were of my boyfriend.

'Slippers.' James grabbed my wrist and jerked me back towards him.

I yanked my hand away and rubbed my skin. 'James, that hurt.'

He kicked something across the carpet towards me. 'Stop making a fuss and put those on.'

I looked down at the beige suedette slippers at my feet and shook my head. They looked like something my grandma would wear.

'You need to put them on, Susan.' He yanked open the cupboard door beside him and pulled out an identical, but larger, pair of slippers and slipped his feet into them. I looked at his face, waiting for him to burst out laughing but it didn't happen.

I looked back at the slippers. I didn't like the way he was telling me what to do but the last thing I wanted was for us to get into an argument before I met his mum for the first time.

I put the slippers on, trying not to think about who'd worn them before.

James looked at my feet then laughed and said they suited me. He slipped a hand around my waist, pulling me into him and his mouth found mine. I relaxed in his arms as he kissed me.

'Come on,' he said, taking my hand, 'let's find Mum. I just know she's going to love you.'

He led me down the corridor and through a white door.

'Mum,' he said, holding tightly onto my hand, 'this is Suzy. Suzy, this is Mum.'

I smiled and held out my other hand as the small, dark-haired woman on the sofa stood up and crossed the room towards me. It remained outstretched as she swerved around me and disappeared out through the living-room door.

'James,' she said from the hallway. 'A word, if you please.'

I was surprised by her strong Welsh accent. I'd assumed she'd be posh like her son.

James followed her wordlessly, without so much as a backward glance at me, pulling the living-room door closed behind him. I stood stock-still, staring at the closed door. When I finally moved it was to perch on the edge of the pristine maroon leather sofa that shared a wall with an enormous mahogany display case. On the wall opposite me, hanging behind a sideboard housing a small grey television and an ancient-looking record player, was the most terrifying batik wall hanging I'd ever seen. It was black with a huge tribal mask in the centre, picked out in blues, whites and purples. The mouth was open, gaping, a black void beneath empty white eyes that stared across the room at me. I looked away, to the bookshelf, crammed with green-spined hardbacks I'd never heard of and then at the table covered with a white lace tablecloth, laden with food. My stomach rumbled at the sight of plates piled high with cucumber, egg and salmon sandwiches, a beautiful fluffy Victoria sponge on a silver cake stand and bowls of olives, nuts and crisps, but I didn't touch a thing.

Instead I wandered up to the bookcase, plucked a green book off the shelf, and opened the cover. Ten minutes later the sound of raised voices filtered into the room. I placed the book back on the shelf and opened the door a crack.

'James?' I shuffled noiselessly towards a door at the other end of the house. It was ajar, light flooding out, turning a triangle of maroon carpet pink. The murmur of voices filled my ears as I drew closer. 'James?'

'How could you?' His mother's voice was strained, verging on hysterical. 'After everything I do for you. How could you be so disrespectful?'

'Mam . . . please . . . calm down.' My outstretched hand fell away from the doorknob. James was talking with a strong Welsh accent too. 'We're a couple of hours late, that's all.'

'For family lunch! Have you no manners? Or did you lose them all the day Da killed his self?'

Killed himself? I rest a hand on the wall. James had told me his father died of lung cancer.

'I'm here now, aren't I?'

'Late. With her. Some tart you've known for ten minutes.'

'She's not a tart, Mam. She's special.'

'And what does that make me? Something the cat dragged in.'

'Of course not. You're—'

'I got up at 6 a.m. this morning to clean the house, James. 6 a.m! I've been scrubbing and cooking and cleaning all day. For you Jamie, for you and that woman. The least you could do is show me some respect and turn up on time. I thought we brought you up better than this.'

'Oh for fuck's sake—'

A sound like a cracked whip cut him short and he gasped. I took a step back from the door. The maroon walls seemed darker and the furniture bigger. Even the photographs were leering at me. I tried to take a deep breath but the air was thick and heavy and I felt it catch in my throat. I glanced towards the front door.

'James! James, I'm sorry.' Mrs Evans' voice was thin and desperate. 'James, please don't go. I didn't mean to—'

I was sent flying as the kitchen door slammed open and James flew out towards me. He gripped my wrist and yanked me after him as he strode towards the front door.

'We're leaving.' He pulled me, slippers and all, out into the front garden. I stretched my fingertips towards my beautiful red patent heels but we were already through the gate and onto the street. 'Fuck family lunches. Fuck her. Fuck it all.'

'Now do you see?' he said, shaking me as he twisted me to face him. 'Now do you see why I didn't want you to come back to my place?'

He didn't say another word to me for the next hour and a half.

Chapter 9

'I don't know why you're looking so stressed.' Brian indicates left and exits the roundabout. 'It's good news.'

I glance at him. 'Is it?'

'Of course. You heard what the consultant Mr Arnold said. Charlotte's tube is out and she's able to breathe unassisted. The damage to her cerebral cortex has healed.'

'How unassisted is her breathing if they're insisting she wears an oxygen mark? And the exact words he used were "the scans show the damage has substantially reduced."'

'Yes. It's healed.'

'Reduced, not healed.'

Brian exhales slowly and deliberately. 'Sue, we both heard him say there's no medical reason why she shouldn't wake up.'

'But she hasn't, has she? I'm delighted that she

can breathe on her own now but it doesn't mean anything if she still hasn't actually opened her eyes and—'

'Oh, for God's sake!'

'Brian! Can I just finish my sentence? Please.'

He shoots me a sideways look and raises his eyebrows.

'I'm worried because of the other thing Mr Arnold said – the part about the longer Charlotte stays in a coma the more likely it is that she could develop a secondary complication. She could still die, Brian.'

'*Could* being the operative word, Sue. You need to stay positive.'

I rest my head against the headrest and stare up at the dull, grey interior of the car. I'm snapping at Brian and it's not fair but I can't shake the feeling that this is all my fault. I've failed as a mother. If I'd been closer to Charlotte, if I'd encouraged her to talk to me, if I'd run up the stairs after her instead of returning to my book maybe she never would have walked in front of a bus and maybe she wouldn't be at risk of pneumonia or a pulmonary embolism now.

'I should have protected her, Brian,' I say quietly.

'Don't, Sue. It's not your fault.'

I look at him. 'I didn't protect her but I can now.'

'What do you mean?'

'If I find out why she did what she did and tell her that I understand, that I'm here for her, maybe she'll wake up.'

'Not this again.' Brian sighs heavily. 'For the hundredth time, Sue, it was an accident.'

'It wasn't. Charlotte tried to kill herself, Brian. She talked about it in her diary.'

There's a squeal of tires on tarmac and my seatbelt cuts into my throat as the car swerves sharply towards the oncoming traffic. I want to scream at Brian to stop but I can't speak. I can't scream. All I can do is grip the seatbelt with both hands as we hurtle towards a 4X4. A cacophony of beeping horns fill my ears and then Brian yanks the steering wheel and we lurch left, speeding towards the grass verge then lurch back to the right so we're back in the centre of the road.

My husband's top lip is beaded with sweat, his face pale, his eyes staring ahead, fixed and glassy.

'You nearly killed us,' I breathe.

Brian says nothing.

He says nothing all the way home then he turns off the engine, opens the car door and crosses the driveway without looking back. I stay in the car, too stunned to move as he lets himself into the house, crosses the kitchen and disappears into the hallway. I don't know what scared me more – the fact we nearly drove head first into another car or the look in Brian's eyes as it happened.

My hands shake as I reach for the handle and open the car door and I pause to collect myself. I'm being ridiculous. Brian would never have risked both our lives like that when Charlotte still needs us. He was angry, I reason as I cross the gravel driveway and approach the house. He asked the other day if there was anything in Charlotte's diary he needed to know about and I said no. I lied to his face and he knows it.

'Brian?' I open the front door gingerly, expecting Milly to come bowling over but she's not in the porch. She must have followed Brian into the living room. I'm about to step into the kitchen when something red and chewed in Milly's bed catches my eye. It's a 'Could not Deliver' slip from the Royal Mail. How did that end up in her bed? I turn and see the mail 'cage' we erected around the letterbox on the floor. It's the third one that Milly has managed to wrench off the door. The older she gets the wilier she becomes. I crouch down and pick up the remains of the card, smiling when I see what the postman has written – 'in the recycling bin'. Brian thinks the postie is probably breaking Royal Mail rules by putting our undelivered parcels in the recycling bin but I think it's a fabulous idea. It saves him from hauling them back to the depot and it saves me a trip to town. I duck back outside and lift the lid on the recycling bin.

I reach down and pick up a green plastic parcel with Marks and Spencer splashed down the side. It's hard, like a shoebox, not floppy like clothes. It can't be shoes. They're the one thing I still insist on buying from the shops. When you've got feet as wide as mine ordering shoes off the internet can be a bit of a gamble.

'Brian?' I carry the parcel into the house and search for my husband. 'Oh, hi Milly.'

She looks up from her prone position in front of the cold hearth then lowers her head and sighs when she realizes I'm not Brian. He must be in his study. Milly knows she isn't allowed upstairs.

'What have we got here then?' I tear into the plastic packaging and discover a cardboard shoebox. 'Very brave of Daddy to choose shoes for Mum—'

The opened box tumbles from my hands and a pair of beige suedette slippers tumbles onto the rug.

They're meant for me. But they're not from my husband.

'Brian?' I push open the door to the study. 'Brian, we need to talk.'

My husband is sitting in his chair, his head in his hands, his elbows on the desk. He doesn't look up at the sound of my voice.

'Brian?' I fight to keep the quiver out of my voice. 'Brian, please. I need your help.'

He raises his head from his hands and slowly tilts back his head to look at me. His expression is blank, his eyes as fixed and dark as they were as we careered into oncoming traffic.

'What do you want, Susan?'

'I . . .' I hold out the slippers but I can't do it. I can't tell him that James sent them to me. There's no note, no purchaser details, no gift card – nothing at all to prove who sent them. And besides, Brian looks like someone just hollowed out his soul.

I perch on the edge of a wooden chair near the door. 'I'm sorry, Brian.'

My husband doesn't say anything but I can tell he's listening, that he wants me to continue.

'I'm sorry I told you there wasn't anything to worry about in Charlotte's diary. There is.'

'What?' Brian is no longer slumped back in his chair. He's sitting up straight, the tips of his fingers splayed on the desk, his eyes fixed on mine. 'Tell me.'

'She . . .' I can't do it. I can't ignore my gut feeling that I shouldn't. Not with Charlotte's safety at risk. 'Why did you lie about going to the pool, Brian?'

'What?'

'Last week, when you took the morning off, you told me you went shopping and swimming.'

'And?' It's just one word but I can hear the irritation behind it.

'The Prince Regent has been shut for renovations for the last two weeks.'

Brian doesn't so much as blink. 'I didn't go to the Prince Regent.'

'Where then?'

'Aquarena.'

'You went all the way to Worthing for a swim?'

'Something wrong with that?'

'Brian, you haven't been for a swim for months.'

'Which is why I fancied a dip.'

'Stop lying.' I stand up. 'Please, just stop lying.'

My husband sits back in his chair. 'Lying? I think we've established who the liar is here, Sue. Or would you like to take back your apology from five minutes ago?' When I say nothing a small smile plays on his lips. 'What did Charlotte write in her diary?'

'Where have you been going at the crack of dawn every day?'

Brian says nothing.

I say nothing.

We stare at each other, eyes locked, neither of us willing to back down.

Ding-dong.

The sound of the doorbell makes me jump. A split second later I'm out of the study, relieved of the excuse to escape. I think I hear Brian call my name as I hurry down the stairs but I don't turn back.

'Coming!' I call as I cross the hallway, pass through the kitchen and walk into the porch. Milly follows me, nudging her empty food dish with her nose as I open the front door.

I can't see anyone through the glass pane so I open the door and peer outside, half-expecting to see someone strolling down the driveway, but it's empty. Whoever rang our doorbell must have sprinted away the second their finger left the buzzer.

'What's that Milly Moo?' I turn back to find the dog gnawing on something in her bed. I take a step closer and crouch down. It's a brown padded envelope.

'Where did you get that?' I distract the dog with a well-chewed tennis ball, slip the parcel away from her and sit down with it at the kitchen table. My name is written on the front in blue biro but there's no address and no stamp. I turn it over. Nothing on the underside either, just a strip of brown packing tape holding the flap closed. Whoever rang the doorbell must have pushed it through the letter box.

I peel off the tape and slip a finger under the flap

to open it. I can barely breathe as I upend the envelope and tip the contents onto the table.

Something pink and glittery lands on the cotton tablecloth with a clunk.

Charlotte's phone.

Saturday 21st October 1990

I didn't hear from James for three days after the incident with his mum.

He finally rang yesterday. I'd expected him to be contrite but he acted like nothing had happened and asked what my plans were for the weekend. I said I'd been invited to have dinner with some mates and he was welcome to join us if he liked. I said how much I'd like him to meet my friends. It was, after all, nearly two months since we'd met and he still hadn't met anyone I was close to.

'Helen and Rupert?' he repeated down the phone, after I told him whose house we were going to. 'The same Rupert you fucked at uni?'

I hated that, the way he said 'fucked' like it was something dirty that I should be ashamed of.

*'No. Rupert my very good friend who I happened to have sex with a very, **very** long time ago. Not that that matters.'*

'It matters to me.'

'Well, it shouldn't. It didn't mean anything then and it certainly doesn't mean anything now. Helen's not bothered so why should you be?'

'Helen's not in love with you.'

'Oh, for God's sake. Don't come then.'

'And leave you alone with some guy who fucked you once and would probably love to fuck you again? No chance.'

'James!'

'What?'

'I'm going to put the phone down now.'

'Don't. Suzy, I'm sorry. That all came out wrong. I'm still smarting from what happened on Tuesday. Forgive me darling, please. I'll be very well behaved at the dinner party.'

'You promise?'

'Of course.'

James was drunk when I met him at Willesden tube. So drunk he could barely stand, never mind speak. I took one look at him and told him he should go home. He refused.

'I'll be the entertainment,' he said. 'I tell really good jokes. What's brown and sticky?'

I couldn't help but laugh and he was being very good natured and affectionate. Maybe it'll be fun, I told myself. At least he won't be uptight about meeting Rupert.

I knew the night was going to turn into a nightmare when thirty seconds after we'd walked into Hel & Ru's flat James pointed at a Formula One framed print on the sideboard and said, 'Only twats are into Formula One. Only a dull mind could watch a car go round and round a track ad infinitum.'

'I think you'll find,' Rupert said, turning back, 'that the number of laps depends on the track and that the sport demands a finite number of laps otherwise there'd be no winner.'

'A blah blah blah blah blah.' James waved a hand in his direction then, just as Rupert disappeared into the living room. 'Posh twat.'

I angled him into the bathroom and closed the door. He stumbled backwards and collapsed onto the (lid closed, thankfully) toilet. 'If you keep this up we're leaving.'

He grinned. 'So we don't have to have dinner with Twattle Dum and Twattle Dumber and two other Mad Twatters? Excellent.' He tried to stand. 'Let's go!'

'Not me.' I pushed him back down again. 'You.'

'No Suzy,' he pulled a face, 'please let me spend the evening with Fat Arse and Dull Face.'

'That's it.' I yanked on his hand so he was upright. 'You're going home. I'm calling you a cab.'

'Noooo!' He wrapped his arms around me and, using his weight advantage, pinned me against the tiled wall. He pressed his lips to my neck. 'Don't leave me. Don't make me go. I promise to be a good boy. Suzy, I want to wake up with you tomorrow morning. Don't send me home to my bitch of a mother. I'm only being silly because it winds you up. I know how much you love Gingerpubes and her Fat Bear.'

'James!'

'See!' He mimed someone pushing a button. 'It's too easy. Please, Suzy. I promise to be good. I'll make polite conversation over dinner and everything. I just need something to eat. I've only had a bowl of cereal all day.'

'James! That's not good for you.'

'See,' he nestled his head into the crook of my neck, 'I knew you still loved me. You care that I'm starving to death.'

'Of course I love you, you idiot.' I stroked the back of his head, relishing the feeling of his hair under my fingers. 'Even when you do behave like this.'

True to his word he did behave, even if his contribution to the conversation around the dinner table was more sarcastic than enthusiastic, but he barely said a word on the tube on the way home. I was grateful for the silence. James didn't have to spell it out but I could tell from his behaviour over dinner that he didn't like my friends, and not just because I'd slept with one of them.

By the time we finally walked into James' living room I couldn't bear the silence a second longer and asked if he was okay.

He ignored me and crossed the room to pull the heavy velvet curtains closed, taking the time to arrange the folds of material so they hung evenly spaced. When he was satisfied they were straight he strode over to the mantelpiece and wound the brass carriage clock. His face was expressionless, his mouth a thin line, his pale grey eyes dull. Only the tension *in his jaw gave his mood away. I stayed by the door, shuffling my weight from foot to foot. The air was electrified, like a dark cloud was hovering overhead, threatening a storm.*

'James?' I said again.

'Would you keep your fucking voice down?' He spun around to face me. 'Mother's asleep upstairs or have you forgotten?'

'Sorry.' I lowered my voice to a whisper. 'I just wanted to check that you're okay. You've seemed a bit . . .' I chose my words carefully, '. . . unhappy ever since we left Hels' house.'

'Unhappy?' James stepped closer, towering over me. 'Why would I be unhappy, Suzy-Sue?'

I wracked my brain, analyzing the conversations we'd had over dinner. Nothing controversial, nothing that referenced my ex-boyfriends (Hels knows not to mention them in front of James) and nothing about my past that he might have found objectionable.

'Nothing?' James took another step closer and tapped me on the forehead with his index finger. 'Really? You can't think of a single thing you might have done to upset me?'

I shook my head. 'No. I can't. I thought we had a lovely even—'

'Liar!' His face was inches from mine, his breath hot and scented with the spices Hels used in the curry we ate.

'I'm not—'

'You are a lying bitch.'

'I'm not, James. I didn't say—'

'Want a cig, Suz?' He said it in a high sing-song voice and I immediately knew what he was getting at. He was imitating Helen, post-dinner, as she leaned across the table and offered me a Marlboro Light before sparking one up herself. My face suddenly felt hot as the blood rushed to my cheeks.

'Hels!' James continued in the same voice, his face bobbing from side to side in front of mine. 'You know I don't smoke anymore. I gave up weeks ago. Remember?'

'She just forgot, James. We used to share cigs all the time at work and it's a habit. She forgot that I gave—'

'FILTHY FUCKING HABIT!'

I took a step back and wiped the spit from my eye.

'My father died from smoking, Suzy. He DIED. A long, painful death. I held him in my arms when he rasped and rattled his way into the next world, gasping for breath that wouldn't come.'

'But your mum said that—'

James crouched down so his face was just milli-metres from mine. 'What did my "mum" say?'

'She said . . .' I rubbed my palms against my skirt, '. . . that your dad killed himself. You were in the kitchen, talking, and I heard her say that. I wasn't snooping, I promise. But you'd been gone so long that I just wanted to check that—'

'Bullshit!' His breath is hot in my face. 'You were sneaking around, listening at keyholes, looking for secrets.'

121

'That's not true.'

'Isn't it?'

'No.' I wanted to take a step back, to widen the space between us and diffuse the tension but I couldn't. James was calling me a liar and yet he's been lying about the death of his father. 'I don't understand. Why would your mum say your dad killed himself if he died of a smoking-related illness?'

'He killed himself alright – with too much booze and too many fags – but she was the one that drove him to it. Always going on and on, nagging and bitching and lying and manipulating.'

'But . . .' I didn't finish my sentence. His mother said 'the **day** he killed himself' like it was suicide, not respiratory disease. Or had I heard that wrong? Now I was doubting myself.

'So tell me,' he prodded me in the chest, again. 'Are you still smoking?'

'No! I haven't started again, James. I prom—'

'LIAR!'

He was right. I was lying. I haven't started smoking again, not regularly but I did have a quick cig with Hels two weeks ago. We met for lunch, had a couple of G and Ts and I just couldn't resist when she offered me a fag. It was just one cigarette but James wouldn't understand that. He'd think I didn't love him enough to keep my promise to quit.

'If you've lied about your dirty, little smoking habit,' he took another step forward, jolting me with his chest so I was forced to take a step back, 'what else have you lied about 'eh, Suzy-Sue?'

I pressed my hands to my mouth. 'Nothing.'

'Really? Really nothing? You're not,' he yanked my hands away from my mouth and gathered them in his, 'secretly shagging Rupert again?'

'No.' I tried to wriggle my fingers free. 'Of course not.'

'Going to our favourite hotels for a hot fuck?'

'No!' I wriggled harder and snatched my hands away. 'Jesus, James you need to let this Rupert thing go. You're obsessed.'

'Obsessed? You're the one that goes for coffee with him several times a week. And I'm supposed to believe that? That two people that used to fuck each other's brains out can sit opposite each other, all alone, without their partners and have a lovely drinky-poo and not be tempted to get it on again? You must think I'm an idiot.'

'Oh, for God's sake, James.' I couldn't believe we were back there again. 'How many times do I have to spell it out? Rupert is a friend and nothing more. I'm as attracted to him as I am to Hels who, before you say anything about my so-called "sexual wild side", I'm **not** attracted in the least.'

James shook his head. 'You don't get it do you, Suzy? I could be friends with my exes too but I'm not because I value **our** relationship too much. I value you too much. I value you more than anything else in my life. I love you Suzy, you know that, don't you?'

'Yes.' My heart softened at his tender tone of voice. No one had ever loved me so passionately or so desperately before. No one had ever become jealous or possessive before. They'd never cared enough. 'And I love you too, James.'

'No.' He cupped my jaw with his right hand and tilted my head up so I had no choice but to look into his eyes. 'I really fucking love you, Suzy. You are everything to me. Everything.'

His left hand snaked around my waist and he pulled me to him, roughly, brusquely as he pressed his lips against mine. He kissed me deeply and, despite the anger I felt at being branded a liar, I kissed him back.

Chapter 10

I snatch up Charlotte's mobile phone and turn it over in my hands then peer into the mouth of the envelope. It's empty. Not a card, not a note, not a post-it. Nothing. Just the phone.

I sprint out of the house and across the gravel with Charlotte's phone in one hand, the padded envelope in the other. I pause when I reach the street. Which way would they have gone? I turn right, towards town, and continue to run. I pass a woman pushing a buggy, an elderly lady dragging a shopping trolley behind her and a teenage couple holding hands. I pass the number 19 bus, *Bills* the newsagents and three or four pubs. Still I keep running. I don't know who I'm looking for or where I'm going but I only slow to a stop when I notice Milly trailing behind me with her tongue hanging out. I'm no spring chicken but she's ten years old with a heart condition and fading eyesight. She shouldn't be running anywhere, never mind down a traffic-fume filled street with dangers at every turn.

'Come on girl.' I reach down and pat her head. 'Let's go home.'

My first instinct, as I walk back in, is to find Brian and tell him what happened but I say nothing. Instead I pour Milly a bowl of fresh, clean water and shut her in the porch then go into the downstairs toilet, locking the door behind me, and sit down on the closed loo seat. I press the button on the top of Charlotte's mobile.

An animation skips across the screen as the phone flashes to life. It takes me forever to work out how to access the text messages but, when I do, a list of names appear. I recognize several of them – Liam, Ella, Oli, Nancy and Misha, two girls from Charlotte's class – and then a couple of names I don't. I feel sick with nerves yet strangely exhilarated as I go through the messages, certain that I am about to reveal the reason why Charlotte tried to kill herself but, the more I read, the more disappointed I feel and my exhilaration is soon replaced by awkwardness as I stumble across a thread of messages between my daughter and her boyfriend. Some of them are sexual but the majority are fun and loving. The text that ends the relationship comes out of nowhere. In the text before Charlotte tells Liam that she had an amazing evening with him and then in her final text to him, the relationship's over and she doesn't want anything to do with him. No wonder he was so angry and confused. What follows are a string of texts from Liam – initially hurt and desperate for an explanation then increasingly agitated and angry. Charlotte doesn't reply to any of them.

I open the thread of messages to Ella. There's a brief conversation, two months earlier, about a project they were working on at school but that's it. There's nothing else – nothing about Liam or Keisha or why they might have fallen out.

I continued to search through her text history – through the ones between Charlotte and her dad (mostly requests for money or lifts), Charlotte and Oli (his version of her request for a hotel room was spot on) and then start going through the names I don't recognize. The texts between Charlotte and the girls from school don't reveal anything apart from a bit of gossip about who fancies who. And that's it. That's all there is apart from one more name – K Dog. My heart sinks as I select it. I really thought Charlotte's phone would provide some answers. I felt sure the mystery would be solved if only—

My skin prickles with goosebumps and I go cold.

My dad's a sick pervert and I don't know who else to talk to. Call me asap. Charlotte x

I read the text again.

No, it's not possible.

He'd never hurt her.

Memories flood my mind. Brian taking Charlotte to the swimming pool. Brian teaching her to ride a bike. Brian giving her a bath. She would have told me if he'd done anything inappropriate or started behaving unusually. Wouldn't she?

No. I give myself a mental shake. Stop it, Sue. Your first instinct was right. Brian would never do anything to harm his daughter. He loves her. He was devastated by her accident. He still is. But . . .

The image of cars hurtling towards us flashes through my mind.

Why did he drive into oncoming traffic when I told him Charlotte had talked about killing herself in her diary? Why turn the argument on me when I asked him about the swimming pool and his early morning walks?

I need to find out what Charlotte's text means. I fumble with the phone as I select the name 'K-Dog' and then press 'Call'.

There's a click, then a dial tone and I'm mentally rehearsing what I'm about to say when a noise from upstairs makes me jump.

Brian.

He's walking around his study.

'Answer the phone,' I urge as the dial tone continues to sound and footsteps cross the landing. 'Please answer the phone.'

Come on. Come on. Come on.

There's a click.

Someone's picked up.

'Hello?' I breathe. 'Hello, my name is Sue—'

This is the Vodaphone voicemail service for 07972 711271. Please leave your message after the tone.

The stairs creak.

'Hello?' I say after the beep. 'You don't know me but my name is—'

'Sue?' There's a sharp knock on the toilet door. 'Sue, who are you talking to?'

'No one!' I frantically stab at the 'End Call' button and shove the phone down my bra. 'I'll be out in a sec.'

I brace my hands against the toilet walls, suddenly lightheaded, and steady myself.

'Sue?' More knocking, louder, more frantic. 'What are you doing in there?'

'Nothing. I'll be out in a second.'

'Okay.' I hear him take a deep breath. 'We need to have a chat, Sue. I'll wait for you in the living room.'

I turn on the cold tap and splash my face then look in the mirror. A tired forty-something with dark circles under her eyes and a haunted expression pats her skin dry with a towel. I barely recognize myself. And what of Brian? Do I still know him or has he morphed into the very worst kind of man? Someone deceitful, someone predatory, someone dangerous. There's only one way to find out.

I drape the towel back over the rail and unlock the toilet door.

Tuesday 24th October 1990

'I'm sorry, Suzy.'

James reached an arm around my shoulders and pulled me into his chest. I closed my eyes, still half asleep. He smelt musky and warm. He smelt like home.

'What for?'

He didn't say anything for a couple of seconds, then stroked my hair out of my eyes and tilted my face up towards him. I opened my eyes.

'For the way I've been recently. For the way I've treated you. I've been . . .' he paused, '. . . unfair.'

I said nothing but a huge wave of relief washed over me. His behaviour over the last couple of days had really worried me. It had seemed so out of character and when he'd screamed at me, calling me a liar, it was horrible.

'I've got a lot of anger in me, Suzy; anger about something that happened in the past that I fight to keep suppressed. Sometimes it explodes . . .' He traced a thumb over my cheekbone. 'I took it out on the wrong person. I took it out on the person who would never hurt me and for that I am truly sorry. I don't want to be a monster. I don't want to be like him.'

'Who was a monster?' I rested my hand on his chest. 'What happened, James?'

He shook his head and a single tear wound its way down his cheek.

'Tell me. Tell me what I can do to help, James.'

He passed a hand over his face, roughly rubbing the tear away and looked down at me.

'See, that's why I love you. You're so incredibly caring.' He pressed a palm to my chest. 'You've got such a huge heart.'

'What is it? Tell me so I can understand.'

He took a deep breath and I readied myself for what was about to come. But nothing came. We lay together in uncomfortable silence for several minutes. Finally James spoke.

'Yesterday was the anniversary of my uncle's death.'

I started to say that I was sorry but he shook his head.

'He died when I was twelve, suddenly, of a heart attack. No one saw it coming. Men like Uncle Malcolm didn't just drop dead in their fifties My mother was distraught, she locked herself in her room and cried and cried and cried. I didn't comfort her. I ran into the woods behind our house and I picked up the biggest branch I could find – so heavy I could barely lift it – and I smashed it against one of the trees until it was splintered and broken and my palms were bleeding and then I screamed at God. I hated him for taking Uncle Malcolm away from me before I had a chance to grow up and I could kill him myself.'

A shiver ran through me. I didn't need to ask him what Uncle Malcolm had done.

'He stole my childhood. He stole my trust. He stole my fucking **innocence**, Sue.' I yelped as he grabbed me by the shoulders and shook me. He was breathing rapidly, his nostrils splayed, his eyes fixed and staring.

'James,' I tried to prise his fingers off my skin but he was holding on too hard, digging in deeply as though he was rooting himself to me. 'James, it's okay. It's over. It's over.'

'It'll never be over.'

'It is. It's over. James, it's over. Please, please let go of me. You're hurting me. James, stop. He's dead.'

He continued to stare at me as though he hated me, as though he wished **me** dead and then, as quickly as the anger had flared, it died. His eyes softened, his face crumpled and he wrapped me in his arms, pulling me into him and he sobbed and sobbed and sobbed.

Chapter 11

Brian is sitting on the sofa, Milly stretched out beside him, her head on his lap. He nods as I lower myself into the armchair.

'Sue.' My name seems to echo off the walls. 'I think you need to see a doctor. You're not well. You need help.'

It takes a while for the words to sink in, for me to understand what he's implying.

'I've rung Doctor Turner. She said she can see you tomorrow morning.'

'I'm sorry?'

Brian leans forward, rests his chin on his hand, his brow furrowed. 'I made you an appointment to—'

'I know what you did. What I don't understand is why.'

'Because I'm worried about you!' He shouts so loudly Milly and I both jump. 'You haven't been yourself since Charlotte's accident and you're getting worse, Sue.'

'Of course I'm not myself. Our daughter is in a coma. She might die.'

'Yes. Yes, she might. And she might not. She might make a full recovery and the doctors and nurses are doing everything they can but you need help too, Sue. I've tried my best to support you, but I don't know how to talk to you anymore.'

'I'm always here for you to talk to, Brian.'

'Physically maybe, but not emotionally. You're so locked in your own head I can't reach you. Whenever I try you give me this wild-eyed look like . . . like . . . I don't know,' he shakes his head, 'like I'm going to hurt you or something. Sometimes you look at me like you don't know who I am.'

My heart aches at the pained expression on his face but I can't say anything to reassure him. He's right. I don't know if I know him anymore.

'Sue?' Brian frowns at me from across the room. 'Did you even hear what I just said?'

I look back at him. Is he trying to get me to see the doctor for nefarious reasons? If the world thinks I'm insane they'll lock me up, leaving him alone with Charlotte. And then he could . . . the thought hangs, ugly and odious, in the air around me.

'I heard what you said, Brian.'

'And?' His eyes search my face. 'What do you think?'

'I'm not going mad. And I'm not going to see the GP.' I speak slowly, calmly and deliberately. If he really does think I've lost the plot I need to prove to him that I haven't.

'I never said you were mad, Sue. I just thought you might appreciate having someone to talk to that isn't me. Someone . . .' he pauses, '. . . professionally qualified to help you.'

'I don't need anyone's help.' The sentence comes out louder than I intended. 'I'm just worried about Charlotte.'

'So am I.'

'Well then,' I shrug, 'so you understand.'

'No, I don't. How can I when you swing between secretiveness and bluntness at a moment's notice? Why do you think I nearly crashed the car when you told me what she'd written in her diary? You can't just throw something like that at me and expect me to just accept it. Show me the diary, Sue. Let me read it for myself. Maybe then I'll understand.'

'I can't . . .'

'Why not?'

'Because I have to protect Charlotte.'

'From what?' He looks at me, uncomprehending, then he pales. 'Not from me. For the love of God, Sue, don't tell me you think *I* had anything to do with her accident?'

'Didn't you?'

'What?!' He throws back his head and makes a noise I've never heard before – half shout, half roar – then springs off the sofa. He crosses the living room and looms above me. 'Tell me this is your idea of a sick joke, Sue. Tell me!'

He rages at me, his confusion, frustration and shock raining down like brimstone and I cross my arms above my head, tuck in my chin and curl into a ball.

'Woah!' The sound makes me peer up through my arms. Brian is shaking his head, his eyes wide with horror. He take a step backwards, his arms outstretched, his fingers spread wide, his palms exposed. 'I wasn't going to touch you. I'd never touch you, Sue. You know that.' He sinks back onto the sofa and slumps forward, his head in his hands. 'Dear God.'

We are both silent. The grandfather clock ticks in the corner of the room and Milly scritch-scratch-scratches at a flea bite.

'Tell me you don't believe that,' Brian says, his voice a distant mumble, his head still tucked into his arms. 'Tell me you don't *really* believe I'm the reason Charlotte tried to hurt herself.'

My heart feels like it's being ripped in two. One part wants to go over to Brian, throw my arms around him and tell him that I love him, that I trust him and that I truly believe that he'd never do anything to harm our daughter. The other part tells me to distance myself, trust nothing, no one.

'Sue?' Hurt is written all over his face. 'Why would you think that? *How* could you think that?'

'Did you?'

'Did I what?'

'Hurt Charlotte?'

'Jesus Fucking Christ!' He's on his feet again, his arms spread wide. 'How can you even ask me that question? I take it back, Sue. You're not stressed, you're insane. Can you hear yourself? Are you even aware of what you're saying? Of what you're accusing me of? You need help, Sue. Urgent psychiatric help.'

'Insane?' Now I'm on my feet too. 'Right. Of course. Is that why Charlotte sent a text to one of her friends calling you a pervert?'

Brian's jaw drops, his body locked in a palm-out pose. He licks his lips, swallows, then licks his lips again.

'What did you just say?'

'I said . . .' I'm shaking so much I have to take a deep breath to stop my voice from quivering. 'There's a text on Charlotte's phone from her to a friend, calling you a sick pervert.'

'Charlotte called me a pervert?'

'Yes.'

He stares at me expressionlessly then blinks as though he's just woken up. 'Show me the text.'

I throw the phone, underarm, at him and he snatches it from the air.

'It's under the name K-Dog,' I say.

Brian looks down at the phone and presses a few buttons. After an age he looks up at me, a strange look on his face. 'There's nothing here.'

'What?' I move towards him, holding out a hand for the phone. 'Of course there is. You need to select the envelope icon and then . . .' I scroll through the text messages, return to the home screen then click on the envelope icon again. 'It's gone.'

'Really?' He raises his eyebrows. 'Or perhaps there wasn't a text to begin with?'

'Of course there was. I—' A cold chill runs through me and I step back.

'What?' Brian looks exasperated.

'You deleted it.'

'Oh, for God's sake, Sue!'

'Brian, it was here five minutes ago. I found it when I was in the toilet. I can remember every word. It—' I stop short. An image of me stabbing at buttons as I frantically tried to end my call to K-Dog as Brian hammered on the door flashes into my mind. I must have accidentally deleted it. I must have obliterated the only piece of evidence I had that my husband was responsible for Charlotte's accident.

'It was here. It was.' I frantically scroll back to the home screen then open the text messages again, but the K-Dog message has disappeared. 'I need to take the phone to Carphone Warehouse in town. They'll know how to retrieve the text and, if they don't, I bet there's someone on the internet who could.'

'Sue . . .' Brian's tone is gentle, comforting. It reminds me of the way you speak to the bereaved. 'Sue, I think you should sit down.'

I let him guide me back to my armchair and nod when he offers to make us both a cup of tea. He pauses as he reaches the door and looks back at me. The expression on his face takes my breath away. Not because it's a look of reproach, resentment or even anger. It's none of those things. It's pity. He thinks I made the text message up.

'Here you go.' Five minutes later he slides back into the room and slips a cup of tea onto the coaster beside me. He puts a plate holding three chocolate Hobnobs beside it and then crosses the room and sits down. He sips at his tea then inhales sharply. It's too hot.

'Sue.' His face is incredibly grey, his eyes impossibly sad. 'There's something I need to say to you and I need you to hear me out. Please don't get angry or defensive, just let me say what I need to say.'

I nod for him to continue.

'I'm only saying this because I love you and I'm worried about you but,' he pauses to take a breath, 'I really want you to see a doctor. Or that therapist you saw before. Your behavior is becoming increasingly erratic. You must realize that.'

I want to give him a hug and tell him that I'm fine and he's got nothing to worry about, but then I remember the text message I read on Charlotte's phone and I shake my head.

'There's nothing wrong with me, Brian. Nothing that a few straight answers wouldn't put right anyway.'

His shoulders slump and he sighs. 'Such as?'

'Why did you let me believe you went to work that morning then lie to me about going swimming?'

'I told you, I—'

'And why have you started taking Milly out at all times of the day and night?'

Brian pinches the skin between his eyebrows and closes his eyes. When he opens them he sighs deeply. 'I've been going to see Tessa.'

'Tessa your dead wife?'

He glares at me from across the room. 'Yes, Sue. My dead wife, Tessa.'

'You lied to me about going to the swimming pool to cover up the fact that you actually went to her grave?'

Brian nods.

'And when you've been taking Milly out for an impromptu walk . . . that's where you've been going?'

He nods again.

'Why?'

He reaches across to ruffle Milly's fur. 'Talking to Tessa helps me clear my head.'

I stare at him, trying to take it in. 'Why couldn't you talk to me?'

'Because you're what I talk about . . .' He rubs a hand over his forehead and squeezes his temples. 'I'm worried that you're going to have another episode, Sue. All the signs are there – the paranoia, the delusions, the obsessions with Charlotte's "accident". I want you to see the GP as soon as possible.'

I turn Charlotte's phone over in my hands and rub my thumb over the sparkly crystals. He almost had me there – with his furrowed brow, soft tone and gentle eyes. He nearly convinced me that he really was worried about me.

'Did you sexually molest Charlotte?'

Brian inhales sharply. 'You didn't just say that?'

I shrug.

'You didn't just accuse me of sexually molesting our daughter?'

I don't move a muscle.

'No.' He shakes his head. 'NO! No. No. No. No. No. No. NO. You've lost it. I will NOT sit in my own front room, in my own house and listen to my wife accuse me of incest. Absolutely NO WAY. I don't care how ill you are, Sue, you *cannot* say things like that. You just can't.'

He springs to his feet but makes no move to approach me. 'I want you to go to the doctor's.'

I say nothing. I feel like I'm in a nightmare where you desperately need to scream and run away but your voice has disappeared and your feet are stuck to the floor.

'I'm serious, Sue. Agree to see the doctor or this marriage is over.'

I should react. I should tell Brian that I believe in him, that there must be some logical explanation for Charlotte writing what she did, that we can work through this together but I feel dead inside.

'Just nod your head, Sue. Nod your head that you agree to see a doctor and . . . and . . .' he tails off as I slowly shake my head from side to side. 'I'll just go then, shall I?.'

He's speaking slower than normal, pausing between sentences and giving extra weight to his words. He's waiting for me to say something. He's giving me the opportunity to interrupt.

I close my eyes.

'Okay.' His voice is even softer. 'Okay.'

The floorboards squeak under the carpet as he crosses the room and the brass discs on Milly's collar clank together as she stands up. A second later I hear a click as the living room door is pulled shut.

The grandfather clock tick-tick-ticks in the corner of the room.

Saturday 18th November 1990

I went to the Southbank to see the World War II undiscovered photos exhibit with Rupert today.

We bought the tickets months ago and, seeing as he's the only person I know who's as fascinated by the Second World War as I am, I expected him to be as super excited. Instead he seemed a bit off, looking at me strangely when I gave him a kiss on the cheek hello instead of a hug, and he barely said a word as we drifted from photo to photo and I wittered on about the cut of this outfit and the shape of that. When we stopped for coffee, I asked what was wrong.

'You and Hels haven't split up, have you?'

'No,' he smiled tightly. 'Nothing like that.'

'What then? You've been weird all afternoon.'

'I've been weird?' he raised a dark eyebrow.

'What's that supposed to mean?'

'You haven't spoken to Hels for four weeks.'

'So?'

'Your boyfriend **ruined** her dinner party and you haven't phoned once to see how she is.'

'James didn't ruin her dinner party!' He'd made a couple of snarky comments maybe, but people had laughed. They weren't that bad.

'Really?' He raised an eyebrow again. 'Is that why Hels burst into tears the second you both left – halfway through dessert.'

'James felt sick. He needed to get home.'

'I'm not surprised considering how pissed he was.'

'So we left early? So what? Is there a law that says you have to stay until after coffee, or cheese and biscuits, or whatever? I can't believe you're giving me a hard time because of that.'

Rupert shook his head. 'I'm not giving you a hard time, Susan. I'm concerned. We both are.'

'I'm fine. In fact, I've never been happier.'

'Really? You're honestly happy with someone who refers to your friends as,' he gazed to the left as though recollecting, 'Fat Arse and Dull Face?'

My cheeks grew hot.

'Tweedle Dum and Tweedle Dumber? Gingerpubes and her Fat Bear?'

'I . . .' I pressed my hands to my face. 'I don't know what to—'

'We heard the whole conversation, Sue. It's not a big flat and the walls are paper thin. Helen was incredibly hurt.'

'I'm sorry.' And I was, really, really sorry. I apologized over and over saying that James was acting out of character because he'd suffered a bereavement and he didn't know how to deal with it.

'I'm sure he wouldn't have been so rude if he'd actually got to know the two of you.'

Rupert sat back in his chair and ran a hand over his face. 'What about you? Whilst you were still in the loo James asked if we were all as slutty as you when we were in our twenties. Why would he say that?'

'To wind you up because he was bored? I don't know.' James' remark stung but Rupert's faux concern and gently, gently way of speaking was starting to irritate me. Could he be more condescending? 'He was probably having a dig at you because we slept together back then.'

'But he's okay with us meeting for coffee, is he?'

I glanced away. 'Actually he's not in London this weekend. He's taken his mother to Cardiff to see family.'

'Right. And would you still have met up with me if James hadn't gone away for the weekend?'

''Course.'

It was a lie and we both knew it. I knew how James would react if he could see me sitting with Rupert.

'Sue.' Rupert reached for my hand. I snatched it away. 'Please ring Hels. She's worried about you.'

'Well, she shouldn't be.' I stood up and put on my coat. How dare they act so sanctimonious and holier than thou just because my boyfriend got a bit drunk and mouthy? 'I'm fine. In fact, I'm more than fine. I'm happier than I've been in a long, long time.'

'You know where we are,' Rupert called after me as I stalked out of the Southbank Centre, 'if you need us.'

Chapter 12

'Charlotte, it's Mummy.' I hold my daughter's slender hand in mine.

Outside it's a glorious day. The sun is shining, the sky is blue and cloudless and the air is thick with the scent of honeysuckle blossom, but when I woke up this morning it wasn't the sunlight streaming through the curtains that I noticed first, it was the empty space beside me in the bed.

'Charlotte,' I run my thumb over the back of her hand. Her skin is incredibly soft. 'I need to talk to you about Daddy.'

The heart rate monitor in the corner of the room maintains its slow steady pace.

'Charlotte, the secret you wrote about in your diary,' I crane my neck to the right to check that no one is hovering in the doorway. The corridor is empty but I lower my voice anyway. 'It was to do with your

Daddy, wasn't it? He hurt you and I . . . I wasn't there to protect you. I didn't stop it from happening. I didn't realize and . . .'

I reach for my glass of water and take a sip, my mouth suddenly dry.

'What happened?'

I spin round. Keisha is standing in the doorway, a cellophaned bunch of daffodils in her hand.

'Sorry, Mrs Jackson.' Keisha half smiles. 'I didn't mean to startle you. I thought I'd pop in so I could . . .' Her expression clouds as she looks at Charlotte. She shakes her head. '. . . It doesn't matter.'

She slips into the room and sits opposite me.

'I didn't mean to eavesdrop,' she fixes me with her dark eyes, 'but what were you saying about Charlotte's dad?'

I look away. 'Nothing.'

'Really?' There's an amused tone to her voice. 'Because I could have sworn you were on about the porn.'

'I'm sorry?'

'The porn,' she smiles as she says the word, 'that Charlotte saw on her dad's computer.'

'What porn?'

Keisha shrugs. 'Charlotte said her laptop crashed when she was messaging a friend so she used her dad's instead. The porn just kind of popped up and—'

'On Brian's computer.'

'Yeah.' She tries to hide her smile with her hand.

'Keisha.'

'Yeah?'

I fight to suppress the nausea rising in my stomach. 'Keisha, did Charlotte call you K-Dog?'

'Everyone does.'

'Charlotte texted you,' I say slowly as the room tilts and I struggle to maintain eye contact with the young woman sitting opposite me. This can't be real. This conversation can't be happening. 'She sent you a text saying her dad was a pervert?'

'Yeah.'

'Because she found porn on his laptop?'

'Yeah, she really freaked out, **totally** over-reacted.' She laughs and my blood turns to ice. 'She said she wanted to leave home and everything. It was only a bit of porn, for Christ's sake not—'

'And she never confided in you that her dad was abusing her or being inappropriate, sexually speaking, with her in any way?'

'God, no.' She looks horrified. 'Of course not. Charlotte adored her daddy. She was always going on about how he was going to save the world from global warming or something. She would have told me if he'd touched her.'

I stare at her, too stunned to respond. I'm relieved and horrified in equal measures. Relieved that there's such an innocuous explanation behind Charlotte's text and horrified at the accusations I leveled at my husband. An image of Brian's hurt expression flashes before my eyes and I jolt back in my chair. What was I thinking? What have I done?

'Mrs Jackson? Mrs Jackson, are you okay? Would you like me to call a nurse?'

149

Keisha is still talking to me but I can't get my mouth to form words.

'Water then?' I hear the creak of a chair, the glug of water as it leaves the jug then a sploshing sound as it's poured into a glass.

'I'm sorry,' she says as she presses it into my hand. 'I shouldn't have told you about the porn. You're shocked. I shouldn't have said anything.'

'No.' I take a sip of water. Swallow. 'I'm glad you told me. Really. It's cleared something up but . . .' I search her dark eyes, '. . . you didn't drop Charlotte's phone through our letter box, did you?'

'Charlotte's mobile?' She shakes her head. 'No. Wasn't me. I don't even know where you live. Are you sure you're okay, Mrs Jackson? I don't mind going to get a nurse if you're feeling a bit faint or something.'

'No, thank you.' I hand her the glass of water and force a smile. 'I'm fine, honestly. I just realized I made a mistake. A terrible, terrible mistake.'

I cry all the way home. I cry when I stand outside the hospital and dial Brian's mobile. I cry when I get his voicemail and I cry when I try the office number and Mark tells me he's in a meeting. And when I start the engine tears roll down my cheeks without stopping as I drive down Edward Street, past the Pavilion, up North Road, down Western Road and up to our house. I'm still sobbing as I unlock our front door. Then, on my doorstep, I spot a snow shaker showing Prague's Charles Bridge and I stop crying.

And scream.

Sunday 17th December 1990

The last month or so with James has been hideous. We've had more ups and downs than a rollercoaster and I've seriously considered leaving him more than once. I'm starting to feel like he can't bear feeling happy and that, whenever things are going well between us, he has to sabotage it by saying or doing something really hurtful.

For example, after we'd been to see Shakespeare in the Park (I actually squealed when he gave me the tickets, I've always wanted to go) we were walking through Regent's Park, hand in hand, laughing about the size of Benvolio's codpiece, when James saw me glance at a man who was jogging past us. I barely registered him but he shot me a smile and then he was gone.

'Fucked him, have you?' James said.

Just like that. Out of nowhere. I told him he was being ridiculous and then we got into an argument where James claimed that I was flirtatious – apparently I was making puppy dog eyes at the actor playing Mercutio when they took their final bow. I told him he was being stupid. He got really defensive then, said it was just like me to lord it over him that I had a university degree while he didn't and if I was so up myself maybe we should just split up so I could go out with someone more educated. He was sick of saying sorry to me and that he felt like he was walking on eggshells around me, having to worry about what he said and maybe we should just split up. That was it, I burst into tears. I couldn't believe we'd gone from laughing and holding hands to being on the verge of splitting up over **nothing**.

I sat on the nearest bench and sobbed and sobbed and sobbed while James just hovered nearby. For a while he said nothing then, when I thought my heart was actually breaking, he gathered me up in his arms and said he was tired of us fighting and that he loved me more than life and he couldn't bear to see me cry. We weren't going to split up, he said, he could never let me go.

That scenario played itself out several times in the last month – a couple of lovely days, then an argument swelling out of nowhere, me crying, James comforting me, a period of calm and then the cycle would begin all over again. I found it so exhausting I started to wonder whether splitting up might not be such a terrible idea after all – and then he sprang a surprise trip on me.

He rang me last Thursday, told me to cancel all my plans and pack a weekend suitcase and a passport and meet him at Gatwick airport. I was gobsmacked. That kind of thing only happens in Meg Ryan films, not in real life. I tried to be sensible, insisted he couldn't afford it but he said that he knew what he could afford and I should just shut up and pack my bag like a good girl or I'd spoil the surprise.

I didn't need asking twice and when I got to the airport, James was bouncing on his heels he was so excited.

'Come on, come on,' he grabbed my suitcase and my hand and speeded me towards the British Airways ticket desk. I gasped when I saw the destination details above the heads of the check-in staff.

'Prague?' I stared at James in astonishment. 'We're going to Prague?'

'Yep.' He squeezed me tightly. 'I thought we could celebrate Christmas early in one of the most romantic cities in the world.'

I threw my arms around his neck and squeezed him tightly. Prague! How had he known? I'd always wanted to go there but I'd never mentioned it. It was like he knew me better than I knew myself.

We spent our first day in Prague happily sightseeing and when I asked James what he had planned for the evening he kept telling me it was a surprise but I should put on my glad rags and do my hair and make-up.

I was relieved when James asked our hotel

reception to call us a taxi (my heels were far too high to navigate the tram system) but I was still no closer to knowing where we were going. I thought perhaps we might be on our way to a jazz club as James is a huge fan but he shook his head and told me to stop guessing. As we sped past the jazz club, I spotted a barge on the river. My heart leapt. I'd never been on a riverboat cruise and here we were, about to embark on one at night with Prague at its most beautiful, lights twinkling on the water, the sky a beautiful mix of royal blue and black.

Despite the boat's glamorous appearance the evening didn't start off too well. James was disappointed by the hot and cold buffet (the tour operator he'd booked the trip from had assured him it was three-course silver service) and the fact there were at least two tables of rowdy hen dos on board. When the barman said there was champagne but it wasn't chilled because of a problem with the ice machine, James thumped the bar with his fist but I managed to dissipate the situation by suggesting we have beer instead as Prague was famous for it. As we sailed under Charles Bridge and past the National Theatre, James started to relax. After half an hour he took my hand and suggested we go and sit on the top deck. I was worried one of the hen do parties would already be up there but luckily we had the entire deck to ourselves.

'This is more like it,' he said, wrapping his coat

around me and cuddling in. 'All this beauty and just the two of us to share it.'

I relaxed into his shoulder. The view was stunning. It was like something out of a dream. London looked positively grimy in comparison. As I took my camera out and started snapping away at the Royal Palace glittering above us as we sailed past, I felt James lean away from me. I assumed he was getting his camera out too and thought nothing of it. A couple of minutes later, satisfied with my shots, I turned to talk to him and he'd gone. Well, he'd disappeared from the seat next to me anyway. He was kneeling on the decking, looking up at me, a nervous expression on his face, a small, black velvet box clasped between his hands.

I could barely breathe.

'Susan Anne Maslin, you are the most beautiful, most warm-hearted, caring, genuine woman I've ever met. You are a precious angel and I don't deserve you but . . .' He opened the box. A beautiful diamond and sapphire ring glinted up at me. 'Will you marry me and make me the happiest man in the world?'

My hands flew to my mouth and I burst into tears. James looked shocked. 'That's not a no, is it?'

'No, it's a yes. Yes! Yes! Of course I'll marry you.'

I can't remember what happened next – whether we hugged or we kissed or James slid the ring onto the ring finger of my left hand – but I do remember him saying that it was his grandmother's ring and he thought he'd never find a woman he loved enough to give it to and how he couldn't wait to spend the rest of his life with me.

The rest of the weekend went by in a blur. It was magical moment after magical moment. I felt like the happiest woman in the world.

Chapter 13

I throw the snow shaker out of the door. It smashes into a thousand pieces against the side of the garage.

'Come on, girl. Quick!' With my hand on Milly's collar I stumble across the driveway to the car and open the driver seat. 'In!'

Milly clambers across the car and into the passenger seat and I hop in after her, lock all the doors and start the engine. The radio explodes with sound as 'Monkey Gone to Heaven' by the Pixies blares from the speakers and I glance at the house, convinced someone is watching me from the window.

'Come on.' I wrestle with the gear stick as I try to get from reverse to first. 'Come ON.'

Milly whines with excitement beside me.

'Yes!' With the car in gear I glance at the rear-view window. A black shape leaps at the kitchen window. Milly scrambles onto my lap, her claws scratching at the window as she barks furiously.

I pull on her collar and push her across back to her seat. 'It's okay. It's just a cat. It's just Jess from next door.'

I pull away, lurching into Western Road and a cacophony of car horns and then I'm away, onto King's Road, speeding along the seafront, past the Marina and on towards Rottingdean. I don't know where I'm going and I don't care.

I hold it together until I pull into the car park of The Downs Hotel in Woodingdean then, as I turn off the engine, I convulse so violently I'm jolted back and forth in my seat. Milly whines in distress as my teeth start to chatter but there's nothing I can do but stare fixedly out to sea and wait for it to stop. After five minutes, maybe ten, the convulsions fade to shakes, then shivers and then disappear. I slump backwards in my seat.

James knows where I live.

The postcard, the slippers – they could be explained away as silly mistakes – someone too distracted to put a name and message on the card and a typing mistake that meant the slippers arrived at our house not somewhere further down the road – but the snow shaker? That was no mistake. He wants me to know he's found me. And if he's been watching us he knows Brian's moved out and I'm all alone.

My hands shake again as I rifle through my handbag for my mobile phone. My thumb flies over the screen as I unlock it, select the phone icon and then tap 9 . . . 9 . . .

I stop, my thumb hovering over the screen. If I call

the police they'll think I'm having another episode and ring my doctor. That's what happened the last time. But I was wrong to call them then. I genuinely *was* ill. Why else would I have believed that James was living in the shed at the bottom of the garden and sending me coded messages via wet laundry and dead birds?

With two taps of my thumb the 9s disappear.

I select Brian's number instead.

It rings then—

'Hello.' His tone is curt.

'Brian, it's me. Listen—'

'No, you listen, Sue. I meant what I said yesterday. You either go and see the doctor or our marriage is over.'

'But Brian something terrib—'

'Are you going to see the doctor, Sue?'

'No, but—'

'Then I've got nothing further to say to you.'

The phone goes dead.

I dial my husband's number again. This time it goes straight through to voicemail.

'Brian, it's Sue again.' I pause to steady my breathing. 'I know you're angry but this is important. *Really* important and I need you to come home as soon as possible. When I got home from seeing Charlotte this morning I . . . no, wait . . . there's something I need to say first. I'm sorry. I'm so, so sorry for what I said last night. Keisha explained to me why Charlotte sent her that message and it was . . . well, I can't begin to apologise for—'

To save this message press 1. To leave a new message press 2. To end the call press 3.

2 . . . 2 . . . 2 . . . I stab at the number. What just happened? Why couldn't I leave a message?

'Hello Brian, this is Sue again. I tried to leave you a message but I got cut off and I'm not sure you got it so I'll try and keep this quick. I'm sorry about last night. I'm *so* sorry. What I said was horrible. It was worse than that. It was unforgiveable and I don't blame you for walking out. I wasn't thinking clearly because James has—'

To save this message press 1. To leave a new message press 2. To end the call pr—

I press the 'end call' button and the voice stops instantly. It's no good. I'll have to wait until Brian gets home. I stare at the phone. Who else can I call? Obviously not Mum. And I can't ask Oliver to go back to the house with me because he's back in Leicester and besides, I'd never risk his safety like that. I can't risk anyone's safety.

I rest my head on the steering wheel and close my eyes.

I don't know how long I stay there, slumped over the steering wheel, but when Milly nudges my hand and whines I open my eyes and sit back in my seat.

'It's okay, girl.' I stroke her woolly head. 'I know what we need to do.'

Wednesday 20th December 1990

I knew it couldn't last, the blissful bubble James and I had been living in since we returned from Prague. I knew he'd have to go and spoil it.

We'd been to Clapham to discuss the new play the company should do next and there was an argument between James and Steve about what they should do. The argument ended with James calling Steve 'an arrogant little prick' and storming out. We went back to mine and James wouldn't speak to me. I lay wide awake in the dark, wondering if I'd done something wrong when James suddenly sat bolt upright in bed and looked at me.

'How many men have slept here?'

'Sorry?'

'In this bed. How many?'

I sighed and rolled over. 'I'm not having this conversation, James. We're both tired. Let's just go to sleep.'

'How many?'

He was itching for a fight and there was no way I was going to let him have the satisfaction of me joining in. 'None.'

'Liar.'

'Okay, one.' I pulled the duvet up around me. 'You.'

'Bullshit.' He gripped the edge of the duvet and ripped it away. 'This mattress is probably soggy with other men's spunk.'

I stared at him in shock. 'That's a vile thing to say.'

'I'm not the vile one.' He jumped out of bed and looked down at me, sneering. 'And I'm never sleeping in this bed again.'

'James!' I pulled the duvet back over my breasts. 'Stop being ridiculous. Come back to bed, for God's sake.'

'You stay in bed. I'm sleeping on the floor.'

'James!'

I watched in astonishment as he marched up to my wardrobe, threw it open and pulled out an old camping blanket. He wrapped it around himself, grabbed a cushion from the armchair by the door and lay down on the floor with his back towards me.

'James please.' I inched towards the edge of the bed and reached out a hand. 'This is ridiculous. You've slept in this bed loads of times and it's never bothered you before.'

He flipped over to face me. 'We weren't engaged then.'

'That's what this is about? Us getting engaged?'

A *wave of fear crashed over me.* 'I don't understand.'

'Us getting engaged changes things.' He sat up, resting his back against the wall. 'You'll be my wife one day Suzy and I can't deal with the fact that you've been with so many men.'

'But I haven't. I've only—'

'Fifteen,' James said and I cringed. Why had I been so honest with him on our second date? 'Why? You gave your cherry away to a one-night stand who used you like a dirty wank rag.'

I prickled but said nothing. It wasn't worth it. At least James had stopped raging and was speaking in a more measured, almost reflective, tone.

'I waited,' he continued. 'I waited and I waited to meet the woman who'd saved herself for me but, time and time again, just when I thought I'd met "the one" I'd find out she was a dirty slag like all the others. Do you know what I did?' He reached up and grabbed my wrist, yanking me towards him so our faces were millimeters apart. 'Do you know what I did when I finally accepted there was no such thing as a soulmate and that the world was laughing at me? I gave my virginity to a prostitute!' He spat out a laugh, spraying me with saliva. 'Yes, an actual slag. Why give it to an amateur when I could give it to a pro?'

I said nothing. James was scaring me, the way he was staring at me, his fingers pressed into my wrist, his hot beery breath flooding my nostrils. I'd never seen him look so angry, never seen him glower at me with such hatred and resentment. I wanted to reason with him, to apologise to him, to commiserate with him. Instead I said nothing and bit down on the inside of my cheek to stop myself from crying.

'I never expected to fall in love with you.' His voice fell to a whisper. 'I thought you were another good time girl I'd have fun with but,' he leaned away and traced the shape of my lips with his index finger, 'there's more to you than a regrettable past. You've got a beautiful soul, Suzy. That's why I gave you my grandmother's ring, the most precious thing I own. I hate that other men have fucked you and they didn't realize what a precious, precious jewel they held in their arms. I want to destroy them, one by one, until your past is obliterated and there's just me and you in the here and now.' I must have made a noise, some squeak of surprise because he added, 'I'm talking metaphorically of course. I'd never hurt anyone. You know I'd never hurt a fly don't you, Suzy-Sue? Never.'

The atmosphere in the room was so thick, so charged with emotion, I felt like I couldn't breathe. I wanted to break out of James's arms, throw open the window and gulp huge lungfuls of night air.

'We're engaged,' he continued. 'It's a commitment to each other but it's also a new start. Let's wipe the past from our lives, Suzy and begin again. Is it too much . . .' he glanced at the headboard then back at me, 'is it too much to ask you to get a new bed?'

I shook my head. Looking at it like that – like we were practically married – it didn't sound like such an unreasonable suggestion. A new life together and a new bed, it made sense.

Chapter 14

'And you're quite sure you saw this person enter your house?'

I'm pretty sure the WPC thinks I'm lying. Which I am.

'Yes,' I say. 'I was sitting in the garden reading a book when he jumped over the hedge, sprinted across the lawn and made a beeline for the porch door.'

The male officer wanders over to where I'm pointing, to the six-foot privet that separates us from next door, and stands on tiptoes to peer over it. He then crouches down and runs a hand through the undergrowth before standing up and returning to where we are standing.

'There are no signs of damage.' He gives me a long look. 'You'd expect there to be broken branches and scattered leaves and twigs if someone just jumped a hedge that size.'

167

I shrug. 'He was very lithe, athletic looking, you know – sporty.'

'So he vaulted the hedge without touching it?' The officer raises an eyebrow. 'That's some athleticism.'

I cross my arms over my chest then uncross them again. 'Well, I didn't actually *see* the burglar jump it. I heard something and looked up from my book to see him sprinting across the lawn towards the side of the house.'

The officers share a look and a wave of nausea sweeps over me. It seemed like such a plausible story when I was driving back from Woodingdean. I'd tell the police that a burglar was hiding in our home and then there'd be no need to mention my ex-boyfriend and the snow shaker he'd left on my doorstep. The police would check my house was safe – and empty – and I'd risk nothing.

'What makes you so sure the "burglar" entered your house through the porch door,' the WPC looks towards the side of the house, 'when you can't actually see it from here? For all you know he could have just run off down the driveway.'

'Because I left the door open.'

She raises an eyebrow.

'To let the dog wander in and out,' I add.

'Right.' She scribbles something in her notebook.

'It's my husband, you see – Brian Jackson, MP for Brighton. We can't be too careful.'

A look of surprise crosses the WPC's face. She looks at her colleague who raises his eyebrows as though he's impressed. Or shocked that Brian would be married to someone like me. Either way, both of them have stopped looking at me like they're considering charging me with wasting police time.

'We've checked your house.' The male officer strolls across the lawn, his car in his sights. The WPC indicates, with a nod of her head, that we should follow him. 'And there was no sign of any kind of disturbance, or an intruder.'

The WPC stops walking. 'You okay, Mrs Jackson? You look a little shaken.'

'I am, yes.' For the first time since they started questioning me I'm telling the truth. Now I know James isn't in the house or hiding in the garden I feel weak with relief.

'We could stay with you, at least until a friend or relative joins you. Is there someone you'd like to ring?'

I shake my head. I need to get inside and look through Brian's laptop. If Charlotte used it to urgently message someone, who knows what clues it might reveal.

'No, thank you. I'll be fine.'

'Are you quite sure?'

'Yes,' I say with more conviction than I feel, 'I'll be okay. Thank you so much for coming out.'

The male officer nods curtly and opens the car door. 'We'll be in touch.'

My bravado disappears the second the police car crunches its way down the driveway and disappears around the corner. What if the police only poked their heads into each room and James is still hiding somewhere? He'll have heard them leave and know I'm alone.

I look from the open porch door to the car. I could just go – jump back in with Milly and drive to my friend Jane's house. I could tell her Brian and I had a row (which wouldn't be far from the truth) and ask if I could stay for a couple of nights. But she and Eric have got two cats and I'd have to put Milly in kennels. Who else? Annette? No. I immediately discount her. She's a terrible gossip. It would only take a matter of days, if not hours, for the news to spread that my marriage was in disarray. I cycle through the rest of my friends – Ellen doesn't have the space, Amelia is knee deep in renovations and Mary is in Spain. The Travelodge just off the A22 takes dogs. All I need to do is pop into the house to grab the laptop and we can be there in under an hour.

I put my hand on Milly's soft head and scratch behind her ear as I mentally rehearse my route through the house, making a list of what I'll take from each room. The house isn't safe anymore. I need to get in and out as quickly as I can.

'Ready girl?' I take a step towards the open porch door.

Every squeaky floorboard, rumbling pipe and creaking wall makes me start as I hurry from room to room, throwing open drawers, gathering up clothes and sweeping make-up and toiletries into a large floral overnight bag. Darting into the bathroom to collect my toothbrush terrifies me when I notice someone staring at me from the other side of the room, only to discover that Brian has left his shaving mirror angled towards the door and it's my own reflection. Milly quickly tires of my frenetic pace and lies down in the middle of the hall and rests her head on her paws.

I leave Brian's study for last and it's only as I turn the handle that it strikes me that he might have taken his laptop with him when he left yesterday. I push the door open and peer into the room.

It's on the desk, closed and unplugged with the lead coiled over the lid and the plug resting on the side like Brian was planning on taking it with him and then forgot. I scoop it up and then—

BANG!

The office door slams shut behind me.

I freeze, half bent over the desk with the laptop in my hands. Every fibre of my body is still, every hair erect. My heart slows to a steady thud-thud-thud as I listen.

Listen.

For the creak of a floorboard, the creak of a joint, or the low sound of a breath.

Listen.

Time slows and I have no idea how long I've been standing here, hunched over the desk, listening, waiting, dreading. My lower back aches, my hip bones hurt from where they're pressing against the desk and the laptop is slipping from my sweaty fingers. If

James is behind me I need to turn around and face my fate head on.

I turn slowly, the laptop still in my hands and brace myself.

But there's no one else in the room.

I take a step towards the closed study door. What if he's on the other side? I take another step forward, place my hand on the doorknob and then twist it sharply to the left. It moves easily under my hand and the door swings open. Milly raises her head from the floor and her tail thumps the wooden floor. There is no one else in the house. I'd know from her reaction if there was.

'Hello girl,' I take a step forward and stoop down to pat her head when,

BANG!

The study door slams behind me.

BANG! BANG! BANG!

This time from the bathroom. I run towards the sound. The window above the bath is open, slamming back and forth, a cold breeze filling the room. I glance outside, half expecting to see someone hanging from the ledge or sprinting across the lawn but the only movement in the garden is the willow tree, bowing and stretching in the wind. I lean out of the window, reach for the catch and yank it closed.

'Come on, Milly.' I hurry back out of the bathroom, grab the laptop and my overnight bag from where I left them in the hallway and speed down the stairs with the dog at my heels. I cast a quick look around the kitchen before I snatch up Milly's food and water dishes and throw them into a plastic bag with a half full sack of dried dog food and then speed out of the house, locking the porch door behind me, and jump into the car. I don't glance in the rear-view mirror as I pull away.

Saturday 4th January 1991

Thank God it's the New Year. That might just have been the most depressing Christmas of my life.

James was really apologetic that he couldn't invite me to spend Christmas with him and his mum but she was still smarting from 'the incident' (when we turned up to lunch drunk and late).

Last year I spent Christmas with Hels, Ru, Emma and Matt but I couldn't see that happening this year.

Instead I scraped together what little savings I had left and booked a train ticket up north and a room at a Holiday Inn so I could see Mum.

To be fair to the care home, they'd made a huge effort to make the place look happy and cheery but the sight of old people dribbling their Christmas puddings down their chins and carers in snowman earrings carrying bedpans along the corridors made me feel sad. Mum was having a lucid period – she didn't lapse once in the whole four hours I was there but instead of feeling pleased I was heartbroken. She kept bursting into tears, begging me to take her back to her house, saying how much she missed Dad. I did the best I could to console her, hugging her tightly, combing her hair, telling her about my engagement in Prague and looking through old photo albums but how can you cheer up someone who tells you they wish they were dead. I offered to move back to York so I could visit her more often but she wouldn't have it – 'I've lived my life,' she said, 'and I followed my dreams and it's time you did the same. I'm pleased you've found love and a job you adore, Susan. All Dad and I ever wanted was for you to be happy.'

On Boxing Day I went to Dad's grave to lay some flowers. It broke my heart seeing his plot so overgrown and uncared for – Mum used to tend to it once a week until she got ill – so I pulled out as many weeds as I could by hand and borrowed a pair of shears from the groundsman so I could trim the grass. I talked to Dad when I was doing it – asked him to look after Mum when I couldn't, told him how much we both loved him and cried when I said I didn't want anyone but him to give me away at my wedding.

I returned home yesterday and found a message on my answerphone from the bed people saying that due to a problem with supply they wouldn't be able to deliver my new bed until after the new year! James and I had already chucked my bed and mattress out before Christmas so, when he came round with my presents on the twenty-eighth we ended up sleeping on blankets on the floor.

The next morning I got up to make us coffee and a fried breakfast and James pottered about, flicking through my magazines and picking through my vinyl. He honed in on my sewing machine table. It's an antique, one hundred per cent oak and beautifully made. He ran a finger over the polished wood.

'Where'd you get this?'

'My parents gave it to me for my twenty-first.'

'Lovely.'

He carried on along the wall, running his hand over the few pieces of furniture I've got.

'And this?' He stopped at my writing desk.

'I picked it up in a flea market. It was only thirty pounds.'

'Nice.'

I froze as his fingers strummed on the wood. If he opened it he'd find—

'What's this?' He held the grey rabbit soft toy by one ear, dangling it from his fingers. 'You've never struck me as the cuddly toy sort.'

'It's . . . it was . . . a . . . a present from Hels.'

'A female friend bought you a soft toy?' My cheeks grew hot as he scrutinized my face. 'That's a little unusual. Are you sure it's not from an old boyfriend?'

''Course not,' I said lightly. 'Hels um, bought it for me as a joke. She used to call me Bunny when we worked together because, um, because I wouldn't sit still. I was always bouncing excitedly all over the room.'

'Bunny?' He raised an eyebrow. 'You?'

'Yes.' The name and the description were true but

Hels wasn't the one who'd given me the nickname or the toy. It was Nathan. I'd grown attached to that little rabbit while we were together and held onto it, as well as a couple of other things he'd given me, after we split up.

'Why are you sweating, Suzy-Sue?' James took a step towards me, the rabbit outstretched. 'You're not lying to me, are you?'

'No, of course not.' I ran the back of my hand over my damp brow. 'It's these eggs.' I jabbed at the burnt offering in the frying pan. 'They're spitting like mad.'

My voice had taken on a strange sing-song character that sounded foreign to my ears. I bent down, ostensibly to check the bacon but actually to avoid James's eyes then squealed as he wrapped a hand around my waist and pulled me into him, pressing my buttocks into his crotch.

'You scared me.' I set the grill pan on the side and, still with his arms wrapped around me, spooned the bacon and eggs onto two plates.

'And you scare me,' James whispered in my ear. 'Because sometimes I wonder how in love with me you really are.'

'Don't be silly.' Blood pounded in my ears. 'You know how much I love you.'

*'Really? Because I'd be **very** hurt if I found out that you were lying to me, Suzy. If you were secretly keeping love tokens from past boyfriends when you know how much that sort of thing hurts me.'*

I reached into the cupboard for the ketchup. 'The bunny is from Hels. I told you.'

'And she'd verify that if I called her up, would she?'

'Of course she would. Ring her now if you like.' I inclined my head towards the phone on the other side of the room, desperately hoping he wouldn't see through my bluff.

He laughed loudly. 'As if I'd talk to that boring cow about a teddy!' He turned me to face him, pressed the soft toy against my cheek. 'You don't have feelings towards this stupid thing, do you?'

I shook my head.

'Good,' he said then launched the toy into the air. It flew in an arc across the room, sailed out of the open window and landed in the road outside.

He kissed me on the lips. 'Is breakfast ready? I could eat a horse.'

Two hours later, after he'd gone, I went through everything I own and threw away everything I've ever been given, or that reminded me, of an ex-boyfriend – photos, letters, postcards, jewellery, books and vinyl. I even sold the vintage Chanel handbag that Nathan bought me for Christmas one year.

Now I'll never have to lie to James again.

Chapter 15

My hotel room is sandwiched between a stag party and a school trip but the noise doesn't bother me. It's almost reassuring, hearing the low ho-ho-ho of male laughter and the hysterical squeal of thirteen-year-olds at play against a soundtrack of blaring televisions and the low bass rumble of dance music.

I move my finger over the track pad of Brian's laptop and click the 'Start' button, then 'Programs', and then pause. The only program I recognize is Microsoft Office. What's a Filezilla? A Photoshop? A Skype? I reach for my handbag.

Oliver answers on the second ring. 'Sue? Everything okay with Charlotte?'

'She's fine. I was just wondering if you could give me some technical help.'

''Course.'

'What software would Charlotte use to chat to her friends on the internet?'

'I don't know,' he says after a minute or so. 'Me and my friends use Facebook chat or MSN Messenger. Maybe Skype. God knows about Charlotte. Why do you need to know?'

I double click a folder that says 'Documents' but it's just Brian's work stuff. 'Someone told me she had a conversation with a friend using software on Dad's laptop and I've got a hunch it might be important.'

'Hmmm.' I can almost hear Oli thinking. 'Chances are you're not going to find anything, not unless you know the application she was using. And even then you'd need to know her username and password. She was using *Dad's* laptop you say?'

'That's right.'

'I could be wrong but I'm pretty certain he uses MSN Messenger to have online chats with his constituents once a week and he logs the conversations so he can't be sued for giving improper advice or making false promises or whatever. If Charlotte didn't change the settings and that's what she used then her conversation should be logged too.'

'Really?'

'Yeah. Do you want me to talk you through how to find the Messenger logs? Actually,' he pauses, 'shouldn't you be asking Dad this?'

'I . . .' I'm not sure how best to handle this. I don't want Oli to know that his dad has moved out. He might be nineteen but the news would still upset him and he's slap bang in the middle of some of the most important exams of his career. 'I haven't been able to get through to him today. Some tedious select

180

committee meeting that goes on all day I think and it's really urgent that I access these messages. If there are any.'

'Okay, no worries.' He seems reassured by my explanation. 'Right, this is what you need to do . . .'

I concentrate hard as he tells me, step by step, where to click and what to open until, finally, we're there, in a folder called 'My Chat Logs'.

'There are loads,' I say as I scroll through the file-names. 'Hundreds of the things. How am I supposed to know which one is Charlotte?'

'You're not. And if she noticed that Dad had the 'save conversation' box checked and unchecked it there won't be any record of her conversation.'

'Oh God.' I keep my finger on the mouse and watch in horror as filename after filename flicks by. It's going to take me a while to go through them all.

'Need any more help?'

'No, no. I'm fine. Thanks so much, Oli.'

We say our goodbyes and I open the first message log. It's a conversation between Brian and a parishioner about school catchment areas. I close it and open the second message. This time someone wants to draw his attention to 'the immigration problem'. Third message – a moan about benefits. Fourth message – a request for help renovating a local children's park. Fifth message – abuse, calling Brian 'an ineffective pretend politician from a party more concerned with planting trees than economic success'. And there are more messages. More and more and more. They never end. It's fascinating and frustrating at the same time. I never realized quite how many small-minded, selfish people Brian has to deal with on a daily basis. I open half a dozen more messages and still there are hundreds more. Where's Charlotte's conversation? I begin clicking randomly, on this conversation and that, hoping to hit the jackpot. Instead I read about allotment battles, property wars, care home scandals and the death of the high street. Everyone is unhappy about something it seems and Brian is the . . . I stop clicking to re-read the line that's just flashed up on the screen.

Charliethecat15: Soz, lappy crashed. Back now.

Charliethecat15. Could that be Charlotte? I read the entire message, my heart beating frantically in my chest . . .

Charliethecat15: Soz, lappy crashed. Back now.
Ellsbells: Like I give a shit.
Charliethecat15: Don't be like that, Els
Ellsbells: I don't know why you're even bothering to contact me. Our friendship is OVER.
Charliethecat15: Fine, but we need to get our stories straight.
Ellsbells: Why don't you get your story straight with Keisha seeing as you and her are SO CLOSE
Charliethecat15: This isn't about Keisha and you know it
Ellsbells: Isn't it?
Charliethecat15: No. Look Ella, I know I pissed you off and that's fine, we don't ever have to

182

talk to each other again but if we don't cover
for each other and Mr E finds out he'll kill us.
Ellsbells: *Fuck Mr E, he's a prick*
Charliethecat15: *I know, right.*
Charliethecat15: *You still there, Ella?*
Charliethecat15: *Ella?*
Ellsbells: *What?*
Charliethecat15: *Will you still cover for me? I will*
for you.
Ellsbells: *Fine. Just don't ever contact me again.*
Charliethecat15: *Fine. I won't. Just wanted to clear*
that up.
Ellsbells: *Whatever.*

I read it again. And a third time. And I still have no idea what they're talking about. Why do they need to cover for each other and who is Mr E? I glance at my watch. 2.45 p.m. I'm going to have to hurry if I want to catch Ella before school kicks out for the day.

I glance at Milly who looks at me hopefully.

'Okay,' I grab her lead. 'You can come too.'

Chapter 16

It feels strange, standing outside the school gates. I haven't picked Charlotte up from school since she was twelve and when I see Ella strolling out of the main doors, her books clasped to her chest, her blazer thrown over one arm I half expect to see my daughter walking alongside her, knocking elbows and laughing at each other's jokes.

'Ella?' I reach out a hand and touch her elbow as she draws close. 'Could I have a word?'

She glances around to check the reaction of her classmates but they don't seem to have noticed me as they stream out of the gates, laughing, chatting and pulling faces at each other. Or if they have they don't care.

'Ella please, it's important.'

'Okay, okay.' She waves a hand to signal that we should move away from the gates, glances over her shoulder – to check for what I'm not sure – and then looks back at me. 'What about?'

'About you and Charlotte covering for each other?'

Her defiant expression fades ever so slightly. 'I don't know what you're talking about.'

'I think you do.'

I could pretend that I know everything but if she realizes I'm lying this conversation is over. 'I read the conversation the two of you had on MSN Messenger. It was saved onto one of our home computers.'

Ella's eyes grow large as she searches my face. She's trying to work out if she's in trouble or not. I need to go carefully.

'Who's Mr E, Ella?'

She glances away, towards the school, then back at me.

'I don't know what you're talking about, Mrs Jackson.'

'Mr E. In the conversation you and Charlotte had on Messenger, Charlotte said that if Mr E found out what you'd done, he'd kill you both.'

She shrugs. 'I think you've mixed me up with someone else.'

'Ellsbells,' I say. 'That was the username of the person Charlotte was talking to. I know it was you.'

She shrugs again, purses her lips into a half-smile, half-pout and turns to go. She knows there was nothing in that conversation to incriminate her and I can't do a thing to persuade her otherwise. How can she be so callous when her best friend is in a coma she might never wake up from?

'Ella, please.' I put a hand on her shoulder. 'I don't care what you and Charlotte did or why you had to get your stories straight. I won't be angry and I won't tell your mum, just please tell me who Mr E is.'

'I told you.' She shakes my hand from her shoulder. 'You've got the wrong person.'

She turns to walk away but I grab her again. 'Is he someone's dad, this Mr E? Or a teacher? Is he one of your—' the expression on Ella's face changes from anger to something else. 'He's a teacher, isn't he?' I can't keep the jubilation out of my voice. 'What's his name, Ella?'

'Get your fucking hands off me!'

Now the other kids are staring at us. The stream of bodies passing by has stopped and I'm surrounded on all sides by staring, surprised faces. Conversations fade and laughter turns to embarrassed giggles. 'Who is she?' I hear someone ask then, 'Oh my God, it's Charlotte Jackson's mum.' 'Shit, yeah! Total nut job. Apparently she wouldn't let Charlotte have a bath or shower for a month because she thought someone had put acid in the water!'

Ella notices the commotion around us too. The base of her throat blushes red but she flicks back her hair defiantly. I know I should remove my hand from her shoulder but I'm terrified that if I let her go I'll never see her again.

'Ella,' I keep my voice soft. 'There's no need to cause a scene. Just tell me Mr E's full name and I promise I'll never bother you again.'

The girl smiles and, for a second, I think that this awful, awkward moment is about to end but then the smile disappears and is replaced by an ugly curled lip.

'Help!' She tosses back her head and screams, 'Someone help! Help! Help!'

I let go of her but it's too late, I'm shoved to one side as someone bowls through the crowd and stands between us.

'Mrs Jackson?' There's an astonished expression on the face of the woman standing in front of me. It's Clara Cooper, Charlotte's English teacher.

'She hurt me. I thought she was going to pull my arm off.'

Miss Cooper turns to look at Ella. A group of girls have appeared around her, forming a protective arc of patting hands, murmured reassurances and raised eyebrows.

'Mrs Jackson hurt you?'

'Yes, Miss. I was just going for the school bus when she grabbed me and wouldn't let me go.'

'Yeah,' says one of the girls behind her. 'Yeah, she did.'

'I thought she was going to hit me.' Ella's face is the epitome of wide-eyed innocence. 'I was really scared.'

Miss Cooper turns back to me and raises her eyebrows.

I feel hot, faint and terribly dry-mouthed. I can't believe this is really happening. I just want to go home. I want to crawl into bed, go to sleep and wake up to find that all of this – Charlotte's accident, James's presents, the argument with Brian and this

– were all just a dream. 'I tapped her on the shoulder,' I say. 'That's all. I just wanted to talk to her.'

Miss Cooper gives me a searching look then turns back to the crowd. 'You lot, go home. Show's over. Ella, go and stand by the gates. I'll have a word with you in a second.'

Ella pulls a face. 'But Miss—'

'Go.'

She pouts, puts her palms out as though she's about to object then seems to think the better of it and she makes her way through the crowd. They disperse slowly, grumbling with disappointment that the spectacle is over.

Miss Cooper waits until there are no children within earshot and then looks at me. The frown has left her forehead now we no longer have an audience. 'How are you, Mrs Jackson?'

The word 'fine' is on the tip of my tongue but there's something about the softness of her tone and the gentle concern in her eyes that makes me say 'Tired' instead.

'I'm not surprised.' She touches me lightly on the arm and then her hand falls away. 'How is Charlotte? She's very much missed.'

'There's no change,' I say, 'but thank you for asking.'

Miss Cooper smiles sadly then glances over her shoulder. Ella is leaning against the gate. She has one foot on the ground, the other kicking the metal fencing beside the entrance.

Clang-clang-clang.

'Ella!'

She stops the second the teacher says her name and shoots a sulky look in my direction. Clara looks back at me.

'What's going on there? With Ella?'

I explain about the MSN Messenger conversation and tell her I'm concerned that this 'Mr E' might be some kind of threat to the girls.

'And you think he might be a parent or teacher?'

I explain about Ella's reaction when I suggested that Mr E might be a teacher and Miss Cooper looks thoughtful.

'There's a Mr Egghart,' she says. 'He teaches Physics.'

I shake my head. Neither of the girls are studying Physics.

'It's definitely a Mr?' she asks. 'It couldn't be Mrs Everett, Miss Evesham or Miss East?'

'No. They definitely talked about a Mr E. One of them called him a prick.'

'I'm struggling to think of any more teachers with surnames beginning with E.' Miss Cooper twiddles her earrings and looks at the pavement, frowning in concentration. 'Jenny Best from the office has a full staff list. She'd be a better person to as— Oh!' She looks up in delight. 'I've just remembered. There's a teacher covering Business Studies for Mrs Hart while she's on maternity leave. His name begins with E. What is it . . . Eggers? No. Ethan? No. It's a very common name. It'll come to me. I know!' She smiles in triumph. 'Evans! That's it. Mr Evans.'

'Evans?' I repeat, suddenly feeling as though I've

been lifted out of myself and I'm watching us have this conversation from ten feet above my head. 'You don't happen to know his first name, do you?'

When Clara's lips part I know what she's about to say before she says it.

'James,' she says. 'Same name as my boyfriend.'

The floating feeling stops as quickly as it started and I'm snapped back into my body so violently I have to take a step to the side to stop myself from falling over.

'James Evans?'

'Yes.' Clara is still smiling. 'Why? You don't think he's somehow respons—'

'What does he look like? Is he over six foot? Blond? Well spoken?'

'Yes.' She looks at me in confusion. 'Yes, he's all of those things.'

'Wait!' She calls after me as I run past Ella and through the school gates. 'Mrs Jackson, please stop!'

Sunday 1st April 1991

I bumped into Hels on Oxford Street yesterday. My first reaction when I caught sight of her, looking beautiful in a black and green polka dot dress with her red hair piled on top of her head, was delight – but then I remembered we weren't friends anymore and darted into HMV to try and avoid her. She must have seen me because the next thing I knew there was a hand on my arm and, 'Sue? It is you, isn't it?' She looked so pleased to see me I could have cried. I didn't though. I didn't want her to see how miserable I'd been without her. I made small talk instead – telling her about the costumes I was making for Waiting for Godot *and how my mum was a little happier in the care home, although her condition was continuing to deteriorate. Hels, in return told me she'd been promoted at work and that she and Rupert had just got back from a week in Florence where they'd got engaged. I hugged her then, I couldn't help myself* and it was only when she pulled away and raised my left hand so she could get a good look at my ring that I remembered that I was engaged too.

'Aren't you the dark horse?' she said but, instead of a smile, a cloud crossed her face. 'Congratulations Susan, you must be very happy.'

That's when I started to cry, right there and then in the middle of HMV surrounded by people picking through the latest chart CDs.

Hels looked so horrified I tried to run off. It was bad enough that I was crying in public without my ex-best friend looking at me like I was some kind of basket case. She chased after me, grabbed my hand.

'Please Susan, let's go for a drink. Tell me what's wrong. I've missed you.'

We went to the Dog and Duck in Soho and found a dark corner where I could talk without too many people seeing my tear-stained face. I told Hels everything. I told her about meeting James's mum, about the trip to Prague, about James refusing to sleep in my bed and him throwing Bunny out of the window and she listened attentively, saying nothing apart from the occasional uh-huh or hmmm. But when I told her how he'd asked me to have anal sex with him to prove how much I loved him she gasped.

'Did you?' Hels looked at me, her big green eyes wide with concern. 'You swore you'd never do it again after you tried it with Nathan.'

'I know. And I kept telling James that I didn't like it and I wasn't going to do it again but he kept going on and on, saying that I obviously loved my ex-boyfriend more than I loved him if I would do it with Nathan but not with him. He brought it into every conversation and it got to the stage where, even if we were having a nice time, I couldn't relax because I was waiting for him to start up again. I figured if I just got it over and done with once then that would be that.'

'And?'

My eyes filled with tears and I looked away.

'You need to leave him, Sue,' Helen reached for my hands, 'and you need to do it now.'

I tried to argue. I tried to explain that James had been abused as a child, that he felt stifled living with his mother, that he'd been such a romantic he'd hung onto his virginity until he was twenty-four and that he really did love me, he was just struggling with disappointment and jealousy but Hels kept on shaking her head.

'That's not love, Sue. The things he says, the way he treats you, that's not love.'

'But . . .' I tried to explain how it wasn't all bad, how things could be magical between us, how we had so much in common, how I'd never felt so alive, how every day could be an adventure when James was in a good mood.

'Exactly – when he's in a good mood. Because we both know what happens when he's not. Is it worth it, Sue? Is it worth being criticized, degraded and judged just for a few happy moments? Is it worth walking on eggshells, constantly wondering when he's going to have a go at you next?'

'But it's not like he hits me. He's never done that, not once.'

'Yet.' She shook her head. 'Just because James doesn't raise his fists doesn't mean he's not abusing you, Susan. You need to get out. Now.'

She didn't need to say any more because everything she had said I'd thought myself a hundred times. But it was different hearing someone else say it, it was different seeing the shock and concern in her eyes. It made me feel like I wasn't overreacting or going mad, that James wasn't treating me how I should be treated, that I'd be happier alone.

So I'm going to do it. I'm going to leave him. I'll do it on Friday when we've agreed to go for a drink.

I just hope I'm not shaking as much as I am now.

Chapter 17

'Brian!' I shout into my mobile as I sprint down the corridor, past artwork displays, sporting achievements and tall metal lockers. 'Brian, you need to come home *now*. James Evans is working at Charlotte's school. I read a conversation on your computer between her and Ella and they were scared of him. Call the police, Brian. I'm at the school now.'

I reach the stairs and speed up them, using the banister to yank myself up, cursing my legs for not moving faster. I haven't been to Brighton Academy for at least a year but I can still remember where the headmaster's office is.

'Can I help you?'

A fair-haired middle-aged woman in a pale pink blouse with pearls at her neck looks up from her desk as I charge into the small room adjacent to the headmaster's office. She's about the same age as me, maybe four or five years older. Her name is Clarissa

Gordon. She was here the last time I came to see the Head.

'I'm here to see Mr Anderson.' I make a half-hearted attempt to pat down my hair. 'It's urgent.'

I can tell from the expression on Clarissa's face as she looks me up and down that she remembers me. Her nose narrows and the hint of a smile plays on her pursed lips. 'And your name is?'

'Jackson. Sue Jackson. It's very important that I see him. The safety of two of the pupils is at stake.'

Clarissa raises her eyebrows. She's remembering the last time I was here – when I stormed into Charlotte's biology lesson and demanded she leave with me. We'd been burgled a month earlier and a news report I'd just watched on the TV about a teenager being raped in a local park had convinced me that James was after her. I was shaking so much I couldn't breathe. Mr Prosser, the biology teacher, took me through to see Mr Anderson and he called the school nurse. I can still remember Clarissa's pinched face peering at me through the glass panel in the head teacher's door as the nurse instructed me to take slow, deep breaths as I desperately pleaded with her to listen to me. Why did no one understand how much danger my daughter was in? I was on high-dose anti-anxiety medication for six months afterwards.

'The safety of two pupils you say? Gosh. Well, if you could give me a few more details perhaps I could call through to Mr Anderson and . . .' she tails off, distracted by half a dozen staff chatting noisily as they stroll past the window behind me.

'There's no time.' I side-step her desk and reach for the door handle to her right. 'I need to speak to him now.'

'Excuse me. Excuse me, Mrs Jack—'

Her chair squeaks as she rises to come after me but I turn the handle and I'm in the headmaster's study before she can reach me.

'Clarissa, I—' the Head looks up from his desk, his lips parting in surprise as I burst into the room, his secretary in close pursuit.

'Sorry Mr Anderson,' she breathes, 'she just burst in. There was nothing I could do to stop her.'

'It's okay, Clarissa.' He nods. 'I'll take it from here.'

'But you specifically said you didn't want to be disturbed. You said you had to prepare a report for the governors about—'

'I'll take it from here, Clarissa. Thank you.'

'Yes Mr Anderson.' She retreats, stepping backwards out of the room. From her expression I'm fairly certain that if we were thirty years younger she'd be waiting for me at the gates later with two of her mates.

'I'll just be outside,' she says, closing the door with a click.

Ian Anderson eyes me from under his heavy brow and waves a hand in the direction of the empty chair in front of me. 'Do take a seat, Mrs . . .'

'Jackson. I'll stand, thank you.'

'Okay.' He leans back in his chair and folds his arms across his broad chest. 'What can I do for you, Mrs Jackson?'

'I'm sorry for bursting in on you but,' I grip the back of the chair, 'it's urgent. One of your teachers poses a very real danger to the children.'

He sits up sharply. 'One of our teachers?'

'I have reason to believe that one of your teachers is working at this school under false pretences. I think he may have harmed Charlotte and possibly her friend Ella too.'

'Charlotte . . .' Mr Anderson looks at me as though seeing me for the first time. 'Not Charlotte Jackson? You're her—'

'Mother? Yes.'

I wait for him to jump to his feet and take action. Instead he keeps staring at me like he's expecting me to say something else.

'Please.' I motion for him to stand up. 'Can we just go and find him? The longer we wait the more chance there is that he'll leave for the day.' Or maybe forever. I can't shake the feeling that James knows I'm onto him. 'Please, Mr Anderson. He needs to be stopped before he hurts someone – if he hasn't already.'

'If who's hurt someone?'

'James Evans.'

'James Evans – our business studies teacher?'

'Yes. No. He's not really a teacher, he's an imposter.' I inch towards the door. 'Please, Mr Anderson. Let's go.'

'Mrs Jackson,' he holds up a hand. 'Sit down for a minute and let's start this again. I'm struggling to keep up.'

'There isn't time.' I cross the room and stoop

down, my hands gripping the edge of his desk, my face at the same level as his. 'Please. I'll explain everything but I need you to find James Evans with me *now*. You have no idea how much danger the children are in. We need to stop him before he can escape.' I can't keep the exasperation out of my voice. 'Please, let's go.'

'We take accusations against our teachers very seriously you know, Mrs Jackson.' He gets up interminably slowly and I wait as he pulls his jacket from the back of the chair and slips one arm, then the other into it then smoothes it over his shoulders. For one terrible second I think he's about to do up his buttons too but he suddenly becomes animated and crosses the room in four large strides.

'Mrs Jackson,' he says as he opens the door and I catch sight of Clarissa's arched eyebrows, 'if you'd come with me.'

Even with Mr Anderson's long-legged strides it takes forever to reach the staff room. When we cross the 'bridge' between the science block and the main building I pause to press my hands up against the floor to ceiling window and search the car park. A dozen or so teachers mill around below, some chatting in small groups, the others letting themselves into their cars. I scan the group for James's face but he's not down there.

'Mrs Jackson?'

The headmaster is standing at the far end of the bridge. I hurry after him.

'Of course he might not even be here,' he says,

holding open the door to the staff room. 'There's every chance he'll have left for the day, be in the business studies room or even . . .'

I don't hear the rest of the sentence because my heart is hammering so hard in my chest I feel sick.

There is a man standing at the opposite side of the staff room. He has his back to us, his blonde head dipped as though he's reading a book or marking a pile of papers. I can still hear Mr Anderson's voice but I can't make out a word he's saying. Every fibre of my being is commanding me to turn and run, but I can't. I can't tear my eyes away from the broad expanse of back and the strong arms of the man across the room. The air stills, the distance between us closes and it is as though I am standing behind him and breathing in his musky scent. I reach out a hand and feel the coarse wave to his hair, the soft skin on the back of his bent neck and the starchy stiffness of his shirt collar under my fingertips. I have seen this shape, felt these things in a hundred nightmares. He just needs to turn around so I can see his face.

'James?' I breathe as the edges of my vision turn amber and then black. It's as though a match is being held to a photograph. I blink to try and clear my vision but now there are black spots and my ears are ringing with the sound of the ocean. I feel like I'm swimming under water, deep, deep down under the—

'Mrs Jackson?'

I feel a hand touch my elbow and try to turn my head to the left to see who has touched me but I'm fighting so hard to keep my balance I feel like the slightest movement will send me hurtling like a stone towards the sea bed.

'Mrs Jackson, do you need to sit down?'

There is another hand, touching my right elbow and I feel something nudge the back of my knees and then I'm pushed/pulled down until I am sitting. Everything is black and the ocean inside my head pounds the sides of my skull. My stomach lurches and—

'Oh God, she's been sick.'

'There are paper towels in the gents. I'll get some.'

'And a glass of water if you—'

'We've got mugs. There might be a clean one some—'

And then there is silence.

'Mrs Jackson. Mrs Jackson, can you hear me?'

'Mrs Jackson?' A different voice, female this time. Then, 'Sue?'

'Brian?' I say but no sound comes out. I try to sit up but gentle hands press down on my shoulders, on my hips and I am forced back down.

'Don't move. You hit your head when you fainted. The paramedics are on their way.'

'James,' I say, staring into the bright blue eyes that are looking at me with a mixture of concern and puzzlement.

'No, Sue. It's Brian.'

'I know. I know you're Brian. Where's James?'

My husband twists around to look at someone behind him, someone out of my eyeline.

'James, she wants to talk to you.'

'No! No!' I try to scream but the words catch in my throat. 'No!'

'Mrs Jackson?' A face I've never seen before appears beside Brian. 'I'm James Evans.'

'No. No, you're not.'

The man smiles. It's a warm smile that lights up his face, spreading his nostrils wide and crinkling the skin under his eyes. 'You can ring my mum or check my birth certificate if you like but I've spent the last twenty-nine years being called James Evans – well, Jamie to my friends – so I'm pretty sure—'

'The other one,' I say. 'Where's the other one?'

I try to sit up so I can look around the room but Brian shakes his head.

'This is James Evans.' He puts a hand to my face and gently brushes the hair from my cheeks. 'Charlotte and Ella's business studies teacher. He's the only James Evans in the school, Sue.'

'But . . .' I look from Brian to the young, blonde-haired man beside him and instantly realize my mistake. James Evans wouldn't be blond anymore – not at forty-eight. 'Oh God.'

I cover my face with my hands and close my eyes. What have I done?

'The girls skived a school trip.' I hear Brian say. 'They were supposed to go to London with Mr Evans but—'

'They called in on the day and said they had food poisoning. Said they'd been to Nandos together the night before and had some bad chicken and were up all night with dodgy stomachs. I had no reason not to believe them although, in retrospect, perhaps I should have called you to check.'

'You should,' says a voice I recognize as Mr Anderson.

'The MSN conversation you read, Sue. They weren't really scared that Mr Evans was going to kill them,' Brian says. 'It was just a figure of speech.'

I remove my hands from my face and look at the four faces hovering over me.

'If they didn't go on a school trip with Mr Evans that weekend,' I say, 'and they weren't at home with us, where were they?'

Brian shakes his head. 'We don't know.'

Saturday 7th April 1991

I've been a mess all week. I haven't been able to sew or sleep and I've barely eaten. Every time the phone's rung I've jumped, certain it was James, terrified he'd found out what I was about to do. As it was he only rang me once this week – and then it was just a brief call mid-week to check where we were meeting on Friday.

I didn't want to go. I kept telling myself James wasn't that bad, that there were a lot of men out there who were worse than him but then, almost as if she could sense my resolve wavering, Hels called me at 5 p.m.

'I'll be there for you,' she said. 'We both will. Rupert and I will help you through this. Be strong, Susan. Remember all the times he's made you cry.'

Typical then that James, sitting alone at a wooden table by the bar, jumped out of his seat the minute he spotted me walking into the Heart in Hand, wrapped me in his arms and told me how beautiful I looked. He was in a fantastic mood, buzzing about a television role he'd seen advertised in The Stage and apologizing profusely for not ringing me because he'd been so busy preparing for his audition.

'It went well, really well,' he said, squeezing my hands between his as we sat down, 'and if I get this I'll be able to afford somewhere big enough for you and I to live with a granny flat on the side for Mum. We'll have our privacy and she'll have the reassurance that I'm close by. And, and . . .' he practically jumped out of his seat, '. . . you can have your own sewing room, maybe start up a business rather than do it for free for the Abberley lot. It'll be perfect.'

We stayed in the pub – him gushing and fantasizing – me nodding and playing the supportive girlfriend for a good two hours until, unable to bear it a second longer I suggested we grab a takeaway and go back to mine. James was surprised, he'd expected to go on to a restaurant but I said I was tired and he acquiesced. The walk home was horrible. I was too preoccupied to talk and we lapsed into an uncomfortable silence, James glancing at me every couple of seconds while I avoided his eyes.

He wrapped his arms around me as I unlocked the front door and nuzzled his face into my neck.

'Maybe coming home wasn't such a bad idea after all. You just wanted to lure me into your bed didn't you, you little minx?'

I stiffened at his touch and slipped out of his arms. He followed me into the kitchen and watched from the doorway as I opened the fridge and pulled out a bottle of wine. I could feel his eyes boring into my back as I unscrewed the lid and poured myself a large glass.

'Want one, James?'

He didn't reply.

I put the bottle back in the fridge then, noticing how messy it had become, set about rearranging packets of ham, cartons of milk and half-empty tins of baked beans.

'What are you doing?' His voice cut through me .

I murmured something inane about a tidy fridge and a tidy mind, unwrapped the cling film from a chunk of cheese then rewrapped it, tighter, and placed it in the top drawer of the fridge door.

'Sue, stop fucking about with the fridge and look at me.'

I turned slowly, my eyes fixed on the tiled floor.

'Look at me.'

I tightened my grip on my glass of wine and forced my gaze upward. A jolt of fear flashed through me as our eyes met. There was no warmth in James's eyes, no humour, no love. He was looking at me dispassionately like he'd never seen me before.

'Let's go through to the living room.' My voice came out as a whisper. 'We need to talk.'

James turned on his heel and left the kitchen. I followed behind, pausing in the corridor to gulp my wine as he disappeared into the living room. I'd barely taken a step through the door when a hand gripped my neck and I was shoved up against the wall.

'I knew you'd cheat on me. You dirty little slut.'

'James.' The wine glass tumbled from my hand as my fingers flew to my neck. I pulled at his hand but he was too strong. 'James, I can't breathe.'

'No one will ever love you as much as I do.' His top lip was curled back, his nostrils flared. 'No one.'

'Please.' I pulled at his hand again, my heels dancing against the skirting as I tried to find my footing. Only my toes were touching the floor. 'Please, James. Please, you're hurting me.'

'Good.' He pressed his face against mine, his breath hot against my cheek, his skin damp with sweat. 'Because you're hurting me.'

'I didn't cheat on you. I swear. I swear on my mum's life. On my dad's grave.'

James pulled back and looked at me through narrowed eyes and then smiled. For a second I thought he was going to headbutt me but then he kissed me full on the lips, pressing so hard I lost all sensation in my mouth. His hand grasped for my breast and then, just as I thought it was over, he threw me across the room. My foot hit the coffee table and I stumbled forward, handing face first on the sofa.

'James,' I twisted onto my side. He moved across the living room towards me, the same dead expression in his eyes that I'd seen in the kitchen. 'James, stop it. I didn't cheat on you. I swear. I—'

He stopped walking and laughed. He laughed so hard he gripped his stomach and gasped, reaching for the arm of the sofa as he doubled over.

'You?' He snorted. 'Cheat on me? As if.' He pointed

and laughed again. 'Have you looked in the mirror recently? Have you? Who'd sleep with you, you fat bitch?'

'I'm glad that you wanted to talk tonight.' The laughter stopped as suddenly as it had started as James pulled himself up to his full height and smoothed down his clothes. 'Because I wanted a little chat of my own. Things aren't working, Suzy-Sue and I think we should split up.'

He stopped talking.

He was waiting for a reaction but I couldn't work out what he wanted me to do. To cry? To beg him not to finish with me? To agree? Too scared to make the wrong decision, I said nothing at all.

'Ah,' he said after what felt like an age. 'No reaction. No reaction to the man you claim you love more than life telling you he wants to leave you. How strange. That's not the behaviour I'd expect of a woman in love.'

'I . . . I do love you James but—'

'LIAR!' He spat the word in my face and I covered my face with my arms, cowering into a ball. 'Filthy liar!'

I felt his fingers on my left wrist and, for a horrible moment, thought he was going to break my hand but then I felt a sharp tugging on my ring finger and I realized what he was doing. I peered through my arms as he crossed the living room and opened the window. The traffic outside roared in response.

'Oh Granny.' He held the ring aloft, between the thumb and forefinger of his right hand. 'I'm so sorry.

I really thought I'd met the one. I thought I'd met my soulmate. But she didn't love me Granny, not as much as she claimed.' He stifled a sob. 'So now it's time to say bye bye. Not just to her, but to your ring too. Sorry to let you down, Granny. I tried. I really did.'

I watched, horrified as he pulled back his arm. He was going to throw the ring – a family heirloom – out of the window and it was all my fault.

'No!' I jumped off the sofa and hobbled towards him, my hands outstretched. 'James, don't. Your Granny wouldn't have wanted—'

But it was too late. The ring flew through the window, arched over the road and landed in the path of an oncoming car.

'It's not too late.' I grabbed James's arm. 'We can still get it. It might not be damaged.'

'You money-grabbing bitch.' He swiped at me and, unstable on my injured foot, I tumbled onto the carpet. 'You don't give a shit about me but you want to keep your precious ring, do you? Well, I've got news for you my darling gold digger,' he stooped down and cupped my chin, forcing me to look up at him, 'it's not a fucking diamond and sapphire family heirloom. It's a cheap piece of shit I picked up from Camden Market. You should have seen your face, lapping up that Great Granny shit like an alley cat with its nose in a bowl of cream. And you claim to be intelligent? Honestly.'

He pushed me away from him.

'Mother said I was worth more than you – some bar scrubber with a sewing machine – and she was right.' He shook his head. 'Poor Mother. And to think I almost abandoned her to spend time with you. You! Jesus. Still, it's true what they say about fat girls being easy.' He crouched down again and ran a finger along the side of my jaw then pinched the small deposit of fat under my chin. 'You might want to keep your legs crossed a bit longer with your next boyfriend. He might respect you a bit more.'

Chapter 18

'Where did you go, darling? It's okay, you can tell Mummy.' I speak little louder than a whisper. It's 5 a.m. and, save a couple of patients being woken for obs, most of the ward is asleep. I can hear the nurses chatting quietly at their station and, every now and then, I hear the creaking of trolley wheels or the squeak of shoes on lino as a member of staff crosses the corridor outside Charlotte's room. The nurse who answered the intercom was surprised by my request to see Charlotte but, when I told her I'd had a terrible dream that my daughter's life was in danger, she relented and buzzed me in. I'm sure I'm not the first parent who's turned up in the middle of the night to check their child is okay and I'm sure I won't be the last.

The dream was a lie though. I haven't actually been to sleep yet. How could I when my mind is so full of questions? We talked for a long time after we returned from the school but, at 1 a.m., Brian insisted we go to bed. I lay next to him, listening to his snores and snuffles for four hours before I slipped out from beneath the duvet, gathered up my clothes from the chair beside the bed and got dressed in the bathroom.

'Mr Evans said you didn't go on the school trip . . .' I watch Charlotte's face, sure there will be a reaction. This – this secret excursion with Ella – it's part of the reason she stepped in front of a bus, I feel sure of it. 'He said you pretended you had a bad tummy from a trip to Nandos. I know that was a lie, Charlotte.'

Nothing. No twitch, no tightening, no tension. If anything her face seems to relax a tiny bit, as though she's just slipped into a deeper sleep. The nurses don't believe me when I say I can tell when Charlotte is asleep. It's a common misconception that comatose patients are always asleep – they're not. They have sleep and wake states like the rest of us, only it's not always obvious when they're in a wake state. I can tell by the heaviness of her eyelids, the shape of her jaw and the looseness of her lips but I can also tell if she's asleep, even in darkness. One of the nurses – Kimberley – gave me a kindly smile when I told her that Charlotte smells different when she's asleep but I knew she thought it was a strange thing to say. It's true though. I know Charlotte's scent better than anyone else's. I know the scent of her skin, the uniqueness that lies beyond her deodorant, her perfume and her hairspray. Sitting

212

by her cot in the dark, when she was a baby, I'd know without touching or listening to her if she was asleep or not. The salty-sweet scent of sleep was all I needed to be sure. Even now, if I hold Charlotte's hand to my face I know from the scent of her wrist if she's awake or asleep.

'Sue?' I jump at the hand on my shoulder and know instantly that Brian is standing behind me.

'Yes, darling?' There are dark bags under his eyes and a grey pallor to his skin. His shirt, the same one he wore yesterday, is crumpled with yellow sweat stains under the armpits. His hair is sticking up at angles. He looks like a scarecrow on nightshift.

'What are you doing?' He glances meaningfully at the clock.

'Visiting Charlotte.'

He squeezes my shoulder so hard I wonder if he's holding onto me because he's too exhausted to stand unaided.

'Come home, Sue.' His voice is loud in the quiet room. 'You need to come home now.'

'So you see doctor, she hasn't been well for a while.'

We are sitting in the Western Road surgery, in Doctor Turner's office – Brian on the left, me on the right and the doctor behind the desk, her red hair tied back in a ponytail, a string of multicoloured beads around her neck.

'I see.' She nods, her eyes still on me. They haven't left my face once since Brian started speaking. He's been telling her about the way I've been acting recently, the things I've been saying, the things I've been doing.

'I'm only here because of the fainting fits,' I say.

Doctor Turner tilts her head to one side. 'Just the fainting fits?'

I feel like she wants me to admit to more than that, that she'll be disappointed if I don't, but I nod anyway. 'Yes. And I wouldn't even have come in for them if the paramedic hadn't suggested I get checked over.'

'I see.' She types something into her computer. 'So you're not worried about the way you've been feeling recently? Everything's been fine . . . emotionally . . . as far as you're concerned?'

'Well, yes. No. Well, I'm obviously very emotional at the moment. My daughter's in a coma.'

'Our daughter.'

I glance at Brian. The last time he took me to the doctor he held my hand all the way through the appointment. He hasn't so much as touched me today – not that I blame him – not after everything I've put him through.

'Our daughter.' I correct myself.

'I see.' Doctor Turner raises her eyebrows. 'How long has she been like that?'

'Seven weeks,' I say. 'Five days and . . .' I look at my watch but catch Brian shaking his head out of the corner of my eye and the words dry in my mouth.

'So you've been under stress for nearly two months then, Sue?'

I nod.

'And all these symptoms . . . they've only presented themselves since your daughter became unwell?'

'Yes,' Brian says before I can object to the term 'unwell'. 'Sue was absolutely fine prior to Charlotte's accident. Well . . .' he glances at me, '. . . since 2006 anyway.'

The doctor made a low hmmm sound and consults her screen. '2006.' Her eyes flick from left to right and then back at me. 'Which is when you were diagnosed with Post Traumatic Stress Syndrome, Sue?'

'That's right.'

'And how did that present itself?'

'Delusions,' Brian says. 'Jumpiness. Paranoia. Heart palpitations. Difficulty sleeping.'

'Sue,' Doctor Turner stresses my name. 'Do you agree with your husband's description of your symptoms?'

I stare at my hands. I don't want to think about 2006. It's too painful, what I put Brian and Charlotte through, particularly Charlotte. 'Yes.'

'And the treatment you were prescribed was—'

'Bloody ineffective!' Brian snorts. 'Talk therapy. Jesus! She may as well have gone down the WI and had a nice chat with—'

'Please.' I put a hand on his knee. 'Please, Brian, don't.'

'But it didn't work, did it, Sue? It might have *seemed* like it did at the time but,' he looks at the GP and holds his hands wide in exasperation, 'it obviously didn't cure her long term or she wouldn't be suffering now, would she?'

I want to tell him that I'm not having delusions, that James Evans knows where we live and that it's dangerous for us to stay in the house but if I do that he'll think I'm mad – more mad than he already does. After what happened at the school yesterday I couldn't refuse when he insisted that I see the doctor, especially when the paramedic chimed in about my fainting fit. Saying that I thought my PTSD had come back was the only way I could explain why I'd run through the corridors of our daughter's school, screaming that the business studies teacher was dangerous. I had to agree to see Doctor Turner – for Brian's reputation if nothing else.

'Sue.' She angles her body in my direction so Brian knows the question is meant for me and me alone. 'How do *you* feel? Day to day. Hour by hour. Now?'

I blink several times, trying to absorb the question. It's huge.

'Don't think too hard. Just tell me the first words that come into your head.'

'Scared,' I say. 'Nervous. Worried. Jittery. Worried? Did I say that already?' I try to block out Brian's nodding head. 'Frightened. Tired. Anxious.'

The doctor nods, her eyes never leaving my face. I feel like she understands me, that if Brian would only leave the room I could tell her all about my worries for Charlotte and my fear of James and she'd calm me with just a single nod of her all-knowing head.

'Do these feelings . . . are they overwhelming sometimes, Sue?'

'Yes.'

'And how would you like to feel?'

'Calmer. Unafraid. Happy. Content. Whole.'

'Whole?' A frown crosses her brow.

'Yes,' I say. 'Whole. I feel split into scattered parts. My heart is with Charlotte, sitting by her bed, holding her hand, even when I'm not actually there. But my head is pre-occupied with my ex-boyfriend,' Brian flinches, 'trying to work out what his next move might be and how best I can protect my family.'

'I see.' More nodding but this time she taps something into her computer. When she looks back at me her expression has changed. The compassion has morphed into professionalism – a bland non-smiling mask meant, I am sure, to calm and reassure.

'There is medication I could give you,' she says, 'to help with the anxiety. It'd help you feel less overwhelmed and more able to cope.'

Brian's face brightens and he parts his lips to speak but is silenced by a look from Dr Turner.

'We could try that,' she says. 'But I would recommend that you take it in conjunction with therapy. Some therapies, CBT – Cognitive Behaviour Therapy – in particular can be hugely helpful when dealing with PTSD. What do you think, Sue? Would you like me to arrange for you to see someone?'

I don't know what to say. I feel awful, like this

poor doctor has been tricked into thinking I'm ill when I'm perfectly healthy.

'No,' I say. Brian inhales sharply. 'To the therapy I mean. I don't have time for a lot of sitting around and chatting and—'

'CBT is more than just chatting, Sue. It's about changing the way you think.'

'I appreciate that. I really do. But I'll just go for the medication, if that's okay.'

'It is.' Doctor Turner's eyebrows are raised but she seems satisfied with my response. She turns back to her computer and clicks several times with her mouse. A couple of seconds later she swivels around to the printer and tears off a green prescription form.

Brian leans over and puts a hand on my knee. 'You're doing the right thing, Sue.'

He smiles, his eyes shining with relief.

I half-listen as the doctor talks me through the medication, telling me when I should take it, what might happen if I drink alcohol or combine it with other drugs, explains about possible side effects and then suggests we make an appointment for six weeks time to review my progress.

'You might feel differently about CBT then,' she adds. 'If you change your mind just let me know.'

'Maybe.' I take the prescription she's holding out, fold it in two and slip it into my handbag.

The doctor smiles a half-smile, nods briefly at Brian and then swivels around to reach for a book on the shelf behind her. Appointment over.

'Come on then, darling,' Brian reaches for my hand and squeezes it tightly. 'Let's go to the chemist and get you dosed up.'

Thursday 31st May 1991

It's been nearly two months now since James and I split up and, despite Hels telling me that time is a healer, I feel worse now than I did the day we split up.

I spoke to Hels the morning after and told her what had happened. She gasped when I told her about James holding me against the wall and said that, if she ever heard me make excuses or blame myself for James's behaviour again, she'd never speak to me again. Then she ordered me to report him to the police. I know she was just worried about me but her comment annoyed me. James wasn't a criminal. He was drunk and scared I'd slept with someone else. Yes, he'd lost his temper and got a bit rough but he didn't actually hit me.

I didn't tell Hels the real reason I was refusing to go to the police – I was secretly hoping that, by the end of the day, James would be on my doorstep with a bunch of red roses and an apology. He didn't. He didn't ring either. And I drank and smoked myself to sleep for a second night.

I saw a lot of Hels and Rupert those first few weeks after James and I split up. One of them would ring at least once a day and they'd take me out – to the cinema, the pub, their house for a meal – two or three times a week. I'm not sure when, or why, we started to drift apart again. Maybe it was after their holiday in Greece, maybe it was when Rupert had to put in a lot of overtime at work or maybe it was because I'd stopped bursting into tears each time James's name was mentioned and they assumed I was over him. Either way, I stopped going out as much and that's when the rot really set in. I'd lie in bed at night, poring over the details of my relationship with James – trying to work out when it had all gone wrong, trying to pinpoint the moment the magic disappeared. I was haunted by guilt and regret – if I hadn't opened up to him about my sex life on our second date he'd have carried on thinking that I was a precious angel, if I hadn't told him about Rupert maybe the four of us would have been the best of friends, if I'd dragged him out of the pub a couple of hours earlier maybe his mum wouldn't hate my guts. I wanted to rewind time – to go back and do everything again differently. Maybe that way I wouldn't feel like I'd lost the love of my life.

The more I thought, the more miserable I became and the more I drank. I'd sit by my phone, repeatedly snatching it up to check it was still working or repeatedly dialling James's number. The first few times I called his mum answered and told me that James wasn't at home. The next time I called the phone went dead at the sound of my voice. By my fifth day of calling there was a 'number not recognised' message on repeat – they'd changed their number.

I started making excuses not to go into work – particularly on a Sunday when I knew rehearsals were on. I lost track of the number of times I had a tummy bug, a migraine or had to rush up north to see my mum – and, when I did go in, customers would comment that something was wrong with my face and ask what had happened to my smile.

Last week my phone rang. I snatched it up, sure it was James ringing to tell me he missed me but no, it was Steve from the Abberley Players. He was in a pub with the other actors and they'd been discussing my mysterious disappearance. They'd figured out that James and I had split up from his surly appearance (I was glad to hear that) and the fact he'd stalk off if anyone mentioned my name in his presence and they wanted to check I was okay (and if their costumes were near completion!). I laughed at the last comment and Steve said, 'See, I told them you wouldn't have lost your sense of humour. Come out with us. We miss you.' I was touched but said no, I was already halfway through a bottle of wine and enjoying listening to my Nina Simone records and chain-smoking. Steve said that sounded like an excellent way to spend an evening and he'd be over with another bottle of wine and some more cigarettes. I tried to dissuade him but *he went on and on, wheedling at me for my address until I finally gave it.*

Within two hours of that phone conversation we were in bed.

The sex was perfunctory and drunken and, when he pulled me onto his skinny, hairless chest afterwards and told me how he'd fancied me for ages and that James was a fool to let me go, it was all I could do not to weep. I thought that, by having sex with another man – particularly a man that James despised – I could exorcise his ghost but it just made me miss him more. Steve was everything James was not. I felt no intensity when he looked at me, no passion when he kissed me and no ache in my heart when he curled up behind me and nestled his face into the back of my neck. I felt more lonely with him lying next to me than I had alone.

I couldn't get rid of him fast enough the next morning. I could see the disappointment in his eyes when I turned down his suggestion of a fried breakfast in a greasy caf, followed by a browse of a local flea market, instead claiming I had a terrible headache and just wanted to go back to bed. He said he'd come with me, that, thinking about it, he could do with a snooze too but just the thought of his naked body touching mine again was enough to make me feel sick. I was brusque, made it clear I wanted to be alone and practically marched him to the front door. Steve stepped onto the street then turned back. His eyes met mine.

'He doesn't deserve you, you know.'

I shook my head. 'I don't know what you're talking about.'

'I'm not an idiot.' He shoved his hands into his jeans pockets, suddenly looking impossibly young. 'I know you still love him. I just thought . . . hoped . . . that if you spent time with me, someone who'd cherish you, someone who'd never be cruel or hurt you then maybe, maybe you'd . . .' he tailed off and shook his head. 'It doesn't matter. Look after yourself, Susan.' He touched the back of my hand. 'Please.'

Chapter 19

Brian hasn't left my side for four days. I've told him over and over again that he should go back to work because I'm not mad and I'm not going to do anything stupid but he won't listen. He keeps telling me that this isn't about me being 'mad', it's about me getting a bit of R&R after a stressful few months and he's only taking time off to ensure that I do actually put my feet up and relax.

'Tablet time!' he says, breezing into the living room with a cup of tea in one hand and a small, white pot of pills in the other.

'Brian—'

'You did promise, Sue,' he says, setting the steaming mug of tea on the table beside me and handing me the tablets. 'You told the doctor you'd take your medication.'

I smile at my husband, unlock the lid of the pill box with a sharp twist and shake two small, white pills into the palm of my left hand. I regard them dispassionately. They'll make me calmer, Dr Turner said. I rotate my wrist so the pills tumble over each other. What is it like not to feel anxious? To feel secure instead of scared? It's been so long I can barely remember.

'Water,' Brian says, standing up suddenly. Five minutes later he returns, a glass of water in one hand, his newspaper in the other.

'There you go,' he says, placing the glass on the table beside me and glances meaningfully at the pills lying on my open palm. I clench my hand shut. I've taken tablets like this before and they work quickly. Within an hour of swallowing them I'll be a more relaxed, immobile, docile version of myself. So docile I will be unable to protect my family from danger.

'Brian,' I say. 'Would it be the end of the world if I didn't take—' but I'm interrupted by the trill ring of the study phone.

'Damn it,' he grimaces, 'I'll have to get it, it might be important.'

'Of course.'

I stay where I am, in the centre of the sofa, the glass of water on my left, the pills in my hand and listen as Brian thunders up the stairs and across the landing. There's a split second of silence as he snatches up the phone then the low rumble of his voice as he answers. He's quiet then there's another rumble, louder this time and then the thump-thump-thump of his footsteps across the landing and down the stairs.

'Goddamn it!' He bursts into the living room and throws himself into the armchair.

'Bad news?'

He slumps forward and rests his head in his hands but says nothing. Neither do I. Sixteen years together have taught me to give Brian his space when he's in a bad mood, they pass quicker that way.

'Hmmm,' he peers at me through his fingers and shakes his head. 'No, I can't. It wouldn't be fair.'

'What wouldn't?'

'They want me to go in. The wind turbine vote has been brought forward.'

'Then go!' I smile. 'I'll be fine.'

'No.' He shakes his head again. 'You need me here.'

'Brian, I'll be fine, honestly. I've got Milly to keep me company. And besides, if you disappear off for the afternoon I can watch *Deal or No Deal* in peace without you shouting at the TV about how there's no such thing as positive bloody vibes or unlucky boxes.'

He cracks a smile. 'I'm not that bad.'

'You are!' I laugh. 'Go! I'll call, I promise, if anything happens. Not that it will,' I add hastily.

'Are you sure?'

'Absolutely. I'll be fine.'

Brian stands up, crosses the room and gives me a kiss on the forehead. 'I'll try and be as quick as I can but you know how these things can drag.'

'Just go. I'll see you later.'

I watch him walk out of the living room and am just about to stand up myself when he suddenly turns back. His eyes rest on the glass of water on the table beside me.

'Did you take your tablets okay?'

'Yes,' I say, smiling brightly as I press the small white pills into the gaps between the sofa cushions. 'I barely felt them go down.'

Ten minutes after my husband's car has pulled out of the driveway I do the same with my VW Golf but, instead of driving to the station like Brian, I head for White Street and a parking space outside Ella Porter's house.

I can see her now, traipsing up the road, her school blazer casually slung over one shoulder, her bag carried loosely in one hand, almost trailing on the pavement. It's killed me, the last few days, being trapped inside with Brian unable to find out where Charlotte and Ella went instead of going on Mr Evans's school trip to London.

'Oh, fuck,' Ella mouths as she spies me behind the wheel.

'Wait!' I call as she hoists her bag over her shoulder and starts running towards her house. 'Ella, wait!'

I jump out of the car and sprint after her as she yanks open the garden gate and hightails it up the path.

'Ella, I know about the business studies trip to London. I know you and Charlotte didn't go.'

She freezes, her back to me, the key held to the lock.

'I spoke to Mr Evans yesterday. I know everything.'

She remains motionless.

'If you don't tell me where you and Charlotte went, and what you did, I'll tell your mum.'

'So what?' She turns slowly, her eyes narrowed. 'She wouldn't believe you anyway. She thinks you're cracked. Everyone does.'

'Is that so?' I try not to think about the rumours that are circulating about me outside the school gates. 'Either way, I know you lied about having food poisoning.'

'No, we didn't. We stayed here all weekend, in my room. Charlotte didn't want to tell you about the food poisoning because that would mean telling you she'd gone to Nandos and then you'd call her fat and tell her off for breaking her diet.'

'I did no such—' I catch myself. She's clever, trying to throw me off the scent by attacking me. 'So if I ask your mum about that weekend she'll corroborate your story, will she?'

'She wasn't here. She and Dad went away for the weekend.'

'Where?'

'None of your business.'

'It is if it meant two fifteen-year-old girls were left home alone.' There's an electronic bleep of a car being locked followed by the click clack of high heels on pavement. Perfect timing.

'That'll be your mum,' I say without turning round. 'Let's ask her shall we, Ella? See if she realizes it's illegal to leave children under the age of sixteen home alone for an entire weekend. Then maybe we'll ring the police and—'

'No!' Ella stares beyond the low hedge, at the blue

Audi and the tall, thin woman walking towards us. 'Don't.'

'Why shouldn't I?'

'Because she'll ground me forever.'

'Then tell me where you and Charlotte went?'

Clack-clack-clack. Ella's eyes grow wider as the sound grows louder.

'No,' she edges away from the front door, as though preparing to make a run for it, 'you'll tell Mum.'

'I won't.'

'She'll kill me.'

'Not if I don't tell her she won't. Your mum doesn't need to know anything about this conversation, Ella.'

There's a jangle of keys and the sharp squeak of a gate being opened. Clack-clack-clack. Clack-clack-clack.

'Tell me,' I hiss. I take a step towards her. 'Tell me.'

'We went to Grey's nightclub in Chelsea with Danny and Keisha.' Her words run into each other she's speaking so quickly. 'Charlotte met a footballer and I had to get the last train back to Brighton on my own. That's it, end of story.'

'You left Charlotte alone in a nightclub in London with a man she'd never met before?'

'And I had to travel across London in the middle of the night on my own to get the last train home. Anyway, she wasn't on her own. Danny and Keish were there too.'

'The footballer – who was he?'

'I don't know. A fit black guy with an accent. Some bloke said he was a premiership footballer but who knows if—'

She stares over my right shoulder, her eyes wide.

'You again!' A cloud of Chanel Number 5 wafts up my nose and there she is, Judy Porter, standing beside me. 'If you're bothering my daughter again I'll call the police. This is harassment, Sue.'

'It's okay, Mum.' Ella flashes me a look. 'She's not bothering me.'

'What did she want then?' She crosses her arms and purses her lips together, waiting for an answer.

'To thank me for dropping off Charlotte's mobile.'

What? I look at her in surprise. She was the one who put the phone through our front door?

'Is that so?'

'Yes,' I look back at Judy. 'It was very kind of Ella and the least I could do was thank her in person, seeing as I was in the area anyway.'

Judy uncrosses her arms, rocks back on a stiletto heel and looks me up and down. 'You'll be going now then?'

Ella nods, ever so slightly. She's begging me not to ask any more questions. To go quietly.

'I'm going. Nice to see you again, Judy. Ella.'

The mobile phone issue will have to wait. There's somewhere I need to go first.

Friday 8th June 1991

Jess, the bar manager, rang me on Wednesday night to ask whether I was over my 'flu' yet and hinted, without actually spelling it out, that if I didn't make it into work on Thursday I'd lose my job.

I had no choice but to go in. What little savings I had are long gone and my rent's due next week and I'm not sure how I'm going to pay it.

My first shift started badly – I dropped a bottle of wine, snapped an optic and overflowed the drip tray when I was changing the bitter – but it was only 6.30 p.m. and the bar was empty and Jess had gone up to the office to work on the accounts so there were no witnesses to my ineptitude. I kept glancing towards the door. James only ever came into the bar on a Sunday and, according to Steve, he hadn't done that for at least a month so why I was so terrified he'd walk in, I don't know.

But then he did.

It was half past eight. The interval had ended fifteen minutes earlier and I was clearing glasses and ashtrays from the tables. He didn't notice me at first, he was too deep in conversation with Maggie, the Abberley Players director, her arm looped through his, but then, as they approached the bar, he glanced up and our eyes met. The colour drained from his face and Maggie, who was in full flow, stopped talking and looked to see what had startled him. Her face fell when she saw me and she pulled on James's arm, stood on tiptoes and hissed into his ear. Her voice was low but I caught the words 'go somewhere else'. James put a hand on her shoulder and, for a second, I thought he was going to angle her out of the bar but then he glanced at me, patted Maggie on the shoulder and headed towards a table at the far end of the room.

I ducked down and clanked a few glasses around in the dishwasher.

'Hello, Susan.'

I looked up, smiled. 'Maggie.'

'We haven't seen you for a while.'

'No,' I had to fight the urge to glance over at James. 'I haven't been well.'

'Oh dear.' It was a good job she was a director and not an actor because her attempt at sincerity was as real as the silk fern in the corner of the room. 'I'm sorry to hear that.'

I was about to ask how she was, whether they'd decided on the next play yet and when she'd want me in to measure up when she said—

'Did you get my answerphone message?'

I shook my head. She hadn't rung me once since James and I had split up.

'Really?' She faked surprise. 'That is strange. I could have sworn I had the right number. Anyway, sorry again that we won't be using you for the costumes any more but a friend of mine recommended this wonderful warehouse near Croydon where they stock a lot of ex-BBC wardrobe. Renting them works out a hell of a lot cheaper than making them from scratch. Anyway,' her eyes flicked from mine to the fridge behind me, 'cheers for all your help. You were fabulous. A bottle of Chardonnay and two glasses please.'

The sound of Maggie's tinkling giggle and James's low rumbling laughter filled the room and I ran from the room and fled to the ladies' loo in the foyer. I bowled into a cubicle, certain I was about to be sick and bent over the toilet. Other than a few dry retches, nothing came out. I stayed there for a couple more minutes then, terrified that Jess would return to the bar and find me missing, I checked my reflection in the mirror, patted my cheeks with toilet paper and opened the door to the foyer. Maggie might have taken my unpaid job away from me but I was buggered if I was going to let her take away the one that paid my rent and—

'Ooof.' I smacked straight into something tall and solid.

'I'm sorr . . .' The words dried in my mouth as James gazed down at me. His hands were on my shoulders from where he'd caught me.

'Are you okay?' His brow was knitted with worry, his voice soft with concern. 'I saw you run out and I . . .' He put a hand to his forehead. 'Sorry, I don't know what I was thinking coming after you. I'm not your boyfriend anymore, I shouldn't care.' He turned to go.

He made it as far as the bar door then turned back. 'No, *fuck it.*' He put his hands on my shoulders again and craned his neck to look down at me. 'I've missed you, Suzy. I've missed you like I've missed a part of me. Like my shadow had disappeared, or my arm or my heart. I tried everything to stop myself from missing you. I tried raging against you, blaming you, cursing you and hating you but none of those things worked,' he thumped at his chest with his closed fist. 'Not a day has gone by where I haven't regretted what happened. I hate myself. Actually **hate** myself for hurting you like that but I had to do it, Suzy. When you looked at me in the doorway of your flat I knew it was time to leave. There was no light in your eyes anymore, no love. You looked miserable and I knew it was because of me. That's why I left you, so you could be happy again.'

I said nothing because I was certain that, if I opened my mouth to speak, I'd choke on my own tears.

'But when I saw you today. When I saw you standing behind the bar that image popped and I realized I'd been deceiving myself. I'd been making up fantasies to avoid finding out for myself how you were.' He cupped a hand to the side of my face and I nearly gasped as the warmth of his fingers flowed into my skin. 'So, I'll ask you now. I'll ask you once *and then I'll never ask you again. And if you tell me yes I'll walk away and never come back.' He paused, ran his thumb over my lips and I tensed, waited for him to kiss me. Instead he let go of my face as though burnt. 'Are you happy, Suzy? Are you happy, my darling?'*

New, hot, desperate tears spilled onto my cheeks as I shook my head. 'No.'

James leaned nearer. 'Say that again.'

I shook my head again. 'No. No, I'm not happy. I've never been more miserable. I've missed you. I still miss you. I miss you every night when I go to bed and every morning when I wake up.'

'Oh Suzy.' James gathered me into his arms and pressed my head against his chest. 'Oh Suzy, my Suzy, my one true love. I'll never let you go again. Never, never, never. I'll never let you go.'

I kept my cheek pressed into his jumper and my arms around his waist for the longest possible time, only opening my eyes briefly as the sound of high heels click-clacking across the foyer floor filled the air and Maggie strode through the open double doors and disappeared onto the street. Then I closed my eyes again.

Chapter 20

'Okay Charlotte, I'm just going to lift your nightdress to clean your legs.'

Two of the nurses – Kimberley and Chris – are giving Charlotte a wash when I arrive at the hospital. I offer to leave but they shake their heads and tell me they're nearly done.

'Now we'll do your teeth.'

I watch as Kimberley gently parts Charlotte's lips and inserts a white stick with a small, square pink sponge on the end, into her mouth. It reminds me of one of the penny sweets I'd buy as a child – a square chewy lolly on a stick.

'Just wiping it around your mouth,' Kimberley says as she leans over my daughter and gently manoeuvers the 'toothbrush' around the contours of Charlotte's mouth. 'And over your teeth and tongue.'

Oli was surprised when I told him that the nurses clean Charlotte's teeth. 'But she doesn't eat anything?'

he said. 'She's drip fed, isn't she?' I told him it was for hygiene reasons. I didn't mention the scent of death and decay and gingivitis that hits me sometimes if I kiss her on the lips. It's a smell so rotten you have to hold your breath not to gag. Charlotte, who's always been so fastidious about hygiene, would be devastated if she knew. Not that I'll ever tell her. There are some things she never needs to know when she wakes up.

'We're just going to change your catheters and then you're done,' they tell Charlotte as they raise her blanket and reach beneath the bed. I instinctively avert my eyes, not because I'm squeamish but because I know how mortified she would be if she knew I'd watched the waste being removed from her body. Before her accident she wouldn't even let me mention the word 'nappy' without throwing a cushion at me and forbidding me from talking about 'gross stuff' to do with her babyhood.

'Okay, Sue?' Kimberley nods at me as she pushes the trolley towards the door. 'I'll be back later. We can catch up.'

'Hi Sue.' Chris touches me softly on the forearm as he follows her. There's compassion in his eyes, even though his tone can be brusque. I see it in the eyes of all the nurses, particularly the mothers. There but for the grace of God go I, and all that.

'Thank you,' I say as they leave the room, pulling the door to behind them. 'Thank you so much.'

'Hello darling.' I pull up a chair so I'm sitting as close to Charlotte as I can. 'Mummy's here. How are you feeling today?'

I reach for her hand, press it to my lips and close my eyes. In a few minutes I'll ask her about Grey's nightclub and the footballer but I need to spend some quiet time with my child first. I need to know how she is.

'Hello?' I press the buzzer and peer up at the CCTV camera half a metre above my head. 'I'm here to see Danny Argent.'

The door entry system crackles then falls silent again. I step back from the door and crane my neck upwards. The neon sign spelling out 'Breeze' over the door is grey and ugly without the fizz of electricity sparking it to neon life. I've never set foot in this nightclub – I haven't set foot in *any* nightclub for over twenty years; James forbade me from going to bars or discos when we were together. They were meat markets where slags went for sex he said, not where monogamous people in relationships hung out. I tried telling him that my single friends weren't slags and that I wasn't going clubbing to cheat on him but to have fun and dance to the music. That's when he reminded me about the conversation we had on our second date when I'd admitted to having five one-night stands. 'You told me you met two of them in a nightclub, Sue,' he'd said. There was nothing I could say to that.

A minute passes, then another and I buzz again. I'm starting to think that this was a stupid idea. It's 5 p.m., of course there isn't going to be anyone in a nightclub at this time of day but I had to come. I need to know more about the footballer Charlotte met in London. I need to know what he did to her.

I press the buzzer again. 'Danny. It's Sue Jackson. Could you let me in, please. It's really very important that we speak.'

I press it again, thirty seconds later and repeat my request then bang on the door with my fist and listen.

Nothing.

There are no windows to peer through and no letter box to rattle. I was resting everything on the hope that Danny might be in his office doing paperwork but it doesn't seem like anyone is in, not even the cleaner. I reach into my handbag and pull out my mobile. I'm just about to call Oli when—

'Sue? What are you doing here?' The speaker above the buzzer crackles to life. 'I'll buzz you in.'

'So, Sue,' Danny places two steaming cups of coffee, complete with saucers and tiny Italian biscotti on the white resin table and pats the velveteen seat beside him. There are half a dozen booths exactly like this one running across two walls of the club. There are three small poufs, decorated in an identical deep red velveteen material around the resin tables, making enough space to seat six. I can almost imagine how this booth will look in five or six hours time – rammed with friends, clinking glasses, downing shots, shouting, laughing and scanning the dance floor for talent. It's been years since the smoking ban was introduced but the air still smells musty – the unique nightclub blend of cigarettes, spilt drinks and sweat.

I perch beside Danny. 'Thank you for seeing me at such short notice.'

'No problem at all. Any mum of Oliver's is a mum of mine.' He laughs and places his hands on the back of his head, pushing out his elbows in an exaggerated stretch which makes his broad chest appear even broader. An effect, I'm sure, that's not entirely unintended.

'So,' he lowers his arms and twists to face me, giving me his full attention. 'This is all very mysterious. Tell all!'

With his bright blue eyes, wide generous smile and strong jaw I can see why Keisha – why most young women – would find him irresistible. There's no doubt that he's an attractive young man but his gaze is that little bit too piercing and his smile a little too arched to be genuine. I've never been alone with Danny before and now I'm starting to understand why Brian doesn't trust him.

'The thing is,' I say, 'I recently found out that Charlotte and Ella skived a school trip.'

Danny laughs, then catches himself. 'Sorry. That was immature of me. You must have been furious, Sue.'

'Not really.' I reach for my coffee, bristling as I take a sip. 'Although I might be with the person who encouraged them to skive.'

'Oh.' He looks intrigued, like I'm about to share some wonderful piece of gossip with him. 'Who's that then?'

I peer at him over the rim. 'You.'

'Me?' His hand flies to his chest. 'Me?' He tosses back his head and laughs but when he checks my reaction the smile has gone from his eyes. 'That's ridiculous, Sue. Whoever told you that obviously has a screw loose.'

'Or they were there too.'

'What?' Beads of sweat shine in his immaculate hairline and he runs a hand over his forehead. 'Who? This is ridiculous. I'm a nightclub promoter not some kind of . . . some kind of weirdo encouraging schoolgirls to skive off.'

I place my cup of coffee back on the table. It slips back into its saucer without rattling. 'So you've never heard of Greys nightclub in London then?'

'Greys in Chelsea?' He sits up straighter. He's on safer ground here. 'Of course I do. It's my job to know what's hot and what's not.'

'Is that why you encouraged Charlotte and Ella to skive their school trip and go there instead? Because it's *hot*?'

'Of course not. I didn't encourage anyone to go anywhere. Why would I? It's not my club. And besides, I barely even know Charlotte. She's Oli's little sister.' He looks me straight in the eye. 'I hope you're not implying what I think you're implying, Mrs Jackson.'

'What's that, Danny?'

'That I . . . that Charlotte and I were somehow involved.'

'Were you?'

242

'God no.' He clutches his chest again but this time I'm tempted to believe him. 'Never. Like I said, she's Oli's kid sister. I'd never look at her that way. Besides, I'm with Keisha.'

'I see.' I glance around the nightclub, taking in the empty DJ booth, the sprawling dance floor and the sparkling bar. 'But you still thought it would be fun to take the girls clubbing in London.'

'No! Why would I do that? What would I possibly gain out of taking two fifteen-year-olds clubbing?' He suddenly becomes very still, very collected. 'Is that what you're implying? That I'm some kind of kiddy paedo? Because if you are—'

'I'm not implying anything. I just want the truth. I've been told that you and Keisha were in Greys nightclub in Chelsea with Charlotte and Ella on Friday, ninth of March. Look me in the eye and tell me you weren't.'

'I wasn't.' His gaze doesn't so much as flicker. 'I wasn't even in London that weekend. I took Keish on a romantic getaway to . . .' he eyes dart to the left '. . . Oxford.'

He's lying through his teeth but giving him the third degree isn't going to achieve anything. He'll just keep lying. James was the same.

I glance at my watch. I've got fifteen minutes to get home before Brian.

'Well . . .' I hold out my hand. 'Thank you so much for the coffee and the chat.'

Danny frowns. 'You're off?'

'Yes.'

'So you . . . you're okay?' He stands up. 'You believe me when I say I didn't go clubbing with Charlotte and Ella?' He bares his teeth in an exaggerated smile. 'You've obviously got the wrong man.'

I smile. 'See you again soon, Danny. I'll see myself out.'

I hurry to the exit before he can follow me and twist the handle to open the side door. I'm just about to yank it open when OOMPH!, it flies open, sending me reeling backwards against the wall.

'Oh my God, I'm so sorry! I totally didn't see you there I – oh!' A face appears around the door. 'Mrs Jackson. What are you doing here?'

'Keisha?'

'Yeah,' she steps around the door, closing it behind her so I'm no longer trapped between it and the wall. 'Are you okay? You look a bit pale.'

I grasp my stomach. 'Just a bit winded. I'll be okay in a bit.'

'Let's get you outside. Some fresh air will soon see you right.'

We perch on the concrete step together, its narrowness forcing us to sit unnaturally close.

Keisha rummages in her handbag and pulls out a crumpled packet of Marlboro Lights and a lighter. She waves them at me. 'Mind if I smoke?'

'Go ahead.'

I watch as she tweezers a cigarette out of the pack with her long nails. She lights it and inhales deeply. Twenty years since I last smoked and I can still remember what that first sweet hit of nicotine feels like when you're desperate for a cig.

'Want one?' she catches me watching and holds out the pack.

'I don't smoke.' I change my mind immediately. 'Actually I will. Thank you.'

I put the cigarette in my mouth, relishing the way it feels so foreign and so familiar at the same time. Keisha lights it for me and I inhale deeply. The smoke scratches the back of my throat. I take another drag. It tastes strong, chemical-like and hot and I'm reminded of the first cigarette I ever smoked, back in 1984, when I was fifteen. I lean back against the door and close my eyes as the nicotine fizzes through me. The cigarette tastes foul but the ritual – lift to mouth, inhale, hold, exhale, lower – and the buzz of nicotine is comforting.

Keisha says something I don't catch and I open my eyes. 'Sorry?'

She tips back her head and blows a perfect, grey smoke ring into the air. 'I said I didn't expect to see you here.'

The smoke ring grows wider and thinner until it breaks up and disappears.

I say the first thing that comes into my head. 'I came to see Danny about a surprise party. It's Oli's twentieth soon.'

'What a lovely idea.' Keisha's face lights up. 'No one's ever thrown a surprise party for me. In fact, I can't remember the last time I had a birthday party. I must have been little. Eight, maybe nine.' She looks wistful for a second then smiles again. 'Are you going to hold it at Breeze then, Oli's party?'

'Actually I was considering Greys nightclub in London. I wanted Danny's opinion.'

She raises her eyebrows. 'I've been there. It's the shit. Expensive though. Seven pounds fifty for a rum and coke!'

'I know, but Oli's been through a lot recently and we wanted it to be special.' I puff on my cigarette, hold the smoke in my lungs for a couple of seconds and then exhale. 'Charlotte was the one who recommended Greys. Before her accident,' I add quickly when Keisha's eyes widen in surprise. 'She said it was amazing, that she went there with you and Danny.'

'It was.' She flicks her cigarette into the gutter. The tip glows for a second then turns grey and goes out. 'Poshest club I've ever been to. There's a woman in the toilets who'll rub hand cream into your hands if you pay her a pound. She'll squirt you with perfume too if you want. She's got loads of different types.'

'Really?' I smile encouragingly. I have to play this carefully. If I spook her she'll clam up. 'Charlotte said a lot of famous types hang out there too.'

'They do.' She wraps her slender arms around her knees and pulls them close to her chest. The sun is starting to go down and there's a chill in the air. 'Pop stars, soap stars, footballers. You don't really get to mingle with them though because they sit in the roped-off VIP bit.'

'So how did Charlotte get to meet her footballer then,' I drop my cigarette onto the pavement and grind it out with the heel of my boot, 'if the famous people are kept separate from everyone else?'

Keisha looks at me in surprise. 'She told you about him?'

'Of course. We're very close. We tell each other everything.'

'Wow.' She raises an eyebrow. 'So Charlotte told you some of what happened that night then?'

I nod. I don't trust what will happen if I open my mouth to lie.

She searches my face. 'And you didn't go mental?'

'No.' I try and keep my breathing slow and measured but my heart is racing from the cigarette. This could be it. This could be the moment I find out what caused Charlotte to step in front of the bus. 'Why would I?'

An empty coke can clatters against the pavement at the far end of the alley. Keisha and I both jump but there's no one there.

'I've got to go.' She leaps up, reaches for the door handle, her eyes still fixed on the entrance to the alley. 'Danny's expecting me and I've said too much already.'

'Please.' I reach for her hand. 'Please. You need to tell me what happened that night.'

'I thought you already knew.'

'I know she met a footballer but that's it. Please Keisha. Please tell me what happened.'

She shakes her head, opens the door, slips one shoulder into the gap. 'If I tell you he'll kill me.'

'And if you don't tell me Charlotte might die.'

It's a low blow but it's enough to make her pause, step back into the alley and close the door. I wait as she shakes her empty cigarette packet, crumples it in her fist then tosses it into the gutter and roots around in her handbag for a new pack. She peels off the cellophane, flips back the lid, pulls off the foil and tweezes out a cigarette. It takes forever and when she roots around in her bag for her lighter I want to scream. Finally she puts a cigarette in her mouth, lights it and inhales deeply. She exhales through her nose and looks at me from under her lashes. 'She had sex with the footballer in the club toilet.'

I stare at the lit end of her cigarette, at the plume of smoke that curls upwards, at the length of ash that grows longer and longer and then falls through the air and disintegrates before it hits the floor.

'Who was he?' I tear my eyes away from the cigarette. 'What was his name?'

She shrugs. 'I don't know. His first name was Alex, I don't know his surname. He was foreign, French, I think. Black. Plays for Chelsea someone said. Or Man U. One of the top clubs anyway, I forget which.'

'This premiership footballer she slept with, this *Alex*.' The words feel like they're coming out of someone else's mouth. 'How can I get hold of him?'

Keisha sucks on her cigarette and opens the side door, her eyes never once meeting mine. 'I don't know, I'm sorry.'

'Okay,' I say and smile, even though I'm pretty sure she's lying to me. They're all lying about something – Brian, Danny, Ella, Liam – and they think I'm too emotionally unstable to see through it.

They're wrong.

I wait for Brian to go to bed and then I creep into his study and turn on his laptop.

Alex famous footballer I type and press enter.

The first entry is for a Brazilian footballer who plays for Paris Saint-Germain. Is that who Keisha meant? Maybe she got confused about whether he was French or lived in France? I look at the next entry, another French footballer – this time he's called Alexandre Degas, but there's no mention of him playing for a British club. Alexandre Laurent then? Or Alex Sauvage? There's an Olivier Alexandre who plays for Tottenham Hotspur but it can't be him, can it?

I push the chair back from the desk. I don't know what I was thinking, expecting that I'd find contact details for this Alex person when I haven't got the slightest idea who he is. I twist from left to right in the chair scanning the room for solutions but none come so I stand up and wander into Charlotte's room. I should have pushed Keisha for more details. I should have asked her how she knew Charlotte had sex in the club toilet. It's so out of character. She was besotted with Liam, absolutely doolally about him. She'd never have cheated on him. It was one thing she felt strongly about because of the fall-out of her own father's infidelity. I just can't imagine her doing something sexual with someone she'd only just met, even if she was drunk and he was a famous footballer and astonishingly good looking and—

I smooth out her duvet then straighten up to get a better look at the posters above the headboard. They're pages she's ripped out of *Heat* magazine's 'Torso of the week' and the wall is crowded with an array of good-looking topless men – soap stars, film stars, TV presenters and . . . footballers. There's David Beckham, Ashley Cole, Ronaldo and . . . someone I don't recognize, a tall, handsome mixed-race man with pale brown eyes, high cheekbones and full lips. Alex Henri, the caption at the bottom says, Striker, Chelsea FC.

I rush back to Brian's study.

Alex Henri Agent I enter into Google.

Details appear on screen for Steve Torrance, 'international sports agent'. I click on his website and an image of a balding, middle-aged man appears, his top lip curled into a half smile, half sneer. I skim read his biography, glance over his list of clients and then click on the 'contact' link. An email address and a PO Box address and London telephone number pop up on screen and I scribble them down. It's too late to call now so I tuck the piece of paper into my purse, leave it on the hall table and then pad into the bedroom. I change into my nightdress in the dark and slip into bed. It's a very long time until I fall asleep.

'Could you tell him it's urgent?'

The woman on the other end of the line sighs. 'Mrs

Jackson, this is the third day you've called. I *know* it's urgent. You tell me every time you call. I've passed on your messages and if Mr Torrance hasn't called you back yet then . . .' I can practically hear her shrug. 'He is a very busy man.'

'Please,' I beg. 'It's vital I get a message through to Alex Henri. My daughter's in a coma and he might be able to help.'

The PA makes a little 'ooh' sound. 'How terrible for you. I've got a daughter myself. She had to spend some time in Great Ormond Street when she was seven and I was beside myself. Made her day when H and Claire from Steps visited the ward. How old's your girl?'

'She's seven too.' It's scary how easy the lie comes out. 'And such a tomboy. Football's her life, her dad's too, they're massive Chelsea fans, never miss a game. Alex Henri's her favourite player, he's on her bedroom wall in pride of place.'

'She wouldn't be the first,' she laughs. 'Look Sue, can I call you Sue?'

'Of course.'

'Well Sue, I probably shouldn't say this but the truth is Steve isn't such a big fan of charity requests. They're good for PR but PR doesn't pay the bills so he only allows his clients to do high-profile gigs – cancer charities, Sport Relief, Children in Need, that sort of thing. You need to approach Alex independently.'

My heart leaps. 'But how? I've searched the internet and the only phone number I've been able to find is Steve's.'

'Now listen,' the PA lowers her voice. 'I could lose my job if what I'm about to tell you gets out.'

'I won't say a word,' I breathe. 'I swear.'

'I would never, *never* normally do this but I'm in a good mood today – my Sean got back from Afghanistan yesterday – and with your daughter being the way she is, well . . . anyway, if you want to catch Alex I suggest you get yourself along to Greys nightclub in Chelsea tonight. He normally goes on a Friday. I'm not promising he'll agree to visit your little girl but he might agree to a signed shirt or a message on your mobile or something. You could play it to her.'

'I could!' I can't keep the excitement out of my voice but not for the reason she might think. 'What a wonderful idea, thank you so much.'

'There's nothing to thank me for. Just promise me one thing, no, two things Sue.'

'Of course.'

'Never mention this to anyone and never call this office again.'

'I won't. I promise. Thank you so much . . . sorry, I didn't catch your name.'

She laughs. 'There's a reason for that. Goodbye, Sue.'

The disconnect tone buzzes in my ear for a good thirty seconds before I place the phone back in its cradle. If she's right and Alex Henri *is* in the club tonight how am I going to get to speak to him if he's in a cordoned-off VIP area? A beautiful fifteen-year-old might be able to bat her eyelashes past security but what about me?

What's a dumpy forty-three-year-old who hasn't been to a club in over twenty years supposed to do? And, more pressing than that, if I can't pop out of the house in the afternoon to buy 'magazines' without Brian checking up on me, how on earth am I going to convince him that it's a good idea for me to go out until the early hours of the morning in London?

Wednesday 27th June 1991

*James and I are living together. Well, James, his mother and I. I moved in just over a week ago. Jess from work cut my hours **again** (I'm only doing fifteen a week now) and I couldn't afford the rent on my bedsit any more. I told James I was going to try and get my TEFL job back to make up the shortfall but he insisted I move in with him instead.*

'Think of it as a new start,' he said. 'Screw Maggie and her tin pot company. You deserve to be paid for what you do. The spare room's big enough for your sewing machine table so get set up, get making some sample pieces so you can apply for a proper wardrobe job or set up your own business and I'll pay the rent and get the food in, don't worry about that.'

It was almost too perfect a solution, the only fly in the ointment being his mum. She didn't come down from her room the whole of the first evening I was there and the next morning, when I came down to

254

breakfast with James at 7.30 a.m. there was a list of *'jobs'* for me to do on the kitchen table. They included grocery shopping, hoovering, toilet scrubbing and weeding and were written in a handwriting I didn't recognise.

'You don't mind, do you?' James said when he saw my raised eyebrows. 'Her carer's gone on holiday for a week and you know what she's like with her arthritis and agoraphobia.'

Arthritis? She'd seemed sprightly enough when she'd stormed out of the room when James and I arrived late for that, now infamous, lunch.

'Besides,' he added. 'You've got a lot of time on your hands now your hours have been cut, haven't you?'

I wanted to remind him that he'd suggested I set up a sewing business in our bedroom but bit my tongue. Helping out was the least I could do considering the fight he'd undoubtedly had to put up to persuade his mother to let me move in and besides, it was only for a week. I could start setting up my business when the carer got back.

By the time James got home from work nine hours later my hands were raw and my forearms were a mess of nettle stings but I'd ticked off every single item on the list **and** had a pot roast happily bubbling away in the oven. He looked delighted and said he knew that his mother and I would get on like a dream if we just gave each other a chance. The truth was I hadn't seen her all day. I'd heard the landing floor creak at about 9 a.m. as she made her way to the bathroom but, other than that, I hadn't caught a glimpse of her. By lunchtime I was worried that she might be ill and I knocked on her door to ask if she was okay and whether she'd like some homemade tomato soup and a cheese sandwich. She replied that she was 'in perfect health, thank you' and told me to leave the food on a tray outside the door. I did as I was told then went back down the stairs and waited silently in the hall. Five minutes later the bedroom door opened, a pair of slippered feet appeared and the tray was dragged into her room.

James couldn't keep his hands off me and, as soon as we'd finished dinner (which his mother had in her room again) he dragged me into the bedroom and threw me onto the bed. I squealed as he pulled off my clothes and buried his face in my breasts but was promptly silenced when he slapped a hand over my mouth and held it there.

'Sssh,' he whispered. 'We don't want Mother to hear us.'

I was just about to reply when he yanked off my knickers and entered me, thrusting so hard I hit my head on the headboard. I gasped in shock and pleasure.

James took his hand off my mouth. 'Or do we?' And slammed into me again.

Afterwards, as we lay in each other's arms, sweat sticking us together, he stroked my hair back from my face.

'You've got no idea how much I missed you, how much I missed having sex with you, when we were apart.'

'Me too.' I ran a hand over his broad chest and raked my fingers through the hair.

'It was torture,' he kissed the top of my head. 'Lying in bed alone imagining you naked in your bed and not being able to touch you.'

'I know.'

'Did you sleep with anyone else while we were apart?'

I looked him in the eye. To look anywhere else would be dangerous. 'No.'

'Really? You didn't mess around with someone because you were lonely?'

'No,' I blocked the image of Steve's face on my pillow out of my head, 'of course not.'

'Kiss someone when you were drunk?'

'No.'

'It's okay,' he smiled tightly, 'you can tell me if you did, I won't be angry. I fucked a couple of people.'

'What?' My chest spasmed with pain. I'd never considered that he might sleep with someone else. Not once.

'I fucked a couple of women.' He shrugged. 'No big deal. We weren't together. Did you?'

Did he mean it? Did he really not care? I looked into his eyes, at the pinprick pupils and the grey iris, flecked with blue. I'd never been able to read him. His eyes were impenetrable.

'No,' I lied. 'I didn't do anything, not even a kiss. I missed you too much to even think about touching another man.'

His shoulders slumped with relief.

'I knew it,' he gathered me into his arms. 'I knew you were special. I knew Mother was wrong.' He pulled away and looked at me. 'I didn't sleep with anyone either. I was just having a laugh.'

A laugh? I nestled my head into his chest and swallowed back the tears that had sprung up in my eyes. It didn't feel very funny to me.

Chapter 21

'A musical?' Brian raises an eyebrow. 'I thought you hated musicals. Opera for stupid people you said.'

'I did not! Those are your words. And I don't *hate* musicals, I just prefer plays. Anyway this isn't about me. It's Jane's birthday.'

'And Eric's got the flu? In May?'

I'm about to protest that there's an unusual amount of it around at the moment and how Jane's husband does work in a school where germs are rife, but there's no need because Brian laughs and says, 'Sounds like he's throwing a sickie to me and who can blame him? I'd rather take to my deathbed than go to a musical too.'

'Jane's wanted to see the Billy Elliot musical forever,' I say. 'It's one of her favourite films.'

'There's a DVD shop down the road, tell her. She can save herself thirty-odd quid a ticket or whatever rip-off prices they charge in the West End these days.'

'Brian!' I pretend to chastise him but I can tell by the smile on his face that he's not going to object to me going to London. It's incredible how easily he's bought into my lie. I could be going anywhere, with anyone and I could go with his blessing.

'Bit late though, isn't it?' he glances at the grandfather clock. 'This show? It's seven o'clock already and by the time you get to Victoria even if you leave *now* you won't be there until eight-thirty at the earliest.'

'I know,' I say. 'I was surprised too. We're going to have to fly across London in a taxi to make it to the West End for nine o'clock. The show's on later than normal because one of the cast is appearing on the Jonathan Ross chat show.'

It's a terrible lie and one that anyone who watches even the smallest amount of television could uncover if they know the first thing about pre-recorded chat shows but, luckily for me, Brian rarely watches TV. Not only does he think it's 'brain rot' but he resents how much non-sustainable electricity it eats up.

'Right.' He nods as though he's bought every word then looks up as I stand up and smooth down my choice of outfit for this evening. It's the most flattering cocktail dress I own.

'Good job you got dressed up before I got in,' he says, raising an eyebrow. 'Anyone would think you were going to go out regardless of what I said.'

I wait for the smile to let me know he's joking and, sure enough, it appears. I didn't assume anything about this evening, not least that Brian would agree to me going but the last few days have passed without incident and I know he's fond of Jane.

'Of course it's fine,' he says. 'You've been with Charlotte all day. The least you deserve is a bit of fun and a night out.'

'You have taken your tablet today, haven't you?' he adds, glancing at the glass of water on the coffee table beside me.

'Of course.'

'And you're feeling okay? You don't think you'll be overwhelmed by the crowded public transport and everything? You haven't been to London for a while. It's pretty frenetic these days.'

'Brian!' I laugh again. 'I went to London a couple of months ago. It can't have changed that much.'

'True.' He glances at the clock again. 'Is Jane coming to get you or would you like me to give you a lift to the station?'

I pick up my handbag, fold my jacket over my arm and slip on my heels. 'Thanks but the taxi should be here in a couple of minutes.'

Brian picks up his newspaper, shaking his head in amusement. 'Have a lovely time.'

I cross the room, crouch down by his armchair and kiss him on the forehead. He looks at me in surprise, his blue eyes searching mine.

'What was that for?'

'Because I love you.'

The grandfather clock in the corner of the room

tick-tick-ticks the seconds away as we look at each other. It feels like the first time we've really looked at each other in a very long time.

'Even after everything that's happened?' he asks softly.

'Despite it.'

He cups the side of my face with his hand and gently strokes my cheekbone with his thumb. 'I don't deserve you, Sue.'

I place my hand over his. 'Yes, you do.'

I can see my reflection in his pupils as his eyes flick back and forth, just the tiniest bit as he gazes at me. I look tired and worried and a million years old. When did that happen? When did I become so old? When did he? Wasn't it just yesterday that we were walking hand in hand along the banks of the Kifissos talking about the future we'd build together?

'I love you too,' Brian whispers. 'I don't know what I'd do without you. I couldn't bear it if anything happened to you, Sue. I'd be lost. Quite, quite lost.'

My chest floods with warmth and I press a hand over my heart because it's almost too much to bear. 'I'm not going anywhere, Brian.'

'And there was me thinking you were off to London!' He laughs heartily. 'Poor old Billy Elliot. I bet he was really looking forward to seeing you too. You're such a fickle woman, Susan Jackson.'

I laugh too then cross the room and peer round one of the curtains. I'm pretty sure I just heard a taxi pulling into the driveway. Sure enough a flash of yellow approaches the house and there's the parp-parp of a horn.

'Don't wait up!' I call as I dash out of the living room. 'I'll be back late, don't forget.'

'Text me if you get into trouble.'

Into trouble? I turn back to see what he means but he's got his nose in the newspaper. It was just a throwaway comment.

I really wish I *had* brought Jane with me. That way I wouldn't feel like such a social leper – a forty-three-year-old woman stood in the queue for one of London's trendiest nightspots with a bunch of clubbers young enough to be my children. A security guard walks past, pauses to glance at me, then continues on down the line.

I thought I'd feel overdressed in my knee-length John Rocha little black dress with its plunging neckline and diamante details on the shoulders but I needn't have worried. Compared to the miniscule handker-chiefs masquerading as outfits that the other women are wearing I'm practically sporting a burka. Other than the beach, I don't think I've ever seen so much female flesh on show in one place. It must be 5°C and yet none of the other women look the slightest bit cold while I threw on my jacket the second I got off the train and wished I'd brought my pashmina with me too.

''Scuse me?' says the willowy blonde behind me. 'Have you got the time, please?'

Her false-lashed gaze is fixed somewhere over my

left shoulder but I'm pretty sure she's talking to me because the only thing behind me is a wall.

'It's ten-thirty,' I say, mesmerised by her pillow-like lips. She's tanned within an inch of her life – a perfect match for the oak coat stand in the cloakroom – and her makeup is so flawless it looks airbrushed on. Her blonde hair is waist length and blow dried *big* so it frames her face like a Farrah Fawcett halo.

'Fanks.' Her glazed eyes flicker slightly.

'Do you come here often?' I cringe at my awkward attempt to initiate conversation.

'Every weekend.' She appears to be looking at the back of the head of the young man three people in front of me now.

'Good music, is it?'

'S'alright.'

'Nice dance floor?'

She shakes her head. 'Don't dance. Not in these heels.'

I look at her feet and am surprised she's even upright.

'I hear a lot of footballers come here,' I say.

Her blue eyes swivel towards me. The intensity of her gaze is unnerving. 'Yeah, they do. Why, you after someone?'

She looks me up and down, as though seeing me for the first time then, having established that I'm about as much competition as Ann Widdecombe, she looks away again.

'I was hoping to meet . . .' I lower my voice so as

not to announce it to the whole queue, '. . . Alex Henri.'

Her brow registers the slightest flicker of interest. 'He's fit.'

I wait to see if she'll say something else but that appears to be it. Half an hour passes before someone talks to me again.

'Sorry love,' The security guard holds up his hand as I approach the gold rope at the entrance to the club. 'Not tonight.'

I look at him in confusion. 'What's not tonight?'

He crosses his arms. 'Being funny won't help. Off you go.'

'No . . . really . . . I genuinely don't understand.' I turn to look at Blondie who's standing behind me looking as bored as she did half an hour ago. 'What did he just say?'

She shrugs a shoulder. 'He wants you to do one.'

'Why?'

Another shrug.

'Is it because I'm old?' The security guard is about the same height as Brian but three times as wide and bald except for a neatly trimmed goatee beard that does little to disguise his double chin. 'Because you can be sued for age discrimination. You know that don't you?'

His facial expression doesn't change. It's still registering indifference. 'You still here?'

'You have to let me in because . . .' I glance down the street, at the crowd approaching the club, the couples walking arm in arm, the groups of girls tottering in their heels, the gangs of lads laughing and throwing back their heads and the wide-eyed tourists consulting their maps and iPhones but my mind goes blank. He doesn't care about Charlotte or Alex Henri or the accident. His job is to only let people in who fit the 'young and beautiful' brief. Neither of which I am. I look at Blondie in desperation but she shrugs her shoulders.

'I'm her agent,' I say in a flash of inspiration. 'And if you don't let me in she, and all her beautiful friends will go to . . .' I say the first thing that comes into my head, '. . . Whisky Mist instead.'

One of Blondie's friends gasps in surprise but is swiftly silenced by a jab to the waist from Blondie herself. She whispers something in her friend's ear as the bouncer looks them up and down, then smiles sweetly at him.

'In,' the bouncer says as he unclips the rope and waves me into the club. His eyes don't so much as flicker from Blondie's cleavage.

It's dark inside and I pause in the entrance, blinking to adjust to the gloom.

'Twenty-five pounds,' says a bored female voice. A black-haired woman is sitting in a smoked glass-fronted booth to my right. I rummage in my purse, pull out three ten-pound notes and slide them towards her. She takes them wordlessly and slides a five-pound note back. When she doesn't say anything I take a step forward, towards the thud-thud-thud of dance music and tiny stream of light that's escaping from double doors at the end of the corridor.

'Stamp,' the receptionist says then sighs.

I turn. 'I'm sorry.'

'I need your wrist.' She looks dead behind the eyes, like she'd rather be anywhere in the world than here, now. I think of my sofa, a book, a glass of wine and Milly's soft head on my lap and empathise.

I untangle my hand from the loop of my handbag, slip it through the gap under the glass and madam stamps my wrist. I'm now the proud owner of a black smudgy 'G' tattoo. I tentatively rub it with my thumb but it doesn't smudge. I'll have to find a way to get rid of it before I get back home.

It's like being in a mirror-balled haulage truck. I have to fight just to get through the door and then I'm stuck, prevented from taking another step forward by the tight throng of bodies that fill the nightclub. There are people everywhere and it's hotter than a furnace. No matter which direction I move in I am knocked, jostled, elbowed and nudged out of the way. 'What?' people shout over the repetitive, thumping dance track that fills the room. 'What did you say?

The bar runs along one side of the room – gold, sparkling and floor to ceiling with bottles of every size, shape and colour. Impossibly beautiful bar staff stalk up and down, reaching for glasses, opening fridges and pouring drinks as though they're working an alcohol-themed catwalk. Seating runs the length of the opposite wall; low leather-backed booths and black poofs are groaning with people sitting around grey smoked-glassed coffee tables. I overhear a girl

267

tell her friend that you're not allowed to sit down at those tables unless you buy a five-hundred-pound bottle of champagne or a three-hundred-pound bottle of vodka. No wonder so many people are standing in the centre of the club, crammed into the narrow walkway between the seats and the bar. I don't bother getting a drink. Instead I inch my way through the crowd towards the other side of the room where I can see the bottom of a flight of stairs. Access is blocked by a rope and two burly security guards – they have to lead to the VIP area.

'Jesus!' I hear a cackle from my right. 'You weren't kidding about going for Alex Henri, were you? The look of determination on your face!'

I spin round. My pneumatic friend from the queue beams back at me.

'It's my agent!' she nudges her friend who giggles like it's the funniest thing she's ever heard.

'Jasmine,' she holds out her hand.

I shake it. 'Sue. Thank you, for what you did outside. I really appreciate it.'

She smiles. 'No problem. If he'd have spoken to my mum the way he spoke to you, I'd have lamped him one. Rude bastard.'

I smile back, unsure how to continue the conversation but Jasmine fills the gap.

'So,' she glances towards the stairs and the security guards. They're turning away a group of three scantily dressed girls. 'How are you planning on getting to Alex then?'

I shake my head. I really didn't think this through

before I left Brighton. I'd assumed I'd be able to talk to him somehow, or at least get a message to him but I can't even see him. The stairs lead to the balcony above our heads but, other than a few pairs of legs, I can't see a thing through the spindly balustrades. I don't even know if Alex Henri is up there.

'Could you introduce me?' I ask, glancing back at Jasmine.

'Me?' She throws back her head and cackles like a fishwife. 'Darlin' if I knew Alex, do you think I'd be standing here now, talking to you? No offence.'

'None taken. I just . . . I mean, you're very glamorous, you could pass for a model and the security guard obviously thought you were successful enough to have an agent so . . .'

'Are you tryin' to chat me up?' She laughs again then, spotting someone across the room, frantically grabs her friend's arm. 'You know that guy,' she says, leaning into her, 'the one I was telling you about that looks like a cross between Andy Carroll and Ben from *Hollyoaks*? He's only bloody here!'

She yanks her friend away and through the crowd without so much as a backward glance. I'm not offended by her sudden disappearance. I'm actually inordinately grateful that she helped me get into the club at all. I look back at the stairs. I'll get into that VIP area if it's the last thing I do.

Thursday 21st May 1992

I can't believe I haven't written in my diary for nearly a year. Initially I hid it in my sewing machine table because I didn't want James to find it and then I guess I just forgot about it until now. So yes, nearly a year since I last wrote an entry and the same amount of time since I moved into James's house. I'd like to say that my life is wonderful, that I'm thinner, happier and more loved than I've ever been but the truth couldn't be more wrong.

I don't know how I ended up here. I feel trapped, unhappy and more lonely than I've ever felt in my life. I feel like my life is on a loop – get up, take a shower, put on jeans and t-shirt (in a size sixteen, I've put on a stone and a half since I moved in), have breakfast with James and his mother (she started showing her face three days after I moved in, sulk finally over) and then complete the list of chores she gives me. If I'm lucky that includes a trip to the supermarket so I can be around real people but, more often than not, it involves cleaning, helping her attend to her personal needs (her carer, if there ever was one, never materialized from her holiday) and sitting quietly in the living room to 'keep her company' while she watches daytime soap after daytime soap. I've taken to watching them too, mostly to try and block out the creepy batik wall hanging that stares at me with its big empty eyes from across the room. It sounds ridiculous but I get really bad vibes from it. It's always watching me, wherever I move.

Unlike the first few months of me living here James doesn't rush through the front door at the end of the day and wrap his arms around me. He doesn't call me his 'angel' or his 'kitten'. He barely even acknowledges me. As for sex I can barely remember the last time we made love. Neither of us sleep naked anymore and, when James comes in from the bathroom he'll say 'night' and turn his back to me. Five minutes later, he'll be asleep.

I started to wonder if it was me. I can't stop comfort eating (chocolate mostly, on the walk back from the supermarket. I don't get the bus anymore, it makes me feel claustrophobic) and I thought maybe he didn't fancy me anymore. I tried wearing a dress instead of my normal uniform of jeans and t-shirt one day but, when James came home and saw me, he shook his head and said I might want to consider getting a bigger size if I didn't want every roll and ripple on show. I ran to the bedroom and cried.

James still makes an effort with his appearance.

Every Sunday before rehearsals, and once or twice during the week, he'll spend over an hour in the bathroom then emerge in a cloud of deodorant and aftershave with a towel wrapped around his waist then he'll spend another ten minutes ironing a shirt, twenty minutes doing his hair and then, when he's checked with me that he looks good, he'll leave. I'm pretty sure he's having an affair – possibly with Maggie – but if I dare say anything he turns it on me and accuses me of flirting with the male customers at work (I had to get a job at Tescos six months ago when Jess let me go from the bar job). I wanted to teach TEFL again but James said he didn't want me travelling up to North London on my own. Besides, his mother needed me he said, and I could get back quickly in an emergency if I worked close to home. What he said made sense but I fought him anyway. I didn't want to work at Tescos. I had a degree. I was a trained TEFL teacher and dressmaker, not a cashier. James didn't listen. Instead he twisted my words and made out that I was a snob, too spoilt to rough it with the normal people for a couple of months while I got back on my feet.

I took umbrage at that but he took my hands in his and said it was okay to have ambition but my sewing business wasn't going to take off immediately and I just had to have patience. I would have laughed if I hadn't been so incredulous. I hadn't touched my sewing machine in months – his mother's demands had seen to that.

I miss my mum so much my heart aches. I haven't

visited her in forever but there hasn't been the time, money or opportunity. I called her a couple of times, a few months ago, but she got upset and confused and that made me feel terrible, like I was the cause of her distress. I haven't rung since and I'm plagued by guilt, terrified she'll think I've abandoned her.

I've nearly called Hels too, dozens of times, but I always put the phone down before the dial tone starts. I can't bear to hear her say 'I told you so' and remind me of all the time and money she and Rupert spent helping me get over James, only for me to go back to him again. And besides, what have I really got to complain about? I'm not starving, I'm not being beaten and I'm not being forced to sleep in the garden shed. I've got a job, food to eat, a roof over my head and a warm body sharing my bed. Sometimes James and I go out together – more often than not it'll be a trip to the theatre, cinema or a restaurant with his mother (she hates being left alone at home) – and, when he's in a good mood, I fall in love with him all over again. He'll wink at me at the table, put a hand on my leg and whisper in my ear that he wants to drag me into the toilets and fuck me. He never does of course but it's moments like that – and him occasionally reaching for me in the night and wrapping his arm around me – that keep me here, that make me think that he does still love me, deep down, we've just got into a bit of a domestic rut and we need to shake things up again so he sees me the same way he did when we didn't live together. I got myself into this situation and I need to get myself out.

I haven't told James this but I've started to stash some of my Tesco wages away so I can get myself a bedsit again. It's not much after I've given him £200 for rent and the same for food each month (he said he'd only agreed for me to live here rent free until I started earning again) but the small pile of notes in the bottom of my rucksack is starting to grow. I've probably got a couple of hundred pounds now, nowhere near enough to put down a deposit and a month's rent but I'm getting there slowly. Another six months maybe? That's what's getting me through this, knowing there's a light at the other end of the tunnel. When I get my own place I'll be able to work full-time at Tescos because I won't be looking after James's mum and I can start eating healthier again and lose some weight. I might even make friends with some of the girls at work. A couple of them have smiled at me but I'm so scared they'll think I'm a snob when they hear my voice I rarely speak (James says I'm so well spoken people find me snobby). I used to be so chatty too. I think back to my first day with the Abberley Players and the way I'd have a banter with everyone. I miss the woman I used to be. And I can't help thinking that maybe James does too.

Chapter 22

'My seven-year-old daughter's in a coma,' I say, hoping the same line that worked on Steve Torrance's PA will work on the Greys bouncer. 'And Alex Henri's her favourite player. I just want a recording of him saying "get well soon, Charlotte" and I'll be off. Honestly, I'll be in and out of the VIP area in no time.'

The security guard crosses his arms but doesn't look at me. He's still scanning the crowd at the bar.

'Please, she's very ill.'

'Look love,' he gives me eye contact at last, 'Your daughter could be drawing her last breath but I'm still not going to let you up the stairs. If I let you go I'll have to let everyone go up there.'

'But they haven't got sick children. Please, I spoke to his agent's PA earlier today and she said it was fine for me to approach him.'

'What was her name?'

'She didn't say.'

He raises an eyebrow. 'Funny that.'

I look at his colleague imploringly. He's wearing a wedding ring and he's got a 'Connor' tattoo on his neck. 'You look like a family man. Have you got kids?'

He doesn't say anything. He doesn't even acknowledge the fact I've just rested my hand, very lightly, on his forearm. 'You'd do anything to protect your children, wouldn't you? Do anything to make them happy? To keep them healthy? I want the same for my daughter. I want her to wake up and I'll do whatever it takes to make that happen. You can understand that, can't you?'

His eyes flick towards me. They're dark and hooded, almost hidden in his big round fleshy face. 'You'd do *anything*?'

'Of course.'

He looks me up and down and grins. A gold incisor glints at me. 'Would you suck my cock?'

I make a sound somewhere between a laugh and a gasp.

'I . . .' I don't know what to say. I've got no idea if he's serious or not. 'I . . .'

'How much are you paying her to suck your cock? Or is she paying you?'

A tall blond man in a white shirt, dark jeans and an expensive-looking black jacket is standing behind me. He looks me up and down then catches the married security guard's eye and laughs.

'What is it, grope-a-granny night? Jesus Terry, your standards have really slipped, haven't they?'

I expect the security guard to punch him on the nose, or at least order him out of the club. Instead he laughs good-naturedly and unclips the velvet rope.

'I take what I can get, Rob, ideally without paying for it.'

'Excuse me.' I side-step so I'm standing between the rope and 'Rob' and pull myself up to my full five foot six. 'I am a person you know. I have got ears.'

'Well fuck me, she's got ears!' He glances back at the group of people gathered behind him and laughs uproariously. 'You're a feisty one, aren't you, darlin'? What happened? Take a wrong turn on your way to bingo?'

'Are you always this rude or just to women who are too old to be impressed by a pretty face and a well-cut suit?'

'Oh,' his face lights up with pleasure at the unintended compliment. 'I get it. You don't go for the pretty boy thing, you're more into a bit of rough like Terry over here.' He nudges the security guard.

'Actually, I'm not interested in either of you. I'm here to see Alex Henri.'

'A French fancier, eh? Like a bit of foreign do you, Granny?'

'Stop calling me that, you jumped-up little twat.' The words are out of my mouth before my brain has time to process them.

Terry takes a step towards me and lays a warning hand on my shoulder but Rob waves him off.

'Leave her, Tez.' He looks me up and down and narrows his eyes. 'Alex Henri, is it? That who you want to meet?'

I nod but say nothing.

He glances at his colleague. 'Has Alex ever had a tart this old?'

I knot my fingers behind my back, suppressing the urge to slap Rob around his smug, patronizing face. The bouncer shrugs non-committedly.

'Let her in. This should be funny.' Rob nods his head at Terry who raises his eyebrows but steps backwards so the way is clear for me to ascend the stairs. I take a step forwards.

'Off you go, Granny. Shag his pants off,' he calls after me as I take the stairs two at a time. The sooner I speak to Alex Henri and leave the better. There's something horribly claustrophobic about this club; the ceilings are too low, there are too many people and it's too hot. It crosses my mind, as I reach the top of the stairs, that if a fire started in here, half the club would be trampled to death in the charge to get out the tiny entrance door. I fight to suppress the thought as my chest tightens and I squeeze past a group of Jasmine lookalikes and dodge around two huge boxer-types with broken noses. The last thing I need right now is a panic attack.

The VIP section is busier up here than it was on the ground floor and it takes me ten minutes to battle through the bodies to the seating area against the far wall. I lose count of the stunning model-like women and athlete-like men knocking back champagne, dancing on the chairs and gyrating against each other. I catch more than one confused look as I make my way through the crowd. I've never felt older, uglier, fatter or more out of place in my life but I plough on anyway.

'Alex Henri,' I breathe his name as I catch sight of him.

I wasn't sure I'd recognize him from a couple of tiny internet photographs and a half-naked poster on Charlotte's wall but there's no mistaking those pale-brown eyes and razor-sharp cheekbones.

'Excuse me, excuse me please.' I wriggle and elbow my way through the throng of bodies surrounding his around his table. 'I need to speak to Alex.'

I receive countless dirty looks, a jab to the hip and what I hope is white wine down the back of my dress but I make it through and suddenly I'm standing a metre away from him. Only a smoked glass coffee table loaded with an ice bucket, champagne bottles and glasses separate us.

'Alex.'

He doesn't so much as glance in my direction. He's got a willowy brunette on one side, a voluptuous blonde on the other and an army of good-looking men and women flanking them. This is what teenagers aspire to, I think as the table cuts into my shins and the white wine seeps through my dress and rolls down my back, gathering in a pool at the top of my buttocks. This is why they want to grow up to be 'rich' or 'famous' rather than doctors, solicitors or air stewards. There are probably a dozen paparazzi crammed outside the front door right now, waiting to earn their share of the riches by grabbing a shot of a footballer leaving hand in hand with a woman who isn't his wife or a glamour girl falling into a car with her knickerless crotch exposed. But Charlotte wouldn't have thought about any of that when she was introduced to Alex Henri – she wouldn't have considered the dark side of this lifestyle – the superficiality, the lies, the drugs and alcohol problems and the hangers-on. She would have been dazzled by the bleached smiles, big hair, designer clothes and fat wallets. And who could blame her? This is a million miles away from the life she normally lives.

'Alex Henri!'

Shouting his name gets his reaction and he looks up. It attracts the attention of several of his friends too.

'Hey Alex, it's past your bedtime!' one of them shouts as the rest bray with laughter.

'Your mum says you're not allowed to play out any more,' shouts someone else.

There's a chorus of guffaws and snorts. Alex smiles too but I can tell from the way he's twisting his cufflinks round and round that he's nervous. He doesn't know who I am or what I want.

'Please maman,' he says, looking me straight in the eye, 'please can I stay out for another hour. I promise to be a good boy.'

The brunette on his right spits out her champagne as she explodes with laughter and one of the men reaches across the table and high-fives Alex.

'I need to talk to you about my daughter,' I continue. 'My name is Sue Jackson. My daughter's name is Charlotte. You met her a few weeks ago. You . . . spent some time together.'

'Charlotte, you say?' He pulls his mobile phone out from inside his jacket and presses a few buttons. I hold my breath, my heart thudding with apprehension. 'A few weeks ago. Charlotte . . .' he looks up and shakes his head. 'Nope, no mention of shagging a fat British girl here.'

For a second I have no idea what he's on about and then I understand. He thinks Charlotte looks like me. I think of my beautiful, slender daughter lying in her hospital bed and anger burns in my chest.

'My daughter's name is Charlotte Jackson,' I repeat steadily. 'You met her on the ninth of March. She's the same height as me but she's young, blonde and beautiful. Her eyes are the brightest green you've ever seen. She's very distinctive looking.'

Alex shrugs. 'I meet a lot of beautiful women.' He looks away, at the blonde to his left and throws a lazy arm around her. She snuggles in gratefully and giggles at something he whispers in her ear. His friends turn away, back to each other and their glasses of champagne. I was entertaining for five seconds but Alex has established that the show's over now.

'You took her into the club toilets, Alex.'

The room falls quiet. The blonde looks at me in surprise, a man in a grey t-shirt and silver cross necklace says 'get in son!' and Alex Henri looks at me blankly. Out of the corner of my eye I spot a bald

281

man in a dark suit and lilac tie frown and try to catch Alex's attention. He looks familiar but I can't work out why.

'You took her to the toilets,' I say again. 'I want to know what happened.'

'What the fuck do you think happened?'

'Want me to show you, Granny?'

'He read her a bedtime story, didn't you, Alex?'

The comments come at me like mortar fire. The laughter has stopped and the air is charged with aggression. The parasites think I'm attacking their host and they're on the defence. I look at the floor, just for a second. When I look back up I've dressed myself in an invisible coat of emotional armour. They continue to shout insults at me but now I shrug them off.

'I'd like to talk to you alone please, Alex.' I say steadily. 'My daughter is desperately ill in hospital and I think that what happened here that Saturday night might have something to do with it.'

'Enough.' Alex stands up, his expression grim, all traces of amusement gone. He looks towards the corner of the room and clicks his fingers.

'Please,' I say as two security rooms start towards us. 'I just need five minutes of your time. I'm not accusing you of anything. I need to find ooph—'

The words are knocked out of me as I'm yanked backwards, out of the throng of bodies, away from the table, away from Alex.

'She was fifteen!' I shout as I'm frog-marched towards the stairs. 'She was underage, Alex.'

'Only fifteen!' I shout again as I'm half-marched, half-dragged across the nightclub. 'Alex Henri, she was *fifteen*.'

People stop talking and stare. The music continues its relentless thump, thump, thump but the room may as well be silent. All eyes are on me. A girl nearby sniggers. 'Your mum's pissed again,' someone says. A man guffaws and spits out his beer.

I stop shouting as the humiliation sinks in.

'Enough!' I dig my heels into the carpet and squirm from side to side to try and loosen the guards' grip on my upper arms. 'That's enough! I'm leaving. You don't have to throw me out.'

They share a look then warily release their grip.

The crowd parts as I step forward, my minders following in my wake, and head for the exit. The doorman I argued with earlier touches a hand to his earpiece as he unclips the rope.

'Don't come back,' he hisses as I leave. I say nothing. Instead I continue to walk, my head held high, past the queue, down the street and around the corner. Only then do my knees buckle and I slump into a doorway. I sink down onto the step and hide my face in my hands. How has it come to this? Lying to my husband, being laughed at by strangers, humiliating myself in public? What happened to Susan Anne Jackson – respectable forty-three-year-old politician's wife – and who is this desperate creature, this figure of ridicule who has taken her place? I might have walked out of Greys with my head held high but that didn't stop me from seeing the horror and revulsion in the eyes of the people I passed. What happened there, Charlotte? Was it as bad as what happened to me? I run my hands over my face. Or worse?

I sit up and look at my watch. It's past midnight. If I don't pull myself together I'll miss the last train to Brighton and Brian will want to know why. I stand up slowly, straighten my skirt, arrange my handbag on my shoulder and set off down the street, my chin pressed to my chest, my arms folded against the cold. Every couple of minutes I wave at a passing cab but taxi after taxi speeds past without slowing. It's only when I reach the end of the street that I realize I have no idea whether I'm even going in the right direction. I glance around, in search of landmarks but the only thing I can see is the neon glow of a tube sign at the end of a narrow alley that runs between two huge Victorian buildings to my right. I'm too short-sighted to make out the name without my glasses but I assume it must be South Kensington. Maybe if I hurry I can get the tube to Victoria? A cab speeds towards me, half blinding me with its headlights and I throw out a hand but it whizzes past, splashing through puddles, then disappears into the darkness, the 'for hire' sign streaking through the night. I look back at the alley and rub my hands up and down my arms. The tube it is.

I set off, tottering as fast as my heels will carry me along the cobbled street, my eyes fixed on the familiar glow of the tube sign in the distance. I keep to the pavement, staying close to the tall buildings on my right and up my pace. I'm halfway down the alley already and now I've left the streetlights and cars of the main road behind. Long shadows and looming shapes appear from nowhere. There are no houses, no flickering televisions and yellow-hued table lamps warming curtained windows. Instead bars, boards and shutters creak and slam as I hurry past. The sound of a can rolling down the street makes me jump and I glance behind me to see where it came from. A man has appeared at the far end of the alley. He's silhouetted against the blurs of cars on the main road, a black shape with broad shoulders and narrow hips, and he's moving towards me. This isn't someone on a late-night stroll through London, this is a man trying to move quickly but without attracting atten-tion. I wait for him to change direction, to cross the road so he's on the opposite pavement – something most men would do to reassure a lone female at night that they had nothing to fear – instead he quickens his pace. I glance at the tube sign. Two hundred metres to go. Two hundred metres to safety. I quicken my pace and start to run. The sound of my heels on concrete echoes through the alley – clip-clop, clip-clop, clip-clop. Seconds later it's joined by a new sound – thump-thump-thump – the man has started to run. He's closed the gap between us. He's wearing an army jacket, the hood pulled tightly over his lowered face but I can still make out the shape of his jaw. It's wide, narrowing to a strong chin, clefted in the middle.

I run. The cold night air whips my face and grabs at my dress, pulling me back, slowing me down, as I run as fast as I can, the underground station in my sights. A woman in a baseball cap and denim jacket crosses the road at the end of the alley and I shout, willing her to turn and see me, urging her to help but no words escape from my mouth. The only sound I can hear is the hoarse wheezing of my breathing and thump-thump-thump of my pursuer's trainers on the pavement. He's getting closer. I can feel him closing the distance, sense him staring at me, his eyes boring into the back of my head. Not much further, just a hundred metres or so and—

No!

A man in a yellow security jacket pulls the metal grating from one side of the tube entrance to the other.

Stop!

I try to shout, to tell him to wait, to let me in, but he disappears through a side door and slams it behind him. I burst out of the alley and onto the main street. I'm panting, my thighs are burning and cramp is ripping at my side but I continue to run – left, after the woman I saw a few moments ago but now I'm closer I can see she's got headphones on over her cap. She doesn't look round. An elderly Asian woman on the other side of the road gives me a curious look then glances away quickly when I catch her eye. I step into the road, to go after her, but a car speeds past and I'm forced to jump back. I'm forced to stop running.

'Sue,' a man breathes my name and my body shuts down. I can't move. Can't speak. Can't breathe. Cars speed past and I wait. 'Sue.'

Wednesday 12th August 1992

I need to write this quickly because James has popped out to go to the hospital and I've got no idea when he'll be back. It's become too dangerous to leave the diary hidden in my sewing room so I've started keeping it under a loose floorboard in the hallway. That way if anything happens to me and the police search the house, they'll find it and the truth about James, and what he did to me, will be revealed.

So I'm going to say it as clearly as I can – I think he's going to kill me.

I don't know when and I don't know how but he said he'd rather spend his life in prison than think of me 'spreading my legs' for another man and, considering what he did to the man I did sleep with, I've got no reason to doubt him.

This is the first time he's left me alone since Sunday night but he's not taking chances on me escaping. He's locked me in the house and disconnected the phone so I can't call anyone for help and I can't hammer on the wall because the couple who live next door have gone on holiday and there's no one on the other side. I've checked all the windows – twice – but they're locked shut and the back door is double glazed so I couldn't shoulder it open even if I could. An hour ago I shouted through the letter box at a woman pushing a buggy down the street but she didn't so much as twitch. I can only assume the traffic is drowning me out or the house is set so far back from the pavement my shouts don't carry.

I can't even ask Mrs Evans to help me – not that she would – because she's not here. She suffered a heart attack while I was in York visiting my mum. That's why James has gone to the hospital, to see her. And I'm trapped and there's nothing I can do but write.

I came back from York on Sunday early evening in a very good mood. I'd finally been to visit Mum thanks to the £50 James had given me for the train fare (I think he wanted me gone so he could spend the weekend with whoever it is that he's shagging) and Mum's mood was brighter than the last time I'd seen her.

Mum had asked how I was and I didn't have the heart to tell her the truth. I told her that James and I were impossibly happy and we'd got engaged (she cried when I showed her my engagement ring and said she wished Dad was around to walk me down the aisle) and I was making a huge success of my costumier business. So convincing was my little tale *that I started to believe it myself and, as I settled myself into my seat on the train home, I was bubbling with excitement. I couldn't wait to get home and tell James about my visit, maybe even grab a little bit of time to organize my fabric whilst Mrs Evans took her daily nap. It was as though stepping outside London had removed the grey fog from my brain. I wasn't neglected and put upon. I'd just become a bit depressed after everything that had happened. I needed a bit of fighting spirit, a bit of positivity back and I could turn things around. Besides, I had nearly three hundred pounds saved up. With the cake tin Mum had pressed into my hands before I left (containing nearly two hundred pounds in assorted crumpled bank notes) that was almost enough for a bedsit deposit and the first month's rent. Maybe, I thought as the train chugged into King's Cross, I won't have to work in Tescos full time after all. If I live with James and his mum for another two or three months and my business takes off, I'll only have to work on the tills part time to cover my rent.*

'James,' I called as I pushed open the front door and stepped into the dark hallway. 'James, are you home? I've had the most wonderful couple of days.'

The answerphone light was flashing red in the gloom but I was only vaguely aware of it as I abandoned my suitcase, replaced my shoes with soft, suedette slippers and padded down the hallway and into the living room. The black mask wall hanging leered back at me as I glanced around but, other than that, the room was empty.

'James?'

'James? Mrs Evans?'

I glanced at my watch. 7.30 p.m. There was every chance James had decided to stay on at the theatre for post-rehearsal drinks but his mother should still be at home. She normally watched Songs of Praise in the living room on a Sunday night. Perhaps she was in the toilet? Or taking a nap in her room? The house was uncommonly quiet and I felt like a burglar, tip-toeing around, barely breathing for fear of disturbing the peace.

'Mrs Evans?' The bathroom door was open so I tapped, nervously, at her bedroom door. 'Mrs Evans, are you okay?'

There was no answer so I poked my head into the room. The bed was made, the curtains were pulled and everything looked normal apart from . . . I stepped closer to the dressing table. Margaret's mother of pearl-handled brush was missing. So was the brown leather case that contained her manicure set and the tiny silver jewellery box that contained her wedding and engagement rings. Where had she gone? She couldn't drive, she was terrified of leaving the house and when she met up with her friends – which was so rare I could only remember it happening twice in all the months I'd lived with her – they came to her.

I shrugged as I made my way to my sewing room. If James and Mrs Evans were both out of the house what better excuse to start sorting through my fabric? Everything was still boxed up and I knew for a fact my silks would need attacking with a cool iron before I hung them up, never mind the lin—

'Oh my God.' My hands flew to my mouth as I pushed open the door to the spare room. My sewing table was lying on the floor on its side. Half a metre away was my machine, a dark footprint staining the body, the delicate thread guides, tension regulators and spool pins snapped and bent, the foot control ripped away, lying on the other side of the room. My boxes of material that I'd so neatly stacked in the corner were upended and crushed, the material spilling out – ripped, mangled and smeared with what looked like red paint. My mannequin leaned drunkenly against the back wall, black-handled sewing scissors plunged into its chest. The floor was a riot of colour – thread, ribbons, buttons, bindings, chords, elastics and tapes, all splattered with the same red gloss paint. The curtains were ripped from the window, the mirror smashed and the upholstery on the chair I'd so lovingly covered before I moved in was slashed open, the white stuffing bursting out like a puff mushroom, the elegant wooden legs snapped clean off.

I backed out of the room, my hands still pressed to my mouth, certain we'd been robbed and the burglar was still in the house. Why else would my room be trashed and Margaret's things missing? But where was she? An image of my mother-in-law, tied up and terrified, flashed into my mind and a cold shiver pulsed through my body. I stepped across the landing as softly as I could – heel, toe, heel, toe – trying to avoid the creaky floorboards. The blood pounded in my ears as

I stepped past mine and James's bedroom door. Did they have her in there? I paused mid-stride, one heel pressed into the floorboard, the ball of my foot raised. All my senses prickled with anticipation as I listened, then as a floorboard creaked behind me I sprinted across the landing, took the stairs two at a time and ran across the hallway. I vaulted my suitcase and sped past my shoes. I had one hand on the front door handle when it flew open and I was grabbed around the neck.

'No!' I slapped at my attacker as I was forced backwards, away from the light of escape and back into the dark hallway.

'Bitch.'

I recognized the voice immediately.

'James, stop.' I tripped over my suitcase as he powered towards me, and fell to the floor. 'It's me. It's Suzy.' I reached my hands up towards him, certain he'd help me up when he realized his mistake. 'James, it's Suzy.'

He bent down and peered at me, his pupils dark pools in the gloom. His fingers made contact with my head and he stroked my hair back from my forehead.

'James,' I reached up and touched his face, 'something terrible has happened. My sewing room . . . it's awful. Everything I worked so hard for has been destroyed. Why would someone do that?'

The pressure of James's hand on my head changed and he began raking his hand through my hair, pressing the tips of his fingers into my skull.

'Ow.' I wrapped my hand round his and tried to

relieve the pressure. 'Could you be a bit more gentle?'

'I don't know. Could you be a bit more truthful?' He stood up suddenly, yanking me up by the hair.

It was as though my scalp was being ripped clean from my skull. I screamed and lashed out but I barely had time to find my feet before James set off, striding towards the living room, dragging me, still screaming, along the hallway behind him. Each step made my head burn like it was on fire. Just when I thought I'd pass out from the pain, James released his grip and threw me across the room. I raised my arms to cover my face as I flew towards the glass cabinet then there was a crash, I hit the floor and a thousand shards of glass rained down on me. I lay still, too dazed to move, and then James was on me again.

'Lying down on the job again are you, you slut?'

He grabbed me by the ankle and dragged me across the room, back towards the door then yanked me to my feet.

'Tell me the truth!' he bellowed in my face then CRACK! his fist made contact with my cheekbone and I fell back to the floor.

'Please,' I tried to scrabble up, my fingers pressed to my cheek. 'Please James, just tell me what I've done wrong. Let's talk about it, let's—'

CRACK! His boot made contact with my shoulder. He towered above me, his face a mask of anger, his eyes black, glittering holes and he raised his boot as if to kick me again when . . .

Ring-ring, ring-ring.

James glanced towards the living-room door.

Ring-ring, ring-ring.

He looked back at me.

Ring-ring, ring-ring.

Beep! This is 0207 4563 2983. Please leave a message after the tone.

The phone went to answerphone.

'Hello? Susan, this is Jake from the Abberley Players. Sorry to call you again but I really need to talk to you. There's been a fight, between Steve and James. Steve's in hospital but we don't know where James is. We're worried about him. And you. He was saying some . . . um . . . unusual things. Could you give me a ring when you get this, please. My number is 0208 9823 7456. Thanks.'

I looked at James. There was a bruise on his cheek I hadn't noticed in the dark hallway and the edge of his mouth was split, caked with blood. There was blood on his neck too, and on his fists. I didn't know if it was Steve's or mine.

He caught me looking at him and the look of worry on his face morphed into disgust.

'Stand up.'

I slowly picked myself up from the ground.

'Take off your clothes.'

I did as I was told, slowly, painfully, undoing the buttons of my shirt before slipping it off – I winced as it caught on my swollen right shoulder – then let it slip to the floor. I undid my jeans, pushed them past my hips and stepped out of them.

'And your underwear.'

'James, please. We weren't going out together when

Steve and I . . . when we . . . it was all a terrible mistake. I didn't enjoy it and I didn't feel anything. In fact, it just made me miss you more and—'

'Your underwear.'

I pushed my knickers to the ground first then reached round to unclip my bra. My shoulder twisted sharply and I gasped in pain but I was more scared by what James would do if I didn't comply so I undid my bra and dropped that to the floor too.

I flinched as he took a step towards me but, instead of hitting me, he side-stepped me and walked up to the window, threw open the curtains and opened the window.

'Stand here, Susan.'

I hesitated. There was a row of houses opposite. They were separated from us by the busy road below but, just as we could see into their illuminated homes on a dark night, so they could see into ours.

'The window, Suzy.'

I walked forwards like I was sleepwalking through my worst nightmare.

'That's it, walk right up to the window. I want everyone to see what a disgusting, fat, dirty whore you really are.'

I gripped hold of the sill and looked out at the cars below. Maybe if one of them saw me they'd realize something was wrong and call the police. I dismissed the thought almost as soon as it crossed my mind. No, they wouldn't. This was London. No one cared enough to call the police. I heard a noise behind me and spun round, sure James was about to push me to my death and came face to face with an anglepoise lamp, the bright bulb pointed upwards, blinding me.

'Turn back around,' James said. 'I want the world to see how ugly and flawed you are. I want them to see how riddled with flab and cellulite and stretch marks and saddle bags. I want them to look at your saggy breasts and your enormous thighs and I want them to wonder how anyone could ever have stomached making love to you. How anyone could have loved this,' he prodded me in the side.

I fought back tears but said nothing. If this was James's punishment for me sleeping with Steve then so be it. There were worse things than public humiliation, far worse.

'Ever wonder why I stopped sleeping with you, Suzy?' He paused for a reaction then continued anyway. 'When this is how you look? Do you have any idea how much of a turn-off men find a body like yours?'

A tear dribbled down my cheek. Fucking bastard. When this was over, when he finally ended my ordeal I'd run so far away from him he'd never find me again.

'And to think I felt guilty for going back to prostitutes?' He stifled a laugh and I realized I must have stiffened in surprise. 'I just couldn't bear making love to a fat, lardy lump any more. And you were never very good at sucking dick.'

'Right.' The sofa creaked as he stood up and the room suddenly dimmed. He must have turned the lamp off. 'Enough entertainment. I want to know why you fucked Steve, how many times you fucked Steve, how you fucked him and whether,' he grabbed hold of my hair and yanked me backwards, 'you laughed at me the whole fucking time?'

'James no!' I twisted and fought, hitting him, scratching him and kicking him as he dragged me across the room and bent me over the glass table in the corner of the room. 'Just let me go. Please.'

'Let you go?' I heard the zip of his fly open and then the weight of his chest on my back as he hissed in my ear. 'Suzy, I'm never going to let you go. Never. You're a filthy whore but you're my whore. And besides,' he lifted my head from the glass then smashed it back down again, 'I want you to apologise to Mother. She had a heart attack when she saw what I'd done to your room, what **you** made me do. I want you to spend the rest of your life apologizing, to both of us. Now then,' he kicked my legs apart and pressed his penis against my anus, 'did Steve fuck you **here**?'

I stared across at the batik wall hanging and let the wide white eyes hypnotise me. My mind went blank as I slipped into the gaping dark mouth and disappeared.

Chapter 23

'Sue, get in.'

I look round, expecting to stare into the cold grey eyes of my ex-boyfriend, but there's no one behind me.

'Sue Jackson?'

A black Mercedes with tinted windows draws up alongside me and a man beckons from one of the passenger windows. He looks familiar but I can't quite place—

'Steve Torrance.' He flashes me an electric smile and I recognize the dazzling white teeth. Alex Henri's agent. I saw his picture on the internet. He disappears back into the car and the door opens. 'Get in.'

I glance behind me again but there's no one there. The alley is empty too. I can't have imagined James running behind me. He was there, I saw his face. Where's he gone? Did Steve's car startle him into the shadows? Is he waiting for him to leave before he makes his move?

'Look, Sue,' Steve's face appears next to the open door. 'I'm a very busy man. Get in or tell me to fuck off, just hurry the fuck up.'

I falter. Try and flag a taxi to Victoria and risk James reappearing or get in a car with a man I've never met before?

Steve's smile widens as I open the door. He moves across into the other passenger seat, leaving the one nearest me empty. I look round one last time – the street is still empty – then slip into the car and lock the door behind me. A shadow crosses my window and I jerk away from the door. 'Can we just go now, please. Drive!'

The driver, an older man wearing a peaked cap pulled low over his eyes twists round. 'Who'd you think you are – Robert de Niro? This is the West End, love, not New Bloody York.'

He glances at Steve Torrance who raises an eyebrow then turns to look at me, the smile still fixed firmly in place. 'Where would you like to go, Sue?'

'Victoria.' I pull my handbag close, one eye still on the street. I keep expecting James to yank open the door and pull me into the street.

The driver shrugs, taps his indicator and we pull away. The road is gridlocked with traffic and it takes an age to get to the end of the street. It's only when we hit a pedestrian-free road that I allow myself to relax.

Steve Torrance glances up from his BlackBerry. 'How much?'

I say nothing, assuming he's talking to the driver.

'How much?' he says again, briefly catching my eye before he looks back at his phone.

I grip my bag to my chest. 'How much what?'

'To keep quiet.'

'Sorry?'

'Look Sue,' he leans back in his seat and tucks his mobile into the inside pocket of his jacket. 'Let's not fanny about. Your big song and dance act in the club got you noticed, congratulations. Let's just hope there weren't any journalists with mobile phones set to record or this conversation is as redundant as Bob Diamond.' He laughs at his own joke. 'So come on, how much is it going to take to stop you going to the papers?'

It takes a couple of seconds for what he's saying to sink in.

'You think that's why I did it? I confronted Alex because I wanted paying off?'

'You don't?'

'No, of course not.' I adjust my seatbelt so I can look at him face on. He can't be much taller than me but his large gut and lack of neck make him look broad and there's a sheen at the top of his bald head. 'I'm not that kind of woman. My husband is Brian Jackson, MP for Brighton.'

'Great.' He reaches into his inside pocket, pulls out a handkerchief and presses it to his brow. 'That's all I fucking need, the bloody government getting involved just because Henri can't keep it in his pants.'

'So he did have sex with my daughter?' I ask the

question as evenly as I can even though my heart is twisting in my chest.

He stops mopping to look at me. 'Hang on one fucking second. It sounded to me – and every other twat with ears – that you were accusing my client of having sex with a minor. Are you saying now that he didn't?'

'I didn't accuse him of anything. I asked him to talk to me.'

'Stop the car!' He leans forward in his seat and holds up a hand. 'Stop the fucking car right now!'

There's a squeal of brakes, a horn honks and then the car jerks to a stop. To our left is a park, an enormous iron fence wrapped around it and to the right there's a row of B&B style hotels. The street lamps either side cast accusing pools of light on the beer cans, cigarette ends and dog poo that litter the pavement. If we're in Victoria we're not in the nice bit.

'Out.' Steve reaches across me and opens my door. 'Get out of my car!'

'No.' I pull the door shut.

'What do you fucking mean no?' His face is inches from mine. I can see the open pores and broken veins around his nose and smell the champagne and curry on his breath.

'I'm not getting out until you tell me what happened.'

'When?'

'When Charlotte and Alex Henri went to the toilets together.'

'You're asking the wrong man, darling, because I wasn't there.'

'Then I suggest you find out.'

'I should, should I?' His top lip curls into a sneer. 'You're not going to the press, you've already admitted as much.'

'No, but I could go to the police.' The sneer instantly disappears. 'My fifteen-year-old daughter is in a coma and I have every reason to believe that what happened with your client may have put her there.'

'Woah!' He raises his hands, palms out. 'Who said anything about a coma?'

'I did, just now.'

'What the fuck?' He catches the driver looking at him and waves a hand for him to start the engine. A few seconds later we pull away.

Steve leans towards me and lowers his voice. 'If you're accusing my client of harming your daughter you'd better have bloody good evidence because—'

'I'm not accusing anyone of anything. I just want to know what happened when they met.'

He sits back in his seat. 'I told you, I wasn't there. I was in New York on business.'

The car turns a corner and there's a sign for Victoria station. I glance at my watch. Fifteen minutes until the last train leaves.

I look back at Steve. 'Can you arrange for me to speak to Alex to ask him what happened?'

'I don't think that's a good idea, do you?'

'Actually I'd—'

'Here,' he reaches into the inside pocket of his jacket and pulls out his mobile. He hands it to me.

'Put your number in. I'll speak to Alex. I'll give you a ring afterwards.'

I key in my mobile number even though I have no idea whether I can trust him or not. He makes his living from painting his clients in the most flattering light so if Alex does reveal something unsavoury he's unlikely to share it with me. In fact, it wouldn't surprise me in the least if he rang to say that he'd denied all knowledge of meeting Charlotte. If he even calls at all.

'All good?' He glances at the entry then tucks the mobile back in his jacket.

The car swings round a corner and then slows to a stop.

'Victoria,' the driver says.

Steve leans across the divide between us and holds out a hand. 'I'll be in touch,' he says as I shake it. The tiniest of frowns crosses his brow, then he sits back in his seat and pulls out his BlackBerry. I open the car door.

Friday 23rd October 1992

James kept me captive for six weeks, only leaving to visit his mother in hospital. Before he left he'd disconnect the phone and make sure that every door and window was locked. After a week, Val, my supervisor at Tescos called, asking to speak to me. I listened from the sofa as James told her I'd moved back to York because Mum's health had taken a turn for the worse. No one else called.

I realized then that James could kill me any time he wanted and no one would miss me. It became my aim each morning just to make it through the day alive. Not that James touched me again – well, apart from the time he caught me waving from the spare bedroom window, trying to catch the attention of an old lady hobbling along the street below – he beat me black and blue for that. Instead he ordered me about – telling me to sit here, stand there, get out of his way, cook his food or else completely ignored me.

He wouldn't let me read a book, watch a film or tidy my sewing room. I was only allowed to do household chores or sit silently in the middle of the hallway where he could see me from the sofa in the lounge.

Three weeks after James raped me I told him I needed to go to the chemist. He laughed in my face and said I should have worried about the clap before I slept with Steve.

'No,' I said. 'My period's a week late. I need a pregnancy test.'

I was terrified as I sat on the closed toilet seat, the pot of my urine and the small white stick on the lip of the bath beside me. Two years ago I would have been over the moon if James had got me pregnant but now I was shaking with fear. I was still clinging desperately to the hope that the memory of my 'infidelity' with Steve would fade and James would get bored of having me around and let me go. But not if I was pregnant. If I was carrying his child he'd keep me prisoner for at least nine months.

'Well?' he burst into the bathroom. I hadn't shut the door, there was no point.

I held the paddle up to him and said nothing.

'Two blue lines?' He frowned. 'What's that supposed to mean?'

'That I'm pregnant.'

I stepped up my attempt to escape the next time he left the house. The first thing I did was rip out a number for an abortion clinic from the Yellow Pages and stash it in the one thing that hadn't been destroyed when James trashed my sewing room – the secret drawer in my table. I tucked it away with my diary and my savings and then searched the house for a way out, going through every drawer, every tin, every cupboard and every wardrobe looking for something, anything to help me. It took five days before I discovered the mink coat stashed at the back of Margaret's wardrobe. I could barely breathe as my fingers stroked something small, cold and metallic in one of the pockets. A key. A door key. She hadn't been out of the house alone for years but maybe someone somewhere was smiling down on me and it would fit the front door. I didn't have a chance to find out because the front door slammed open as I closed my hands around the key. Panicking, I shut myself in the wardrobe and hid, as best I could, behind the mink coat. James's footsteps reverberated throughout the house as he climbed the stairs.

'Suzy?' he shouted. 'Suzy, where are you? I can't smell dinner cooking. Have you been watching TV all day, you lazy bitch?'

'Suzy?' The landing floorboards creaked as he crossed towards the sewing room, then again as he made his way back. 'Suzy?'

The footsteps grew louder. He was in the same room as me. I held my breath, sure my thudding heart would give me away then, 'Suzy?' James's cry was quieter, he'd gone back down the stairs.

I crept silently out of the wardrobe, pushing the key deep into my sock before I left, and hurried down the stairs.

James looked up in surprise as I burst into the

307

living room. 'Where the fuck have you been? I looked for you upstairs. You weren't there.'

'Attic.' I gestured at the dust on my cheek (swiped from the top of one of the shoeboxes in Margaret's wardrobe). 'I remembered your mum saying she'd stored your baby clothes up there and went to have a look.'

'You did what?'

'I'm sorry,' I pressed my hand to my non-existent bump. 'I just wanted to make things nice for the baby. I thought we could turn my sewing, I mean, the spare room, into a nursery. I thought it was a nice thing to do.'

'But . . .' James's face returned to its normal colour and his jaw softened, ever so slightly. 'I didn't see the step ladder. The hatch was shut.'

'I closed it,' I said, my hand still on my belly. 'I didn't want to risk tripping and falling through it. I didn't want anything to happen to the little one.'

It made me feel sick, talking like that, like we were all going to play happy families and waltz off into our perfect primrose-coloured future but the 'baby' was the only Achilles heel James had.

He looked at me for a second, his eyes flicking from my face to my belly and back again. He knew I was lying but he so desperately wanted to believe.

'Don't do it again.' He waved a hand for me to leave the room. 'What's in the attic doesn't concern you. If the baby needs anything I'll be the one that provides for it.'

'Okay.' I felt the key press into my ankle, hard and

reassuring as I turned to go, 'I'll go and get tea on then, shall I? It's turkey stir-fry tonight.'

I left the next day. I watched from the spare room window, the curtains open a millimetre, as James left for work, crossed the road and stood at the bus stop. Terror ripped through me as he glanced up at the house but then he looked away again, down the road. Thirty seconds later he stepped onto the number 13 bus and was gone.

I flew through the house, jamming clothes, toiletries, a nightie, a towel and food into a bag. I had no idea how long a private abortion would take or how long I'd have to be in the clinic. I didn't know anyone who'd had an abortion so had no idea what it would cost, never mind entail but I didn't want to think too much about the latter. I already hated myself for what I was planning on doing. As for the cost, I just had to hope that £600 would be enough to cover it and get me a cheap flight abroad because, if James ever found out what I'd done, I needed to be as far away as possible.

I was standing in the sewing room, the diary and advert in one hand, a pile of notes in the other when I heard it – the sound of a fist thumping on glass. I threw my secret spoils at my bag, tossed a paint-stained sheet over it, crept onto the landing and pressed myself up against the banister. The noise was coming from the front door. Had James come home early? I dropped to my stomach and inched my way across the landing. If I could just get to the top of the stairs I'd be able to see.

I shuffled forwards slowly, freezing each time there was another knock. I was almost there when the metallic clatter of the letter box made me jump. I peered down the stairs. A white card lay on the front mat. A 'sorry you were out' card from the gas man.

Thirty seconds later I was on my feet again, this time with my bag in one hand, the key in the other, and speeding down the stairs.

'Please,' I prayed as the tip of the key jiggled against the lock. 'Please fit, please fit, please—'

The door swung open.

I ran down the pathway and along the street and didn't look back. Not as the evil white eyes of the batik wall hanging were burning into the back of my head. Not as an upstairs window slammed shut in protest at my escape. And not when the vague memory of a yellow piece of paper fluttering to the floor of my sewing room as I tossed my diary at my bag flashed across my mind and then disappeared.

Chapter 24

'Good night?' Brian peers at me through bleary eyes as the alarm clock beep-beep-beeps 6 a.m. on the table beside him.

'Lovely, thank you.'

He yawns and stretches his arms above his head. 'What time did you get in?'

I consider lying but have no idea what time he fell asleep so can't pretend I slipped in next to him. 'It was after two.'

He raises an eyebrow. 'You weren't drinking, were you? I don't think you're allowed to take alcohol with the tablets you're on.'

'Of course not. There was a lovely late-night coffee shop just around the corner from the theatre so Jane and I had a catch up. We just lost track of time, that's all.'

Brian shifts in the bed, to get a better look at me.

My stomach churns and I look away, praying he won't cross examine me.

'Just as long as you had a good night, darling.' I feel his lips on my cheeks and then a blast of cold air as he throws back the duvet and sits up. The mattress squeaks as he stands, a floorboard creaks as he crosses the room and then there is silence.

I pull his pillow to my chest and hug it tightly. I'm getting closer to discovering what happened to Charlotte but I'm so very tired. I want to roll over, to sleep for a million years and wake up when this is all over but I can't. I can't do anything as the coma robs Charlotte of her health, her mental faculties and possibly her life.

But what can I do but wait? The path ran as far as Steve Torrance and there's nothing I can do until he calls.

I throw back the duvet and sit up.

Yes, there is.

'Sue?' Danny peers out at me from behind the front door. His face is crumpled and sleep-lined, his eyes bleary and unfocussed. 'It's eight o'clock on a Sunday morning.'

'I know.'

I don't want to be here either. I want to be in the hospital with my daughter – and I will be once we've spoken – but I have to find out what he's hiding first.

'How did you get my address?' He runs a hand

through his tousled blonde hair and his white towel-ling dressing gown slips open.

'I rang Oli.' He wasn't delighted to be woken up early either.

'Right.' Danny yawns and glances back into the apartment. 'So what can I do you for, Sue?'

'I'd like to come in if I may.'

'Um,' he pulls his dressing gown closed. 'It's not really convenient right now.'

'Keisha in, is she? It's okay, I can say what I need to say in front of her.'

Danny shifts from one foot to the other. 'She's not here.'

'Oh.' There's a pair of vertiginous black high heels scattered across the hallway. Danny turns to see what I'm looking at.

'It's not what . . .' He shakes his head. 'What's so important anyway?'

'You lied,' I say, 'about going to Greys nightclub with Charlotte and Ella. I know you were there.'

'Sue, I swear,' He holds out his palms like an innocent man surrendering, 'I wasn't there. There are a lot of malicious people in Brighton and if someone's been spreading rumours that—'

'Danny.'

'Yes?'

He's smiling, his eyebrows raised cordially, his thumbs hooked into his dressing gown pockets. Like James, he's a consummate professional when it comes to lying. I wonder what he's told the woman lying in his bed – that his relationship with Keisha is over, that they're just casual, that they have an open relationship? And what of Keisha? What lies has he told her so she doesn't suspect that he's sleeping around?

'No one told me anything, Danny. The police accessed the CCTV footage that Greys have of that night. I saw you enter the club.'

'The police . . .' He searches my face but I maintain my composure. Two can play at this game.

'Just tell me what happened, Danny.'

He steps back into the hall. 'You'd better come in.'

Fifteen minutes later and I'm back on the doorstep, this time saying goodbye.

'It wasn't my fault,' Danny says again. 'Ella over-heard me and Keish talking about going to Greys and she and Charlotte turned up on the same train as us on Saturday night. I tried telling them to go back to Brighton but Ella said—'

'That she'd report you for letting underage girls drink in Breeze.' He's already told me this. Several times.

'Exactly.' He crosses his arms, tucking his hands under his armpits.

'But why Greys? Why follow you there?'

'Because it's glamorous?' He shrugs. 'Because you see pics of celebs falling out of it in all the papers? Because Ella's got a crush on me?'

'A crush?'

'Yeah, Charlotte told Keisha about it. I think that was part of the reason they all fell out – because

Ella heard me talking to a mate about going to Greys and she got the impression that Keisha wasn't coming and thought that if she turned up in a miniscule dress and a load of slap,' he smirks, 'that she could pull me.'

I look again at the pair of high heels in the hallway. How old is the woman in his bed? 'And did you?'

'Shag Ella? Are you fucking kidding me?'

'You let her into your club.'

'Look Sue,' he holds his hands wide. 'I let the girls into Breeze because of Charlotte. She's my best mate's little sister and she's as good as family.'

'So you'd encourage your sister to drink if she was underage, would you?'

'No, of course not—' He becomes very still, very composed. It's as though a shutter falls over his face. 'You can blame me all you want for what happened to Charlotte, but she's not my kid. Where did you think she was when she was out until two or three in the morning? Playing hopscotch? What kind of mum doesn't know where their daughter is at that time of night?'

I reel as though slapped.

'Sorry, but I won't have you paint me as some kind of paedo just because I let my mate's little sister and her best friend into my club.'

I can't speak. I'm too stunned by his previous remark to reply.

He's right. I hate to admit it but he is. Where *did* I think Charlotte was on a Saturday night?

I know exactly what I thought – that she was

staying in London in an over-priced YMCA hostel with her classmates and several of her teachers from school. 'Did you meet him?' I ask. 'Did you meet Alex Henri?'

He shakes his head. 'I didn't go into the VIP enclosure. I didn't stay that long. Charlotte, Keisha and Ella all got pissed and then had an argument. Keisha was swaying all over the place and slurring her words, accusing me of secretly fancying Ella, saying I'd invited her along so we could have a threesome. Which was bollocks, I should add.' He shrugs. 'So I left.'

'You left all three of them in the club?'

'Yeah. Keisha's not a kid and I figured if the other two were old enough to get a train to London they were old enough to get one back. Like I said, I didn't invite them along.'

'But they were only fifteen, in a club with men twice their age.'

'Do I look like a fucking child-minder?'

'Danny, I hardly think—' I'm interrupted by the sound of a phone ringing. 'Hang on a second.'

I fish my mobile out of my handbag. I don't recognize the number.

'Hello, Sue Jackson speaking.'

'Hello Sue, it's Steve. Steve Torrance.' For a split second I have no idea who I'm speaking to then I remember.

'How are you?'

'So I spoke to Al . . .' I gird myself, waiting for the inevitable denial.

'He says he did go into the loos with your girl but nothing happened. The plan was for her to give him a blow job but she got stage fright. Burst into tears and said she couldn't go through with it. Told Alex some fella was blackmailing her. Got into a right state, he said. He didn't know what to do so he left her there, in the ladies' and went back to his mates. After that he didn't see her again.'

'She . . .' I step backwards, grasping at the air but there's nothing to hold onto, nothing to steady myself with. 'She was being blackmailed?'

'That's what he said.' He sighs. 'Look darlin', I don't know how well you and your daughter get on but if she was my kid I wouldn't let her hang out with pimps and prostitutes, not if she doesn't want to be taken for a whore herself.'

'A prostitute?' I fight to steady my voice. Danny is staring at me, his eyes wide with curiosity, but I don't care. I feel like I'm in a play speaking someone else's words. 'My daughter was mistaken for a prostitute by Alex Henri?'

'No one's saying anything about Alex using prostitutes, you hear me? No money was exchanged between Charlotte and Al, and if you try and sell a story to the papers that he tried to bed a hooker in the bogs of Greys I'll slap a lawsuit on you faster than Red Rum ended up in a dog food factory.'

Danny frowns and crosses his arms over his chest.

'What did they look like?' I ask. 'These . . . people . . . she was with?'

'How should I know?' Steve yawns loudly down

the phone. 'What do you want? A fucking photofit? Al just said something about a guy and a fit black girl.'

'Did he mention either of their names?'

'Pinky and Perky. I've got no fucking idea. He didn't say and I didn't ask. Look love,' his voice takes on a new steely tone. 'This is all very lovely, having a nice little chat with you but I'm a busy man. We made an agreement and I've kept my end of the bargain. The question is – are you?'

'What?'

'Going to the police? Not that you've got a leg to stand on because, as my client said, he didn't lay a finger on your daughter.'

'No,' I say. 'I'm not.'

The phone goes dead.

'You alright, Sue?' Danny asks.

'Who're you talking to, Dan?' A heart-shaped face framed by a mass of blonde curls pokes around a door halfway down the corridor. 'Come back to bed, I'm getting cold!' Her eyes meet mine. 'Oh shit, is that your mum?'

'It's not what you think—' Danny starts as she disappears back into the bedroom but I hold up a warning hand.

'I don't care who you're sleeping with, Danny.'

'Cool.'

'Just one thing before I go.'

'Yeah.'

I could confront him. I could tell him that, unless he tells me the truth about what happened in Greys that night I'm going to tell the police that he's a pimp but there's a quicker way to find out what I need to know.

'I'd like your girlfriend's address, please.'

Chapter 25

'Keisha?' I prod the letterbox with my fingers and force it open. 'Keisha, are you in there?'

A shadow crosses the wall at the far end of the seafront basement flat and a seagull squawks overhead.

'Keisha, it's Sue Jackson, Charlotte's mum. I really need to talk to you.'

The shadow grows longer.

'Keisha?'

I hear a floorboard squeak then, 'Are you alone?'

'Yes.'

A foot appears from the shadows, the toes painted pink, a silver chain shining around the ankle, then the rest of Keisha appears. She's wearing a short pink nightdress with a Disney cartoon on the front with a thin grey cotton dressing gown hanging from her shoulders. Her hair is wild and frizzy and, make-up free, she looks impossibly young. I let go of the letterbox as she draws near and stand up. The door opens a second later.

'Sue! What are you doing here?'

'Danny gave me your address. I just wanted to see how you were doing.'

'Oh.' She looks delighted and worried at the same time. 'That's very kind of you. Come in.'

I follow her into the living room and, when she tells me to sit down, I sink into a black leather armchair. Keisha crosses the room to the window and reaches for the blinds. For a second I think she's going to open them – it's a beautiful day outside – instead she parts two slats with her fingers and peers outside.

'Did anyone see you, Sue? Come here, I mean.'

'Not that I noticed. Why?'

'No matter.'

She lets go of the blinds, jumping as the slats clack back together and rubs her hands over her arms. She looks cold but her basement flat is boiling. I've already removed my coat and cardigan.

'Would you like a cup of tea, Sue?'

'No, thank you, I just—' but she's already gone, padding along the carpet towards the tiny galley kitchen at the other end of the flat.

'Keisha.' I go after her. 'Is everything okay?'

She glances towards the front door then motions for me to step into the kitchen and shut the door behind me. As I turn to pull it to I hear the swish of curtains being pulled and the room dims.

'Keisha, what is it?' She moves from the curtains

to the counter and reaches for the kettle. She fills it and turns it on then reaches into a cupboard and starts rummaging around.

'Where's the damned tea? Ester better not have used up the last of it.'

I stand silently by the door as she moves jars, cans and packets from one side of the cupboard to the other then begins lining them up on the counter.

'It's okay,' I say as her movements become more frenzied. 'I don't need a tea. Coffee would be fine.'

'Fuck!'

A jam jar tumbles from the cupboard, it hits a glass which rolls off the counter and explodes onto the tiled flooring showering Keisha's bare feet with a thousand tiny shards.

'Fuck!' She hops backwards but there's nowhere to escape in such a small kitchen and a large piece of glass sinks into her heel.

'Have you got a first-aid box?' I ask as she stares in horror at the blood pooling around her foot.

She shakes her head.

'Clean tea towel?'

She points at a drawer to the right of the sink.

'Antiseptic cream?'

'There might be some in the bathroom cabinet.'

Fifteen minutes later and we're back in the living room, Keisha is in the armchair, her injured foot dressed as best I could in a clean *Coronation Street* tea towel and raised on a couple of stacked Amazon boxes I found in the backyard.

'I appreciate your help, Sue,' she says as I perch beside her, 'but I'm not going to A&E.'

'But it's a deep cut.' I think of the pool of blood I mopped up in the kitchen and the deep laceration in the sole of her left foot. 'You might need stitches. It's stopped bleeding but the second you put your foot down and your circulation returns you could be in all kinds of trouble.'

'I already am.'

'Sorry?'

She glances away. 'Nothing.'

'I've got my car,' I gesture towards the window and the street outside. 'It wouldn't be any trouble. It would only take—'

'I told you I'm fine.'

'Keisha, I couldn't forgive myself I left you here and—'

'I'm not going to the fucking hospital!'

Neither of us say anything for a couple of minutes. I twist my hands in my lap and stare around the living room – at the ugly gas fire, the vase of wilting roses above it, the mountain of DVDs stacked up by the television next to a framed photo of a woman I don't recognize standing in front of Buckingham Palace. Is that her flatmate?

'I'm sorry, Sue.' Keisha raises her face to look at me. 'You didn't deserve me to swear that.' She glances at the blinds and slips lower in her seat.

'Is everything okay?' I glance towards the window too but see nothing, 'you seem a bit jumpy today.'

'Do I?' She laughs. 'I'm just a bit clumsy that's

all. You ask Danny. I'm forever dropping and breaking things. It's a surprise I didn't brain myself sooner.'

'Anyway,' she pushes her hair back from her face. 'How are you, Sue?'

'I'm okay.' I reach for my cardigan and pull it into my lap. Without a cup of tea to hang onto I need something to do with my hands. 'Keisha, why would someone accuse you of being a prostitute?'

I expect her to gasp in protestation. Instead she reaches for a cigarette and lights it. She inhales deeply but her hands don't stop shaking.

'Does he know?' Her voice is so quiet I can barely hear her.

'Who?'

'Danny.' She looks at me, her eyes wide and beautiful and brimming with tears. 'Have you told him?'

'Danny?' I shake my head. 'I . . . I don't understand. I thought he was your pimp.'

'My pimp. You're kidding me, right?' She gives a little laugh. 'Danny thinks I'm an angel. That's what he calls me – his precious, perfect angel. Can you imagine what he'd call me if he knew what I do,' she covers herself, 'what I *did*.'

'Did?'

'I gave it all up when I met him. I don't want to work behind the bar in the club but it's the only way I can pay my rent ever since . . .'

'Ever since what?'

'Nothing.'

'It's not nothing.' I look at the cigarette quivering

between her fingers. 'What happened? Why were you so scared to answer the door just now? And why were you so jumpy outside the club the other night?'

She glances looks down at her hands. There's bruising around her wrists. She catches me looking.

'It wasn't Danny if that's what you're thinking.'

I stand up from the sofa and crouch down beside her. The bruises on her wrists are purple, perfectly-shaped fingerprints. Whoever attacked her had a strong grip.

'Who did this? A client? Your pimp?'

'I told you,' she looks up angrily. 'I'm not on the game anymore. I love Danny and I'd die if he found out. If he left me I don't know what I'd do. I'm nothing without him.'

She sounds like me twenty years ago.

'I'm sorry, Keisha.' She flinches as I gently touch her arm. 'I didn't mean to upset you but someone's hurt you and they need to be stopped before they do it again. Have you been to the police?'

She shakes her head.

'Would you like me to come with you?' Just the thought of stepping into a police station makes me feel sick but she needs my support, even if I can only make it as far as the entrance.

'No.'

'But you'll go? Alone if you have to?'

'No. I can't go to the police.'

'Why?'

'It doesn't matter.' She attempts to stand up, groaning as her injured foot touches the carpet. I try to help her but she waves me away and I trail behind as she hobbles into the kitchen and opens the fridge.

'Wine?'

When I shake my head she pulls out a bottle, unscrews the lid, swallows down a couple of large mouthfuls and then grabs an oversized glass from the rack beside the sink.

'I don't want you to get involved, Sue,' she says as she empties the bottle into the glass. 'I've already told you too much.'

'You haven't told me anything.'

'Best we leave it that way.'

'Keisha,' I say as we return to the living room and she lowers herself into the armchair and hooks her leg over the armrest, 'if you're not on the game why would someone tell me that you were in Greys night-club with your pimp?'

She looks at me for a couple of seconds as though deciding what to say.

'Who told you I was a prostitute?' she says finally.

'Steve Torrance. Alex Henri's agent.'

She raises an eyebrow. 'That makes sense.'

'What do you mean?'

'I've known a few footballers.'

'Known?'

'Fucked.' She looks me straight in the eye. 'For money. When I was a whore and lived in London.'

I don't know what to say. Despite her feisty tone she looks uncomfortable and I'm still no closer to understanding what happened to Charlotte. I don't want to hurt Keisha more than she's already suffering but I can't walk out of here without uncovering the truth.

'I don't understand,' I shake my head. 'Danny told me he left the club before you and Charlotte met Alex Henri which suggests he didn't go into the VIP section.'

'That's right.'

'So who did Steve Torrance think was your pimp?'

Keisha glances towards the window again.

'What is it? You don't know or you can't tell me?'

She says nothing.

I look at her, taking in the beautiful almond shape of her eyes, her full sensuous mouth and slim lithe body and I wonder what terrible trauma forced her to sell herself to make a living. She's so stunning she could be a model or a television presenter and yet she values herself so little she'd let anyone with money have her body and a man who doesn't really love her steal her heart. I could tell her a hundred times over that she's worth more but I know she'd never believe me.

'Have you ever been blackmailed, Sue?' She speaks no louder than a whisper.

I shake my head. 'Is that what's happening to you? Someone who knows you used to be a prostitute is threatening to tell people? Threatening to tell Danny.'

She nods and a single tear rolls down her cheek.

'What did they make you do, Keisha?'

She shakes her head.

'Was it sexual?'

She nods minutely.

I inch forward so I'm sitting on the very edge of the sofa. 'Was he a client?'

She nods again.

'What's his name?'

I stare at her lips as she mouths a word.

'Mike.'

'Mike what? Do you know his surname?'

'No.'

'What did he want in return for keeping your secret, Keisha?'

'I can't tell you.' She covers her face with her hands and starts to cry.

'Charlotte,' I say, and it's as though someone has poured ice into my veins. 'Did it have something to do with Charlotte?'

Keisha howls in anguish.

'Tell me.' I grab her hands and gently pull them away from her face. 'Tell me what you did. Tell me what he made you do.'

'No.' She slaps my hands away and clamps them back to her face. 'No, no, no, no, no. I can't. I can't.'

'Keisha, please.' She knows. She knows what happened to Charlotte.

'I can't.' I can barely make out her words between sobs. 'He'll kill me. He said if I breathed a word to anyone he'd hunt me down and—'

She's interrupted by the sound of my phone ringing. I snatch it out of my bag ready to end the call without even answering it but it's Mum's care home.

328

'Hello?' I put a hand on Keisha's shoulder – partly to reassure her, partly to let her know I'm not about to drop the subject. 'Sue Jackson speaking.'

'Hello Sue,' says the voice on the other end of the line. 'This is Mary. It's about your mother. I'm afraid I've got some bad news.'

Chapter 26

'I should have been there.' I dissolve into tears, my face buried in the crook of Brian's neck. It's the third time this morning I've broken down and it's only 9 a.m. 'I should have been the one to hold her hand, not a stranger.'

Brian wraps an arm around my shoulders and pulls me close. 'It wasn't a stranger,' he says softly. 'It was Mary. She looked after her for a very long time.'

'But I'm her daughter.' I barely recognize the sound of my own voice it's so thin and wretched. 'And I wasn't there for her when she needed me most.'

'Sssh.' He strokes my hair and lets me cry onto his shoulder. 'Sssh, sssh, sssh.'

Sobs continue to wrack my body but I'm soothed by the pressure of his hand on my head and the soft sound of his voice in my ear. It reminds me of scooping Charlotte up when she was a toddler and had a nasty fall or bump. I'd press her to me and stroke her hair until her tears dried up.

'That's it,' Brian says as I shift in his arms so I can press a tissue to my nose. 'We don't want to upset Charlotte, do we?'

We're in the hospital. I asked Brian to drive me straight here after I'd visited the care home. I was terrified of leaving Charlotte alone in case she died too.

'There's nothing you could have done,' Brian says as he helps me into the chair next to Charlotte's bed and presses a box of tissues into my lap. 'It was too sudden, Mary said.'

She said the same to me. One minute Mum was right as rain, shuffling her way from the dining room to her bedroom with Mary at her side, propping up her elbow, and the next she was a crumpled heap on the floor. 'She just collapsed,' Mary said. 'There were no signs, no warning at all, she just went.' A doctor was called but, even though he arrived within ten minutes it was too late. She'd already gone.

I couldn't, wouldn't believe it. Mum was lying on her duvet in her grey tweed skirt, white blouse and beige cardigan. When I gently stroked her cheek I was shocked to find she was still warm.

'Quick!' I stared up at Mary. 'Get the doctor back. There's been a mistake. She's still warm.' I stood up and put a hand on Mum's chest. 'Do you know CPR? It might not be too late.'

'Sue.' Mary put a hand on my shoulder. 'She's dead. I'm sorry.'

'But . . .' I looked at Mum's cheek, expecting it to twitch in her sleep, to see a thin line of drool winding its way down from her open mouth to her jawbone, but I saw nothing. She was utterly still. That's when I accepted that she was dead. Not because her mouth was closed and her hands were crossed over her chest but because the room was too still, too quiet, even with Mary and I talking. I'd never seen Mum so peaceful before.

'She'll be warm for a little while longer,' Mary said softly. 'They don't go cold until about eight hours after they've passed.'

'Can I hold her hand?'

She nodded her head and I lifted my mother's hand from the duvet, cradling its sparrow's weight.

'I'll leave you alone,' Mary said, 'I'll be in the office if there's anything you need.' And then she was gone.

I don't know how long I stayed in that room – ten minutes or ten hours – but it wasn't long enough. Even after I'd said my goodbyes, even after I'd told Mum everything I wished I'd told her when she was alive, even after I'd run out of things to say and sat there with my head nestled into her side, her hand still in mine, it still wasn't enough time. I wanted to stay there forever because I knew, the second I stepped out of that tiny eight by six room, that I'd never see her again.

At some point Mary appeared with a cup of tea. She pressed it wordlessly into my hands and made to move off but I called after her.

'Yes?' She turned back.

'She didn't have any visitors, did she? Mother.

Her . . . nephew didn't come back after the last time?'

She shook her head. 'Your mother hasn't had any visitors since you were last here. Were you expecting someone?'

Relief flooded through me. 'No. No one.'

'Have you told her?' Brian presses a polystyrene cup into my hands and glances at Charlotte. 'About her Nan?'

'No,' I take a sip of boiling tea, my eyes on my daughter's sleeping face, 'I want her to wake up thinking the world is a beautiful, safe place, not somewhere dark and sad.'

'It's not all darkness and sadness,' Brian says, 'though I understand why you'd say that given what's happened but the world doesn't have to be . . .'

I stop listening. Charlotte's too afraid to wake up. I know she is. I've felt sure ever since I was told about the accident and now I know why. I was *so close* to finding out more about her blackmailer yesterday but then Mary rang and I sped off in my car leaving Keisha peering out through the front room blinds. I couldn't tell if she was relieved I was leaving, or scared.

I've texted her four times since I left yesterday and called twice but I haven't had a reply. I tried again, about five minutes ago, but her phone went straight to voicemail. I'm sure there's a rational explanation – the ankle, an extended trip to A&E, changing her mind about going to the police – but it doesn't matter which excuse I feed myself, I still can't unknot the tight twist in my stomach. Something's happened. Something terrible.

'What's up?'

I jump at the sound of Brian's voice.

'You're not still blaming yourself for what happened to your mum, are you?'

I shake my head but I'm astonished at how insightful he can be. Right sentiment, wrong person.

'I need to go,' I say. 'There's something very important I need to do.'

Brian nods and reaches for his newspaper. 'Your mum would be proud of you, Sue.'

'And you're quite sure?' I say into the phone as I park outside Keisha's flat and turn off the engine. 'You're quite sure that's she's gone to Ireland?'

'You tell me.' Danny sounds irritated. 'You were the last one to see her. What the hell did you say?'

I can't work out if he's genuinely concerned or worried that I told her about his infidelity with the blonde.

'Nothing.'

'You promised me, Sue. When I gave you Keisha's address you promised me you wouldn't say anything.'

'I know, and I didn't.' And not because of any misplaced sense of loyalty to him. 'How did she sound the last time you spoke to her?'

'We didn't speak. She texted about midnight last night to say she was going back to Ireland for a bit because she was homesick. I was asleep and didn't get the message until this morning. I tried ringing her but she wouldn't pick up. I've rung three more times since . . .' he tails off. 'I've tried the bar manager, her mates and her flatmate but no one knows anything. None of them have seen her since you did. Are you sure you didn't accidentally let something slip?'

'No,' it comes out curter than I meant it to. 'You weren't even mentioned, Danny.'

That's a lie, but I'm not about to tell him *why* Keisha mentioned his name or what it was in reference to.

There are no lights on in her flat and the blinds in the living room are still drawn. I crouch down, holding onto the flowerpot by the front door for support and peer through the letter box. The concrete makes my knees ache.

'But—' Danny says.

'I'm sure she'll be in touch,' I reply as a shadow crosses the hallway and my heart leaps with relief. 'And if I hear from her I'll let you know.'

'Will you?' He sounds genuinely desperate. 'I'd appreciate that.'

I tuck my phone back into my handbag and peer through the stained-glass panels in the door.

'Keisha?' I knock heavily. 'Keisha, it's Sue again.'

There's no reply.

I wait a few seconds then knock again. I'm just about to shout through the letter box when the door opens an inch and a face I don't recognize peers out at me.

'Hello?' says a woman with a violent red bob and a blunt fringe. I immediately recognize her from the photograph in the front room. She stares up at me with big, critical green eyes, her long tangerine-coloured fingernails wrapped around the door. 'Can I help you?'

'You must be Keisha's flatmate?' I glance into the hallway. 'Is she in?'

She shakes her head. 'She's gone.'

I detect something unusual about her accent, an intonation that isn't English. Polish perhaps. 'Do you know where?'

'Ireland.'

Maybe Danny was right. Maybe she has pulled a disappearing act. 'Do you know when she left?'

Her flatmate shakes her head. 'No. She left a note. On the fridge. It just says "Gone to Dublin", that's it.'

'Would you mind if I popped into her room before I go?' I say as a thought strikes me. 'I lent her a book that I need back quite urgently.'

She gives me a look. 'You tell me the name. I find it.'

'Well, the thing is I also need . . .' I don't know what to say. I need to see Keisha's room. I don't know what I'm expecting to see but, no matter how many people tell me she's gone back to Ireland, I can't shake the feeling that something has happened to her, '. . . to look for another book,' I finish weakly. 'There was one she recommended to me but I can't remember the title. She did describe it to me though so I'm sure I'll be able to find it really easily. I'll be in and out in less than a minute, I swear.'

The flatmate looks me up and down. 'Who are you?'

'Sue. Sue Jackson.'

She shakes her head and closes the door ever so slightly. 'Keisha never mentioned you before.'

'That's because we've only recently become friends. She's knows my daughter better. Charlotte, perhaps you've met her?'

'Charlotte?' Her face lights up. 'Pretty Charlotte who get hit by a bus?'

'Yes,' I say. 'That's my daughter.'

'Oh gosh.' Compassion floods her face and she throws the door open wide. 'Of course you must come in. Anything I can do to help you let me know.'

On first glance Keisha's room doesn't look all that dissimilar from Charlotte's. There are photos of half naked men on the walls, the chest of drawers is crowded with perfume bottles, hair products and make-up and clothes are strewn over every available surface. Unlike Charlotte's room there's a clothes horse in the corner, decorated with drying underwear – bras, knickers, basques, suspenders – in every conceivable fabric, colour and cut. It makes my drawer of M&S five packs and lace-trimmed black and white bras look positively pensionable.

'She's so messy,' her flatmate, who introduced herself as Ester five minutes ago, comments from behind me. 'She never do the washing up, always leaving cups and plates in living room but I like live with her.'

Keisha's room looks like an explosion in a clothes factory but there's a suitcase and several overnight-type bags stuffed on the top of the wardrobe and her hairbrush, deodorant can, perfume bottles and black satin make-up bag – with pencils, lipsticks and concealers spilling out – are fighting for space on the top of her chest of drawers.

I look at Ester. 'Is her toothbrush still in the bathroom?'

She raises her eyebrows. 'You want to borrow that too?'

'No, but it doesn't look like Keisha has packed anything for her trip home and I was wondering if she left her toothbrush.'

The look on Ester's face changes from bemused to worried. 'I check the bathroom.'

Whilst she's gone I step through the magazines, bills, bank statements and clothing on the floor and approach her chest of drawers. I glance back towards the hallway then yank open the top drawer. More paperwork and bills. I slide them to one side and discover a rabbit-shaped vibrator, several tangled necklaces, a broken watch and a pair of hair straighteners. I feel like a burglar ransacking her things but I need to . . . ah! I swoop down on something maroon and leathered, peeping out from beneath an old Christmas card.

'What you doing?' Ester stares at me from the doorway, a blue toothbrush in her hand, a horrified expression on her face.

'It's Keisha's passport.' I pull the book from the drawer and flick through it, looking for the date stamp and photo then hold it towards Ester. 'Look, it doesn't expire for three years. How would she get back to Ireland without it? You can't get in with just a driving licence these days.'

'But . . .' She shakes her head. 'Why say she go home in her note?'

'I don't know.' I look at the toothbrush in her hand. 'But wherever she did go, she went there in a hurry.'

Chapter 27

'Alright, Mrs Jackson,' Ella doesn't look the slightest bit surprised to see me as she opens her front door. 'Mum's in the back. Want me to get her?'

I shake my head. 'Actually it was you I was hoping to talk to. Is there somewhere we can go?'

'Let's go to the park.' She glances back into the hall. 'I'll just grab my coat.'

The front door closes and I hear her shout something about popping to the corner shop and then she reappears in front of me, a crisp ten-pound note in her hand.

She grins. 'Mum asked me to get her some fags while I was out.'

'If this is about the phone,' Ella says as we sit down on a weather-worn bench on the edge of Queen's Park, 'then you're wrong if you think I nicked it. I didn't. I only had it because me and Charlotte had

340

a row at school, in the changing rooms after a games lesson. It was a couple of days before, you know . . .'

'Her accident?'

'Yeah. She left it behind on the bench when she called me a jealous cow and stormed off. I thought I'd keep it for a bit and make her freak out that she'd lost it but then she got hit by a bus.' She peels the cellophane off her mother's Marlboro Lights, tears off the foil and prises out a cigarette with her fingernails. 'I didn't want to give it to you because everyone would think I'd nicked it so I kept quiet. But then the stuff you said to me made me feel really guilty so I, you know . . .'

'Posted it through our letterbox?'

'Yeah.'

'Thank you, Ella,' I smile. 'Really, thank you for telling the truth and giving the phone back. But that's not why I'm here.'

She raises her eyebrows. 'Really?'

'Yes, I need to know who Mike is.'

'Mike?' She blinks as the wind changes direction and her exhaled smoke is blown back in her face. 'How'd you know about him?'

'Keisha told me.'

'Oh.' She rolls her eyes. 'That figures.'

'What does that mean?'

'Nothing.' She puts the cigarette to her lips again and inhales. She smokes like a fifty-year-old grandmother on forty a day.

'Come on Ella, it's not nothing.'

She tips back her head and exhales. 'They're just

dicks, that's all. Both of them. No wonder they hang around together.'

I frown. 'He's her friend?'

'That or her minder.' She laughs. 'The only time they're not together is when Keisha's with Danny and that's because he refuses to have him anywhere near him. He thinks Mike's a creepy gay, which he is.'

'A gay?' I assume she means that in the derogatory sense.

'Yeah,' she glances at me, 'you know, he likes men.'

What? That contradicts what Keisha told me last night. How can Mike have used a female prostitute and be a gay man? It doesn't make sense. I look at the packet of cigarettes in Ella's hands. There's nothing I'd like more than to spark one up. Instead I cross my arms against the wind, tucking my hands under my armpits. 'How well did Charlotte know him?'

'Pretty bloody well!' She gives me a sideways look. 'You know, don't you? That's what this is all about? You're pretending like you're clueless but actually you're trying to catch me out.'

'Something like that . . .' I say tentatively, knowing my lie could be discovered in a heartbeat.

'Oh, thank God!' She throws her spent cigarette at the ground then slumps back on the bench. 'I thought about telling you, after what we talked about the last time you came round but Charlotte made me swear not to tell anyone. I mean, I know we're not friends anymore but I'm no grass.'

'I think this is a pretty unique situation, don't you,

Ella? Grassing someone up to their parents is a bit different if they're on life support, right?'

'Yeah.' Her head drops and she fiddles with the toggles on her coat.

'Tell me what you know,' I say softly.

'Neither of us liked Mike the first time Keisha introduced him to us,' she says. 'He was old and overly friendly and there was something really sly about his eyes.'

I nod for her to continue.

'But, after Keisha went off to find Danny, Mike offered to buy us some drinks. We thought he was on the pull, dirty old git, so figured we'd get the most expensive cocktails we could out of him before we did a runner. I had a . . .' she dismisses the thought with a wave of her hand, 'doesn't matter what we had but while we were drinking them Mike started telling us how he was new to Brighton. He said he'd moved here from London to make a fresh start after splitting up with his boyfriend and losing his niece Martha to cancer. He said he really loved her, said she was like a daughter to him and that Charlotte reminded him of her. I thought that was a bit creepy but Charlotte thought it was sweet.'

That's my daughter, always thinking the best of people.

'So,' Ella licks her lips then pops another cigarette into her mouth, 'once we'd finished the cocktails I gave Charlotte a look like "let's get out of here" but she ignored me and kept on talking to Mike. He bought us some more drinks and they kept talking – about his niece and his job as a photographer – which Charlotte thought was way cool – for ages. I thought we were going to spend the rest of the night chatting to his Royal Gayness,' she shoots me a look. 'Sorry, but he wasn't bothered about talking to me, just her. Anyway, I only managed to drag her away when 'Love it When You Lie' came on and we went for a dance.'

'Did you see him again?'

She shakes her head. 'Not that night, no. But he was there the next time we went. Keisha wasn't there that time and he just strolled up and said hello.'

'So Charlotte and Mike became friends?'

'Yeah.' She shrugs. 'That's part of the reason why we fell out, the fact that she was getting all these new friends and hanging around premiership footballers in Greys and I felt like I wasn't good enough for her anymore, like she was really up herself. I called her on it but she said she was just living her life and that it was cool to have a gay friend and that Mike was funny and gave her good advice on clothes and stuff.'

'Clothes?' A sick feeling rises from my stomach as I imagine my daughter in a changing room, parading around half naked in front of a man she barely knows. 'What do you mean he gave her advice on clothes?'

'He took her shopping.' Ella pulls a face. 'I know, I was totally jealous, I'm not even going to lie. He must have spent hundreds of pounds on her and got her all designer stuff – the proper labels and everything, not reject stuff from TK Maxx. It wasn't just clothes either – he got her sunglasses, CDs, DVDs,

344

loads of shit. Said it made him happy, like he was still buying stuff for Martha.'

Ella's face is animated as she continues to describe, in minute detail, everything 'Mike' bought for my daughter. I recognize some of the descriptions – I saw them in Charlotte's room and bought her explanation that they were fakes from a market stall at a car boot or love tokens from Liam – others I've never seen. The story is plausible enough, a recently bereaved single gay man in a city where he knows no one spots the doppelganger of his dead niece and showers her with presents in return for her company and yet, why do I feel like the temperature just dropped twenty degrees?

'What does Mike look like, Ella?'

She shrugs. 'Old.'

'How old? As old as me?'

Ella screws up her eyes and scrutinizes me. 'Probably, yeah.'

'What else?'

'He was just a bloke, an old bloke with grey in his hair, like any old bloke you see in the street.'

'Think . . . please, it's important. How tall was he? Was he fat or thin? What kind of clothes did he wear? He did wear any jewellery? What were his shoes like? Did he have a moustache, beard, glasses?'

'Like I said,' she twists in her seat and gazes across the park at a bunch of teenagers swinging back and forward on the children's swings, 'he just looked normal, apart from being really tall.' She looks back at me. 'He was probably about the same height as my dad.'

So he was about six foot four. 'What else?'

'He always looked smart – dark trousers and a shirt, that sort of thing. I never saw him in jeans. I don't remember what shoes he wore.' She glances back at the teenagers. 'He had a watch, I think.'

'And his build?'

She sighs. 'Medium. He wasn't fat and he wasn't thin. And he didn't wear glasses or have a moustache or beard,' she adds before I can ask. 'Oh yeah . . .' she puts her feet up on the bench and hugs her knees. 'His eyes were a really odd colour, kind of grey-ish and he had quite a big nose and a strange accent. Birmingham? Liverpool? I'm rubbish with accents but he definitely wasn't from round here. That okay?' She looks back at me but I can't meet her gaze. I can't tear my eyes away from the teenagers at the other end of the park. She's just described James, twenty years after I last set eyes on him.

'Sue?' Out of my peripheral vision I can see Ella unclasping her legs. 'You okay? You look weird.'

I was wrong about the school teacher Jamie Evans, but I'm not wrong about this. I can feel it in my bones, the marrow-deep certainty that, somewhere in Brighton and Hove, my ex-boyfriend is watching and laughing, proud of his newest role – bereaved gay man – delighted that he managed to wheedle his way into my daughter's life right under my nose.

'Did he ever touch her?' I snap round to look at Ella. 'Did he hurt Charlotte in any way?'

'Why would he? I just told you, he bought her loads of stuff. He treated her like a princess.'

'What was he blackmailing her about?'

'Blackmailing her?' She shakes her head. 'Charlotte never said anything about that. Mike acted like he worshipped the ground she walked on – little miss "My dead niece".'

'Have you got his number? Or his address?'

'No. Liam will though.'

'Liam?'

'Yeah,' she looks at the surprised expression on my face and laughs, 'Charlotte wasn't going to have sex on her own in Mike's flat, was she?'

Chapter 28

'Sue?' I can hear the concern in Brian's voice. 'Where on earth are you? You've been gone for hours.'

'I'm sorry,' I turn off the engine. All the curtains are open in Liam's house but there's no movement beyond any of the windows. 'I got caught up at the funeral home.'

'Really?' The change in the tone of his voice is immediate. 'Is that why they rang up to offer their condolences and ask when we'd like to come in?'

'I . . .' My brain scrabbles for a way out. 'I haven't been there yet.'

'Obviously.'

'I went for a walk along the beach instead. To clear my head.'

'For three hours?'

'Yes, three hours.' There's something about his tone that irritates me. 'My mother just died for God's sake, Brian! Is there a time limit on grief? Was there a

348

motion passed in Parliament that you didn't tell me about?'

It's unfair but lashing out is easier than lying, even when it's not deserved. And I'm so close to finding out what happened to Charlotte.

Brian says nothing for a very long time and I'm just about to take the phone from my ear to check whether he's ended the call when—

'Tell me where you are and I'll come and collect you.'

He may as well have offered me the other cheek.

'There's no need. Really. I brought the car.'

'Then I'll join you. We'll get a coffee. Have a talk.'

There's a cough to my left and I remember that I'm not alone. Ella is tapping away at her phone like her life depends on it but I can tell by the hunch of her shoulders and the fact her body's angled away from me that she finds this whole situation hideously awkward. And who can blame her? I asked her to come along to convince Liam to tell me the truth, not to bear witness to my marital problems.

'I don't want any company, Brian,' I say and then I realize that's exactly why he's checking up on me. He's not trying to control me, he's worried. My mother has just died, he thinks I'm suffering from depressive anxiety and post-traumatic stress disorder and I'm insisting he leave me alone. He probably thinks I'm about to do a Sylvia Plath and walk into the sea.

'I'm sorry,' I soften my voice. 'I know you're just trying to look after me but this is something I need to get through on my own and—'

'But—'

'Not forever, just today. I just need to get through today on my own. I'll be back by this evening. Please, Brian. Please trust me.'

'Of course I trust you, Sue. I just don't want you to—'

'I'm not going to do anything silly,' I say, even though I know there's every chance I might do the opposite, depending on what Liam has to say. But I don't feel silly. I feel like I'm regaining control of my life, twenty years too late. 'Please Brian, I need to do this.'

'Okay,' he says. 'I understand. Just . . . please don't stay out too late. Don't make me worry unnecessarily.'

My heart twists in my chest. He is a good man. Despite everything he's a good man and I'm lucky to have him in my life.

'I love you, Brian.'

Ella squirms in her seat but I don't care.

'I love you too, Sue. Take care of yourself, okay and I'll see you later.'

I end the call but I don't immediately turn to Ella. Instead I stare out of the windscreen, at the thin blue line of sea on the horizon and I say a small prayer. Not to God, the Universe or anyone in particular but I ask for strength, courage and protection for my family. I ask for a twenty-year nightmare to be over.

'Can I put the radio on,' Ella asks, reaching towards the CD player, 'if you're just going to sit there and be weird. I can't stand it when it's quiet.'

I smile. 'No need. We're going to go and see Liam now and I hope you'll do the talking.'

If Liam's older sister was surprised to see his girlfriend's mum and ex-best friend standing on the doorstep, she didn't let on. Instead she pointed in the direction of Lewes Road and told us that he and Last Fight, his band, were rehearsing. She didn't know what time they'd finish but suggested we wait in The Gladstone, the pub round the corner, where they always headed afterwards.

'You didn't have to get me a Diet Coke,' Ella grumbles as we take a seat at one of the wooden tables in the back of the pub. 'I've got ID you know.'

I raise an eyebrow. 'Should you be telling me that?'

She grins and it strikes me how different she is from the first time we talked after Charlotte's accident. The brittleness, the anger, the hurt – all gone. She's like a little girl again, like the darling playmate Charlotte would bring home to bake cakes and decorate with fairy wings and sprinkles.

'There he is!' She points across the room.

Liam, surrounded by dark haired, similarly dressed young men, saunters across the pub, a guitar bag slung over his shoulder. He does a double take when he spots us.

'Liam!' I raise a hand and wave him over.

He nods then turns to his bandmates, says something I can't make out and splits off from the pack.

'Mrs Jackson.' He looks at Ella and frowns questioningly. 'Ella.'

351

'She knows,' she leans back in her chair and widens her eyes, 'about you and Charlotte having sex at Mike's house.'

'What?' He pales.

'But she's not angry,' she adds quickly, pulling out the chair beside her. 'She wants to know more about Mike. She thinks you might know something that could help Charlotte wake up.'

Liam glances at his bandmates, laughing and drinking, crowded around a table on the other side of the room.

'Please.' I force a smile. 'I'm not angry. I promise. I just need to ask you a few questions.'

'Okay.' He reaches a tentative hand towards the chair next to me. 'I can't stay long, we've got band stuff to talk about.'

'It was Charlotte's idea,' he says before I have chance to draw breath. 'She was the one who pushed for us to have sex. I wanted to wait until she was sixteen and legal.'

I don't believe that for one second but what Oli told us about the hotel room suggests that Charlotte was as keen as Liam, if not more.

'Was she the one who suggested that you have sex in Mike's house?'

'No.' He eyes our drinks. 'Well, not straight away.'

'What do you mean?'

'She told me that she'd met this rich old gay bloke in Breeze who thought she looked like his dead niece and wanted to buy her stuff. I thought

352

it was creepy.' He rubs a hand over his stubble. 'But then Charlotte said Mike could probably get me stuff too and my guitar was knackered so . . .' he tails off.

'He bought you a new guitar?'

'Yeah.' His eyes dart to the guitar case propped up on the wall beside him. I'm no muso but even I know that Les Paul guitars aren't cheap. 'I told her not to ask him to get me one but she thought it would be funny. If he had the cash he should be able to spend it however he wanted, she said and besides . . .' He picks up a bar mat, pulls off the paper advertisement and rolls it into a ball. '. . . buying us, buying *her* stuff seemed to make him happy so why not?'

A shiver runs down my back at the thought of my daughter being so Machiavellian. I thought I'd brought her up better than that. I'm not sure how much more I want to hear.

'So how did the two of you end up having sex at his house?'

'Mike suggested it when Charlotte got drunk one night. She'd been shooting off, telling him how crap it is being a teenager these days because, if you want to lose your virginity, you have to do it on the school fields or in someone's car. That's when he suggested we use his flat.' He lowers his eyes. 'He said he was going away for the weekend, to see some mates in London and that he'd put clean sheets on his bed and food in the fridge and we could treat the flat like it was ours for two days.'

353

I can see why two teenagers would have jumped at that offer.

'So you took him up on the offer?'

He doesn't look up. 'Yeah.'

'And?'

'And nothing.' He pushes back his chair, rests a hand on his guitar case. 'Can I go now?'

'Mike didn't turn up while you were there? Nothing bad happened? Nothing out of the ordinary?'

'No.' He shakes his head, his cheeks colouring slightly. 'It was cool.'

He's halfway out of his seat and I realise I'm about to lose him. How long did I expect my daughter's ex-boyfriend to talk to me about sex for? Even Ella, across the table from me, is staring at the cocktail menu like it's the most fascinating thing she's ever read.

'Then why would Mike blackmail Charlotte?'

'What?' He looks down at me, his forehead creased.

'Keisha told me Mike was blackmailing Charlotte about something. Do you know what?'

'No.' He shakes his head, his expression incredulous. 'She never said anything about . . .' He looks at Ella. 'Did you know about this?'

She raises her eyes from the menu. 'Nope.'

'She didn't give you any clue?' I look from one to the other. 'Nothing at all?'

Two blank expressions meet my question.

'So if I were to tell you that she wrote *"keeping this secret is killing me"* in her diary you wouldn't know what she was talking about?'

They look shocked but shake their heads.

'Liam,' I stand up too, 'one more thing before you go back to your band.'

He shrugs. 'Sure. What?'

'Show me where Mike lives.'

Chapter 29

Liam and I are alone in the car. Ella received a phone call from her mum while we were leaving the pub asking where the hell her fags were so I dropped her home. I wasn't just returning her home because her mum was suspicious, I wanted her safe and, now we're outside number 117 Highgate Road, I need to make sure Liam is too.

'This is definitely the house?' I ask.

'Yeah.' He nods at me from the passenger seat. 'I'd know it anywhere.'

'Thank you, Liam.' I look in the rear-view mirror and flick the indicator, 'I'll take you back to The Gladstone now.'

'Nah.' He shakes his head. 'I'm staying here. If you're going to confront that mincing fucker I'm coming too. I'll punch his fucking lights out.'

That's a lot of bravado for a seventeen-year-old but it doesn't raise a smile. Liam has no idea how much danger he'd be in if he so much as looked at James the wrong way.

'No, you won't.' I pull out into the road, ignoring his protestations, 'we don't want two people in the hospital.'

Liam laughs, flattered I'd think him capable of hospitalizing a grown man. I don't bother to correct him.

Fifteen minutes later and I'm back outside the flat. It looks innocuous enough – marine-blue front door, brass knocker, bay windows with curtains ever so slightly open – but I'm having a hard time opening the car door. My brain is urging me on, telling me to get out, knock on the door and confront the man who's been terrorizing my nightmares for the last twenty years, but my body is holding fast, refusing to move. I look down at my right hand, at the diamond band Brian bought me during a 'make up' holiday in Rhodes after the affair. I refused to wear it – his guilt gift – for a long, long time and then suddenly it was our fifteen-year anniversary and the affair was a distant memory and the ring felt like a symbol of positivity, of a fresh start, so I started wearing it. I try and will the hand to move from the steering wheel to the door handle.

The hand refuses to move.

I look back at the house.

Maybe confronting James is more than foolhardy or idiotic, it's downright dangerous. What if I've made the same mistake again – what if 'rich gay guy Mike' really is a rich gay guy? What if I ring Brian, or the police, or whoever and tell them that my psycho ex-boyfriend has tracked me down to Brighton, falsely befriended my daughter and then blackmailed her and I'm wrong? How many times can you cry wolf before the men in white coats come out with a nice white coat of your own to wear? Ella described someone who could be James twenty years down the line but I thought the description of Jamie Evans the school teacher matched him too. I've been wrong once, I could be wrong again. I need proof. Concrete proof.

The fingers of my right hand twitch on the steering wheel and the next thing I know the driver side door is opening.

Somehow I make it from the road to the pavement and from the pavement to the gate. I keep looking from the front door to the windows to check for signs of life, for danger, for a sign that I should RUN, but when my shoes hit the pathway and I try and walk towards the house it's as though I've stepped into a magnetic field. My body lunges forward but something pushes it back. Go back. Go back. The air is thick, charged, protecting the house, urging me away. Go back. Go back. I take another step forward, my car keys clutched tightly in my hand. I just want to peer through the small gap in the curtains. Just one small look. I take another step, starting when a gull squawks overhead. There are no lights on in the living room, no warm flicker from a television set. I make a deal with God. When I peer through the gap in the curtains, I pray, don't let James peer back.

I take another step forward, then another. I'm so close now I only need to move a couple of centimetres to my left to see through the gap in the curtains. I exhale as quietly as I can. The street is silent now. There are no gulls, no cars, no children screaming or playing, just me, this house and the thud, thud, thud of my heart.

I hold myself very still and slowly, slowly, tilt my head to the left, towards the gap in the curtains, towards the window into James's life.

I don't know what I expect to see – an exact replica of his room twenty years ago perhaps – but I don't expect the characterless room behind the curtains. A single armchair – black leather with a matching foot-stool, a leather sofa – same fabric, a pine side table, a beige carpet, stained with what looks like coffee by the fireplace, an entertainment unit holding nothing apart from a large flat screen television and a DVD player. And that's it. No books, no scripts, no coffee cups, no shoes, no ornaments, no photographs. This could be a show home, a flat designed to appeal to the modern bachelor, devoid of character, colour and warmth and yet . . . I press a hand to my heart as it lurches in my chest . . . there is something that stops this room from being completely bland.

A batik wall hanging over the fire.

Chapter 30

My hands shake as I pull my handbag off the passenger seat and onto my lap. I was right all along. I didn't imagine the cards and parcels that were left at our house and I wasn't chased down the street by a shadow in London. James Evans was responsible for Charlotte's accident. I was right all along.

I check that all the doors are still locked and the street is still empty then I delve into my bag. I find my purse, my address book, my make-up bag and a handful of till receipts but not my phone. I tip the handbag upside down. The contents spill onto my lap and my hairbrush hits the keys, dangling from the ignition, as it tumbles. I stare at them as they swing backwards and forwards. Maybe it's a sign. I should just go. Ring Brian when I'm somewhere safe. Yes, that's what I'll do – my fingers make contact with something smooth and buttoned as I sweep the debris from my lap.

My phone.

I scoop it up and press the on button.

Nothing happens.

I sweep my finger down the screen. Jab at the buttons. Press the on button again.

Nothing. Nothing. Nothing.

I shake it, bash it on the steering wheel and press the on button again but nothing works. It's out of battery.

Please, I pray as I turn the keys in the ignition. Please let Brian be home.

Never have I been so relieved to see my husband's car in the driveway. I sound the horn as I pull up next to it and glance at the house for signs of life.

There aren't any lights on in the kitchen or upstairs landing. Brian's probably in his study.

Milly launches herself at me the second I'm through the porch door. She frantically licks my face, her thick tail pounding the air.

'Hey girl,' I rub her head then gently push her down. 'Sorry, got to find Daddy.'

I ignore her whined protestations and go into the kitchen, shutting her in the porch behind me.

'Brian!' I call as I glance around the living-room door. It's empty, exactly as I left it.

'Brian?' I call again as I run up the stairs, cross the landing and push open the door to the study. 'Brian, we need to call the police.'

The room is empty, the laptop lid closed, the chair pushed into the desk, the paperwork piled up neatly in three piles beside the phone.

I head for the bedroom. Maybe he decided to have a nap. 'Brian, are you—'

But the bedroom is empty too.

It doesn't make sense. How can Brian's car be in the drive but he isn't? His car's in the drive so where is he?

I run from room to room to room, scanning the floors, the walls and ceilings for signs of a struggle, for – my stomach constricts so powerfully I think I might be sick – evidence of an attack, but everything is in order. There are no smashed ornaments, no overturned furniture, no broken glass and no blood.

I drift out of the living room and into the kitchen, my terror replaced by confusion. There's no scribbled note on the pine table, no scrawled 'gone to the pub' on the whiteboard above the microwave. Maybe Brian texted my phone and I didn't get it because it's out of charge. I head towards the charger, plugged in by the kettle, when a scratching sound makes me jump and I'm knocked to the floor.

'Milly!' She nudges me with her nose then licks my face. I gently push her away and glance at the porch door. It's wide open. I mustn't have shut it properly.

I scrabble to my feet and cross the kitchen. I'm about to pull the porch door closed when I spot the white padded envelope in the cage below the letterbox. I fish it out. My name and address are written in a fine cursive handwriting I haven't seen in over twenty years.

'Milly, quick!' I grab her by the collar, yank open the front door and stumble across the driveway.

Ten minutes later we're parked up by the Marina. It's late and the seafront is empty and silent. The only sound is the rage of the black sea crashing against the pebbles over and over again. A streetlight casts an eerie glow into the car, turning the white parcel in my hands blood-orange red. I shouldn't open it. I should take it straight to the police and tell them what I know about James Evans, but I can't. I can't risk this being some kind of sick joke, a kitchen implement, cuddly toy or something equally innocuous that would get me laughed right out of the station.

I fish a tissue out of the small pack in the glove compartment and cover my fingers with it then pick at the envelope's seal. If James's fingerprints are on it I don't want to smudge them. It's fiddly and takes forever for me to peel back the flap but I get the parcel open and peer inside. It's too dark to make out the contents and I don't want to reach inside so I manoeuver Milly onto the backseat and upend the package on the passenger seat.

Two exquisite baby's booties tumble out. Knitted from the finest yarn in tiny delicate stitches, overlaid with lace and tied with ribbon around the ankle they're exactly the kind of expensive, impractical footwear I coveted for Charlotte when she was a baby. I reach for one, overcome by memories and bring it closer to my face. I'm not sure what happens next – whether the smell of iron hits the back of my throat or the thick viscous liquid rolls down the side of my hand and curls around my forearm – but

I scream and toss it away. It smacks against the windscreen and drops into the passenger seat footwell.

Even under the burnt amber glow of the streetlight I know that's what it is, clinging to my fingers, smudged on the windscreen, soaked into the fine ivory wool of the booties. Blood.

A cold calm descends on me. James knows. He knows the secret I took with me twenty years ago. I can stop being afraid now. He knows. I can stop.

I reach for the card that's lying beside the remaining bootie and wipe it with the tissue, smearing away the blood so I can read the message written on it in the same neat handwriting as the envelope.

'Life shall go for life, eye for eye,
tooth for tooth'
DEUTERONOMY 19:21

I turn the card over,

A life for a coma? That doesn't sound right.
We have some unfinished business,
Charlotte and I.

The card falls from my fingers in slow motion, arcing backward and forward until it flutters to a stop by my foot.

I have to get to the hospital before James does.

Chapter 31

I run from the car park to the double doors at the entrance of the hospital but I don't feel the wind on my face. I don't hear the mechanical voice tell me the doors are opening as I step into the lift or smell the sharp sting of antiseptic as I squirt sanitiser onto my hands at the entrance to the ward. I don't see, hear, feel, touch or taste anything. I am in limbo, I am running through a nightmare, chasing the spectre of my sleeping child. She hovers in front of me, so close my fingertips are millimeters away and then – gone – she darts away before I can touch her.

She will die unless I get to her. I know it with a certainty that runs deeper than bones, flesh or thought. I would stake my own life on it. Give my own life. James will not take her. He can have me. I will make him have me. I will give him no choice.

I can see the door of her room, further down the corridor. It is ajar, light spilling through the gap.

Someone is in there with her. I run but now I'm wading through mud, each footstep sinking lower than the next and I move slower, slower.

I took James's baby from him because I knew that I would never be able to escape if I gave birth to his child. And it wouldn't have been a child – it would have been a leash around my neck, a choke collar to be jerked whenever he wanted to control me, whenever he needed to abuse me, whenever he had to punish me.

I was dry-eyed and resolute when I walked into the clinic. I took the tablet without a moment's hesitation, lay down on the bed without a second thought and gripped my stomach stoically, silently when the cramps came. I didn't even cry when blood trickled down my leg and I hurried to the toilet and felt life slip out of me and into the pan. But half an hour later, as I lay curled up on the bed and a nurse put a hand on my head and said, 'You're a strong one, aren't you? You haven't had so much as a paracetamol for the pain,' I sobbed like the world was about to end.

Strong? I was impossibly weak. I'd spent four years of my life with a monster of a man, being tortured by hate dressed up as love. I'd been humiliated, belittled, berated and cross-examined. I'd been judged, ignored, criticized and rejected. I'd cut myself off from my friends and my family, lost my job and been made to choose between my life's dream and my love for James. And I hadn't walked away. I tried, several times but I was weak. He always talked his way back into my life and into my heart. Strong wasn't lying silently on a hospital bed as I aborted his child so I could be free. Strong would have been walking straight out of the World Headquarters club in Camden three years, two hundred and seventy days earlier when he laughingly called me a slut. Strong would have been refusing to ever see him again the night he refused to sleep in my bed because other men had been there first. Strong would have been reporting him to the police the night he raped me. Strong would have been stopping him from doing the same to another woman ever again.

I didn't cry for the baby I aborted that day but I did every year afterwards, on the anniversary. I cried because it didn't deserve to lose its life and I cried because I felt angry with James for forcing me into that situation. Mostly I felt guilty – if I hadn't been so weak when I left him – if I'd had the tiniest bit of resolve left – maybe I could have taken him or her to Greece with me, somehow made it work as a TEFL teacher and a mother.

I thought I'd be punished for what I'd done. I thought I'd never conceive again but then Charlotte, our miracle baby, appeared a year into my marriage to Brian. I felt blessed, forgiven, like a new chapter of my life had opened up, that I was truly free. And then we tried to give her a sibling and I had four miscarriages in three years.

My miracle baby.

I put a hand to the door and push it open.

Charlotte is lying prostrate on the duvet-less bed,

an oxygen mask covering her mouth, her chest polka-dotted with multicoloured electrodes. The heart monitor in the corner of the room bleep-bleep-bleeps, marking the passage of time like a medical metronome and I close my eyes.

'Sue?' There is a hand on my shoulder, heavy. 'Would you like a cup of tea?'

'Brian?' I blink several times.

'Sue?' He's looking at me and his brow is furrowed but I have no idea what he's thinking. 'Sue, are you okay?'

'Alright, Mum?' I twitch at the word 'Mum' but it's not Charlotte speaking it. It's Oli, sitting at her bedside. He's got a pile of *National Geographic* magazines in his lap and my best hairdressing scissors in his hand. There are a stack of cuttings on Charlotte's bedside table.

'Mum?' he says again.

I can't remember the last time he called me that.

'I . . .' I look from him to Brian and back again. What are they doing here? It's as though my world has switched from the hyper real, a living technicolour nightmare, to the monochrome of the mundane. Why are they sipping tea? Don't they realize how much danger Charlotte is in? I look at Brian questioningly.

He smiles, his hand still on my shoulder. 'Oli popped by to pick up his magazines and said he'd like to visit Charlotte before he went back to uni. We came in his car.'

'You came in Oli's car . . .'

'Yes. Mine's still at home. It won't start, some kind

368

of problem with the fuel pipe, I think. The sooner I get myself an electric car the better.' He squeezes my shoulder. 'We waited for you to come back from the beach so you could come with us but when you said you wanted to be alone I thought . . .' he tails off. 'I would have left a note but, somewhere between grabbing my jacket and leaving the house, I forgot.'

Oli laughs. 'Not like you to be forgetful, Dad.'

I stare at the two of them. They're laughing and smiling but lying on the passenger seat of my car are two blood-stained booties and a card threatening our daughter's life.

'You look a bit pale.' Brian angles me into the empty chair on Charlotte's left and crouches beside me.

No one says anything for several minutes until he inhales noisily through his nose. He's steadying himself to say something big.

'I found these.' He plunges a hand into his trouser pocket then uncurls his fingers to reveal two small white pills. 'I was having a bit of a tidy up. I thought you'd appreciate it after everything that has happened but,' he looks at the treasures he has uncovered, 'I was wondering if there was anything you wanted to tell me, Sue.'

'Yes.' I sit upright, suddenly, which makes him lurch back in surprise. 'Charlotte's in danger. James has found me. I'm not imagining it this time, Brian. I've got proof. It's in my car. Blood-stained booties. He knows about the abortion and he's trying to get his revenge through Charlotte. He blackmailed her, that's why she's in the coma, that's what made her walk in front of the bus that Saturday afternoon. But it's not enough for him to hurt her,' I grip Brian's wrist, 'he wants her dead. He's going to kill her.'

I stare at his face, waiting to see rage, violence or murder but I see nothing at all, save a quick glance towards Oli.

'Brian?' I tighten my grip on his wrist. 'You do believe me, don't you? Look at my hands they're . . .' But my hands aren't bloodied in the slightest. 'Clean. But only because I used the hand sanitiser when I came in. If we go down to my car I can show you the booties and the—,' I try and stand but Brian pulls me back into the chair. 'Brian please! Why are you looking at me like that?'

He looks at Oliver and nods again. Three seconds later he's standing beside me too, a plastic cup in his hand.

'Sue,' Brian eases my fingers off his wrist. 'I'd like you to take a couple of these tablets.'

'No!' I look imploringly at Oli who looks down at the ground. 'There's nothing wrong with me. I only went along to the doctors because I made a mistake about that teacher at the school but I've got *proof* this time. I haven't made another mistake. Please! Let's just go down to my car and I'll show you.'

'Sue.' Brian presses the tablets to my mouth. They graze my bottom lip. 'Take the tablets and then we'll talk.'

'No!' I try and stand up but he puts a hand on my shoulder. The pressure is gentle but insistent. He's not going to let me up.

'Please, Mum.' Oli takes a step towards me, holding out the plastic cup like it's a sacred chalice. 'Take a sip. It'll help the tablets go down.'

'Oliver, no.'

'It's just water.'

'I don't care what it is. I'm not going to—'

'Mum please! We're worried about you. We have been for a while. You . . .' he looks away, unable to sustain eye contact, '. . . you haven't been yourself since Charlotte's accident. All that talk about Keisha and Charlotte and who was best friends with who and asking for Danny's number and address and . . . well, I thought it was a bit odd but I wouldn't have said anything until Dad mentioned that he'd found your tablets down the side of the sofa.'

The haze that hit me when I walked into the room clears and I stare at my husband and stepson as though seeing them for the first time. They think I'm mentally ill. I can see it in their frowns, in the hunch of their shoulders, in their whispering voices. They've put one and one together and come up with 'mad' and nothing I do or say will convince them otherwise. What can I say? That I've spent more time with Charlotte's friends recently than I have my own daughter? That I went to a club in London and got in a blacked-out car with a footballer's agent? That I've been peering into the front rooms of strangers' houses? They wouldn't believe a word. Worse than that, they'd think it was all part of the delusion. And of course I'm deluded – I haven't been taking my tablets, have I?

I could show them what's on the passenger seat of my car but they'd probably think I did it myself, for attention or because I'm disturbed. Brian would take one look at the blood-stained booties and be on the phone to the GP quicker than you can say 'psychiatric unit'. There's only one option left to me. One thing I can do.

I look at the tablets in Brian's fingers. 'If I take them,' I say steadily. 'Will you listen to me then?'

A slow smile crosses his face. 'Of course I will, darling.'

Chapter 32

'So we'll go to Millets then.'

'We won't be long.'

'Just need to pick up a few things for Oli's next trip.'

'I need a coat that's actually waterproof. This is a proper Lake District downpour we're talking about not some kind of light drizzle.'

'Two man tent.'

'Hiking socks.'

'Carry mat.'

My husband and stepson are talking to me. Their jaws are going up and down, their eyebrows are wriggling and twitching and their eyes are widening and narrowing, but nothing makes any sense. I can hear words, lots of words, rolling together like waves of sound then crashing together above my head but I can't distinguish one from the other and when I open my mouth to ask what they're talking about nothing comes out. After two attempts I stop trying and allow the heavy feeling in my bones to roll me back in my seat, my head resting against the wall, my eyes drawn to the strip light on the ceiling. It flickers, pulses and hums and I remember Charlotte, three months old, lying in her pram, looking up at the blue and grey Habitat lampshade in our living room, her eyes wide with wonder.

'An hour.'

'Hour and a half tops.'

'Come and collect you afterwards. Oli will go back to uni and I'll drive us both home in your car.'

'You look a bit more relaxed.'

'Is that a smile? I can't remember the last time . . .'

My eyes swivel towards them and I'm vaguely aware of my mouth moving and words coming out. They sound nonsensical in my head but Brian and Oli smile and nod and it appears I've said something that reassures them that it's fine to leave me on my own, because the next thing I know there are lips on my cheek, a squeeze to my shoulder, a pat to my head and then they are gone.

Without the roar and crash of their voices the room hums with silence. It hurts my ears and then . . .

Bleep-bleep-bleep.

I make out the sound of the heart monitor in the corner of the room. The medical metronome – Charlotte's constant companion and now mine too.

Tick-tick-tick. Bleep-bleep-bleep. Tick-tick-tick.

We are in the living room. I am lying on the sofa, Charlotte is sitting on the floor. She picks up a plastic brick, throws it half a metre, crawls after it, picks it up, throws it again. Her face is a picture of happiness and pride – she has conquered throwing and crawling, now she can take on the world. I want to freeze the scene. I want to re-live it over and over again.

I glance at my daughter, asleep on her hospital bed, and reach out a hand to touch her hair. I am surprised when I don't feel the fine silkiness of a baby's curls but I continue to stroke anyway, the follicles of her hair soft and smooth under my fingertips.

I was afraid. A memory stirs in my mind but it is ephemeral, transient and slips away as my brain tries to anchor and examine it. I feel the pressure of Brian's lips still warm on my cheek and Oli's hand on my head. My life is perfect. I have been blessed.

There is a squeak, an interruption to my reverie and I am aware of the door opening. Did Brian and Oli shut it behind them when they left? I didn't notice. A figure – a man in a dark suit – drifts past me and crosses the room. He stands by the window, his back to me, looking out.

Consultant.

The word pops into my head and I smile. He has arrived to give me good news, to tell me that Charlotte will wake up soon, that I can take her out of her incubator, give her a cuddle and bring her home.

'Mr Arnold?' I rise effortlessly, as though in a dream, and take a step towards him. 'Will my baby be okay?'

There is something about the shape of the back of the doctor's head that makes me pause mid-step, and halts my progress across the room. There is a spot of black in the glorious technicolour haze of my happiness and, as I gaze at the width of his shoulders and the uneven balance of his stance, it spreads, like black ink on a wet watercolour. My fingers twitch at my sides as if they've developed pins and needles after hours of sitting on my hands. My thighs twitch too, then my shoulders, my calves and my feet. My body is waking whilst my mind still snoozes and I feel a sudden compulsion to run but why would I? My child is here. She needs me.

'Mr Arnold?' I say again. 'Is it bad news? Is that why you won't talk to me?'

Yes, I have sensed that what he is about to tell me is bad news and my body is preparing itself for the worst, it is trying to shake my mind out of its soporific slumber.

For a couple of seconds the consultant does nothing and I wonder if he has heard me then his shoulders rise as he takes a deep breath and he turns to face me. I don't immediately recognize the grey eyes flecked with blue, the large nose and the wide, thin mouth because I'm thrown by the thatch of grey hair, the deep lines around the mouth and the heavy stubble that covers his top lip, jaw and throat.

'Hello Suzy-Sue.'

The shudder that goes through me speeds from my head to my toes then explodes back again and I shake violently, as if the temperature has dropped by forty degrees.

I thought I was ready for this moment. I thought I

was old, strong and resilient enough not to be affected by the sonorous timbre of his voice but it's as though I've stepped into a time machine and I am twenty-three again, hiding in the wardrobe, quaking as he walks from room to room, calling out my name. I take a step backwards, instinctively pressing a hand to my stomach, to hide my secret, to cover what is no longer in my womb. James notices and the blank expression he was wearing morphs into something else. His lip turns up in a sneer, his eyes narrow and his nostrils flare and then the revulsion is gone, replaced in a heartbeat by a wide, natural smile. I blink several times.

'Hello Sue,' he takes a step forward. 'How's Charlotte?'

The mention of my daughter's name is all I need to snap out of my shivering stupor and I spring to her side, my hand on her shoulder, my eyes on James as he moves to the foot of her bed and unclips her notes and flicks through them making small uh-hum noises as he scans the pages. On the last page he purses his lips and shakes his head.

'I'm no doctor but, even to me, the prognosis doesn't look good. Unless I'm very much mistaken your daughter is minutes away from death.'

'Get out.' I say it as calmly and steadily as I can and point at the door. 'Get out or I'll—'

'Press this?' James steps nimbly to the other side of the bed and thumps the taped emergency button with his fist. 'Oh dear, it appears it's broken. The NHS do try hard but honestly, their equipment just isn't—'

'I'll scream then.'

'You could do that,' he places a hand on Charlotte' pale neck and drums his fingers slowly and deliberately on her pale skin, 'but she'll be dead by the time you pause for breath.'

Lying on the bedside table beside him is Oliver's pile of *National Geographic* magazines with my best hairdressing scissors on the top. If I threw myself across Charlotte I could reach them but James would still get to them first.

'There you go,' he says, misreading my silence. 'There's no need for histrionics. No silly screaming, no heroics. Not that you could move quickly enough for heroics.' He removes his hand from my daughter's throat and sculpts a beach ball in the air. 'You always were on the chubby side but you're veritably matronly these days.'

'Childbirth, was it?' He glances at my daughter and I suppress the urge to leap across the bed and tear out his eyes. 'Did carrying your ugly spawn around for nine months turn you into a fat bitch or did you mainline cream cakes and butter?'

James laughs and I am glad he's gone straight for a verbal assault. My fear was that he'd wrong-foot me by being charming and apologetic. Still I say nothing. I'm waiting for the sound of footsteps or chattering voices in the corridor so I can scream for help but the wing is unusually quiet, there's not so much as a squeaky trolley or a slamming door.

'She's not as gargantuan as you but it's only a matter of time.' His eyes are still on Charlotte. 'I still shudder when I remember those rolls of flab on your back, your stomach, your thighs . . . how you found someone else who could bear to make love to you, I don't know.'

'Is that what you call rape these days?'

'Rape?' His dead eyes flick towards me. 'Rape implies taking something of virtue from someone innocent but you were never innocent were you, Suzy-Sue? You were a dirty slut who'd been putting it about for years.'

'No, I wasn't. I was a normal twenty-something who'd had a handful of boyfriends and a few one-night stands. I wasn't a party girl or wild or unusual or dirty or used goods or any of the filthy things you called me.'

'The truth hurts, Suzy-Sue.'

'But it's not true.' The words spill out of me and there's nothing I can do to stop them. For twenty years these thoughts have blistered and festered inside me, dying to be spoken. I tried to block them out but the more I ignored them the stronger they grew. No wonder they spilled into my dreams. '*None of it* was true. You tried to make me feel ashamed, James. You tried to make me regret the life I'd lived because you couldn't accept that I'd had a life before you. But most twenty-somethings don't come with a blank slate, James, no matter how much you might wish it, they are who they are *because* of their past.'

He shakes his head. 'Still proud to be a slag I see. Twenty years and you still haven't learnt.'

'Did you love me, James?'

e jolts, as though mentally disarmed by the ques-
on, then steadies himself with one slow blink. 'Of
course I did. You were the love of my life.'

'No, James.' I slide the top drawer of the bedside
table open and spider my fingers, searching for a
biro, a letter opener, a syringe, anything sharp I can
use as a weapon but all I find is an unopened box
of tissues and something smooth, square and leathery.
'I wasn't. If you'd really loved me you'd have accepted
my past. Instead you made me suffer because I
couldn't live up to the idealized woman you wanted
me to be.'

His mouth narrows in disgust. 'You tricked me,
Suzy. You let me think you were different – that you
were special, a beautiful angel – but you were the
same. You were like every other dirty slag in London.
You weren't special enough for me.'

He inches closer to Charlotte, runs the back of his
index finger over her cheekbones then touches the
crown of her head and strokes her hair from root to
tip, then does it again. His eyes are intense and staring
and he's breathing deeply in and out through his
nose.

'Is that what your mother told you?' I say when
he rests the tip of his index finger on one of her
closed eyes. 'That her special little boy deserved a
good girl? That God would send Jamie an angel
who'd saved herself especially for him?'

'I saved myself for *you*.' His hand leaves Charlotte's
face and he lunges at me across the bed. I dart backwards as his fingers graze my neck but then step

forward again. If I can't get help I need to get him away from my daughter, use myself as bait.

'No, you didn't, James. You lost your virginity to a prostitute.'

'And how proud do you think I am of that? Something that should have been a beautiful meeting of souls was instead a dirty fumble with a whore.'

'That wasn't my fault.'

'No.' His eyes fill with tears and he reaches for Charlotte's hand and presses it to his lips, his head bowed. 'No, it wasn't.' A single tear rolls down his cheek. 'I'm sorry, Suzy. I'm so sorry for what I put you through. You're not a slut or a slag. You're a beautiful, kind, tender-hearted woman. I never felt I deserved you. That's why I was cruel to you. I was trying to push you away.'

I stare at him in astonishment as another tear follows the first, then another and another. We stare at each other, neither of us saying a word, until the silence is broken by the excited chatter of two female voices in the corridor. I look towards the door. Do I shout? Run? But running would leave Charlotte with James. It would be too dangerous. Shouting it is then. I open my mouth and—

SNAP! There is a sickening crunch like a chicken bone being bitten in half by a dog and I spin round. James is holding Charlotte's right hand around the wrist. The little finger of her right hand is bent backwards at ninety degrees, the nail brushing the back of her hand.

'Hello Mummy,' he says in a little girl's voice as

he waggles my daughter's hand at me, mimicking a wave, the broken finger flopping limply from side to side. 'Look at my wibbly, wobbly finger.'

'Leave her alone!' I launch myself towards them, clambering onto the bed with one knee as I throw myself at James in an attempt to knock him away from my daughter but he's too quick and knocks me sideways so I topple on top of my daughter instead. I struggle to right myself but James grabs my right forearm and, as he twists it so it's lying across Charlotte's throat, the oxygen mask over her mouth is knocked free. There is a deep rumbling gurgle from within her chest and she gasps for breath.

'Leave her alone?' James says as he digs his fingers into my arm, his face millimeters from mine, my cheek pressed against Charlotte's ribcage. 'Like you left my Mammy alone? She died, Sue. No, you didn't know that, did you? You didn't know because you ran away and left her to rot in a hospital ward. You didn't just abandon me, Sue. You abandoned her too.'

'I didn't know,' I whisper, 'I had no ide—'

'Shut up. I'm sick of the sound of your whinging, whining voice. Make one more noise and I will break the rest of Charlotte's fingers, one by one, while you watch and then I will wring her neck. Do you understand?'

I nod silently.

'Now get up.'

I try to stand but James grabs me by the hair. He drags me, bent double, towards Charlotte's feet then yanks me around the end of the bed so I'm bowing in front of him. A jolt of fear courses through me as he tightens his grip on my hair and presses down on my head so I fall to my knees.

Nothing happens for several seconds. The only sound in the room is the bleep-bleep-bleep of the heart monitor in the corner of the room and the deep rasp of Charlotte's unassisted breathing. I close my eyes and steel myself for a blow, a kick, or worse but nothing happens. Finally there is the squeak of chair legs on linoleum and James speaks.

'It broke my heart when I realized where you'd gone,' he is speaking softly, his voice barely a whisper and I risk a glance up at him, through my hair. He is sitting on the chair next to Charlotte, his head in his hands. 'I'd been to the florist during my lunch break and bought you flowers and then, on the way home from work, I spotted a children's clothes shop on the High Street that I'd never noticed before. The window display called out to me and I couldn't resist going in. Do you know what I bought?'

I don't move a muscle.

'Do you know what I bought, Suzy-Sue?'

I shake my head.

'A dress. A beautiful red dress with tiny white daisies embroidered on the skirt. It was tiny, Suzy. For nought to three months old. I'd never seen anything so exquisite in my life and I couldn't wait to show you. I knew you'd be as excited as me.' He clears his throat. 'I told you I'd always wanted a daughter, didn't I?'

I nod.

'I was over the moon when you told me you were pregnant.'

I bite my lip. James wasn't delighted when I told him I was pregnant. He accused me of cheating on him and spent three hours screaming at me in the kitchen demanding to know whose baby it was while I curled up in a ball on the floor and sobbed into my knees.

'It was the most wonderful thing in the world – the fact that you were carrying my beautiful, innocent child – I thought I might burst with pride. Finally I'd be able to love someone without restraint, hurt or fear. I'd love and be loved in return. Forever.'

Charlotte's breaths are coming unevenly now, the rasping replaced by a high-pitched wheeze. I need to get the mask back on her as soon as possible. Without enough oxygen to her brain . . . I close my eyes and say a quick prayer for the second time since her accident. I'm not sure anyone was listening the first time.

'So I returned to the house, full of love, full of happiness, full of hope with an armful of flowers and a beautiful dress and you were nowhere to be found.' An edge creeps into James's voice and I tense. 'I couldn't work out where you could have gone, especially as I'd made sure to lock the door when I left. I felt lost Suzy, so terribly lost without you there to welcome me home. And then angry – how dare you spoil my surprise by being selfish and creeping out the way you did?'

There's a space under Charlotte's bed that I should

be able to fit under. If I fall to my stomach maybe I can scrabble under it towards the door. James will leave Charlotte's side and try to go after me but if I scream, maybe someone will get here before he has chance to do anything.

'You thought you were so clever didn't you, sneaking out and leaving me all alone without so much as a kiss on the cheek after everything we'd been through, but I was cleverer Suzy.'

I place a hand on the linoleum and lean towards my right. I have to be quick or James will grab hold of my ankle and yank me backwards.

'I went into your sewing room and I found a piece of paper on the floor. A piece of paper torn from the Yellow Pages.' He shakes his head. 'I knew you were a lot of things, Susan but I never suspected, I never . . .' his voice quivers, '. . . imagined you would murder a child.'

I scream as James pounces, his hand over my mouth, an arm locked around my throat.

'Get up, you baby-killing bitch.'

He hoists me to my feet and shoves me towards Charlotte's bed. My hip hits the metal bedstead and, as I put out my right hand to steady myself James grabs it and holds it over Charlotte's mouth and nose.

'Love her, do you?' he hisses in my ear. 'Think she's beautiful and pure and innocent do you?'

'Please,' I mumble against his hand, 'don't do this. She hasn't done anything wrong.'

'Because she's not innocent, Suzy-Sue, you know that don't you? I heard her moaning like a stuck pig when she fucked her boyfriend in my spare room. I saw her fucking him doggy-style like a dirty pro and, when she's dead, I'm going to make you watch it too.'

'No.' I try and twist away from him, to pull my hand from my daughter's face but James holds me firm. There's suction on my palm as she tries, and fails, to inhale and a strange snuffling noise fills the air.

'You took something beautiful and precious from me. You killed my child and now you're going to kill yours.'

He leans his weight so heavily onto my hand that Charlotte's nose makes a terrible clicking sound and I know instantly that it's broken. The heart monitor in the corner of the room bleeps urgently and the red line that used to undulate up and down like a gentle wave oscillates erratically as the colour drains from my daughter's face and her eyeballs roll wildly under her closed eyelids.

'Not long now,' James hisses in my ear as Charlotte's body jerks and her hands twitch at her sides. He glances at the heart rate monitor and reaches for the off switch. 'We don't want to alert the cavalry when she flatlines, do we?'

'No!' I wriggle desperately as he drags me away, towards the other side of the room, my left hand flailing desperately as I knock at his head, his hand, his hip. My blows bounce off him but then, as my hand hits the bedside table, two things happen simultaneously – the bed is showered with a stack of *National Geographic* clippings and my fingers make contact with the hairdressing scissors. I reach high into the air then, using all the strength I can muster I twist to the left and dig them deep into James's thigh. He howls and falls to the ground, clutching his leg.

'Help!' I shout as lean over Charlotte's body. Her lips are blue and she's barely breathing. 'Somebody help me! Please!'

I try to push the bed, to wheel her out of the room but the brakes are on and no amount of kicking will get them unlocked.

'Somebody please—' the words are knocked out of me and I'm pinned on top of Charlotte, my head twisted to the right, hands in my hair. I can see James above me, the bloody scissors in his right hand, his eyes black with rage. I close my eyes as he raises the scissors into the air and pray that, even if it's too late for me, someone will have heard the disturbance and save Charlotte before he can kill her too and then—

'No!'

The bed shakes violently and I feel weight on my shoulders and back then hear a thud, like bodies falling to the floor and the sound of men grunting and metal scraping across paintwork. I try to stand up, to free Charlotte from the weight of my body, but there's a searing pain in my right arm and then everything goes black.

Chapter 33

'Do you recognize this woman?' The lawyer, Gillian Matthews, hands me a photograph of a slightly overweight young woman with dark hair, hazel eyes and a beautiful smile.

I shake my head and push it across the desk towards Brian. 'No, should I?'

'Not unless you were watching the news twenty—'

Brian gasps and we both turn to look at him.

'What?' I say.

'Can't you see it?'

I shake my head. 'See what?'

'The resemblance. She's the spitting image of you when we met.'

There's a vague similarity; the hair is certainly very alike and our mouths have a similar shape but her eyes are prettier than mine and her cheekbones higher.

'Interesting that you should say that, Mr Jackson,'

Mrs Matthews reaches for the photograph and tucks it back in the paper wallet in front of her.

'Why? Who is she?'

She leans her weight on her forearms and looks me straight in the eye. 'The prostitute James Evans murdered twenty years ago.'

I stare at her in disbelief. 'What?'

'My God.' Brian reaches a reassuring arm around my back and I wince as his hand makes contact with my shoulder. My arm's been in plaster for seventy-two hours but I've already taken a week's worth of painkillers. 'You said he was dangerous and I didn't believe—'

'James murdered someone?' I can't stop staring at the paper wallet in front of the lawyer. What else is in it? A photocopy of the card he enclosed with the booties? Shots of Charlotte's blood-splattered room? A photo of the severed artery in his leg? 'When? Who was she?'

She flicks open the notebook that's lying beside the wallet. 'Sarah Jane Thompson. The autopsy states the date of her death as 2 October 1992.'

'That's three weeks after I left him.'

'Yes,' she looks down at her notes. 'The police say they tried to contact you but no one knew where you were and there were a lot of Susan Maslins on the electoral register. The search was stopped after a few weeks and they went to trial anyway. Evans pleaded not guilty but the police had enough evidence to convict. Apparently he spent a while looking for a prostitute who fitted his precise requirements,' she

389

looks back up at me, 'someone who looks like you it seems.'

'But he got out.' I shake my head. 'How can that happen? How can he murder someone then be set free twenty years later to come after me? How is that even possible?'

She shakes her head. 'He served his time and fulfilled the conditions of his release by reporting to his parole officer once a week. He even had a job,' she checks her diary again, 'working in a nightclub in Chelsea. Greys. Apparently he was very popular, particularly amongst the VIPs.'

'Keisha!' I say. 'How is she?'

A dog walker found her naked body, bloodied, beaten and barely recognizable, in woodland near Devil's Dyke. She hasn't been able to tell the police much but what she did manage helped fill in the missing pieces of what had happened.

James found out that I was married to Brian and living in Brighton by searching Google – it was that easy. Once he had my new surname and the town where I lived it was easy for him to track down the Facebook profile Charlotte forced me to create a year ago to prove I 'wasn't living in the dark ages'. I hadn't looked at the thing in months so wasn't surprised when the police told me that my security settings were so poor James had access to all of my updates, photos and, worst of all, a link to my daughter's page. Her page was as public as mine and when he read that Breeze was her favourite club it was the link he needed to wheedle his way into her life.

He already knew Keisha, he'd been one of her clients when she was sleeping with the footballers and rock stars that frequented Greys and she'd liked him enough to tell him she was leaving London because she'd met a great guy in Brighton who managed a club called Breeze. He visited the club on the pretense of being Keisha's friend but, when he spotted Charlotte and Ella, and Keisha told him that Ella had a crush on her boyfriend he'd made his move – he told Keisha that unless she introduced him to them and kept her mouth shut he'd tell Danny about her past. She thought that was it, and it was for a while as James got to know Charlotte better and lent her his spare room so she and Liam could lose their virginity to each other. She had no idea that James would use that most intimate of moments to blackmail her.

'Keisha's not great,' Mrs Matthews closes her notebook, 'but she's stable. Twenty-four hours longer and she wouldn't have made it.'

'My God.' I press my hands to my forearms but my warm palms do little to flatten the goosebumps that have appeared on my skin.

'We need to go and see her,' I look at Brian. 'If she hadn't told me what she did. If she hadn't told me—'

'Sssh.' He pulls me towards him again, but his time I don't complain at the pain in my shoulder.

'When will the recording be destroyed?' he asks the lawyer, his tone hushed. 'If Charlotte wakes up we want to be able to tell her that it's gone.'

'When?' I say. Yesterday her eyelids fluttered when I told her there was no need to be scared of 'Mike' anymore. The doctors say I mustn't read anything into it, not when she'd just come out of an operation to reset her nose and little finger, but I know it's a sign. She's trying to come back to us. She's fighting harder now she knows it's safe.

'Recording?' The lawyer frowns at Brian. 'The sex tape, you mean?'

He cringes at the description. 'Yes.'

'I'm afraid the police will have to hang on to it as evidence. Evans was threatening to send it to the papers and post it on the internet. If he'd done that he'd have done more than tarnish Charlotte's reputation,' she looks at Brian, 'he'd have destroyed your career too.'

'But why try and pass her off as a prostitute?' he says. 'That's what I don't understand.'

She shakes her head. 'All part of his plan to get revenge on Mrs Jackson, I'm afraid. When I spoke to DCI Carter he said Evans's initial idea was to seduce Charlotte and convince her to run away with him but when he realized that most fifteen-year-old girls wouldn't look twice at a forty-three-year-old man, he decided to play the part of a lonely gay man and become her friend that way. Once she trusted him enough to go back to his flat he blackmailed her about the sex tape and then forced Keisha to pass her off as a prostitute at Greys. We don't know what he was going to do after that although I've got a pretty good idea it wouldn't have been very . . .' she purses her lips, drawing a line under that line of thought.

'My God,' I breathe the words as the full impact of the situation hits me, 'no wonder Charlotte did what she did. She'd broken up with Liam, fallen out with Ella and she couldn't trust Keisha anymore and there was no one left for her to talk to so . . .' The words catch in my throat as I look at my husband. 'Brian, Charlotte tried to kill herself because she couldn't confide in us.'

'No.' He tightens his grip on my hand. 'She did it because she was trying to protect us. She knew what would happen if Evans's recording got out. It would have been all over the papers – "Politician's Daughter in Underage Sex Scandal". Charlotte was so sensitive, there's no way she would have wanted to put me in that position.'

'But none of this would have happened if it wasn't for me, if it wasn't for my relationship with him. He never would have found us if I hadn't, if I hadn't—'

'You stopped him, Sue.'

'No.' I shake my head. 'You did.'

Brian had left Oli at the counter of Millets with an armful of supplies and a promise that it wouldn't take him long to pop back to the hospital to get the wallet he'd left in Charlotte's bedside drawer. Ten minutes he'd said but, instead of walking in, grabbing the wallet and walking out again, he'd burst into the hospital room to find his daughter fighting for her life and his wife about to lose hers. He'd launched himself at James, knocking him to the floor. Seconds later, alerted by the noise, several nurses came rushing in to find him sitting astride his chest, thumping him repeatedly in the face.

'No, Sue.' He presses his face into my hair. 'You knew Charlotte hadn't just had an accident and you refused to let it lie, even when I took you to the doctors, even when your mother died, even when no one believed you. Even when,' he pulls away and looks at me, 'I didn't believe you. I put you all in danger. You, Charlotte and Oliver, you're my family. And you protected us. Alone.'

I touch my left hand to the side of his face and wipe a tear away with my thumb.

'Excuse me.' Mrs Matthews delicately clears her throat and we turn to look at her.

'So are we clear?' she says, closing her notebook and laying the pen on the top of it.

'Clear?' I shake my head.

'Yes. The toxicology report suggests that Evans died as a result of MRSA rather than the wounds inflicted by Mrs Jackson,' she looks at Brian, 'or the head trauma inflicted by Mr Jackson. As a result, and in the face of overwhelming evidence that you both acted in self-defence, the prosecution are dropping the manslaughter charges against you both.'

I reach for Brian's hand and squeeze it tightly. 'So does that mean . . .'

The lawyer smiles for the first time since we stepped foot in the police station. Her mouth opens and closes as she talks, looking from me to Brian and back again, but I only hear one word.

Free.

Book club questions for THE ACCIDENT by C.L. Taylor

1. As Susan searches for the truth behind Charlotte's accident she realises she had no idea what was going on in Charlotte's life. Was that her fault, or Charlotte's, or is it normal in a mother/teenaged-daughter relationship?

2. The novel alternates between the main storyline and Sue's diary entries from fifteen years earlier. How effectively do you think this works as a literary device in this novel?

3. Brian lies to Susan several times throughout the course of the novel. Was he justified in doing so, or should he have been completely honest with his wife?

4. There are several clues in Susan's early diary entries that James is controlling. At what point did you notice the warning signs?

5. Discuss the theme of 'secrets and lies' in the book and impact they have on Sue's attempt to find out why Charlotte stepped in front of the bus.

6. How does forty-three-year-old Sue change over the course of the book?

7. Sue won't go to the police because she doesn't think they'll take her seriously (because of an incident that occurred during one of her PTSD 'episodes'). At which point would you have gone to the police?

8. Susan sees a mirror of her relationship with James in Keisha's relationship with Danny. Is she justified in being concerned?

9. Could young Sue's friends and co-workers have done more to help save her from James?

10. What do you think would have happened if Charlotte had woken up before Liam admitted to Sue that they'd been sleeping together in 'Mike's' house?

11. Susan doesn't turn to her friends for help during her search for answers. Why do you think that was?

12. At the end of the novel, when James and Susan face each other in Charlotte's hospital room,

Susan asks if he ever really loved her. Do you think he did?

13. What did you think of the ending? Would you have liked it to end differently?

14. What do you think the future holds for Susan and her family? What effect do you think what happened will have on their relationships?

15. What other books would you compare this to? What books would recommend to other readers who have enjoyed this book?

A conversation with C.L. Taylor

Q. Where did you get the idea for THE ACCIDENT?

I was pregnant with my son when the idea first came to me. I wanted to write a novel about 'keeping secrets' but I had no idea who would be keeping the secrets or what those secrets would be. Then one day, when I was walking back from the supermarket – waddling along under the weight of my groceries – the first three lines popped into my head:

'Coma. There's something innocuous about the word, soothing almost in the way it conjures up the image of a dreamless sleep. Only Charlotte doesn't look as though she's sleeping to me.'

I heard Susan's voice as clear as day and I knew immediately that she was the mother of a teenaged girl who'd stepped in front of a bus. I kept repeating those three lines over and over again as I walked home so I wouldn't forget them, then frantically scribbled them down. I kept writing and, less than two hours later, I had the first chapter.

I didn't write any more until a couple of months after my son's birth. As a new mum in a new town I was lonely, and very sleep deprived, and I missed writing so, in his naps, I started plotting the rest of the story. I finished the first draft in five months.

Q. How did your personal history inform the novel?

Like Susan I was once in an abusive relationship. Unlike Susan it wasn't physically or sexually abusive but it was emotionally abusive and, over the course of the four years it lasted, it changed me as a person. It took me a long time to find the courage to leave the relationship, and even longer to heal from it.

When my son was born I was overwhelmed by how protective I felt of him. I barely slept for fear something might happen to him in the night and I watched him like a hawk in the day. When I started plotting *THE ACCIDENT* I began to wonder how I'd react if my son was in danger from something very different from SIDS or choking or falling or any of the other 'normal' dangers. What if there was a person who meant him harm? I never really believed that that would happen but I channelled those fears into Susan who'd been through a much more horrific experience than me. What if she'd taken something precious from her abusive ex and he wanted revenge? And what if that revenge was wreaked on her own child?

Q. Why did you use diary entries alongside the main thread of the story?

I felt it was really important that the reader understands why Susan is the way she is. She's nervy, neurotic and paranoid and, without the diary entries, it would be hard to be sympathetic towards her. During the course of the novel Susan moves from whole to broken, to whole again and I thought it was important for the reader to see – via her diary entries – how very broken she was. Both threads of the stories build at the same time and I hope the climaxes are as satisfying for the reader as they were to write.

Q. Your main character, Susan, is a very 'unreliable narrator'. Did you find her difficult to write?

Not really. Once I'd heard Susan's voice in my head the words just spilled out of me. That said there were times – when she was lashing out at people who didn't deserve it – when I just wanted to shake her and tell her to trust people, but I totally understood why she was the way she was and why it was so important that she discover what had happened to Charlotte in her own way.

At the beginning of the novel Susan says that she feels like she was 'sleep walking' through her own life but, by the end, she's totally in charge of it. That was incredibly satisfying to write.

Q. Did you always know how the novel was going to end? Did you ever consider an alternative?

No, I always knew that James would die at the end and Charlotte would wake up. I did consider Susan killing him but I didn't want her to become as vicious as he was. I also umm'd and ahh'd about whether or not Brian should return to the hospital room. I didn't want him to be a 'hero' and save the day but I liked the idea that the habit that had annoyed Sue so much at the beginning of the novel (of him always returning to collect something he'd forgotten) actually helped save her life at the end. I also thought that, given how Sue had done so much over the course of the novel without Brian's support, it would prove his love for her if he came to her aid.